PRAISE FOR

Kaaterskill Falls

"*Kaaterskill Falls* continues where [Goodman's] last book, *The Family Markowitz,* left off—and then goes further, cutting new ground. . . . Her truest talent is for imposing a shape on the little, everyday disturbances that distract most of her writing peers; she has an almost 19th-century ability to create a sense of linkage, of one existence impinging on the next."
—Daphne Merkin, *The New York Times Book Review*

"Admirably rich in nuance and detail, *Kaaterskill Falls* sets out to compose an entire tapestry, and certainly in its gradually realized world of interrelated friends and neighbors, it succeeds."
—*The Boston Globe*

"Like Jane Austen, Goodman locates the universal in the quiet doings of small, honeycomb societies, deftly tailoring the particulars of her characters to generic moments of self-awareness."—*Elle*

"[Goodman] writes with such winning grace, such deftly evocative intimacy of detail."—*The Wall Street Journal*

"A delight, stem to stern . . . Goodman has often been singled out for her eye, which like Arnold Bennett's or Vermeer's never loses a significant detail or blurs its focus. . . . This young Mozart of Jewish fiction has pulled off another major feat."—*Newsday*

"A carefully observed and haunting novel . . . Like the late Nobel laureate Isaac Bashevis Singer, Goodman wrings ineffable strands of passion from the quietest of hopes and disappointments."—*People*

"[An] inventive first novel . . . Goodman's writing is nuanced, graced with subtle imagery and flashes of insight."—*USA Today*

"A writer of uncommon clarity and grace . . . Goodman's handling of incident is masterly."—*The New Yorker*

Please turn the page for more extraordinary acclaim. . . .

"Ms. Goodman does a marvelously sympathetic job of conjuring up the circumscribed world of the rabbi's followers. . . . [She] writes with such supple understanding of her people that the reader quickly . . . become[s] absorbed in the small, daily dramas of their lives. So authoritative is her storytelling that she is able to move from one character's point of view to another's and back again to an omniscient overview without missing a beat."
—Michiko Kakutani, *The New York Times*

"*Kaaterskill Falls* is a kind of heaven . . . complex and brilliant. . . . Allegra Goodman has not so much created a world as given us entry into one that, for many, will seem almost unimaginably foreign. But Goodman's talent runs so deep that to step into it is to live there for a while."—Mary Cantwell, *Vogue*

"Goodman's portrait of the Rav is a marvel of research and imagination, a fascinating multifaceted profile of power and rigidity based on utter devotion to Jewish law and prayer. . . . *Kaaterskill Falls* is a different, surprising kind of Jewish novel . . . one that isn't afraid to both question and embrace *Yiddishkeit* and spirituality."—*Los Angeles Times Book Review*

"[Goodman] creates a world that gives the natural wonder of Kaaterskill Falls its full due. In short, occasions to admire the shape and ring of her sentences abound. . . . Few putatively 'Jewish novels' manage the tricky business of giving equal weight to substance and style. *Kaaterskill Falls* does—and does so brilliantly."
—*The Washington Post Book World*

"An elegant portrait of orthodox Jewish life in the modern world."
—*The Forward*

"A stunning story . . . As warm and knowing as her acclaimed story collection, *The Family Markowitz*."—*Glamour*

Kaaterskill Falls

A NOVEL

Allegra Goodman

DELTA TRADE PAPERBACKS

A Delta Book
Published by
Dell Publishing
a division of
Random House, Inc.
1540 Broadway
New York, New York 10036

ISBN: 0-385-32390-5

Reprinted by arrangement with The Dial Press

Manufactured in the United States of America
Published simultaneously in Canada

August 1999

10 9 8 7 6 5

BVG

In memory of
Madeleine Joyce Goodman
mother, scientist, administrator,
and baker extraordinaire

Kaaterskill

Falls

I

June–July '76

We, I may say, fortunately, missed the direct path, and after wandering a little, found it out by the noise—for, mark you, it is buried in trees. . . . First, we stood a little below the head about half way down the first fall, buried deep in trees, and saw it streaming down two more descents to the depth of near fifty feet—then we went on a jut of rock nearly level with the second fall-head, where the first fall was above us, and the third below our feet still—at the same time we saw that the water was divided by a sort of cataract island on whose other side burst out a glorious stream—then the thunder and the freshness.

—JOHN KEATS
Letter to Tom Keats, 1818

1

FRIDAY afternoon, Edelman's Bakery in Washington Heights is like the stock exchange—paper numbers strewn across the floor, everybody shouting orders: "Give me two! Seedless! No, make that four."

"A dozen onion!"

"What?"

"A dozen onion rolls—and I'm in a rush."

"Six challahs!" Isaac calls out. Suit jacket slung over his shoulder, he leans against the glass counter where Mrs. Edelman presides at the cash register. Isaac's white shirt is drenched with sweat, his tie folded in the pocket. The air conditioner is feeble, and the bakery is mobbed with sweating customers: the women, in their long skirts and long sleeves, all covered up, even in the heat. The men, just off from work, their faces flushed under their black hats. The bakery floor, and even the walls, are scuffed and dirty, the glass cases empty except for a few babkas on curled wax paper. Edelman's is rich only in the fragrance of its bread.

Plucked from wire bins, Isaac's challahs are so fresh that Mrs. Edelman's fingers dent them. The loaves are magnificent, over a foot long, artfully braided, glossy with painted egg white, but time is short. Mrs. Edelman dumps them unceremoniously into brown paper bags. Isaac snatches them up with his change and runs out to his station wagon.

He drops the bread and his suit jacket into the scorching-hot backseat and starts the car. He does not take off his hat; Isaac wears a black felt fedora, even in the summer. He is a small man, slightly built. His eyes are not dark, but light brown, and luminous like amber. His hair is brown, too, and like all the men in Washington Heights' Kirshner community, he is clean shaven, almost modern looking, with neither beard nor peyyes. Isaac rolls up his shirtsleeves, and the veins stand out on his bare forearms. The steering wheel burns his fingers, but he has a wiry strength, a commuter's stamina.

Easing out into the traffic, Isaac passes shop windows armored with metal grilles, cement walls spray-painted pink. He drives past Auerbach's butcher shop, Schwartz's kosher cheese, Grimaldi's corner store, and the Kirshner synagogue with its barred windows and combination locks. In 1976 the neighborhood is small and shabby and tight. The Kirshners' apartment buildings are built close together of red brick, their few stores clustered as if for safety. Flights of stairs, hundreds of cement steps, provide shortcuts from the streets above to those below, and always, on the cement stairs, mothers and their babies, grandparents and teenagers, are passing each other. Everyone takes these stairs to get up and down, as if the neighborhood were a single house. There are no stairs, however, to the top of the Heights. No Kirshners climb up to Fort Tryon Park or go to the museum there, the Cloisters, with its icons and crucifixes, its medieval sculpture carved in cool gray stone. The Kirshners never think of the Cloisters. They are absorbed in their own religion. Although they have no paintings, or stained glass, or sculpture, they array themselves with gorgeous words.

PULLING into the upper Port Authority, Isaac sits with the engine running and scans the crowds for his car pooler, Andras Melish. Loudspeakers in the bus terminal blare destinations in New York State: Syracuse, Albany, Schenectady. Isaac is surprised not to see Andras standing there, waiting. He does not think he could be overlooking him. Andras is not easily overlooked. He always stands out, much taller than the others in the waiting crowd.

A shadow darkens the passenger side window. Andras climbs into the car and slams the door behind him.

"Where were you? I was trying to phone you," Andras says.

Despite his fifty-seven years he has the challenging voice and arrogant black eyes of his youth.

"I got held up at the bakery." Isaac is polite but unapologetic.

They had hoped to beat the rush-hour traffic, but at two o'clock they're crawling over the silver George Washington Bridge. Isaac's Mercury does not have air conditioning. Stuck in traffic, the car gets so hot, it hurts to breathe. As if to taunt them, the Hudson below glistens in the sun. Through the bars and cables of the bridge Isaac watches sailboats puff up with the river breeze.

"Why don't you try the other lane?" Andras asks. He is a stickler for punctuality. Habitually, as if to hold it against Isaac, he times their commute.

"This lane is fine," Isaac replies.

There is still a distance between them left over from the winter. In the city the men almost never see each other; they lead such different lives. Isaac's gritty neighborhood is nothing like Andras's on the Upper West Side. Isaac's clerical job in the Department of Public Works is far from Andras's position as head of his own import company. And, of course, Isaac's upbringing and convictions are nothing like Andras's. Young and fervent in his observance, Isaac was born into the separatist Kirshners in Washington Heights. But Andras is twenty years older, an immigrant from Budapest. He comes from an expansive, assimilated Jewish community that, like Andras's belief in God, has scarcely existed since the war.

By the time the gray Thruway spreads out before them, and the station wagon picks up speed, Isaac is exhausted. His legs ache. He wishes away the two hours ahead. His wife will be waiting for him. He hasn't seen Elizabeth all week. She will come out to the car and help him carry in the armfuls of fresh bread. The girls will be playing in the yard. Soccer, hopscotch, tetherball, jump rope. They will jump up to see him.

Through the open window, in the dry breeze, Andras watches trucks heaving past—eighteen-wheelers with smokestacks of their own. He's brought in a new line of toy trucks at the warehouse. Tonka trucks, blue and white, logger trucks loaded with miniature pine logs, orange U-Hauls with detachable six-inch trailers. They've even got tiny SPIRIT OF '76 bumper stickers for the Bicentennial.

What Andras really needs is a second car. His wife won't hear of it, of course. It would be a waste of gas, she says. Nina's conserving energy for the whole country, car-pooling.

Often Andras thinks that he wouldn't mind spending a few weekends alone in the city. He could use the time to do his books. But his sisters, Eva and Maja, are waiting for him in their brick house in Kaaterskill. Even now, as he and Isaac are driving up, Andras's older sisters are baking rugelach, prune cake, and mandelbrot. They still bake for him, just as they did when he was a boy.

"Our exit," Andras says suddenly.

Isaac turns off, at the last minute, onto 23A.

"You didn't see it, did you?" Andras asks.

Isaac smiles, a lightning-quick smile. "I was waiting for you to remind me." He can tease Andras now that they are past the heavy traffic and making better time. They are closer to Kaaterskill. Everything is easier.

Even as they take the exit, the wind softens. The Thruway is now four lanes instead of eight. Billboards for Catskill Game Farm appear, ads for the petting zoo with pictures of goats and lambs blown up giant-size against the trees. The hills on either side are green, thick with oak and pine. Nothing but trees on either side, and the broad road slowly rising. The wind seems to comb the trees upright so that they stand thick and straight.

Turning onto Washington Irving Highway, they enter the forest. They exchange the sunny afternoon for shade, and the light breeze for damper, stiller air. The highway cuts around Cole Mountain, peeling away in a slow spiral from the trees. As the road rises, the lanes narrow, pressed together by the heavy woods. Transmission humming, the car climbs past shattered boulders, enormous shards of rock. Old oaks overhang the road, roots flung up from the ground, while younger birches shoot up toward the light in thin stalks, like grass. And yet there are houses here behind the trees. One on the right with peeling white paint, another freshly painted turquoise with a baby barn, and an enormous mailbox. This is Palenville. The mountain villages announce themselves with motels and signs: WELCOME TO PHOENICIA, and ENTERING COOKSBURG. Sudden flashes of sun, Floyd's Motel and Cooksburg's main street radiate light as clearings in the shade.

Isaac's car hugs the tightly coiled road. The low safety rail bolted to the road's edge isn't much to keep a car from tumbling down into the deep gorges, hundreds of feet below. Isaac drives above the gorge called Devil's Kitchen, and the ravine called Devil's Dam. There are car wrecks rusting down there under the leaves, and boulders bigger than the wrecked cars. And there is the sound of water, the rustling water, to Isaac's ears, like a thousand men praying together, davening and turning pages. Little by little the rustling water gathers strength, the gathering of voices growing louder and louder, until, as the road turns toward Kaaterskill Falls, the water begins to roar.

The road is high, clinging to the mountain. The rapids rush white over the green rocks, then tumble down into pools far below. From the car Isaac and Andras can't see the swimmers playing and diving in the rock pools. Only the falls pouring down over the upper face of the rock, a blasting of all the long spring's rains and winter's melted snow.

It's darker and greener here than anywhere else. The gorges and ravines broaden into a deep valley, and across the valley, far away in the trees, are Victorian mansions, tiny in the distance. Fairyland, Isaac's girls call the hillside, and the faraway houses do look like fairy palaces, delicate as chess pieces, exquisitely carved rooks.

Past Fairyland, past Kendall Falls and Bear Mountain, Isaac drives. Past the roadside spring bubbling into its mossy barrel, past granite boulders, past thousands upon thousands of trees standing together, the young and old in congregation, until, at last, he enters the town of Kaaterskill, bright with white houses set against dark trees.

Kaaterskill's Main Street is five blocks long. The buildings are all clapboard with porches, except for the brick firehouse, just built to replace the old station that burned down a year ago. Rubin's Hotel is the biggest building on Main Street. The line of rocking chairs on the hotel porch is positioned for a view of the whole town. Across the way the post office also has a porch, and is freshly painted Williamsburg-blue with cream trim. Then there is the Taylor Building, where the Taylor brothers practice law, and trade in real estate; Hamilton's

shingled general store; King Real Estate; Boyd's Garage, with its
dusty, glassed-in office at the back; the Orpheum, showing *The God-
father Part II*. The Main Street buildings nestle together companion-
ably, as they have for years. They match each other, with their
shutters and twelve-paned windows, and their creaky front steps.
Only near the end of the street does the old style give way to the
new. Here, like the village dragon, the chrome-and-glass A & P
sprawls in its black-paved parking lot.

Isaac turns off Main Street just before the A & P, and drives down
Maple Street, gently sloping, broad, and gracious. The trees on Maple
are gigantic, so old, they arc over the road in a canopy of leaves. Their
shade extends to every house, from the big summer places like Andras's
with sweeping lawns in back, to the rental bungalows like Isaac's, small
and square. Under the trees Isaac parks the car, and he and Andras step
out. The city is gone and the world is green. Green trees, and green
grass, and green leaves all around.

As he does every Friday, Andras goes directly to see his sisters, but
Isaac walks across the street. A crowd is gathering at the Curtis place.
Will Curtis's new house has finally arrived. It has come in two sec-
tions, preassembled, and mounted on an enormous flatbed truck. A
white-sided rectangular shoe box of a house with a green front door
and matching ornamental green shutters.

"Daddy!" Three-year-old Brocha runs toward Isaac. "Up!" He
hoists up his youngest daughter onto his shoulders and they watch as
the huge truck backs into the Curtis lot with half the house clamped
on its back.

Isaac's wife, Elizabeth, makes her way to him through the crowd.
She doesn't kiss him. Not in front of all these people. But Isaac stands
so close to her that her skirt brushes against him. Elizabeth is wearing
a long twill skirt and a pinstriped man-tailored shirt buttoned all the
way up. In summer she is so covered up in her long sleeves, long
skirts, and white stockings that only the backs of her hands are freckled, and her face. She wears small gold-rimmed glasses. Her cheek is
curved in a smile, her hazel eyes green in the shade.

"Isn't it marvelous?" Elizabeth says to Isaac. Her voice is distinc-
tive. Her accent English. "Look, even the carpet is down in the

rooms already!" She watches the men maneuver the second half of the house into place.

"Well, it's just a prefab, Elizabeth," says Isaac, amused.

"Oh, I know that," she says, eyes on the closing seam between the two halves. "But it's marvelous. It's like a doll's house."

Nearly the whole town has come to watch. The year-rounders and the summer people, who are mostly from the city, Kirshners from Washington Heights, families from Borough Park, Lubavichers from Crown Heights. They all stand together, chattering excitedly, watching the delivery of the new house. The old place is gone, burned to the ground, and now the insurance money's come in. Everyone's busy pointing and shouting out directions to the movers and the trucks. "A little more, a little more," urges one of the teenagers from town.

"You've got a mile!" screams a Talmud scholar, up for a week's vacation.

The trucks pull the two halves of the house in close, but there is still a gap between the walls. The crowd stirs, frustrated, surging forward to give advice—fair-haired children along with young men in black hats.

"Nu? What gives?" demands a silver-bearded man in a frock coat. And just then the seam vanishes and the house is finished. The whole town and the summer people break into applause.

"More. More," protests Brocha from Isaac's shoulders.

"It's all done," he tells her. "It's time to go home."

"Again!" she says, pointing to the house, but Elizabeth is already crossing the street, and Isaac follows with Brocha swaying on his shoulders. He puts her down on the porch.

"Go on," Elizabeth tells him. "Go on inside." And she calls the children to help her unload the car. "Ruchel? Sorah? Take the bags. Chani?" She looks over to the tire swing, where their oldest daughter stands, storklike, watching the trucks pull out across the street. "Chani, could you bring your sisters back? They're still out with Pammy Curtis."

Elizabeth's English accent hasn't rubbed off on her daughters, but they all have English names. No one ever uses them. To their friends they're just the Shulman girls, five rattled off in a row: Chani, Malki,

Ruchel, Sorah, and Brocha. But Elizabeth gave them other names, and she repeats them to herself: Annette and Margot, Rowena, Sabrina, and Bernice. These are her daughters' real names; the ones on their birth certificates; extraordinary and graceful—princesses and dancers. It's true, of course, the nickname Malki by itself means "queen," and Sorah means a "princess." But those are words the children drag around the house. There must be twenty Sorahs at the Kirshner school. Elizabeth wanted something remarkable and elegant —beyond the usual expectations. She didn't name her daughters to be rattled off. She named them to have imagination.

As a girl in Manchester, Elizabeth played tennis. When she was sixteen, she even got a job teaching it to younger children at her school. But the interschool matches in the district were all on Saturdays, and she couldn't play on Shabbes. Hers was a small school built by the Kehilla of observant families. Her father taught Talmud in the upper division. Elizabeth had prepared to teach Hebrew herself, and took her certificate at Carmel College in Henley before she married. Then she settled down to raising children. None of this was unexpected. Meeting Isaac in New York was not arranged, but it was natural. Elizabeth was twenty, and her parents said she ought to move about and see things. Not exactly travel, but visit the family, her aunt's family in New York. And there was Shayni's wedding that summer anyway. Elizabeth would be their emissary.

She is unusual in her community, an Englishwoman among the Kirshners of Washington Heights. She reads Milton on her own. She's spent her pregnancies with Austen and Tolstoy. With Brocha she was the most ambitious and tried to read all of Sandburg's biography of Lincoln. She should get back to that one, she thinks, as she sets the table for their late dinner. They don't have a separate dining room, of course. It's a small bungalow. Just three bedrooms. The girls' rooms are so narrow, there is barely any space between their beds. They don't mind, though, because they spend their time outside. The living room is shadowy, with only one dim ceiling fixture and two windows. Elizabeth keeps the front door open to let in more light.

In the evening the trees rustle together. Not a single car passes by. Elizabeth prays, standing in the living room, with her tiny siddur, its pages thin as flaky pastry. She recites the Friday-night service to herself, rapidly, under her breath. She is not tall, only five foot six, but she holds herself straight. In the way she holds herself, in the way she moves, she has a kind of athletic grace. She is slender, although she has five children. She grew up early, marrying young, having her first child at twenty-one. Still, at thirty-four, she is excitable, eager to speak, and quick to laugh. She is, more than anything, curious, delighted by paradoxes, odd characters, anything out of the ordinary. She looks forward every year to Kaaterskill and the people there: Andras Melish and his South American wife; Professor Cecil Birnbaum; the Curtises with their tomboy daughter, Pammy; the Landauer family, Lubavichers from Crown Heights. In the summers she can see these friends again, and they are both exotic and familiar, like distant relatives.

Both Brocha and Sorah are asleep by the time Isaac comes home from services, and so Elizabeth and Isaac sit down for blintzes with the older girls. Twelve-year-old Chani looks most like her mother, with her fair skin and hazel eyes. She has Elizabeth's black hair, though a stranger wouldn't know. All Elizabeth's sheitels are auburn. She'd always loved auburn hair, and so when she married and had to cut hers short she decided she might as well become auburn haired. She bought auburn wigs in different styles: pageboy, straight, short, and wavy. Most often in Kaaterskill she wears a kerchief over her hair, but she brings the sheitels up, and keeps them on the top shelf of her closet on faceless white Styrofoam heads.

Next to Chani at the table, Malki eats her blintzes without sour cream or jam. Ever since she could talk it was always "plain, *plain*" for her food. No jam on blintzes, no gravy on her meat, no mustard on her salami sandwiches. She's a solemn girl: light brown hair, brown eyes, a little wall-eyed even. A quiet child, not a biker like Chani or a tree climber like chattering nine-year-old Ruchel. Ruchel's legs are scratched from her expeditions climbing birches. She comes home covered with mud. She and Sorah and Pam Curtis with her red wagon seem to be dredging Bramble Creek behind the Birnbaum place.

"Daddy," Ruchel says now, "you know down there at the creek?"

"Yes."

"The blackberries down there are the biggest ones I've ever seen in my life. But Mr. King came out with his *dog*."

Elizabeth laughs. "You mean his poodle?"

Ruchel keeps talking. "He said we were trespassing on his property and we had to get off. But he doesn't own the creek, and I was standing in the creek."

"But the bushes belong to him," Elizabeth points out. "You shouldn't pick from his bushes."

"He's a Norka," Ruchel says oddly. She's been reading the *Red Fairy Tale Book*.

"He's a real estate developer," Isaac says. "Do you know what else he owns? He owns this house."

Ruchel dismisses this. "I don't believe you."

"When we went up to the lake I squashed the tire on my bike," says Chani.

"Sh. We'll talk about it later," Isaac tells her. Drowsily he leans back in his chair. Across from him Malki cuts her blintz and Ruchel chatters about bicycle pumps.

"Cecil Birnbaum brought his wife up," Elizabeth tells Isaac. Cecil is the Brooklyn College professor who summers across the street. "And do you remember Regina from Los Angeles?"

"Cecil's sister."

"She came up for the week. She's having a wedding reception for Cecil and Beatrix tomorrow. His wife's name is Beatrix."

"Cecil and Beatrix Birnbaum," Isaac says, trying out the names.

"Yes. I said we'd come."

"We'll see," says Isaac. He can barely keep his eyes open.

Isaac goes to bed right after dinner, and Elizabeth tucks in the children and washes the dishes alone. The candles are burning down in the little silver travel candlesticks. Elizabeth wipes the crumbs off the counter and then walks out onto the front porch stacked with bicycles. The house, small and close, is filled with the rhythmic breathing of Isaac and the children, but the air outside is cold, and it wakes her. She peers through the thick maple leaves, trying to glimpse the stars. What are they dreaming about inside? Blackberries and poodles, speckled newts, "The Twelve Dancing Princesses" in Ruchel's *Red Fairy Tale Book*. Are her daughters now tiptoeing down the secret staircase to the enchanted lake? Perhaps now they are dreaming of the silver wood with the trees spangled in silver, and the golden wood where the trees are spangled with gold, and at last the diamond wood where the trees are hung with drops of diamonds. They are wearing out their shoes dancing. Elizabeth had loved that story when she was a child, and the idea that there are secret forests where you can become someone else.

2

—

THE Kaaterskill shul is an old, steep-roofed clapboard building, prim and white. It was built long ago for a Reform congregation, but in the past twenty years the synagogue has filled with Orthodox vacationers. Its arched windows frame men davening in dark suits and black hats.

Elizabeth and the girls walk through the vestibule, where only the racks of wire hangers and an abandoned blue scarf remain of winter. The paneled synagogue is narrow but deep, with rows of long, high-backed benches cushioned in red plush. A mechitza of polished wood and glass separates the men from the women. In front, in the men's section, the seats surround a raised bima fenced with newel posts like a dark porch railing all around.

Sorah and Brocha are still little enough to sit with Isaac in the men's section. It's not sitting they like, though—it's running back and forth. They squirm their way between the dark-suited men to the front wall where the ark stands, its red velvet curtains decorated with gold tassels and lions embroidered in gold thread. Above the ark hangs the ner tamid, the eternal flame encased in red glass. The girls tilt their heads back and dizzy themselves looking all the way up at the embossed tin ceiling, painted robin's-egg blue. Back and forth Sorah and Brocha wriggle between the tall dark rows of men. They like the bima best, because it's in the center and it's crowded. Sorah pushes her little sister in front of her, and the two of them work their way over to the dais, where they grasp the base of the railing and look at the polished shoe tips and trouser cuffs in front of them. Whenever the reading stops and the Torah rises above them, they look up expectantly. Maybe old Mr. Heiligman will see them; maybe he will give them candy from his blue velvet tallis bag. Small, thin lollipops or sour balls. Either way the choices are orange, red, green, purple, or yellow.

Elizabeth and the three older girls sit in the front row of the women's section. Chani daydreams, siddur open on her lap, while Malki bends over her prayer book, catching up on what she missed by coming late. Ruchel is neither quiet nor industrious. She's leaning forward, blowing the curtain on the mechitza to make it flutter against the glass, rubbing the velvet chairs back and forth with her fingers so the nap stands up rough and then slides down smooth. Elizabeth scans the room for Cecil's wife, but she doesn't see anyone new. She turns to her Tanach and follows the Torah reading. She cannot see the men on the bima, but she knows them all by voice. There is the rich bass of the Hasidic rabbi, Reb Moshe Feurstein, and then Rav Joseph Butler with his strong, slightly acerbic tenor. And then reedy Pesach Lamkin. Although much younger than his colleagues, Pesach Lamkin is the official rabbi of the synagogue. Every summer the shul is full of great rabbis, exacting and learned men who come up to the mountains with their own constituencies. In order to avoid disputes and interrupted vacations, they chose Lamkin to officiate in Kaaterskill. Young, pious, inexperienced, he was likely to offend the fewest people.

Rabbi Lamkin is well liked, but the synagogue hushes as Elizabeth's own rabbi, Rav Elijah Kirshner, reads from the prophets in his precise baritone. Rav Kirshner was the first of all the rabbis to come up to the mountains, and he has hundreds of followers in Kaaterskill. Just after the war, the Rav decided his community should migrate in the summers. In 1938, just before Kristallnacht, they had left Germany en masse from Frankfurt, and resettled in Washington Heights. Then, in the fifties, those with reparation money bought summer houses together in Kaaterskill. The Rav is a grandson of Jeremiah Solomon Hecht, the founder in Germany of neoorthodoxy, who wrote in his elegant and stylish German, arguing that the generations to come should study science and languages, law, and mathematics—and yet none of these could come before religious law. Rav Elijah Kirshner was born in 1898, only ten years after Hecht's time, and it is said his mother was Hecht's favorite daughter. He earned a doctorate in philosophy at the University of Frankfurt am Main, and then rose to take his grandfather's place. Rav Kirshner brought Hecht's books and his community to America—only a small part of what there once was, but a remnant that he has guided and strengthened. He has founded the Kirshner school and the yeshiva, sustained his people in Washington Heights, even now in the battered parks, the narrow alleyways. The Rav is an extraordinary man. And famous. He knows the mayor of New York, has led prayers in the state legislature. *The New York Times* calls him "the Reverend Doctor."

As usual, at the end of the service, one of the Landauer boys sings the hymn "Anim Zmiros." There is always a Landauer boy to do this, as each succeeds to the position when he turns eight. Isaac watches in the men's section as Avromy Landaur pulls the gold cord and opens the ark curtain for his brother. In their small dark suits they look like miniatures of their father. It is always quite a contrast, the little boy—just a pipsqueak—singing at the front, and the spectacular thirteenth-century poetry, the reedy voice singing the mystic love song to God: *Anim zmiros, vishirim erog, ki elechah nafshi tarog.* . . . I sing hymns and compose songs/Because my soul longs for thee./My soul desires thy shelter,/To know all thy mystery. . . . Landauer's son rattles off the verses. It's like a kazoo performance of Beethoven.

Isaac has always liked Joe Landauer's sons, but his own daughters laugh at them and their nasal voices. The girls pretend they can't tell the Landauer boys apart. After the service, when everyone is talking, crushed together, trying to get out, Isaac says to Elizabeth, "That was a good job Boruch did with *'Anim Zmiros.'* "

And Chani says, "No, that was Yakov-Shloimie."

And Ruchel contradicts, "It was *not* Yakov-Shloimie. It was Avromy. I recognized his voice!" Then they start giggling among themselves.

Near the door, Elizabeth and Isaac catch sight of Cecil Birnbaum with his sister, Regina. Cecil is wearing his old blue suit and wire-rimmed glasses, and he has a vaguely dissatisfied look. His parents, of blessed memory, were pillars of the summer community and the synagogue, but in ways Elizabeth can only marvel at, Cecil has become a gadfly and a malcontent in Kaaterskill.

"Mazel tov," Isaac says.

Elizabeth looks around for Cecil's bride. "Nu, where is she?"

"Oh, Beatrix doesn't come to services," Cecil says grandly.

Elizabeth smiles. Cecil likes to shock people, but she's known him since their first summer in Kaaterskill five years ago and she is used to him. "When did you get back from England?" she asks.

Before Cecil can answer, they are both crushed against the wall as the crowd parts for old Rav Kirshner. Seventy-eight and frail, the Rav is borne forward by two of his nephews, one on each side. His thin hands rest on his nephews' arms—his pale fingers translucent skinned against their dark suits. The Kirshners pull back the children in the Rav's path.

The crowd closes up quickly behind the Rav. There are many Kirshners in Kaaterskill, but they mill about in shul with Hasids and their little boys with peyyes, modern Orthodox, with wives in hats instead of sheitels. There is even a Conservative rabbi named Sobel, who is revered by no one in the synagogue but Cecil, who shows him the utmost courtesy, partly out of real respect, and partly in order to pique his orthodox neighbors. Rabbi Sobel is struggling to get out in the crush of people, and Cecil holds the door for him. "He walks over here every week," Cecil tells Elizabeth after he passes, "and no one gives *him* the time of day. This is a world-renowned historian—"

Elizabeth doesn't hear him. She is staring after the Rav and his entourage. There, in that mass of black hats and jackets, is a man in a cream suit. It is, unmistakably, Jeremy Kirshner, the Rav's firstborn son. Jeremy Kirshner, Dr. Kirshner, as he is called, is an enigma. He is a rabbi, like his brother Isaiah, but he works as a professor at Queens College. No one speaks about him. If his name comes up, people just say one thing—"He never married, you know"—and they leave it at that.

"Did you see him?" Elizabeth asks Isaac as he joins her.

"I couldn't tell who it was," says Isaac.

"Oh, that was Jeremy Kirshner," Cecil says. "Why?"

"Nothing—just, he never comes up here," says Elizabeth.

"But he came to see me," Cecil says with a flourish.

"I didn't know you were friends," says Elizabeth. It astonishes her.

"Yes, we are friends," says Cecil, "despite the fact that I'm a commoner."

THE old Birnbaum house stands alone, set back from the street. Years ago, when Cecil's parents bought the place, they planted the rose-bushes on the side of the house, and dogwood trees that now over-hang the front walk. Taller than the tall house stands the silver spruce tree, planted when Cecil's sister Regina was born.

"Welcome, come in," calls Regina to Elizabeth and Isaac and their daughters. The girls hang back on the porch, but Elizabeth and Isaac enter the shadowy living room. They see that they are the first to arrive at the party. "This is Beatrix," Regina says, "—from England, like you, Elizabeth."

Beatrix is a thin woman in a sleeveless dress. A mass of coarse black hair falls stiffly around her shoulders. "Hello, very pleased to meet you." Beatrix innocently puts out her hand to Isaac, who draws back. "Don't you shake hands?" she asks.

Quickly Elizabeth shakes her hand instead. She and Isaac sit on the couch, careful not to brush the bunch of wildflowers lying on the coffee table.

"I picked these this morning." Beatrix lifts up the bunch of goldenrod. "I'm going to put them here. What do you think?"

She props the flowers in the twin vases standing on the piano and pours in water from a long-spouted watering can.

"Beatrix," Elizabeth ventures after a moment, "I think it's com-ing out the bottom."

"What is?" Beatrix lifts one of the vases to check, and a stream of water along with the flowers courses out onto the Steinway.

"They're ornamental vases!" Regina calls, rushing from the kitchen with a dish towel. "Cecil. Could you bring me another rag for the piano?"

"Not on Shabbat," he answers precisely. "I never touch the pi-ano on Shabbat."

"You see, they're ornamental," Regina tells her sister-in-law again as she sponges up the water. "They're from the thirties. They don't have bottoms."

"Oh," Beatrix says. Then she laughs. "How frightfully bourgeois!"

WHEN the other guests arrive and Regina begins to serve, Elizabeth wishes Isaac trusted Cecil's kitchen. "How about some meringues?" Regina offers. "They're just eggs and sugar." Elizabeth hesitates, but then declines.

More than fifty of Cecil's neighbors fill the house. Jeremy Kirshner, however, is absent. Elizabeth looks at the dining-room table set out with Linzer tortes, rugelach, and cheesecakes, an apricot jelly roll, and miniature Danish. There are lattice-crust pies on the sideboard under the freshly dusted painting of a ship tossed in a violent blue-green sea.

"I cleaned this week, of course," Regina tells Elizabeth. Regina has a wry way of talking, although she is much gentler than her brother. She wears glasses as he does, but hers have stylish tortoiseshell frames; her skin is fair and her hair curly and almost red. She doesn't cover it. She is the only person Elizabeth knows who actually lives in California. Regina tells Elizabeth, "I decided the house couldn't wait for Cecil and Beatrix to pass into a domestic stage."

"No, Cecil is more interested in gardening," says Elizabeth. "But you do the house justice." She has never seen it like this—silver polished, Persian carpets vacuumed.

"Well, you didn't know my mother," says Regina. "She really kept at things, and she decorated. She had the eye for it. She had a gardener who painted these flowers up here." She points to the plaster flowers that serve as upper moldings for the walls. "And she picked out the green and gold colors for the dining room."

"That's right," says old Esther Ergman, who knew Regina and Cecil's parents. "And you, Regina. You have to come up and take care of it."

"Not now," Regina says, with a funny little grimace. "They left it to Cecil, not to me. I can't come up and pick up after him. Believe me, it's exhausting. One of these days he'll have to struggle along with his own vacuum cleaner."

Esther asks Elizabeth, "Do you know what Regina said about her brother when she was a child? She said, 'Cecil, you are a monstrosity.' I remember when she said that. She was just a little girl wheeling her doll's carriage in front of my porch, and she wore a little leather purse on her arm—the sweetest thing. And what she said was absolutely true. He was a little imp, Cecil. And if you ask me, he still is."

Elizabeth has noticed this about Cecil and Regina: Though they are in their thirties, both professors at universities, when they return to Kaaterskill, they carry the reputations they had as children. It doesn't matter that Cecil is a learned scholar, expert on modernism and Shaw. Nor does it matter that in his way he is strictly observant. He's still a little mazik to the old people. They haven't forgotten when he lost control of his bicycle and crushed old Friedman's flower bed. And in just the same way Cecil's sister, the research oncologist at UCLA, will always live in the old-timers' memories as the girl with red curly hair and the wicker doll carriage.

"No one since her mother," Esther tells Elizabeth, "—no one else makes rugelach like this."

"I'd like to have the recipe," Elizabeth says.

"Oh, it's very simple," says Regina on her way to the kitchen. "But I've got to go back to L.A. tomorrow. You should watch it being done. And there's a secret," she calls over her shoulder.

"Really?" Elizabeth asks.

Regina disappears behind the swinging kitchen door, and her voice floats out. "Don't overwork the dough."

Elizabeth moves back to the living room, where Cecil and Beatrix stand at the center of a large group of people, Isaac among them. "There is no sign on the synagogue," Beatrix says. "Doesn't it have a name?"

"Of course. But not as good a name as the old one," Cecil says.

"What old one?" asks Joe Landauer, the father of all the Landauer boys in their miniature black suits and hats.

"Ah," says Cecil. "You betray your fleeting residence on the mountain. The original shul, which was Reform, was built by old man Rubin in the 1880s on Bear Mountain, to serve both Bear Mountain and Kaaterskill. And it was called Anshei Sharon."

"Why People of Sharon?" asks Cecil's wife. "How very odd."

She knows Hebrew, Elizabeth thinks. How is that?

"Well, the founders got confused. They thought *sharon* meant 'mountain.' They tried to change it later, but the incorporation papers were filed already, and Judge Taylor refused to bother with them. No, it wasn't our Judge Taylor. It was his great-uncle. But he was a Taylor, so he wouldn't change the papers. Now in due time the shul founder, Rubin, fought with the people in Bear Mountain and moved to Kaaterskill. And he took his shul with him. He put it on rollers and shlepped it down the mountain on a sledge with his team of oxen."

"Cecil, how do you *know* these things?" asks Joe.

"Anyone a resident for over thirty years knows this," Cecil replies airily. "When Rubin deposited the shul in Kaaterskill, naturally he renamed it—and the Bear Mountain shul got a new name too."

"And?" asks Beatrix.

"Well, that's the end," Cecil teases.

"But what were their *names*?" his wife demands.

"Oh, that should be obvious," he says. "What are all breakaway synagogues called? Rodef Sholom—because they're seeking peace. And what are all the parent shuls renamed? Sharei Tzedek!"

"Gates of Righteousness," Beatrix cuts in. "Because they were *right*! Of course."

Elizabeth whispers to Isaac, "He's really in love. I've never seen him let someone run away with his punch line before."

THE children are feasting on the porch where the grown-ups have left their hostess gifts of Barton's candies. There is a huge selection piled on the green wicker sofa and chairs. Chocolate truffles, cherry creams, bitter mints. The Landauer boys are plastering caramel over their front teeth. The girls move to the other side of the porch in protest.

"Let's go look for snakes," Chani says. She jumps off the porch rail, and her sisters and Esther Ergman's two granddaughters run after her. They run down the little hill at the side of the house and into the acre-deep back garden. Small green apples squeak and mush underfoot as they race over slippery pine needles. They skid around the spruce tree. Hot and out of breath, in their fancy dresses, they run all the way to the unmown grass at the ragged edge of the garden. The girls are wearing scuffed white patent leather shoes, dresses printed with bouquets of flowers, lockets and big sashes, white piqué collars.

Overgrown blackberry bushes separate the Birnbaum and the King lots. White currant bushes and red. Scraggly old raspberry canes. There are no snakes, but the blackberries cluster in the brambles, shining dark and heavy as carpenter bees. Ruchel and Sorah stand in the Birnbaums' blowsy garden with its tall grass and old-fashioned lilac arbor, and they stare at Mr. King's new swimming pool, surrounded by cement and striped lounging chairs. Just yesterday Mr. King yelled at them and Pammy Curtis for eating his blackberries. Admittedly they ate a few. The girls want to go play somewhere else, but they can't stop looking next door. Mr. King's pool is dazzling, an unearthly aqua blue.

Then the girls hear raised voices coming from Mr. King's painted aluminum utility shed. Two men come out arguing onto the terrace. The girls can see them clearly above the bushes. Mr. King, broad and tall, and red in the face. And Mr. Knowlton, a much smaller man, Lark's father from across the street.

"You are never working for me again," says Mr. King.

"Why?" demands Mr. Knowlton, "because I took some extra flagstones?"

"Extras! Knowlton, I hired you to lay down my deck, not your chimney! I'm going to prosecute this."

"You're paranoid," Mr. Knowlton says. "Curtis badmouths me, and you believe it."

"Paranoid? I don't have to listen to Curtis when I can *see* across the street that you've been building your chimney with my flagstones."

"Who said—"

"I don't want to hear it," King snaps. "You can tell Taylor in court." Then he turns and sees the bunch of girls staring at him. He doesn't say a word, because they don't give him a chance. Instinctively, like rabbits, the girls run away, back through the tall grass, past the spruce tree, and up the slippery apple-littered hill.

———

IN the house Elizabeth is asking Beatrix, "How is it you know Hebrew?"

"Oh, I learned it one summer in Israel."

"You must be clever with languages," Elizabeth says. "What sort of mathematics do you practice?"

"Differential topology and things."

"It does sound interesting," Elizabeth says.

"I shouldn't think so," Beatrix demurs. "Not for most people. Who's at the door? Oh, Jeremy!"

The front door opens and Jeremy Kirshner walks in. "Mazel tov, mazel tov," he says to Cecil and Beatrix. "And my apologies for being late." He wears a straw hat with a jaunty air, as if he were going to a garden party in a Renoir painting. He is perhaps forty.

"Good to see you, Jeremy," says Beatrix, "Are you staying all weekend?"

"No, no, I'm leaving tomorrow, early in the morning," he says. "I have to go back for the Summer Institute."

"We should introduce everyone," says Regina, intervening as hostess. "Andras and Nina Melish. Saul and Eva Rubinstein. Philip and Maja Cohen. Esther Ergman, Elizabeth and Isaac Shulman, Joe and Leah Landauer," she goes around the room. "Jeremy was at Columbia with Cecil," she explains.

"But he's my colleague now," Beatrix says lightly. "So you should really say, he is at Queens College with Beatrix." Then she tells Jeremy, "You shouldn't do institutes in the city. You should do them here. It's so much prettier. Much cooler."

"But no one wants to come up here," says Jeremy.

"No, it's just that you don't want to," Beatrix says, and all the satellite conversations in the room dip down a little. They seem to dim. Cecil grins; he loves this kind of thing, creating a frisson, a slight static in the air, a storm warning. Cecil loves watching Beatrix in Kaaterskill, sharp and intellectual, asking questions with all her pointed, worldly innocence.

Jeremy stiffens, surrounded in the living room by his father's followers and their friends. On the couches and on the chairs they sit dressed in their plain clothes, their straightlaced finery. Jeremy

Kirshner looks at them with his dark eyes and clever, intent face. He has a young face for his age. He wouldn't look forty, except that his watchfulness gives him away. There is something concentrated and even a little hard about him. He affects a kind of nonchalance in the way he sits and speaks, but he does not carry it off completely. He is self-assured, but he is also studied. He is a specialist in Castiglione and in Renaissance courtly handbooks.

"Well, I'm going to have lots of mathematicians up," Beatrix says, "and we're going to do research under the trees. I'm going to hold a Kaaterskill mathematical institute. Right here."

Jeremy says nothing to this. Regina offers him coffee and a plate of rugelach. He takes one. His father's people are pretending not to look at him, eating food made outside the community, pastry from Regina's alien hands. They are pretending not to watch him taste the crushed nuts and cinnamon, and he is pretending not to notice them watching.

"Dr. Kirshner," Elizabeth says, "if you do come up again, do you think you might be interested in speaking—"

"Speaking?"

"Yes, giving a drash for our ladies' shiur," Elizabeth says.

"Well, if I were here," Jeremy says. He speaks as if from a great distance. "If I had something to say."

Elizabeth blinks. It is as if he were asking her, And who are you? Of course, she is no professor. There is a feeling with Cecil, and even more with Beatrix, of a kind of brisk and academic egalitarianism, as if in their house anyone can say anything. Elizabeth forgot for a moment that it is only they who really can say anything. Cecil is very strange. And his wife, too, with her strange sleeveless tunic of a dress, her loose hair, her Oxford ways. Knowing Hebrew without going to shul. Cecil and Beatrix cast a kind of spell. All the rules are different with them. It strikes Elizabeth that Beatrix and Cecil are so different from the Kirshners she lives with that she doesn't even disapprove of them. Ironic that last summer she was appalled along with all the other Kirshners that a woman from shul was seen in trousers in the park. But if Cecil's wife drove her car down Main Street on Shabbat, Elizabeth wouldn't be shocked at all. It really would be quite natural for Beatrix; it wouldn't be offensive in the same way.

"But what do people do here?" Beatrix asks again. "What is there to do? Besides eat rugelach, of course." She flashes a smile at Regina, who looks stoic.

"Go hiking," Cecil says.

"Play badminton," Elizabeth suggests.

"Oh, badminton, I love it!" Beatrix cries with real enthusiasm. "I'm appalling now, but I used to play at home. It was my only game at school, and I used to practice madly, to show I was proficient in *some*thing physical, because I was hopeless for their ghastly hockey teams. I've found a net, you know, in the cellar, and we could set it up in back. It's still light out. We could chalk the ground. I could do it this afternoon while you're up there praying."

"You could wait till Sunday. Then I'll help you," Elizabeth says, alarmed at the thought of causing Beatrix to transgress.

"Not at all," Beatrix says. "Division of labor. Leave it to me. Leave it to the secular arm." And she stretches out a sinewy bare arm.

WHEN the long day ends and the evening settles over the trees, the men walk back to the synagogue for services. The women sit in their glider rockers and their porch swings and they look into the fading light and talk. They talk about their children and their husbands and the traffic from the city. They talk about berry picking, the blackberries now in season and the blueberries to come. Then they lower their voices so the children will not hear. They speak of Israel and the hijacking of the Air France flight. The hostages in Uganda. The talk of politics mixes with the scent of roses.

Elizabeth sits with Regina on Cecil's porch. "Can't you stay a little longer?" she asks.

"No," Regina says, "I have to get back to the lab."

"Tell me about California," Elizabeth says.

Regina smiles. "Why don't you come out and see for yourself?"

"Oh, I don't think I'll ever have a chance to go to Los Angeles," Elizabeth says. "Tell me what it's like to live there."

"What do you want to know?"

"What's the Jewish community like?" Elizabeth asks. Her question sounds parochial, but it isn't meant that way. She asks out of intense curiosity. She wants to know what it is really like to live there, and so she tries to imagine herself in that place, a part of that community.

"We live in the Pico Robertson area," Regina says. "On a beautiful flat street with palm trees."

"All lined with palm trees?" Elizabeth asks.

"Yes," says Regina, and she looks out at the great trees on Maple, and the tiny jagged pieces of sky cut out between the leaves.

"And where do you daven?" Elizabeth asks.

"In a synagogue that used to be a movie theater."

"No!"

"Really. It's a grand old movie palace with the lights and the curtains and everything. And the women sit in the balcony. The name of the shul is outside on the marquee. And believe me, there isn't any coatroom like there is here."

"No one wears coats?" Elizabeth asks.

"Maybe light jackets in the winter—or a sweater."

Elizabeth laughs in delight. "You must love it there."

"No," Regina says. "I love it here."

3

RAV Kirshner's house has a closed look; the porch glassed in. The rooms are cool and quiet; the furniture dark wood. The upholstery and curtains are heavy and floral, with dust in the pleats—dusty Schumacher prints of roses. They have not been changed since the rebbetzin, Jeremy's mother, was alive. Rav Kirshner's daughter-in-law Rachel keeps up everything herself. She cooks and cleans, with only a little outside help once a week. Jeremy's brother, Isaiah, bears the brunt of the Rav's secretarial work, but it is Rachel who must run the household.

Rachel is a thin woman, almost childlike, with her slight figure and slender, nervous fingers. Her deep-set eyes are blue, her skin pale. She suffers from migraines so terrible she must take to her bed and lie in a completely dark room for hours until they pass. Rachel is the only child of the famous Rabbi Guttman, and her father gave her everything—even sent her to college at Barnard. She commuted each day to the college from her home in Brooklyn. Music was her subject, and she studied piano. Of course, her goal was never a performing career. She does not play for anyone, although she still plays exceptionally well. Her husband listens to her sometimes. He sits with his books and listens to her practice at the old Steinway in Kaaterskill or on the Bosendorfer in the city. Isaiah is not musical, but he admires Rachel's skill.

Rachel and Isaiah have only one child, a thirteen-year-old boy, who is not spoken about for his brilliance but always praised for his behavior. He is dutiful and meek. On Sunday morning the boy sits at the dining-room table, bent over the great black-bound volumes of Talmud, from which he learns each day. Briskly Jeremy flicks on the light over the table. "Don't read in the dark, Nachum." Through the open double doors to the library, Jeremy can see Rachel and Isaiah helping the Rav to his desk. They are easing him slowly into his leather chair, one on each side.

Everything in the house is old. The china is old, so are the candlesticks. They are not from this lifetime, but from another place and another world, the house in Germany in the 1930s. The place is so oppressive, Jeremy can hardly bear it. He avoids coming up to the house as much as possible. And yet Jeremy loves antiques; he collects early printed books—only small volumes, of course—very small ones in fine leather bindings. He doesn't collect extensively. But when a good piece comes up for auction, or when he sees one in the catalogs, if the book is learned and not too expensive, he will buy it. He loves the touch of soft leather and smooth paper. He loves antique furniture, especially small traveling cases, fitted boxes, inlaid lap desks, travel libraries with miniature volumes, travel apothecaries. He cannot afford to indulge his appetite for these, of course. He reveres certain manuscripts in the great libraries; he is moved by certain paintings, portraits of small dark beauties looking over their gilt windowsills into the vast museum rooms, nervous, like train passengers arriving at unfamiliar stations. All these are wonderful to him, but he cannot bear the old furniture and the books in his father's house— watermarked as they are, rescued from the library of the house in Germany. There is a stench about all the old things in the house. They reek. They are like freshly killed birds with the flesh still on them. They have no delicacy, no formal and anonymous beauty; they smell only of death.

Jeremy stands and watches his father at his work, frail and intent, reading letters, sorting them into piles. Slitting open envelopes with his silver letter opener. Isaiah comes out to the dining room. He looks a great deal like Jeremy. He has the same sharp features. But the pointed nose and sharp chin look different on Isaiah, not shrewd, but delicate.

"Are you going back today?" Isaiah asks Jeremy.

"I'm getting ready."

"If you want to stay . . ." Isaiah trails off.

"No, I'm going today. I'm stopping for coffee at Cecil Birnbaum's and then I'm going home."

"I only asked because he said he wants to see you before you go."

"Why?" Jeremy asks.

"He wants to talk to you."

Jeremy looks past Isaiah to where their father sits working in the library. "He's tired," he says.

"You think so?" Isaiah demurs. He is extremely cautious. He is conscious of his public position. In the eyes of the community he is his father's heir.

"He looks worse," Jeremy says. "He's taking the new medication?"

Isaiah doesn't answer, but Rachel has come up beside them. "He takes it every three hours," she says. "But the problem is that his condition changes. Then sometimes the medication is too much and it makes him shake, or sometimes it's too little, and his muscles freeze, and then he can't move." Her voice is perfectly quiet, but authoritative in tone. It is she who gives the Rav his medication and watches the clock constantly through the day. At night there is a male nurse to care for him. The Rav has Parkinson's disease. No one outside the family knows this.

Jeremy stands with his brother and sister-in-law and he feels their unhappiness, their unspoken reproach. After all, he helps neither with the correspondence nor with the medication.

He turns abruptly and strides into the library. "Father," he says, "did you want to talk to me?"

The Rav looks up from his mail. His eyes are black and sparkling in a face and frame diminished by age and illness. His features are small but deep cut so that his face seems cast in shadow. His hair is thin, but even now mostly black. He sits up straight in his chair. He holds his letter opener firmly. He is not too weak to hold it, but his hands shake. It's not that he has too little energy, but that he has too much. His fingers tremble with life. "Close the door, Jeremy," he says.

Jeremy closes the door and then returns to stand in front of the desk.

"Thank you," the Rav says. He looks at Jeremy carefully, but he does not ask him to sit down. "I have a question for you," he says. "Where the *baal koreh* shifts the emphasis of the word at the end of the sentence. What is the word for it? The English term?"

Jeremy's heart beats faster—not from fear, but pride, the desire to pull the word out somehow. He did know the word once, he is sure of it. He knows exactly what his father is talking about; he could come up with examples. The reader of the Torah is finishing a sentence and he pronounces the last word differently, shifts the stress on the vowel. Jeremy searches his memory. He does know the word. Not just as a child, but later, all the way through college, Jeremy pursued the rigorous Jewish curriculum devised by his father. Jeremy and Isaiah had exactly the same education. They studied the same texts, sat together at the same table. The Rav himself examined them. The term is on the tip of Jeremy's tongue. It is a Masoretic rule, recorded in the fifth century.

"Your brother did not know it either," the Rav says calmly, and he goes back to his letters. For a moment Jeremy watches him, sitting there, absorbed in his correspondence. His father is not interested in waiting for an answer. When he asks a question he wants results immediately. If he gets them later he is not interested.

Jeremy stands there for a moment.

"He wants me to do less," the Rav says suddenly.

"Who?" Jeremy is taken aback.

"Your brother wants me to do less."

"Is that what he told you?" Jeremy asks.

"No, we have not spoken about it," the Rav says.

"Then how do you know?" asks Jeremy.

"I know. I see. I hear. I don't need him to tell me." The Rav's tone is denigrating. "He is not an artful person. He is not a subtle person."

It is strange for Jeremy to hear his father talk like this. To hear him speak so openly. There is something in the Rav that he rarely shows, a steeliness, a shrewdness, and a kind of calculation, something political, something self-aware. It's startling, because the Rav is so learned. He is steeped in ancient language, and seems far removed from the world. He seems completely disengaged. And, of course, he is insistent, he absolutely insists, not only for himself, but for Isaiah, his successor, for everyone who follows him, on a religion of strict observance. Slowly and firmly with the passing years, the Rav has guided his community into a life of increasing restrictions. He has moved in his exegesis of Jewish law toward an interpretation ever more bounded and punctilious. What he truly values, it seems to Jeremy, is not deep thought about the sacred, but obedience. Gradually, irrevocably, the Rav is drawing his people after him, in study, in word and deed, into a realm of obscurantism, a life encumbered and weighed down by tradition and endless layers of legalism and strict observance. So it is strange to feel at times the secret disdain that the Rav carries within him, even for his own followers, even for Isaiah, his own son, the good son, after all. To hear him say in that dismissive voice, he is not an artful person, he is not a subtle person. The Rav can show that to Jeremy because he thinks Jeremy is full of scorn already. Cynical and detached enough to enjoy his father's sense of irony. He has flattered Jeremy and rebuked him at the same time.

"What will you do?" Jeremy asks his father.

The Rav does not answer. His silence excuses Jeremy from the room.

Closing the door behind him, Jeremy sees Isaiah in the dining room helping Nachum through the day's Talmud passage. The two of them sit together in their white shirtsleeves bent over the open volume on the table, the folio pages with their ganglia of texts. In the kitchen Rachel is already preparing dinner. Methodically she is putting up a large brisket for the evening. There will be lunch and afternoon prayers; there will be dinner. There will be evening prayers. There will be blessings for washing hands, blessings for breaking bread, blessings after all the meals. There will be prayers before bed. The house is filled with blessings. All time and all activities are regulated by them. It was different when Jeremy's mother was alive. The blessings, the prayers, were hardly noticeable then. They were like the ticking of clocks. Inaudible, except in the dead of night.

Jeremy doesn't like to come to Kaaterskill in part because he feels his mother's absence there. When his mother was alive she ran the house. She insisted on having things done properly. The windows washed, the baseboards dusted. She kept his father's work at bay, never allowing books in the dining or living rooms. Now the Rav's reading, his notes, dictionaries, and volumes of Talmud, seem to creep through the house like tendrils of ivy. Jeremy's mother, Sarah, was a pious and imperious woman, his father's match in the standards she set, although, of course, her interests were different from his, focused on the kitchen and the table, the lighting of candles and polishing of candlesticks, flower arranging, needlework, knitting, painting—she painted well and knitted exquisitely. She was meticulous about her home. She set a gorgeous table on the holidays with crystal and silver, and she had a set of Limoges china, used only two nights a year for Pesach. When she baked, she baked with passionate intensity, destroying any batch that fell below her expectations. When she entertained she exhausted herself. She made herself ill. When she shopped for clothes or furniture, she looked in the stores uptown and then bought on the Lower East Side. She bought there and yet she never bought cheap things. Everything had to be solid. The furniture was solid wood, the silver sterling. The candlesticks she bought at the time of Isaiah's engagement were not hollow like the pretty ones she saw in Tiffany, but solid silver down to the base.

But her real passion was for Jeremy and for his education. Isaiah was never interested in literature or in art, but Jeremy had been different, and she fostered that difference, nursed it tenderly, insisting that his father hire a French teacher at the fledgling Kirshner yeshiva, a history instructor, even an English teacher with a doctorate, a former professor at Brooklyn College. She changed the faculty and the entire curriculum of the school for Jeremy, because, as she put it, she wanted him to have opportunities. Of course, she wanted him to be a rabbi. It was her deepest wish that he succeed his father, and yet succeed to the position with an extraordinary range of skills. Not merely ordination, but with degrees from secular universities as well. Always, she was his champion and advocate, constantly spurring Jeremy on, constantly pushing the Rav to recognize his accomplishments. And yet, even then, his father was turning away.

When his mother died, Jeremy was only twenty-five. Suddenly her advocacy and interest were gone. There was only awkwardness between him and his brother, and with his father, an increasing tension, an icy cold that worsened every year as Jeremy still did not marry. His mother had always assumed he would marry, as she had assumed he would succeed his father, but it was just love; just the force of her love that made her assume these things. In all his studies and his travels, Jeremy has never had a teacher or a friend who has loved him as much as his mother. She lived to see him ordained as a rabbi, but she died before he received his doctorate. She had wanted him to achieve both, as his father had so many years before. She had wanted him to become the rabbi and the scholar that his father was, or might have been if not for the war. Jeremy's mother spurred him on; she gave him language teachers, trips to Europe, books of poetry. She gave him a secular education rare anywhere and unheard of in the Washington Heights community. Even she did not fully understand the value of her gift. She educated her son to rise to the Rav's position. She wanted to give Jeremy the key to his father's kingdom. She gave it to him and set him free.

"REALLY, it's odd to see you here, out of school," Beatrix tells Jeremy over coffee. "The scion of the famous rabbi. I had no idea." They are sitting in the kitchen of Beatrix and Cecil's house. A sunny spacious room with a black potbellied stove as well as a modern oven, a round table tucked into a bay window, a curvaceous 1930s refrigerator with a decal of strawberries. There is no dishwasher, and there are few counters, but there is a blue-and-white delft coffee grinder attached to the wall. "It's like discovering someone has a fortune— someone you thought you knew quite well. But it's more spectacular than that; a whole kingdom in the mountains . . ."

"Only in the summer, Bea," says Cecil.

"Yes, yes, a summer retreat, like the Indian princes retreating during the monsoons."

Jeremy raises an eyebrow. The comparison is odd. His father's middle-class New Yorkers and the bejeweled mogul princes.

"So are you a courtier prince?" Beatrix presses. "Is that why you study all those little princely books? Everyone talks about Jeremy's clothes," she tells Cecil. "They say he finishes his lecture and puts on his coat, and it's as if he were putting on his cape. Because he gives his lectures in character. *You* can do that. I could never do it teaching my miserable freshmen calculus."

"You could try," says Cecil. "Haven't you seen Richard Feynman lecturing? He says he just thinks—If I were an electron where would I be?"

"Sh. Sh," Beatrix says, and then to Jeremy, "What's it like to be in the line of succession, as it were?"

"Well, I'm not—"

"But you are in line, aren't you? Just think—to be inheriting all those souls."

Jeremy sips his coffee. He can't begin to explain any of it to Beatrix. Not merely the politics of the community but those of his family as well.

"I think you've got it backward," Cecil says to Beatrix. "In a situation like this you wouldn't be inheriting souls at all; they would be inheriting you."

"No one is going to be inheriting me, I'm afraid," Jeremy says dryly.

"But suppose you grew a white beard and became all wrinkled and sagelike," Beatrix proposes.

"Tell me about the wedding," Jeremy says.

"You were supposed to be there," Beatrix says.

"If I hadn't been in Spain, I would have been," says Jeremy.

"He's very strange," Beatrix says to Cecil after Jeremy leaves.

"Of course you know he isn't Kirshner's scion at all," Cecil says.

"Yes, I suppose he had to give it up when he started teaching on the outside. A profane university. All sorts of atheists. But then, can you ever give it up completely? Isn't it bred in the bone?"

"I think he does what he wants," says Cecil.

"Oh, a secret identity. Different rules for different places."

"Different manners, in any case. He didn't like all your questions."

"No, I suppose not."

"I liked them, though."

"So you say he has all sorts of secrets."

"Not secrets. Personas."

Beatrix thinks for a moment. Then she grins. "Of course. He must. That way he can be Jack in the country and Ernest in town!"

ELIZABETH and the girls arrive that evening carrying their badminton racquets, and Elizabeth can see that Cecil's wife is a true geometer. Beatrix has surveyed and chalked a real court over the levelest place on the hilly Birnbaum lawn. The lines are all measured out, the corners square, the net pins driven firmly into the ground.

"Are they *all* yours?" Beatrix asks, looking at the girls. "How very clever of you! A captive audience. What do you usually do with them during the day?"

Elizabeth herself used to wonder how to occupy her daughters. She's found, though, that with a steady stream of projects, puzzles, and excursions she and the children survive quite well in the summers. She goes to flea markets and buys odd lots of yarn and fabric remnants. And so under the trees each girl works on handicrafts according to her age and skill. Chani embroiders, although she doesn't much like it. Malki crochets. Ruchel is learning bargello. Sorah is learning to crochet, but she can only make chains. She plays with Brocha in the pine cones.

"Don't you worry they'll become overly domestic?" asks Beatrix. "Too—too little-womanish?"

Elizabeth shrugs and concentrates on her game. She does look Victorian in her long dirndl skirt and white blouse, kerchief over her hair, but running over the lawn she's much faster and more fluid than Beatrix. Watching the two of them from the window in the pantry, Cecil calls out, "She really has you, Bea! You're all over the court!" Elizabeth is hot, but she loves badminton, and she has so little opportunity for exercise. She's always envied Isaac's ability to sit and be content. Somehow she can't savor quiet the way he does. She loves to run. She whips her badminton racquet and the birdie whooshes through the air.

"I'd like to play against you," Cecil tells Elizabeth after she's beaten Beatrix twice.

"Oh, good," says Beatrix. "Now she'll trounce you, my boy." And she retires to watch in the shade.

Elizabeth's daughters stare at Beatrix in her shorts and tank top. Her legs show, and her arms and shoulders.

"She's got *you* all over the court now!" Beatrix calls out gleefully to her husband. And Cecil, breathing hard as he stretches for elliptical shots, looks at his neighbor with new respect.

Partly because Elizabeth has an insurmountable lead, Cecil pauses before his serve. "Listen," he says.

They all look up, and they can hear faint music drifting in the trees.

"I think you're stalling for time," Elizabeth chides Cecil.

"It must be from the Sobels in back," Cecil says. "The wedding reception for their niece. I remember they were going to have a trio up from Palenville."

"Let's dance!" Beatrix springs up from the grass.

"Absolutely not." Cecil rejects her outstretched hands. "You know I never dance."

"Oh, all right then." Beatrix claps her hands on Elizabeth's shoulders. Despite her protests that she doesn't know how, Elizabeth finds herself twirling to the music with Beatrix, her skirt billowing between the mathematician's bare legs.

"Oh, no, I can't, I've never waltzed," Elizabeth gasps as they waltz across the grass.

"I do think we're corrupting her!" Beatrix calls out to Cecil.

Kerchief loosening, Elizabeth protests, "Oh no, it's quite permissible for women to dance together." And then, over Beatrix's shoulder, she sees her children sitting under the tree, all looking at her. Five pairs of disapproving eyes.

4

NOISE fills Andras Melish's house. Andras's daughter, Renée, is practicing piano, banging away. His son, Alex, clatters up and down the
stairs with the old fish tank he's converted into a terrarium. Outside,
the Curtis boy is mowing the lawn. Andras hides upstairs in the
bedroom, reading about the Syrian invasion of Lebanon in the *Econo-
mist,* and hoping Nina won't call him.

Often he avoids her. It makes him feel guilty, but he can't help it.
She is beautiful, his young wife. Her red hair, her Spanish accent—
even her sharp temper—seem to him exotic, a remnant of her childhood in Buenos Aires. Andras still carries with him his first seventeen
years in Budapest and the corresponding mystique of the tropical, the
sun, the flaming colors, on the other side of the world. Nina is all that
to his cool gray eyes. He likes to buy her clothes and jewelry. He
bought her a square-cut emerald ring, and it sparkles as she gestures
with her hands. You wouldn't know she's only five foot one, the way
she moves, the way she lifts her chin to look you in the eye. She
makes Andras smile, impresses him with her determined voice, her
clear ideas about whom to see and how to educate the children. And
he tells himself she's sensible, insightful, about certain things. But
always, after he tells himself, he comes to the fact no catalog of Nina's
virtues can change: he doesn't take her seriously.

He's known this for some time, and it disturbs him. He doesn't
really listen to her. She chatters and she sermonizes. She sounds so

pompous, coupling her pronouncements, for example, about large cars and safety with her insistence that Andras should save gas by driving up with Isaac. She speaks the same way about religious rituals, insisting on minutiae like fish forks that Andras really doesn't care to know about. Over time Nina has become more and more tenacious in her observance, so that while the family used to eat in unsupervised restaurants when the children were small, now Nina mistrusts such places entirely. Andras would be perfectly happy to stay home and sleep through services on Shabbat, but Nina insists that he set a good example for the children, and so he goes. Strictly speaking, morally, Nina is right to insist. Andras's parents taught him that if you are going to be religious, you have to do it all, observing every holiday and law. They believed that when it comes to God you can't do things by halves—which was why they did nothing. Andras humors Nina, lets her have her kosher food and synagogue services. To his skeptical mind they don't mean much. That's the problem, as he sees it: he allows her all the trivial, superfluous decisions. He defers to her judgment about car pooling and the brand of cheese they buy. In appearance Andras lets Nina rule and dictate every least little thing. And in fact, the things Nina determines are least and little to him.

There are moments when Andras looks at his wife and remembers how he first felt about her. But the memories themselves are embarrassing to him now. Even his first love for her, he thinks, was middle aged. He used to prize everything Nina said to him, as if she were a child speaking each word for the first time. Later, when the words weren't new, when her opinions no longer seemed like new creations, he let them sink back into the everyday sound of things.

As Nina has grown more observant, Andras has become distanced from her. Her religious fervor doesn't interest him. Coming to tradition late, Nina has all the pedantry of an autodidact. Her strivings seem inauthentic to Andras, and not at all spiritual. Really nothing more than an expression of Nina's ferocious domesticity. He isn't involved with his wife. He knows it's wrong. Even his gifts to Nina trouble him; he gives her rings instead of his own good opinion. He feels sometimes that he demeans her even with affection.

Sunday afternoon Andras and Nina sit with his sisters on the porch, and Nina pours iced tea.

"I've always felt," Nina says, "that for the children a Jewish education must come first."

Eva and Maja nod politely from the glider. They are always polite to Nina, although she amuses them privately. She seems to them more like a daughter-in-law than a sister-in-law. Nina is seventeen years younger than Andras, and more than twenty-five years younger than they are. Certainly, she is young enough to be their daughter. But Eva and Maja sit together in their print dresses, and they listen, as they always do, occasionally exchanging glances. A stranger would think the two were spinsters, they look so close, so complete, sitting next to each other. But, in fact, they are very much Mrs. Cohen and Mrs. Rubinstein. Very much matrons, although they married late, well after the war and their emigration. Those years still cling to them and make them a pair; long years when they subsisted on each other. Now, in their sixties, Eva and Maja together have a kind of burnished glow.

"I was talking to Regina about this," Nina says. "She sends her children to the public schools in Beverly Hills. She doesn't mind them studying among goyim. But I, for one, would never take the risk. If you're with the others you forget who you are. Assimilation." She pronounces the word slowly, as if she doesn't want to set it off.

Eva steals a look at Maja. This red-haired girl from the ends of the earth, preaching to them about assimilation! Their little sister-in-law from South America telling them it's dangerous to keep an open mind to different backgrounds.

"I know about this," Nina says, refilling their glasses. "Believe me, I know. It goes very deep in Buenos Aires. The Saints days. Parades in the streets. It goes very deep. They talk about this pluralism in the *Jewish Post*. They should talk about Jewish education. Renée?" she calls to her daughter as she comes out of the house.

"I'm going into town," Renée says.

"She practiced today," Andras says.

"She practiced today fifteen minutes," Nina corrects him.

But Renée is already running down the walk to the street, dragging her bike behind her, taking a running start.

"You could go see the Shulman girls and say hello," Nina calls after her daughter. Renée keeps pedaling. "I don't know what's wrong with her this summer," Nina frets.

"She just wants to get out of the house," says Andras. Even he does not realize how true this is.

RENÉE pedals up the street as if her mother and her brother, and even her aunts with their iced tea, were chasing her. She used to love to come up in the summers and play with the Shulman girls across the street. Even last summer she didn't mind them, but this year Renée is fifteen, and suddenly everything in Kaaterskill is too short and too small. All the wrong size. "You should use the time to practice," her mother says. "You should read a book." But Renée isn't going to sit around reading books. School is over, after all.

Renée is a bit spoiled, although her mother never meant her to be. Nina is strict with her, but neither her father nor her aunts even try. Renée is too pretty. Her hair is shoulder length and copper brown. Her brown eyes are flecked with gold. She is small, and her skin is fair and lightly freckled. When she was a very little girl in curls and white dresses, no one could resist her. Her face is still pretty, but becoming more interesting, more self-aware. She still wears dresses because her mother makes her. The hems get tangled up in her bicycle, but she has to wear them all the same. Her mother doesn't like girls to wear anything but skirts and dresses.

In town Renée walks her bike up Main Street. She watches the children from the city camp march by in double lines. She sits for a long time on the steps of the post office. Then she wanders on in a desultory way, cutting through the parking lot of the A & P, walking her bike up the street past the launderette to where Main Street becomes a bridge over Bramble Creek. She leans her bike against the railing and looks down into the streambed below, where the water bubbles in silty pools between the rocks. She is surprised to see that someone is down there in the creek.

A girl in rolled-up jeans is picking her way across the stream—slowly, as if looking for something. Renée scans the creek and spots an old straw hat near the bank. "Is that it?" she calls down.

The girl looks up, startled. Then she sees where Renée is pointing. She hops from rock to rock and picks up the hat. Renée can see that the hat is a little wet, but the girl puts it on anyway and clambers up the bank and back around to the bridge where Renée is standing. "Thanks," she says.

"You're welcome." Renée can't help staring. The girl is tall, much taller than Renée. Her skin is tanned, her eyes dark brown. She has long straight hair, brown streaked blond.

The girl stares back at Renée. She asks, "Are you one of the summer people?"

"Yeah," says Renée uncomfortably.

"I am too," says the girl. "My name is Stephanie Fawess." She rubs her hand off on her jeans and holds it out to Renée.

"Renée Melish," says Renée. And she shakes Stephanie's hand, although it seems an odd thing to do.

"Want to get a cheeseburger?" asks Stephanie.

"No, thanks."

"Why not?"

"I can't," says Renée, embarrassed.

"Why? Diet or religion?"

"Religion," says Renée.

Stephanie nods matter-of-factly. "You're one of the Orthodox," she says. "I have an aunt who's Orthodox too."

"She's Jewish?" asks Renée.

"Greek," Stephanie says. "She converted, and now she's Greek Orthodox. My grandmother had a conniption cause we're Maronite Catholics."

"Oh," says Renée. "You're not Greek?"

"Syrian," says Stephanie. "That's my bike over there." She points to a ten-speed bike tossed on its side on the other side of the bridge. "I'm going down to Lacy Farm to see the cows. Want to come?" Stephanie ties the straw hat under her chin. "It isn't all that far."

Renée hesitates a second. Then she begins to pedal behind this strange abrupt girl with straight hair spilling out from under the hat and down her back.

"Do only the men wear black?" Stephanie calls over as they ride.

"No," Renée says. "Anyway, my parents—most people—just wear normal clothes. Where do you live?"

"Mohican Lake," says Stephanie. "We have a boat too. My parents went fishing. That's why I'm going to the farm. I want to be a veterinarian," she adds. "Large animals."

"What grade are you in—in the city?" asks Renée.

"Ninth. St. Ann's."

Stephanie's father and her uncle are independent truckers, she explains. They truck between New York and Montreal. It's a good business, since they're independent; but they have to work summers too. They drive for days up and back from Canada, and Stephanie wants to go with them but she isn't allowed. Stephanie's uncle rents the other house on the lake, and he also comes up with his wife and daughters, Michelle and Monique. These cousins of hers—Stephanie is worried about their minds. She herself is a feminist and successfully accused her math teacher of intimidation and harassment over his use of sexist jokes in the classroom.

"You got him fired?" Renée is amazed.

"Yup," says Stephanie. "Tape recorder in my desk. Turn right here on Mohican. They're a bunch of racists in there, you know." She waves her hand at the gatehouse off Mohican Road. A private road arcs upward into the leafy hillside. "The owners have a secret covenant."

Renée doesn't know what a covenant is, but she doesn't ask.

"I'd love to infiltrate them," says Stephanie. "If I don't work with large animals, I want to expose social injustice. I think I'm going to become an activist. What do you want to do?"

"I don't know," says Renée, feeling eclipsed by the decisive and far-reaching plans of Stephanie.

Renée's ideas seem unimportant next to Stephanie's agenda. Stephanie talks about the news and the election, inflation, abortion, and nuclear proliferation. "I mean, one girl in my class asked me: 'What's the Cold War?'" she tells Renée. "This was a girl at a selective private school, for God's sake! I just wanted to find a place where I could quietly commit suicide, you know?"

"Yeah," says Renée, and she plans to find out what the Cold War is as soon as she can get her father alone.

Where the road flattens again, the houses are year-round places, ranches fixed up with American flags in front and white wagon wheels. There are flower beds planted with petunias and vegetable patches sprouting tomato plants and giant pumpkin vines. At the turnoff onto the farm road, they find a vegetable stand with peaches, lettuce, watermelons, and barrels piled with fresh ears of corn.

The Lacy Farm visitors' path leads up through pastures to a great red barn and two towering aluminum silos. Dressed in overalls and serious boots, the official Lacy Farm visitors' guide is Bebe Lacy, an in-law of the family. Mrs. Lacy leads Renée and Stephanie into the cow barn thundering with the sound of hundreds of cows chewing, snorting, swatting flies, placidly rubbing flanks against the partitions between them. The girls watch the milk machines from the wooden walkway between the double rows of stalls. Above each cow hangs a white plaque painted with her name, weight, and pounds of milk output per day. "When you leave, you girls'll have to sign our guest book," Mrs. Lacy says. "We always have guests sign the register because we run out of names for the cows. This is Stephanie." Mrs. Lacy pats the rump of a huge red cow. "She's a good one. Good milker." Stephanie the girl looks up, as if uncertain whether this is offensive. The cow swats off a fly.

"And what did you say your name was?" Mrs. Lacy asks Renée. She lights up when Renée tells her. "Terrific. We haven't got a Renée. How do you spell that?"

"Do you feel honored?" Stephanie asks Renée as they bike home.

"What?" Renée breathes hard as she pedals to keep up with Stephanie.

"They're planning to name a cow after you. Don't you feel honored?"

Renée laughs. She feels hot and sweaty, and happy. It probably wasn't a big deal for Stephanie, but it was an adventure for Renée to bike all the way out to the farm. She's certainly done something not allowed. "I can think of lots of good names for the cows," she says.

"Yeah, but they already have most girls' names you can imagine," says Stephanie.

"How about Esther?" Renée starts to giggle. "Or Eva, or Beyla?" Then she remembers the Shulman girls, "How about Chani, Malki, Sorah, Ruchel, and Brocha?"

"What is that—one name?" asks Stephanie.

"Five," says Renée.

"You said them all together. Anyway, they're too hard to pronounce. Do you want to go swimming?"

Renée thinks for a minute. "I should go home," she says.

"So let's go tomorrow. Let's go to North Lake."

"All the way up there? It's far."

"So we'll take the bus," Stephanie says. "What's the matter with you, woman?"

Renée chokes up again with giggles.

"What're you laughing about?" Stephanie asks, half joking.

"Just the way you talk," says Renée.

"What do you mean?"

"Just—calling me a woman."

"That's what we are," says Stephanie, and she looks over at Renée and her eyes sparkle, and her hair streams out like a banner behind her.

"Okay," Renée says, "we are."

RENÉE'S aunts are gone, but her parents are sitting on the porch when she comes home. Nina smells manure instantly.

"Renée! Take off your shoes," she says. "Where have you been? Don't bring those shoes into the house!"

Renée does as she is told, and takes some cookies from the table on the porch. Tired out from biking, she settles down next to her father on the glider.

"You thought I was wrong about what I said?" her mother is asking.

"Well . . ." Andras hesitates.

"You agreed with them," says Nina. She shakes her head. "I still say, a sense of identity is what young people need."

"No, Nina, no one was arguing about that," he says. "It's just a question of how much a school can provide—that's all Eva meant. There is only so much a school, even a private school, can do. And as for public schools, they have a certain mission to—"

Impatiently, Nina begins clearing away the empty glasses of iced tea, and puts the dessert plates on a tray. "The children don't know their history," she says. "They know nothing about the war. Nothing. Who will teach them this in the public schools? I spoke to Regina about this. What do her children learn? They learn *American* history; they learn about Pearl Harbor. To them that's what the war is. They don't learn about their heritage. They don't learn about Israel. It's a shanda."

"All right, fine," says Andras, "it's a shanda." He gets up and stretches.

"Renée, do you want a glass of milk with that?" Nina asks.

"No, thank you," says Renée, and she pushes the glider with her feet as her mother bustles around, clearing the dishes. Of course Renée doesn't mention that she and Stephanie have decided to go to North Lake tomorrow.

THAT afternoon Andras walks up Mohican. The sky is growing cloudy, the light dim. On either side of the road the forest grows thick and lush. Secretive. Nina's words echo in Andras's mind. She believes in education. She thinks that finding the right school, insisting on the best teacher, will solve every problem. When the children learned about the Holocaust in school, Nina wanted Andras to talk to Renée's class about how he got out of Budapest. He wouldn't do it. He's never talked about it, not even to Nina. There are people who lecture about that sort of thing, so it won't be forgotten. Andras can't do that. It's not because it is too painful for him. That isn't the reason at all. He wasn't in the camps. It's because there is no way for him to convey his experience. It lies within him, a separate place within his present life. He couldn't begin to explain it to his children, really just born and unscratched, all of a piece; knowing just one world, one language.

It's disingenuous, he thinks, to teach that kind of thing, that tragic history. You can never fully tell another person what you know. You can't imagine what you don't know. There is no way to conceive, to picture, someone else's life. There is no way to transfer memories. His own experience of the war is one of confusion, ignorance. When Andras was sixteen his parents said good-bye to him. They put him on a train and sent him to France. Andras had not wanted to go; his mother cried. But his father was adamant. He

nearly pushed Andras away at the station. The urgency of the moment prevented any long good-byes. The train bearing down into the
station; the heaviness of the time. In France, alone, Andras made his
way from safe house to safe house. He hid alone for months, alone
with his thoughts, awaiting and yet half dreading the release his parents had purchased for him, the passage to New York. In New York
Andras found his sisters. They had to make their way on a different
route. As for Andras's parents, his aunts and uncles, his grandparents,
his childhood sweetheart, none he left behind survived.

Nina thinks he has a responsibility. She's told Andras it's his
responsibility to record his suffering on tape, or write it down. Survivors are witnesses, and when they are gone there will be nothing left.
This is one of her opinions, earnest and fierce and full of the phrases
of articles in Jewish periodicals. Survivors have to tell their stories
before it's too late. But how can he describe a vacancy, an absence?
That was his past life. He has no way to explain it to Nina, who
thinks he has been shutting her out. Nina thinks the problem is the
age difference between them. The seventeen years Andras lived before she was born: Andras's childhood in Budapest, the years working
in New York. Nina thinks those years account for the difficulty they
have understanding each other. What she doesn't understand is that,
like hers, Andras's knowledge of the war is full of gaps. He left before
the end. It's an emptiness within him, his escape.

Andras walks down the cool road, no cars in sight. The forest
towers over his head on both sides, thick with ragged branches, and
soggy leaves. He is about a mile from Kendall Falls when a doe and
her fawn step out from the trees ahead. Andras holds still, and the
deer freeze a moment, too, their bodies taut, ears opening, slender
legs poised, ready to fly. Andras hardly ever sees deer on the road, just
the yellow signs warning motorists of deer crossings. Driving up
once, he saw a buck, but it was far away and vanished quickly into the
trees. These are close; Andras can even see their eyes, dark, passive,
impressionable, he thinks—although the word couldn't apply to
them. They haven't anything to learn. He hardly breathes; he doesn't
want to frighten them. But in the next instant they are gone. The
deer slip into their own shadowy light, and leave him at the edge of
the forest.

He wishes he could see the deer again, if only for a moment. He wants, somehow, to come closer. He bends his tall frame under the branches at the edge of the road, and follows them into the trees. Cautiously, tentatively, Andras picks his way through the woods. He feels foolish, and awkward, out of his element, but he keeps walking. He keeps pushing away the branches in his path. He knows he won't see the deer again, but he walks on, as if by walking far enough he'll find them. He'll stop in a minute, he thinks. He'll turn back on Mohican Road for home. But in the meantime he steps farther in. The forest floor is soft under his feet, and damp, and all the rocks are velveted with moss. The place is wet under the trees, and its sounds surround him. Mosquitoes and distant water. He walks on in a kind of haze, absorbed with the place, the dark tree trunks and the thick carpet of dead leaves.

The sight of a house stops him short. It is really just a shack, not much bigger than his own toolshed. The walls are weathered wood, and the roof covered with loose, sloppy shingles, growing lichen. In front, in a rough sort of clearing, two white goats are wandering loose. There is a musty smell about the place, the scent of cats and urine. A woodpile stacked up high stands at one side of the house. Leaves rustle; something moves. Out from behind the woodpile steps a tiny old woman. She is extremely small, her hair gray, pulled back in a bun; she wears a blue windbreaker over her dress. In the city she might be a bag lady; in the woods Andras isn't sure what she is. She is holding white plastic cider jugs, two in each hand. She looks surprised to see someone on her property, but she puts her cider jugs on the ground and comes toward Andras, as if to show him she is unafraid.

"Are you lost?" she asks.

"I don't think so," Andras says.

"Do you need help?" she asks.

"I hope not," Andras says.

"Did you come for a reason?" she asks.

"I was just walking," Andras says.

"Oh, all right, then. I'm pleased to meet you," she tells him. "My name is Una Darmstadt-Cooper."

"Oh," Andras says. He has heard of her from Cecil. She is a

photographer and writer of children's nature books. In fact Cecil once gave some of her books to Renée and Alex. "My name is Andras Melish," he says.

"Summer people," she says.

"Yes." His eyes glance over her worn cabin. "Do you live here all year?"

"Of course I do." She seems amused by his reaction. "Are you thinking it's strange?"

"No, I was just thinking it must be difficult."

"Do you mean the winters? Oh, no. Winter is my favorite time. In the city the winters are all the same. Up here they are magnificent. Like the wrath of God."

"I suppose you get used to them," Andras says. "Were you born here?"

"No. Born and bred in New York City. But I left in 1938. I escaped with my life."

"Did you," Andras says.

Una explains, "There was the pollution, and the overpopulation. And then there was the war. I was against that. The artists were just starting to leave in those days. They had their colonies, and their little enclaves. But that was not for me. When I left, I left for good. I don't go to the city, I don't talk to the city."

"No telephone?"

"Oh, not at all. If it's for my books, my publishers, you know— they leave word for me at Kendall Falls Library."

She picks up her jugs of springwater and carries them to the door of her house.

"May I help you get those inside?" Andras asks.

"Oh, no, you'd better get back home," Una says. "Better hurry. It's going to rain."

Andras makes his way back to Mohican Road. The sky does look threatening, and he walks quickly. The old woman's roof must leak when it rains. And the cabin must be miserable in the snow. How does she manage in the winter? She can't depend on wood alone to heat the place.

Raindrops pepper Mohican Road's gray asphalt. Andras can't imagine that Una is as independent as she seems. Someone must come by to care for her in winter. Some relative, perhaps, comes by with food or helps her with her heat. She must buy fuel in Kingston.

A honking car startles Andras and he looks up to see Rabbi Lamkin's battered station wagon. Pesach Lamkin and his wife, Beyla, are ferrying a load of their own children, and their children's friends.

"You want a ride home?" Pesach calls out.

"It's going to pour," Beyla says, unrolling her window.

Andras hesitates, but he knows that Beyla is right. He'll get soaked if he keeps walking.

He squeezes into the backseat, and just manages to shut the door. The children are packed in the car, two perched illegally in front between Pesach and Beyla, three in back, and at least three curled up in the very back of the wagon.

Andras sits with his arms drawn in at his sides. Noisy with children's voices, the crowded car is a shock after the still forest. The car is filled with crumbs and potato chips, stuffed with toys. Still, Andras is grateful that the Lamkins stopped. As soon as they are on their way the rain comes down, pounding, streaming over the windshield.

"Slower, Pesach," Beyla warns, and then to Andras, "I hope on the Fourth it doesn't rain like this. You're coming on the Fourth?"

"What's on the Fourth?" Andras asks.

"Opening day."

"Oh, of course." The Fourth of July is opening day for the Lamkins' day camp.

"We're having a treasure hunt," Beyla says, "and prizes. Food, great food from New York. Tug-of-war, softball. Everyone's coming. It'll be nice. We're doing it up by the falls. You know."

Andras nods. The camp is of huge importance to the Lamkins. Really a windfall for them. Last summer there were great debates about whether there should even be a summer camp. The shul owned property, the old Thorne estate that Cecil's father had bought years ago when he was treasurer. Mr. Birnbaum had bought the land as an investment for the shul, and now it's worth some money. At the shul board meeting last summer the Lamkins proposed that they lease the land for just a few dollars a year, so that they could get a summer camp off the ground. Of course, old Mr. Birnbaum was not alive to respond to the suggestion, but Cecil stood up in his father's place and declared that the land should be sold or rented at market value, not for a pittance—and if it wasn't, he was quitting the board. Some people said that if Cecil wanted to quit, fine. The shul should invest in the children above all, not in real estate. Others said that starting a day camp was too difficult, and the children should stay home.

Meanwhile, all through this controversy the Lamkins were holding their Shabbes afternoon onegs for girls and boys. Rabbi Lamkin was telling his group of thirty boys that they would have a basketball court if a camp were organized, and shiurs at picnic tables outdoors. And Beyla Lamkin was subtly campaigning among the girls. She would pass out Stella D'oro cookies, juice, and nonpareils; then she would launch into her stories: the little shul all alone and abandoned in the forest, discovered by a hunter who heard it weeping; the poor man who spent his last pennies so he could buy a fish for Shabbes, and then, cutting open the fish, found a priceless diamond there; the rich man and the silvered mirrors he learned to give up, exchanging them for clear glass so that he could look out onto the suffering of the world; the little Jewish boy who was stolen away and became pope. And she told tales of selfless men. Men who gave tzedakah at the highest level. They didn't merely give gold and silver; they helped the unfortunate help themselves. Not only that, but they gave in secret. Such was the modesty of these saints that their work was known only after they had died. So tenderhearted were they that they wept to see a Jew breaking Shabbes. Beyla dwelt on the importance of a generous heart over and above all practical considerations, and even told the children of a piece of land left to a city, and how the king debated what to do, until finally he decided he would give it to the children for them to play in.

The Lamkins got up and spoke before a meeting of the Kaater-skill parents, and they explained why it was necessary to establish a summer camp. The camp would protect the children from the dangers of summer; it would keep them learning, even when the weather was nice, so that they wouldn't run wild and forget everything from the school year. Hashem shouldn't be in one ear and out the other, but all year round! Of course, Andras thought these arguments were absurd. He would have walked out of the meeting, if it hadn't been for Nina. Andras has no patience for this kind of thing, this cringing from the world in little enclaves, this desire to keep the children from outside influences, the building of a European ghetto in America. He grimaces now to hear the Lamkins go on about the camp. He came from the Old Country himself, after all, and he chose the new.

THE rain splashes Elizabeth and her daughters as they dash from their car into the Kendall Falls Library. They come every Sunday, because during the week they don't have the car.

Elizabeth opens the jingling glass door, and the girls walk past the box of sale books, twenty-five cents each. "Wipe your shoes, please," the librarian, Ernestine Schermerhorn, tells the children. The girls are a little afraid of her. She is a proud librarian, watchful and keen, with short salt-and-pepper hair, a tall, straight back, and the elegant, slender arms of a trained dancer. Mrs. Schermerhorn often tells how in her youth she studied modern dance at Bennington College. Now she lives with her husband on Mohican Road. Not in the Mohican Road estates, but in the gatehouse. Her husband serves as guard for that exclusive community, and Mrs. Schermerhorn is proud of that. Her own family is old, pre-Revolutionary, she has told Elizabeth, descended from the earliest Dutch settlers on the mountain.

Mrs. Schermerhorn's assistant, Janet Knowlton, is young and fair and likes to read stories to the little girls, but Mrs. Schermerhorn just watches them from her desk. When the children come up to her to take out their books, Mrs. Schermerhorn examines each selection, and looks each girl in the eye as if to judge whether she is worthy.

The walls of the library are decorated with posters depicting "Common Birds of the Northeast," "Leaves of the Forest," and "Woodland Flowers." All the posters have a cameo picture of Smokey the Bear and his famous saying: "Only YOU can prevent forest fires." The children's books are on short bookcases. Also for children, there is a corner with a burnt-orange rug, pillows, small chairs, and a long coffee table covered with glass. Under the glass lies a map of Fairyland in ink and watercolor, an intricate, glowing map the color of sunsets, with fairies and sea monsters, Sleeping Beauty's castle, Sinbad's ship, the wicked witch's gingerbread house sharing the dark forest with

Robin Hood's men. There is Cinderella's coach on the way to the
ball, the cottage of Snow White and Rose Red, the four winds blowing with squinting eyes and billowy, puffed cheeks.

Chani wanders around while her mother helps Sorah and Ruchel
find their books, large ones with their clear plastic library covers. *B Is
for Betsy*—all the Betsy books; *Ramona the Pest, Bread and Jam for
Frances.* There are tall boxes of records on one of the tables. Chani
remembers once her mother took out some records of poetry, and
they all went over to Cecil Birnbaum's house to hear them, because
Cecil had a record player. There were records of Robert Frost, and
Dylan Thomas, and Edna St. Vincent Millay. Old voices that creaked
and swung in rhythm, their long phrases like the screen door on the
bungalow, closing slowly, partway, a little more, and then, with a
long sigh, thumping shut.

Elizabeth marshals the girls at Ernestine Schermerhorn's desk,
and deliberately, formally, but with a kind of humor the girls miss,
the librarian calls each one before her.

"Hannah." Mrs. Schermerhorn hands Chani *Nabby Adams's Di-
ary.* "You have two weeks. Sarah"—she summons Sorah up to the
desk. Mrs. Schermerhorn glances at the windows streaming with
rain. "I'm surprised you came in this downpour," she says.

"I thought it would let up," says Elizabeth.

"It shows no sign of letting up," Mrs. Schermerhorn says.
"Sarah, you have two weeks. Rachel," she calls to Ruchel. Mrs.
Schermerhorn says to Elizabeth, "You must be extremely careful
driving home in this. We've had some accidents on these roads, cars
swerving, trucks losing control. As you know, it's a straight drop
down to Devil's Kitchen."

"We've been hiking there," Elizabeth says. She has always
thought Devil's Kitchen a lovely place, dark and green, its great boulders strewn in the cleft of the gorge.

"You may have seen the wreck," Mrs. Schermerhorn says.

"No," says Elizabeth.

"Well, I suppose it's grown over now. It's been ten years. Has it
been ten years, Janet?" she asks the assistant librarian. "Young people
driving home in the rain. Flew right over the guardrail and down in
the gorge. That was how we lost Billy Walker. He used to stand here

just where you're standing now. He would come in at all hours. His sweetheart worked here. Candy Kendall. And they were just married when he died. Married just a day."

The car is silent as Elizabeth drives home in the rain. Thoroughly subdued by Mrs. Schermerhorn, the girls clutch their books as Elizabeth eases the station wagon around the curving mountain road.

The rain shakes down from the mountain like loose pine needles. It floods the sidewalks on Maple and collects in ponds under the bushes. Running up the path to the bungalow, the children brush between overgrown hydrangeas, and a waterfall drops down on their heads.

Inside, the older girls go off to read on their beds; but Brocha doesn't know how to read yet, and she cries, because no one will play with her. "Be quiet and I'll read you a story," Elizabeth promises.

"No! No!" Brocha wails. "*I* will tell it."

"All right," Elizabeth says, sitting the three-year-old down in a chair.

"Three bears," Brocha says.

"All right." Elizabeth waits.

"You tell it," Brocha says.

Outside, the trees shake with thunder; the bungalow rattles. Elizabeth tells Brocha "The Three Bears" and "The Three Little Pigs."

"Different story," Brocha says.

Elizabeth gets out one of the new library books, *Rip van Winkle*. "This is a good story. Look, Rip van Winkle is watching the elves make the thunder." She holds up the picture for Brocha to see. The elves are dancing up and down in the mountains in their peaked hats and pointed shoes. They are playing ninepins with the mountain boulders.

"Three bears," Brocha says.

"Once upon a time in the great big forest there were three bears," Elizabeth begins, looking out at the rain.

The rain is still falling after dinner that night. Elizabeth and Isaac sit on the couch and listen to it thumping on the roof, and Elizabeth thinks how quickly the weekend slips away. Tomorrow is Monday, and Isaac will have to get up before six to drive back to the city.

There was going to be a sort of theater party tonight. Beatrix and

Cecil, Leah Landauer and Elizabeth, were planning to see *A Midsummer Night's Dream,* but it's playing all the way down in Lexington, and in this storm it isn't safe to drive there. Beatrix wants to try again during the week, but Isaac will be in the city and won't be able to watch the children. Elizabeth is a bit disappointed. She hasn't been to a play in years. Isaac doesn't go to them. Plays aren't exactly forbidden, but they aren't encouraged. The behavior onstage is so often violent, improper, everything painted in garish colors. Plays are vulgar entertainment.

"I was hoping it would clear up, so I could go to Lexington," Elizabeth says.

Isaac doesn't answer.

"You think it's silly—to go?" she asks him.

"Well . . ." he begins. He doesn't have to say it; she knows what he is thinking. It just isn't something that they do. They never go to plays in the city. And is it because of Beatrix? he is wondering.

"I wouldn't go to plays—in general," she tells him. "But this is different—because it's Shakespeare."

Elizabeth has a romantic streak. But hers is romanticism of an unusual kind. Unlike many of her neighbors Elizabeth does not romanticize religion. God and the scriptures, worship and ritual, are all simple, practical things for her. She never sheds a tear during Yom Kippur, and she doesn't sit in her car and look heavenward, thanking God after near accidents. She isn't a skeptic like Andras, or a gadfly like Cecil. For her religion is such a habit, ritual so commonplace, that she takes it for granted. She worships God three times a day in her room, and while she would never say she felt a familiarity with her Creator, the prayers are familiar, and she's used to approaching him. The sacred isn't mysterious to her, and so she romanticizes the secular. Poetry, universities, and paintings fill her with awe. Museums, opera houses—although she has never been inside one. It might come from being English. Her family in Manchester was strictly observant, but her mother, who spoke Yiddish, was a collector of China teacups and an avid royal-watcher who wept to hear the king's abdication address on the radio and later shamelessly named her daughter after the princess Elizabeth. When Elizabeth was a child, her family all sat together and watched the queen's coronation on television, the grand procession in the vaulted abbey, the crosses, robes, and crowns, dazzling even in black and white and shades of fuzzy gray.

"What are you thinking?" Isaac asks.

"I wonder if Esther Ergman's niece could watch the children," Elizabeth says. "If I go during the week."

THURSDAY night is clear, the weekend storm long gone. Elizabeth puts up a meat loaf for Chani to serve the little ones. She shows Amy Ergman where the nightgowns are, and the puzzles, and then Cecil and Beatrix zoom up, honking their funny Hillman Minx, and they're off to the play with Leah Landauer and her oldest boy, Chaim.

The theater is a red barn in Lexington with lights hung from the rafters. There is no curtain, just a sudden blackout before the play begins. Then the barn is like a planetarium. Instinctively, Elizabeth looks up for the stars. Titania and Oberon appear instead, their flesh rippling in the speckled light. They seem constantly to be shedding skins, half dancing, half copulating, on the stage. Elizabeth has read, but never seen, the play. On the page *A Midsummer Night's Dream* was lovely but elaborate, like old embroidery. Onstage the fairy-spirits leap like cats.

"This *is* good," Beatrix says during intermission, and she sounds surprised.

"Their enunciation is excellent," Cecil says.

Elizabeth sees that the Landauer boy looks truly ashen. She feels sorry for him in his gray hat, dragged along by his more cosmopolitan mother. But she can also see him through Beatrix's eyes, and it occurs to her that in some strange way he probably feels obligated to look ashen—that he finds his downcast look and embarrassment are requirements of his social situation.

"Do you like it?" Beatrix asks Elizabeth.

They are all looking at her, and so she smiles. "I hadn't imagined that the poetry was so athletic," she says. "It's very modern. But I think all the dancing makes it otherworldly—and that's what Shakespeare must have intended."

"Now, that's telling," Cecil says, rattling his program with a gleam in his eye. "That you talk about Shakespeare's intentions—as if he intended something."

"Well, didn't he?"

"He could have—but it's wonderfully archaic of you, talking about authors' intending things and carrying them out. You betray your archaic theology," Cecil says. "Talking about texts as the products of authors, and authors meaning what they say. I suppose you'll say next that God sat and wrote down the Torah and all the commentaries, all seeing and all intending, of course—"

"He's just baiting you, Elizabeth." Beatrix rolls up her program and whacks her husband on the knee. "Pay no attention to that man in the corner."

"I don't really see the connection—between God and Shakespeare," Elizabeth says.

"Bardolatry," Beatrix tells Cecil repovingly.

"Traitor," he shoots back.

Beatrix confides to Elizabeth, "Cecil's a literary critic, so he can't believe people simply have ideas and write them down. He has to make it more complicated so he'll have something to do."

"Now, that isn't fair," says Cecil. "And I wasn't asking you. I was asking Elizabeth, do you think Shakespeare might have imagined this sort of . . . slithery production?"

"Well . . ."

"Absolutely not. This was a—"

"Sh. They're starting," says Beatrix. Elizabeth leans back and watches the rest of the play, through Puck's last monologue, delivered with a final pelvic thrust.

By the time Elizabeth gets home, everyone is sleeping, even the baby-sitter. She wakes up Amy Ergman and pays her, and Amy walks off to her aunt's across the street. Then Elizabeth puts on her nightgown. It's too late to phone Isaac in the city.

She wasn't sure exactly what Cecil meant by bringing up theology at intermission. Theology and Shakespeare have nothing to do with each other. She supposes he was just trying to tease her. It didn't surprise her when he said she was archaic; he thinks all the Rav's followers are old fashioned. He's told her before that he doesn't see why people should revere one man's authority, or one family. She imagines Cecil thinks reverence is confining. Of course it isn't, when you grow up with it. Her family had always followed their Rav in Manchester; and when she married Isaac and moved to America, Elizabeth simply took up his community and his Rav. It was simple, almost nothing, like taking Isaac's last name. There are slight differences in the Kirshner traditions, different niggunim, and minhagim, but the standards aren't much different from those in Manchester. In any case, the things she does and doesn't do, the things she eats, even the words she utters, are all external for her. Not superficial, but fixed and homely. They don't really control what she is on the inside; they don't have anything to do with what she thinks or what she wants.

Elizabeth partly recognizes her romance of worldly things, art and theaters, exotic people. Regina from Los Angeles, where the shuls are movie palaces. Or Beatrix, who is from the very citadel of poetry and numbers, Oxford, with its gargoyles and museum-churches, its gardens kept for scholars and their robed processions. This love of the outside world is a kind of voyeurism for Elizabeth, and realizing that, she is dissatisfied. If she could do more than watch; if she could participate—do something or create something in the shimmering, spinning secular world. If she could move outside the fixed and constant realm in which she lives. But, of course, without giving it up, without exchanging it. Her religious life is not something she can cast off; it's part of her. Its rituals are not rituals to her; not objects, but instincts. She lives inside them and can't hold them up to look at. That is the beauty of the secular world—she can examine it. And yet she'd like to hold it more closely; really touch it. That's what makes her restless.

5

MICHAEL King walks up Maple, glancing at his bungalows, all rented, all summer. He owns eighteen of these in Kaaterskill, including Elizabeth and Isaac's, and three chalets in Bear Mountain. He has built up his real estate business gradually over the years, buying up lots, tearing down old houses, making subdivisions. He started out as one of the summer people, and then, when his father moved permanently to Florida, he went into business renting out the family summer house and buying another. Nearly all the outside real estate deals in Kaaterskill, Bear Mountain, and Kendall Falls pass through King's office—the loose stuff, that is—everything not sucked up by Victoria Schermerhorn's agency or by Judge Taylor and his nephews. He is a shrewd investor, King, a tight landlord. He always has his eye on new property, new investment openings. He's developed part of the lakefront on Mohican Lake, built the two luxury houses there that the Fawesses rent each summer, big two-story lodges with terraces for the lake view and a pier for sailing. And now he has his eye on the nonconservation land just above Kaaterskill on Coon Lake. Lakefront houses bring in as much as three bungalows together. This is the kind of development King wants to move into. He sees Kaaterskill as more than just a bungalow town. After all, up behind Mohican Road are mansions worth one, two million each. Why shouldn't King rent places on that scale? He's getting top dollar for the houses on Mohican Lake. Coon Lake could be even better.

vs,

King had some wild summers up in Kaaterskill wh n he was a kid. He didn't care much about development in those day or where his future came from. He liked to drink. He liked to fight. He used to smoke with a bunch of kids in the back lot behind the s nagogue. That was before the telephone company bought that little corner piece and put in the unmanned switching system, taking Kaaterskill off the four-digit exchange. King didn't have an eye for old houses in those days—he speculated on the Kaaterskill girls instead. Later the girls grew heavy; they married and had children. He watches them now wheeling strollers. King is heavier himself, at thirty-six, but he's tall; he carries it. He stands out in Kaaterskill with his western clothes. He wears boots and red plaid shirts. The hunters stare at him and his open-necked shirts—no buttons, metal snaps instead, covered with mother of pearl. But King is a permanent resident now in Kaaterskill. He and his wife, Jackie, spend their weekends shopping at auctions in the antique barns outside Phoenicia and the converted mill in Palenville. A quiet life for a young man who was once threatened by old man Kendall brandishing a rifle.

King has changed. He has grown from a nuisance discussed at the Town Meeting to becoming a selectman on the Three Town Council. Grown from a "bragging, bullying menace that has to stop" into a landlord with contractors and workers in all three towns and strict standards for his men as well. He runs a lean, high-profit office, and he punishes dishonesty, waste, and graft. He has actually become a Rotarian.

King walks up Main Street into the Taylor building, announces himself to Judge Taylor's secretary, and takes a seat in one of the hard-backed chairs in the reception room.

Taylor keeps him waiting. It's always a ten-minute wait for King in Taylor's reception room with the ancient *Yankee* magazines.

When Taylor's secretary finally ushers King into the judge's inner office, Taylor looks up and asks briskly, "Well, Michael, what can I do for you?" He does not offer King a seat.

King sits down in the chair in front of Taylor's oak desk anyway.

"I want to swear out a complaint against Stan Knowlton," King says. "He's been stealing from me for months and I've had it. I've had enough."

The judge raises his eyebrows. Taylor knew King's father, Herb Klein, and he's known Michael since he was just a boy. Taylor caught him setting off smoke bombs fifteen years ago Fourth of July. It doesn't matter how much of Kaaterskill King tries to buy; to Taylor he will always be one of the summer people. The rich, loud, fast-driving, deer-scaring kind. The kind teeming in the woods like ticks, shooting in the bird sanctuary, plowing the fishing places with motor boats. King is a landlord now, but he'll always be one of them. He hardly keeps up the bungalows he rents out. He's a landlord as sloppy as the skiers who invade Bear Mountain in winter, tramping in the snow and drinking, pocking the hardwood floors with their ski poles.

Miles Taylor is an orderly man with an ordered mind. He has a clear ethic that he uses every day. Not a dusty emotional morality examined only in church, but a practical system. His ethical accounts have columns for credits and debits: what is done for him and what he does for others. And his goal, it must be said, is not an equilibrium of favors done and favors rendered. Not that Taylor is crassly manipulative, or merely self-aggrandizing. He seeks an advantage for himself, but he identifies himself with his family—his brother and his nephews —and further, with his town. On a more ethereal level Taylor has a kindly feeling for those he doesn't deal with directly: his country, his world, his God. He believes in the fellowship of man and the immortal soul. He has loved deeply, although his wife has been dead fifteen years. He has principles and a heart. But the summer people do not inspire his sympathy, generosity, or fellow feeling. And looking at the Klein boy, self-styled King, Miles Taylor feels only anger to hear he's fired poor Knowlton, who has never had anything except for Janet Kendall, his childhood sweetheart, now his wife. A pretty girl, and a good family, too, except that the Kendalls haven't any money. There are too many of them these days in Kendall Falls.

"Why should I bother with a few flagstones?" Taylor asks now.

"He took over a hundred," snaps King. "Aren't you going to prosecute a thief?"

"Oh, he's not a thief," says Taylor.

"What would you call him, then?" asks King.

"He's just a young man, who made a mistake."

"You're going to sit by and—"

"You made some mistakes when you were young, as I recall."
King doesn't answer.

"Well," says Taylor, "if you want me to publicize Knowlton's
peccadilloes, hadn't you better start with your own?"

"This is ridiculous," King says.

"Why?" asks the judge.

"Are you threatening to blackmail me over a pile of flagstones?"

"It does sound trivial when you put it that way," says Taylor.
"Not worth a fuss, eh? Big smoke, no fire."

King gets up. "I'm going to hire a lawyer," he says.

"You do that," Taylor says, as King walks out the door.

The judge opens his desk drawer and takes out his lunch, a cheese
sandwich and two apples. He eats the first apple and he frowns. In the
past five years he has watched King snap up properties all through
Kaaterskill, tear down fine old houses on Spruce and Maple, and
subdivide the lots within inches of the zoning laws. Taylor's family
real estate company has kept to certain standards about quality and
price control. He and his nephews know the history of the place, and
what the town could be. King just puts up bungalows and rents to
Orthodox Jews, one family after another. He gives no thought to the
effect the Jews make when they come up for the summer, Russian
kerchiefs over the women's hair. Cultish attendance at the synagogue.
There has been a small cohort of them in town since the fifties, but
King is attracting more and more, with his cheap house-building and
low-rent cottages. The worst of it is the way King has got poor
townspeople like Knowlton to sell out their property and take bungalows themselves. They need the money, and they haven't anything
else to sell, so King buys them out. Like Jacob the usurper, he approaches them to buy up their inheritance.

Now King is expanding into virgin territory. Buying up at Mohican Lake like a slash-and-burn farmer, planning to expand into
Coon Lake, too, on speculation. Methodically Taylor eats a second
apple, all the way around, and then the top and bottom ends. He eats
every bit except the stem and seeds.

In Plattville a visitor can find a little country charm, the church
with its steeple, a New England village green. But Kaaterskill has
nothing left of that. There is the forest, and the falls, but the town has

been trampled and badly run down. The year-round residents are
demoralized. Few are house proud. What can they do, living among
the subdivisions? The town looks nondescript, Main Street nearly
empty. The only real reputation Kaaterskill has is as a summer home
for the ultrareligious Jews. And with their modest incomes, big families, parochial tastes, these Orthodox don't nurture boutiques and
restaurants, parks, or college scholarships for the town children. There
was a time when these people had their own resorts outside of town,
self-contained hotels. But one by one the hotels closed, and emptied
out like Trojan horses into the countryside. The Jewish summer people settled on the little towns themselves.

The Mohican Road community could have saved things, if
they'd invested in Kaaterskill; but the residents have retreated farther
into their wooded estates, and there is no prying them loose now to
help remedy the sorry state of things in town at the foot of their
private mountain peak. Those rich introverts have no interest in the
real people who live in Kaaterskill. As for the religious introverts in
the town itself—they have their synagogue and their own day camp,
and every summer they send up flags to attract more like them. It's
distressing. But it isn't right or even useful to resent groups of people.
The one Taylor blames is the Klein boy, Michael King.

6

___

ELIZABETH and Isaac and the girls watch the Fourth of July parade from Cecil's porch. It's a short parade, but a loud one. Every year the volunteer fire department polishes up the engines, two red, two canary yellow, and they set off, sirens blaring. Up and down Main Street they fly. Down Maple and around up Spruce Street in a loop back to the fire station.

Cecil has his portable radio set up on the porch so they all can hear about the big parades for the Bicentennial in the city. "Thousands of people are thronging the bridge! The coast guard estimates thirty thousand yachts and small craft cover the river," cries the announcer on Cecil's tinny receiver.

"Well, we don't have throngs," says Cecil. "But I think King's dog puts on a good show." The fire engines scream down the street, and King's gray poodle chases after the last one, barking ferociously.

"And the ships are beautiful!" screams the announcer. "The cruiser *Wainwright* leads a flotilla of warships from twenty-two nations. Each one covered with pennants, and rigged as they would have been two hundred years ago today!" The receiver begins to crackle.

"Don't you wish you were down there in the city?" Elizabeth asks as Cecil fiddles with the dial.

"God, no," Beatrix says. "It's not *my* holiday. Nor yours either," she points out to Elizabeth.

The radio comes to life. "This just in," says the announcer. "We have confirmation that in the small hours of the morning Israelis executed a daring rescue mission at Entebbe Airport, Uganda. One hundred five hostages of the Air France hijacking have been freed. We have unconfirmed reports that an unknown number of airborne Israeli commandos swept down on the airport in a predawn raid."

"Commandos!" Beatrix exclaims.

"What happened?" asks Ruchel.

"Sh."

"What was that?"

"Allegedly they overwhelmed the pro-PLO hijackers who last week took over the Air France flight from Athens to Paris. There are no details on casualties."

"What happened, Daddy?" Chani asks.

"I can't hear," says Cecil.

They end up walking over to the Melishes to see if Andras is getting better reception. Chani, Malki, and Ruchel pedal in front on their bikes, and their parents and the Birnbaums trail after them with the little girls. They listen to the news on the Melishes' stereo, and later, on the Melishes' porch, they pore over Andras's *Times,* even though it is already out of date. They spread it over the glider, drinking lemonade. The articles about the raid are sketchy, padded by interviews with foreign ministers, and speculations about the events of the night.

"If they really pulled it off, it's incredible," says Andras.

"Extraordinary," Elizabeth says.

"When you think of all the things that could have gone wrong," Andras says.

"But they had split-second timing," says Cecil.

"And luck," says Andras. "There were so many variables. They all could have been killed."

"It was a *nes min hashamayim*"—a miracle from heaven, Chani says suddenly from where she's sitting on the porch rail.

There is a startled silence. Everyone looks up. "Yes, it was," Elizabeth says at last.

"And do you think Israel is a miracle too?" Cecil asks, grinning.

Chani doesn't respond, but Cecil folds his arms. "I think we have a Zionist in the family," he says impishly.

Elizabeth's cheeks burn. It may be a joke to Cecil, but this is not something they talk about. There are no Zionists in their community.

The Kirshners are waiting for the perfect Israel, as the Rav puts it. They won't settle for less. No Israeli jets for them, no modern Hebrew newspapers. Hebrew is a holy language. The Kirshners are anti-Zionist. They are not militant. They don't campaign for an end to Israel like that tiny community near Jerusalem that actually allies itself with the PLO. The Rav would never countenance such actions against fellow Jews. Nevertheless, his people stand apart from Israel with its atheist socialists. They haven't softened, like the Lubavichers. The Rav's yeshiva remains in New York. He rarely speaks of Zionists, and when he does, he merely remarks that they are a troubled lot. Elizabeth actually had a cousin who left England and went to Israel; that was a terrible thing, a scandal, and a great heartache for her grandmother.

Sitting in his chair on the porch, Andras watches the unease settle on his neighbors in the wake of Cecil's remark. Much as he disagrees with, and even disparages, the Orthodox in his mind, Andras hates to see them provoked. It seems unfair, unmanly. Like hitting a girl. He looks at Isaac and Elizabeth and feels protective of them, almost proprietary of their narrow experience and messianic politics. He feels concerned, somehow, for the integrity of their quaint closed worldview. Smooth, small, delicate, useless as a robin's egg.

Nervously Nina flits from one person to another, offering more lemonade, more ice. "Well, Cecil," says Andras, "it's about time for us to go to the Lamkin Camp's opening day."

"You're going to that?" Cecil asks quickly.

"Of course," says Andras. He knows it angers Cecil even to hear the camp mentioned. As Cecil says, his father had bought the land as an investment for the synagogue and not as a free gift to a third-rate rabbi. He puts it that way, as if the camp were just poor financial judgment. But Andras knows Cecil's true feelings: that leasing the land to the Lamkins for their camp is an insult to his father's memory. "You're going, I take it," Andras says to Elizabeth and Isaac.

Cecil reddens to the edges of his ears.

Andras just sips his lemonade and says coolly, "Of course, it's easier to boycott a summer camp when you don't have children."

For once Cecil doesn't know what to say. For a long moment he is silent.

They are all surprised at Andras. He is usually so controlled. Even Elizabeth and Isaac don't fully understand his motivation: his irritation at Cecil for provoking them about Zionism. His motive was too complex. And here is the mystery of Andras's character: he is cold, but deep, too deep, within him, his heart is chivalrous.

THERE are so many people at the camp opening that Elizabeth and Isaac are lucky to squeeze in at a picnic table. A crowd of sixty, maybe even seventy, fills the park above the falls. A mixed group, some Kirshners, some not. At one table, clustered together in dark trousers and white shirts, sit the five teachers Rabbi Lamkin has brought up from the city to instruct the children. They look pale and a little worried in the gold summer light. All this commotion bothers them. They bob back and forth respectfully, trying to hear Rabbi Lamkin's speech.

Elizabeth can't hear Lamkin well either. He's standing up on a rock, talking excitedly, although few are paying attention. He wanders between topics, and quotes profusely from the Torah and the prophets, but without much art in the quotation, so that instead of embroidering his drash he seems to bury it. The feeling is there, the knowledge is there, but he seems unsure of his direction. He just flits from one idea to the next, weaving like a drunken bee; mixing up the events of thousands of years of history, tangling up texts and commentaries. At first Elizabeth thinks he's talking about youth, "bonayich, your builders," but, suddenly, he is speaking about the destruction of the Temple and the dispersion of Israel. He takes a turn back in time to speak about the encampments of Israel in the desert, only to jump forward to the Maccabees in their rebellion against Antiochus. He skids back again to Biblical times, and at last he settles, heavy with quotations, on the blessings of the prophet Balaam, "who was at first unwilling to bless the people of Israel. But Balaam saw, finally, after three times he was warned, that he had no choice but to say: *'Mah tovu ohalecha Yaakov, mishkenosechah Yisroel'* "—how beautiful are your tents, O Jacob, your dwelling places, Israel.

Lamkin looks out at the picnic gathering. "And the question is— was Balaam seeing the tents of Israel in the valley, the camp of Israel? So we know that was not what he saw. This vision"—he pauses, drawing the words out—"this vision was not about the physical tents. It was at the deepest level the Torah that was meant. That's what the tents were. We know that the tents were Torah, and the camps in the desert were places of Torah. For forty years in the desert, as the midrash says, the children of Israel were learning Torah and mitzvos. Was it any wonder they didn't want to give this up—this life of learning—to enter the land promised to them? These were the years they were learning *intensively,* having unbelievable insights and understanding. All the books of Mishnah and Talmud and all the commentaries were spread out before them. This was a yeshiva of spectacular learning in the desert that was going on for forty years. That was what the camps of Israel were. Now, when we look at *our* camp"— Pesach glances at his wife, but quickly turns back to his speech, anxious not to lose his point—"we look at our camp, now, and hopefully what we are going to see is what Balaam saw, a whole yeshiva of learning outdoors. A whole wonderland of Torah. Which is for us lofty like the wild ox, strong like the lion. . . ."

"Like the wild *ox?* That's the wrong verse. That's not very apt," Elizabeth whispers to Isaac, at the picnic table.

"I didn't hear," Isaac says. "It's all right."

Elizabeth just shakes her head. Lamkin's words seem to her hopelessly muddled.

When Rabbi Lamkin is finished, Beyla's promised feast begins. There are platters of cold cuts, plastic tubs of potato salad and coleslaw, attracting wasps; pickles, potato chips, and scores of hot dogs curling up on the Lamkins' brand-new grill.

The parents are gathering together to talk. The children are screaming under the trees, clambering over rocks, skinning their knees, dripping ketchup onto the grass. And above all the waterfall roars, rushing down into the gorge below them. In this din Elizabeth feels a little sad. It occurs to her that she doesn't particularly like Rabbi Lamkin, and she isn't happy about his running the summer camp. He isn't the sort of rabbi she respects. She and Isaac are different this way. Isaac knows very well that Lamkin isn't well spoken or intelligent or practical; but he believes the young man has a good heart, and so he won't think ill of him. Elizabeth often thinks ill of people. She is critical; she resents them, and she can't help it. She accuses herself sometimes of being a snob, or even slightly mean-spirited. She hates incompetence. On Yom Kippur in the city, for example, there is one old codger who always leads musaf, and he sings out of the side of his mouth in such a harsh and tuneless way that Elizabeth burns with indignation. On Yom Kippur of all days! But she can't help herself. She stands there fasting and exhausted, and when she hears this man sing she actually wants to do him harm. Isaac, who davens beautifully and has a lovely voice, never leads the services on Yom Kippur. He is not a big macher in the community by any means. In fact there is not a single great rabbi in his family.

The problem isn't that people show Lamkin undue reverence. No one accords him great respect; and yet, for that very reason, it seems wrong to entrust him with the summer camp. It seems a kind of mutual exploitation. Community baby-sitting in exchange for rabbinical power.

"What's wrong?" Isaac asks her as he comes up with a plate of food. "You're not enjoying it?"

"Lamkin jumbled everything together," Elizabeth says.

"He was nervous." Isaac makes allowances, as he always does. "It's going to be a good camp. And you'll have some time to yourself."

"All right! All right!" Beyla Lamkin is announcing. "All children come here to get ready for the treasure hunt. One, two, one, two—if you're a one, you're on team one; if you're a two, you're on team two. One, two, one, two . . ." She taps each child lightly on the head. The Lamkins' new campers mill around for the treasure hunt. "Pinchas! Stop that!" Beyla calls to her youngest son.

Elizabeth remembers the summer three years ago when Brocha was just a newborn. Brocha and Pinchas had the same birthday, and Beyla joked about making a shidduch between them. Pinchas is three now, a little monkey running around with his shirt untucked, and the fringes of his tallis katan flying. With his long, pale face and wispy black hair, he looks just like his father. Elizabeth would not be happy to see her daughters marrying Lamkins. Although, of course, they are good people; they are a pious family.

When Elizabeth thinks about her daughters, she thinks of them living extraordinary lives. She can't speak of it aloud—all that she wants for them. She doesn't have one simple idea, only a fervent, unarticulated wish. The girls' future is just something Elizabeth imagines, nothing whatever to do with reality. They're very good children. They expect to marry scholars and then support them while they learn. But Elizabeth imagines someday her daughters could be scholars themselves—not of Talmud, of course, but perhaps Tanach. Or at other times she thinks one of them could become a writer, or an artist. Perhaps a journalist. It would have to be a Jewish newspaper, so that she could keep Shabbes. Naturally, becoming a mother, keeping a Jewish home, is the most important thing. But somehow she can't see it as the only thing for her girls. There must be, there ought to be, something else as well, a second purpose. Perhaps Elizabeth's dreams for the girls are really only what she desires for herself. She is by nature discontented, she thinks; by nature the opposite of Isaac. For he never had money, never had a great family name, and he seems happy anyway.

"Mommy, can we go down to the water?" Chani asks her.

"And can I come?" Ruchel asks.

"I'll come down with you," Elizabeth says.

Carefully, she and the girls climb down the long dirt path into the gorge. They climb all the way down from the park to where the falls pour louder and louder into great pools of rippling water, green and brown. The rock pools are cool under the waterfall. Elizabeth and Chani and Ruchel take off their shoes and socks and stand in the shallowest water, smooth mossy pebbles stroking the soles of their bare feet. The wet hems of their skirts slap against their legs. In the distance they hear the cries from the treasure hunt, a confused yelling about team one and team two, and then Elizabeth hears Isaac as he comes down the path to the falls. He waves at them, and laughing, calls out the line from the Book of Isaiah: *"Kol tzameh l'chu lamayim."*

Let all who thirst come for water. The water of Torah, the thirst-quenching truth of God's law.

"ISAAC," Elizabeth asks that night in bed, "how are you so content? I try, but . . ."

He smiles at her in the dark. She can make out the shape of his quick smile, the curve of his cheek, the parting of lips. "How are you so patient?" she asks. "Tell me."

"Just habit," he whispers. "It's only habit."

"Tell me how," she says. "So I won't want things."

"I couldn't teach you that," he tells her.

He has had his disappointments. Because he wasn't a particular favorite of the Rav, and had no distinguished relatives, he didn't get a stipend from the yeshiva to continue his studies. No one wanted him to leave, but his family didn't have the money to support him for so long. And yet, for all of this, Elizabeth can see that his private learning outside the yeshiva sustains him. He doesn't want a second purpose. His life is all one. His books are part of him. Truly, his books quench his thirst; he is more than satisfied, while Elizabeth's reading only whets her appetite, fills her with confused longings for change and new experiences. She sighs. Too often reading makes her feel incomplete, impatient.

"Here's the trick." He kisses her. "You have to want what you have."

She props herself up on one elbow. "Really, Isaac, are you such a fatalist?"

"No," he says, and already, as he touches her, his hands erase her words. How can there be room for questions? He is her whole landscape, his body next to hers, his arms around her. She lies in the valley of his arms.

7

THE picnic over, Renée sits at the piano under protest. She's been ordered to practice an hour before she can go to the Fourth of July barbecue at Stephanie's. Her mother hadn't wanted her to go at all. She's seen Stephanie, and the girl looks wild. Nina doesn't know much about the Fawess family, but they aren't Jewish, she knows that. They don't belong to Nina's circle of acquaintances, and it hurts her that with all the Jewish children to choose from, Renée runs around with this Arab one. Nina isn't racist exactly; it's just that she remembers such isolation as a child. She had so few Jewish friends. Her own parents in Buenos Aires sent her to a Catholic school. Even then, she hated sitting alone, different from the others though she wore the uniform. She begged to go to the Jewish school, but it was far away, and her parents wouldn't let her board. They hired a Hebrew tutor for her instead and pretended they were like their neighbors, living in the suburbs with servants and big gardens.

The world is very big, very dangerous. Full of enemies of Israel and of Jews. There are people who make crime and hate their business. These terrorists, these hijackers. Naturally, Nina wants her daughter to be safe, and to be sheltered by the kind of community she herself had longed for as a child: the Jewish school in which Renée can know her whole class, the summer place where she can play with the neighbors.

Renée, of course, knows better. She complains all the time about her Jewish school, where she has two friends and hates everyone else. Nearly everyone spends the day backbiting and acting vicious. And she's tried to explain why the Shulman girls are so dull. All they want to do when they grow up is marry rabbis and then support their families by teaching Hebrew. In the Kirshner school, of course. And as soon as they're married they'll all cut their hair and wear sheitels just like their mother. No one Renée knows in the city does that. But Nina still can't see why her daughter suddenly doesn't like Chani Shulman anymore.

At the piano Renée fiddles with the metronome for a while and then looks at the clock.

"I don't hear it," Nina calls from upstairs.

Renée crashes down on the first page of Chopin's *Fantaisie-Impromptu*. She is advanced enough to play difficult music, but not to play it well. She skips a few notes on the first runs and starts again, banging down even more violently. "Like a feather," her piano teacher told her at her last lesson before she left for Kaaterskill. "Think of the Chopin like feather dusters on the keys." She smashes some more chords and then sees her father come in, about to go up the stairs. She runs up to him.

"I have to go to the party," she says. "I can't practice on the Bicentennial!"

"Oh, all right," he says absently, and walks on up the stairs.

"Renée?" Nina calls out again from the upstairs bedroom.

"I let her go out," says Andras from the doorway.

Nina turns on him. "I told her one hour piano." In the light of the window she looks as if she could catch fire. Her red hair flames in the sun. "How can I control her if you undermine everything I do?" She tilts back her head to accuse her tall husband.

"I wasn't thinking," Andras says.

"You're never thinking about the children."

Why is she so shrill? he asks himself. The afternoon sun pours into the upstairs room, and Andras retreats into the dark closet to change his shirt for a fresh one. He hates the heat. Even in the mountains he can feel the afternoon glare.

Nina pulls the closet door open into the sun. "Andras, listen to me! Renée isn't practicing, and you just let her get away with it."

"All right, she can practice tomorrow," he says.

"She isn't practicing at all," Nina tells him. As always when she is angry, her Spanish accent flares. "She isn't making any progress."

"Well, she doesn't have any talent," Andras says matter-of-factly.

His wife throws up her hands. "All right," she cries. "Fine, all right. We stop the lessons!"

"Good," he says.

"No!" she rages. "It's a waste! Ten years of lessons and she wants to stop. That's what I'm trying to tell you!"

"Nina." He takes her hand. "Why do you care?"

THE Fawesses' mailbox is decorated with balloons, the deck railing hung with red, white, and blue streamers, the front yard full of cars. Enormous cars. Navy-blue Lincolns and black stretch limousines. Renée hadn't realized the party was so big.

"It's a family reunion," Stephanie explains.

"Are all these people your relatives?" Renée asks. There must be sixty people milling around the grand modern house by Mohican Lake. The house itself is strange. The side facing the lake is almost all glass; and, unlike the painted old-fashioned summer places in town, this house is just stained wood.

Stephanie's father and uncles are firing up the barbecue. "They're mostly my relatives," says Stephanie. "Some of them I'm not quite sure how we're related, though."

They watch the musicians unloading their instruments from a van. Drums and steel-stringed lutes, strange pipes that look like recorders. The musicians set up on the deck, and gradually the tuning and experimental thumping builds into a real melody carried by pipers and twanging lutes, music flung far out into the lake with long, singing drumbeats.

At the grill one of the chauffeurs is roasting chicken pieces over the fire. Stephanie's mother brings out platters of raw lamb and rice. Mrs. Fawess is heavy, and short of breath from bringing out the food. Her face is round and earnest, her hair threaded with gray and pinned up out of the way. Her body looks tired.

"My mom loves cooking. It's her solace," Stephanie tells Renée. Stephanie seems to enjoy that word. *Solace.* "That's why we don't have a cook. And you know what else she does? She gambles. Just for like ten dollars at a time."

The men are dancing near the band. Mr. Fawess dances at the center, lifting his arms above his head. He seems much younger than his wife. Slender, dark, smiling, far more relaxed, as if he were the one spending his weeks in the country. He is handsome, Renée thinks. Almost like a movie star. He has a mustache and dark shining eyes.

Stephanie and Renée help bring out more food, more meat for the grill, more rice. They carry platters of tiny cookies shaped in wreaths, a pistachio nut at the center of each one, like a little button. They keep bringing out the food and nibbling as they go, especially the tiny cookies. At last, when all the food is out, and everyone is eating, Stephanie's mother sits at a picnic table with four other women. She shuffles a deck of cards so that they melt together, dissolving and then melting back into the pack.

"See," Stephanie says. The women put in five- and ten-dollar bills, while the girls stand and watch Mrs. Fawess shuffle. Her fingers move like a magician's, so that the deck becomes an accordion, a book, a fluttering bird's wing.

"You stand it," Mrs. Fawess is telling her friends. "After twenty years you stand it." She cuts the deck and deals out around the table.

Stephanie whispers to Renée, "Come on, they're going to be there for hours. Hey, I have a great idea. . . ."

Renée looks up warily. All Stephanie's ideas are great. And strenuous. Stephanie doesn't take walks, she goes on all-day hikes. She doesn't just swim, she sails and water-skis. Renée follows along cautiously on these excursions, hurrying after Stephanie up the Escarpment Trail, shuddering in the wind while her friend navigates the sailboat. It's new for Renée to be a follower. Renée's friends at school never do anything adventurous enough to demand one leader. With Stephanie, Renée is for the first time the squire.

"Come on, come on." Stephanie drags Renée away to where the limos are parked. "Let's take one of Dad's cars and go dancing."

Renée laughs.

"Oh, come on," Stephanie says.

"Can you even drive?" Renée asks.

"Sure I can. Mom lets me drive all the time."

"You have a license?"

Stephanie sighs long-sufferingly and takes out a folded paper. "Temporary license," she says. "I got it from my cousin, Stephen, when they sent him his card. See, I added the *ie* onto his name. And I drive better than he does. We can go to Bear Mountain. There's a place there where my father knows the owner. They'll let us in."

"I can't," says Renée.

"Why?"

"Because my mother would die," Renée says.

Stephanie puts her hands on her hips. "You're fifteen years old! How can she be so overprotective?"

"I don't know," says Renée, but secretly she is glad to have the excuse of an overprotective mother. She is a little frightened at the thought of driving on the mountain road with Stephanie. And she has never been dancing. She wouldn't even know how. She just tells Stephanie, "I think my mother used to be better when she was young, but she got religious and decided everything was immoral. Wouldn't your mother be upset?"

"Oh, she's used to me," Stephanie says. "I've trained her. I started by using horrible language when I was twelve. I had this baby-sitter, Malaya, while my parents were in Europe, and she taught me all about the women's movement and stuff. That's when I became a feminist. My baby-sitter was amazing because she just took me with her wherever she went. My parents are really paranoid, so the one thing while they were gone was Malaya couldn't leave me alone in the apartment. So she took me to her women's group. She taught me to draw. She used to have all these pads of drawing paper and she would fill them up drawing imaginary faces. She never drew the whole face, though. Only half a face. I forget why she did that, but she had a really cool reason. She also had a guru; she carried his picture in her wallet. And she belonged to an ashram on Central Park West. Basically you sat on the floor in this dark living room and you chanted. They passed out the chants on these photocopied sheets, and they lit candles. There were some little bells too. Once I got to play the bells. I was so annoyed when my parents came back and they kicked her out. She was kind of strange, but she was a very . . ." Stephanie stops, searching for the word, and then she gets distracted. "Do you ever feel like just standing on your head?" she asks Renée.

"No," says Renée.

"Watch," says Stephanie, and right there on the grass she does a perfect handstand, with legs together and pointed toes. "Do you want me to teach you?" she asks Renée.

"Well, I'm wearing a dress," Renée points out.

"Let's go inside and change you!" Stephanie says.

THE party is still in full swing when Andras comes to pick up Renée. He looks for her uncertainly among the chairs and picnic tables.

"Welcome! Welcome!" Michael Fawess runs up and clasps Andras on the shoulders. "You are Renée's father? Have some food. Have a drink. They are over there." He points to the yard, and Andras sees that Renée is wearing blue jeans like Stephanie. Nina doesn't let Renée wear jeans. She believes religious girls should not dress immodestly like that.

"Have a cigar," Fawess urges Andras.

"I don't smoke," Andras says.

Fawess looks surprised. "A cigar on a beautiful afternoon? A beautiful evening like this? This is not smoking."

"I gave it up," Andras says. But he does take a plate of grilled lamb and rice. The cookies are delicious. Renée waves at him, and he sits in a deck chair while she and Stephanie cartwheel around the yard.

"These girls are good friends," Fawess says. "It's a good thing for Stephanie. A good thing for both of them, is it not?"

"It is," says Andras. He leans back and listens to the music, the thrumming melody. He has a beer. Nina would not approve of this. The food is not kosher, the music loud. These people are Syrian. They are Syrian Christians, and they are truckers—prosperous ones, from the looks of this house on the lake.

The evening is settling over the water, and as it gets dark, a string of lights rigged up in the trees blinks on. Renée and Stephanie are flitting around, fooling with a pair of flashlights. Andras knows he should tell Renée it's time to go. It is getting late, and he will bring her home late. Nina will be waiting for them, sitting on the porch and worrying. She will ask what took them so long.

Sometimes Andras laughs and teases Nina about her worrying. He can play a certain role, the sardonic older husband, the provider with a sense of irony. He can joke with his sisters about his wife. "And how is Nina?" they ask him.

"Oh, Nina," he says. "She insists the vacuum cleaner isn't big enough. She wants an indoor-outdoor Hoover."

"That's a tank, Andras!" They find the stories about his wife entertaining. Eva calls her General Nina. Sometimes, even, Nina from Argentina.

Andras sits back at the party. The men are dancing, and the women gambling. The lights quivering over the twilight blue of the lake. The dark limousines shimmer on the grass, moored there like boats. Renée and Stephanie flash by. He should tell Renée it's time to go, but she won't want to leave. He doesn't want to go home either.

THERE are times Nina wants to strike Andras like a flint and make him burn. And there are times when she is patient and steels herself with more strength than he knows. But mostly Nina is lonely. She manages everything during the week—the bills, the shopping, the children—and then when Andras comes up, he spends hours walking, or visiting his sisters, sitting in their kitchen with a glass of ice coffee.

Often, Nina looks across the street at the yellow bungalow where the Shulman girls jump rope, or spin on the tire swing Elizabeth has rigged up. Nina admires Elizabeth. Her life is so organized. So neat and disciplined, precise, like her English enunciation. Above all Nina admires Elizabeth's religious observance, natural to her as breathing. Nina always gets to shul before Elizabeth, davens rapidly, fervently, always in the right place in the siddur. She has to try harder, because she didn't grow up with the kind of background Elizabeth had. She'll never have Elizabeth's assurance. It seems to Nina that Elizabeth fits perfectly into her community; she never has to worry about belonging. Nina loves to imagine that, the shelter Elizabeth enjoys, the consistency, the little bungalow where Elizabeth doesn't have to insist, as Nina does, that the family say the blessing when they wash their hands. None of this extra effort is necessary for Elizabeth. She keeps the laws with such élan.

Monday morning when the children are all at day camp, Nina walks over to see Elizabeth, and raps on the frame of the screen door.

"Hello," Elizabeth says, answering the door with her book in her hand. *Abraham Lincoln: The War Years.*

"I wondered if you would like to come to Olana with me," Nina says.

"And what is that?" asks Elizabeth.

Nina is surprised. "You've never been?"

"No," says Elizabeth.

"Oh, it's a magnificent house," says Nina, "Built by Frederick Church. It's a museum now, for Hudson River School paintings. There is a traveling exhibition there—"

"We could take the children," Elizabeth says immediately. "Do you think we could fit all of mine and yours in the car? Is it open this afternoon?"

Nina doesn't want to offend Elizabeth, but hesitantly she suggests, "I thought you might like to come without the children."

Elizabeth looks startled for a moment. Then she says, "Even better!" and she laughs, as she runs in to look for her purse, and she calls back to Nina, "I'd forgotten we could go without them."

The hum of Nina's Buick is wonderful to Elizabeth. Zooming out of Main Street onto the open road, Elizabeth feels like she's flying.

Wind and sun ruffle through Nina's hair. Like red gold, Elizabeth thinks. Like the first letter in an illuminated manuscript. She's always looked at her neighbor with some awe, because she is so beautiful. She admires Nina's clothes—the cut and colors. In a pressed linen dress Nina sits straight and slim behind the wheel. Her Catholic school emphasized ironing, Nina told Elizabeth once.

They pass Kaaterskill High, a brick fortress of a school built in the 1930s, to last centuries. "Look at the apple trees," Elizabeth tells

Nina. There is a whole orchard on one side of the school. The high
school seems somehow manorial, the school on the hill, like Pen-
shurst made over for America. Or perhaps the trees were planted for
the students as some lesson in economy. Were pupils expected to
learn the tending of these orchards? "Lovely," she says to Nina, "to
build a school and set it out with apple trees."

As Elizabeth speaks, the words remind her of a snatch of Kipling:
"the great gray-green greasy Limpopo River all set about with fever
trees." That isn't the idea at all, but the rhythm is right, and the words
hum inside of her. Her mother used to read those *Just So Stories* at
bedtime, and especially the long captions Kipling wrote for his illus-
trations. All Kipling's explanations of the details in his drawings, and
his descriptions of the colors he would have used if the printers
hadn't restricted him to black and white. As they drive, it seems to
Elizabeth that every sight sparks in her some memory or odd new
thought. They speed by, and the wind licks the hills. The mountains
beyond Kaaterskill are fresh to her eyes.

Now that the children are in camp, Elizabeth is having her first
summer to herself. She doesn't have a baby at home. No one in
diapers, or waking up at night. All the children can walk now. There
is no one to carry or push along in the stroller. For years she's waited
for this. Now that it's happened, it feels strange. It's as if a fog has
lifted. At thirty-four, after thirteen years of pregnancies and babies,
the constant responsibility, the wide-open eyes and curling fingers,
the rocking to sleep, the wiping of noses, she has at last passed into a
new stage of life. It's like waking from a dream—an exhausting, beautiful dream. But on waking Elizabeth doesn't feel relieved or peaceful.
She is ravenously hungry. She needs something to do.

She'd had all kinds of plans for these hours with the girls at camp,
but baking and reading are far less tantalizing with so much time to
get them done. In past summers she read her books in snatches, and
they were always new. She had only stolen hours to spend with the
characters in novels, and so when she could hear about their lives,
about Pierre or Emma, Milly Theale or Lydgate, when she picked
them up from where they slept beside her bed, she read with emotion
and anticipation. Reading was like visiting distant friends. Gibbon

held a charm when Elizabeth hadn't time to read. *The Decline and Fall* spread out before her like a great unfinished afghan. But now, with whole mornings on her hands, she finds herself dissatisfied.

Time or no time, Elizabeth wants to do something. She feels pangs of impatience, and at night after the long sunsets, she can't sleep. She lies in bed with her pile of books, words floating around her, the pollen of other people's dreams. She'd resolved to go swimming every morning, but even that didn't work out.

Two days ago she ventured out to swim in Mohican Lake. It was lovely there. Not a soul on the pebbled beach. She left her dress and towel on a flat gray rock and swam out to the middle of the lake. Carefully she swam, head above the water in a kind of breaststroke. That was all she had learned from her brief lessons at school in England. But even swimming slowly was invigorating. The water rippled cold between her legs, although just skimming the surface with her arms, she could feel a warmer layer on top. She would have liked to float on her back and look up at the sky, but the lake was so quiet and deep, she was afraid. She paddled out slowly and watched the pine trees on the encircling bank.

Then, "Hey!" she heard a man calling from the shore. "Hey, over there. This is a private beach. Are you a guest at Mohican Road?" After all her resolutions to get some exercise, the empty beach was private. She was not allowed.

"You seem quiet," Elizabeth says to Nina now.

But before Nina gets a chance to speak, they enter the estate. Olana.

Through ornate wrought-iron gates the long approach to the mansion is dark with forest, but the house itself rises up clear of the trees on a hill covered with wildflowers. Olana is a palace, vast and delicate, its bricks and roof tiles set in intricate geometric shapes. There are terraces and balconies, fluttering with striped awnings. The whole construction outlandish and Arabian, more fanciful than any of the Victorian spires Elizabeth has seen in the mountains.

When they park the car and come inside the house, they pass through rooms of treasures; jeweled stained glass and Persian carpets the color of dusty rubies. Inlaid tables, and marquetry floors, and tapestry cushions, are all intricately patterned. There is nothing rustic here. Only when she looks at the paintings does Elizabeth remember the dark approach through the forest. These are outdoor paintings, trees and wild cliffs, huge sunsets. Elizabeth sits with Nina on a divan before a cluster of Bierstadts. Deep trees and cerebral winter skies.

The museum is nearly empty this weekday morning. The elaborate gallery still. Elizabeth looks intently at the winter landscapes. And as she looks, she whispers to Nina, "It's marvelous, just sitting here while the girls are at camp."

Nina looks at the floor. Renée is working as a junior counselor at the camp. It was Nina's idea. She thought the job with the Lamkins would be good for her daughter, that it would teach her responsibility and how to care for children. But Renée made a fuss. Nina had to threaten and cajole and, in the end, force Renée to go. There were tears and threats up to the day she started. Even now, Renée is sulking about working there with the little children.

"Renée doesn't like the camp," Nina says. "I think she'd rather waste her time wandering around, doing nothing, playing with that Arab girl. Andras doesn't care. I hear the father owns a trucking business—he just drives trucks from New York to Montreal—" She breaks off, frustrated.

"She's a good child, really," Elizabeth says.

"But Andras spoils her," says Nina. Then Elizabeth sees that Nina is really upset. There are tears in Nina's eyes. It's hard for her to speak. Elizabeth sees it, and doesn't know what to do. They are close neighbors, but they are not intimate friends. Beautiful Nina in her crisp dress, downcast among all these paintings. "He's very . . . indulgent of the children, both of them," Nina says. "He used to take them to the warehouse and let them pick out any toys they liked."

"At least he's not in the candy business," Elizabeth says. "Toys won't rot their teeth."

"He's going to let Renée quit piano," Nina says bitterly, utterly serious, "and she'll regret it all her life."

Elizabeth tries to look sympathetic. She's heard Renée play.

"And now that Renée is working at the Lamkins' camp, she wants to quit that too."

"He wouldn't let her do that," Elizabeth ventures.

"I don't know," Nina says miserably, and Elizabeth looks over at

her, and she wants to say, It can't be so bad. It isn't so awful. She can't
know what Nina really wants—that somehow Renée might be
friends again with Chani, in fact, with all of Elizabeth's own children,
so sweet to Nina's thinking, so pious, utterly sheltered from the outside world. So safe, they don't even know it.

"Let's go over there." Nina points to another group of paintings.

"Oh, look." Elizabeth points to the painting that has caught her
eye. A luminous work on the east wall, unmistakable, even from a
distance, Kaaterskill Falls. She rushes over to examine it, leaning forward, hands clasped behind her. FALLS OF THE KAATERSKILL,
THOMAS COLE, reads the plaque on the wall. Cole must have set up
his easel on the trail—just where she and the girls climbed down from
the overhanging park, far down until they reached the stream, the wet
hems of their skirts slapping against their legs, the water pouring
down from above them over the cliff. She has stood there like Cole's
tiny painted Indians, barely visible on the rocks. She has looked out to
those mountains and that sky. The place is much more dramatic on
canvas, of course, the exuberant water flinging itself below—nothing
dirty in this froth. Cole's trees are straining upward toward the clouds,
leaves just turning—burnt orange and gold mixed with green. Elizabeth would have dismissed the whole thing as overblown, clichéd,
except that she's been there so many times. She's seen the falls
streaming down and the enormous smoke-blue sky, the wild mountains. The unabashed, romantic colors are right. It's worth the whole
exhibit to see this painting. Knowing the site as she does, she realizes
Cole's integrity, and now, among the exhibit's many paintings, this
particular landscape seems to mark the truth in all the others.

She moves about, forgetting Nina at her side, just looking at the
painting from different angles. She knows so much about the place.
The drive up past the waterfall every summer—the children sleeping
by this time in the back. The curving footpath down from the road to
the pools under the falls. She can see it drawn here by Cole. The sky,
luminous above the trees, the crash of water. Piles and piles of yellow
leaves pillowing the trail. Elizabeth slipped in them hiking once with
Isaac and the children, and she fell right on her face, deep, deeper,
falling gradually, losing her balance by degrees. She kept waiting to
hit hard ground, expecting something sharp. But she never did hit.

The leaves were so deep that she felt as though she were falling in a dream; falling farther and farther until she landed in her own bed. She just laughed; she couldn't get her feet under her; she couldn't stop laughing.

She loves the place; she loves the painting by association. The painting is all associations. All familiar to her; reminding her, inspiring her. It brings back her own half-buried wish to capture and even recreate a place and time that beautiful. More than ever she wants to do something of her own. She has to make something; she has so much energy, she feels so strong. Fearless. She imagines for a moment she could learn to paint, except that she never could draw. She thinks perhaps she could write something. But she's not that sort; she reads too seriously. She couldn't separate her own words from the books humming in her head. She's filled with other music, not her own. Elizabeth looks intently at the painting, that brilliant piece of the world, and gazing at the color and the light of it she feels the desire, as intense as prayer. I want—she thinks, and then it comes to her simply, with all the force of her pragmatic soul—I want to open a store.

II

July and August '76

In my front yard grew the strawberry, blackberry, and life-everlasting, johnswort, and goldenrod, shrub oaks and sand cherry, blueberry and groundnut. . . . The sumach (Rhus glabra) grew luxuriantly about the house. . . . In August, the large masses of berries, which, when in flower, had attracted many wild bees, gradually assumed their bright velvety crimson hue. . . .

—HENRY DAVID THOREAU
Walden

1

AT THE Lamkins' camp Renée has charge of the three-year-old girls. Watching them in the sandbox, she sits on a swing and drags her feet in the dirt.

"This is the most difficult job of all," Beyla Lamkin told her. "This is the crucial age." It may be true, for all Renée knows, but she spends all her time stopping fights and tying shoes.

She is supposed to read the children midrashes, illustrated in picture books, but she never gets to that. She's always marching them off to play in the wading pool the Lamkins have rigged up, and then trying to put the right clothes back on them afterward. The activities the Lamkins plan all happen at such a distance from Renée's post at the sandbox that she can't even see the watermelon hunt or the idiotic boccie games. Renée can't go on the rebbetzin's nature walks, because her girls are too little. One of them is bound to get lost. The girls are so small, Renée can't leave them for a minute, and so she doesn't get a chance to talk to the other counselors when they get together and commiserate about how boring Pesach Lamkin's shiurs are—descriptions of how a pure red heifer was used for purification in the days of the Temple, the rabbi droning on while everyone sits at a picnic table, watching a spider hanging from a tree.

Renée glares at the girls playing in the sand. No one asked her if she wanted to take care of them. After two weeks she doesn't think they're sweet at all, and she doesn't feel in the least bit motherly toward them. Watching the little campers dump sand on each other, she thinks dark thoughts. She wishes she had some other mother, not her own. Stephanie's mother wouldn't make her spend all day with three-year-olds. Mrs. Fawess lets Stephanie wander wherever she likes, bike to Lacy Farm, even go swimming alone all the way up at Coon Lake. Stephanie never has to follow rules, except be home by dark. Renée feels an overwhelming need to talk to Stephanie, to ride her bike with Stephanie far away.

She doesn't have a plan. She just hops down from the swing. Slowly, she walks over to the other counselors where they sit at a picnic table. She looks at them, the good teenagers, the responsible girls. "I have to go," she whispers. She doesn't explain. She just walks off.

Away from the sandbox, away from the grassy field where the boys are playing flag football, Renée skirts the picnic tables and the grand old house with peeling paint, the old Thorne house, where the Lamkins now live. Head down, she walks out to the road and past the scores of small bicycles lying against the fence. The little girls' bikes with their handles decorated with streamers and baskets adorned with plastic daisies. The little boys' bikes, sleek and black with decals of rocket ships and fire. Renée extricates her own three-speed bicycle from the pile, and she pedals off quickly, almost afraid the Lamkins will notice and run after her. Of course, they are far too busy to realize she has gone. Her heart is pounding all the same.

She has never done anything wrong before. Never done anything interesting, as Stephanie has pointed out. Renée has always been a dutiful sort of girl, campaigning for attention, and getting it mostly by being pretty. Now she's run off.

She rides her bike to Stephanie's house.

"Renée!" Stephanie says when she answers the door. "What are you doing here?"

"I left," Renée says.

"You mean, you quit," Stephanie says.

"Yeah," Renée admits.

Stephanie's eyes sparkle. "I'll lend you a bathing suit! We're going to Coon Lake."

Coon Lake is gray and green, the water cold. Stephanie makes a face, but she plunges in right away. Renée shudders and holds back, but Stephanie splashes her.

"Now all you have to do is tell your parents," Stephanie says, treading water.

"I can't," Renée wails.

"Got to," Stephanie says in her blunt way. "What are you going to do, send them a copy of your resignation letter?"

"I didn't write a—"

Stephanie looks at her.

"Oh," Renée says.

Stephanie dives under the water and comes up with her long wet hair plastered down over her face. It looks as though she has her back to Renée, but she is still facing her. "Renée, Renée," Stephanie says from behind her long thick hair. "No guts, no glory."

"I'M not going back," Renée announces at Friday-night dinner in front of her entire family, including aunts and uncles. She says it just as her mother backs into the dining room from the kitchen with a platter of roast capon.

"Going back where?" asks her aunt Maja, at which point little Alex knocks over a wineglass on the embroidered white tablecloth.

"Alex, Alex," chides Uncle Saul.

"Sh, Saul, he's coughing," Maja says.

"Blot, don't wipe it," Nina tells Andras.

"Raise your hands over your head," commands Aunt Eva, as poor Alex coughs, cheeks reddening.

"Give him some water," Maja says.

"Give him a piece of bread," Uncle Philip chimes in. "How about a piece of challi?"

"Let him be!" Nina begs her elderly in-laws. "All right, there you are." She pats Alex on the back and he stops coughing and Andras begins carving.

"I'm not going back," Renée repeats.

"White meat, please," requests Maja. "What did you say, dear?"

"I'm not going to be a counselor. I hate it," Renée says.

Nina puts down her fork, appalled.

"I never wanted to do it. I *told* you I didn't like it. I just can't go back. I'd rather sit and play piano all day," Renée blurts out.

"Well, you'll have to go back," Nina murmurs, deathly quiet.

"I won't," Renée says.

"We'll discuss it later." Nina's face is flushed. Renée is humiliating her in front of Eva and Maja and their husbands.

"I'm not going," Renée says.

Nina turns to Andras.

"Renée," Andras says, "are you contradicting your mother?"

"I won't go back," Renée mutters to her plate.

"Yes, you will, young lady," Andras tells her. "It's high time you learned the meaning of a day's work."

"I will, I will. I'll do anything else," Renée says. "I'll get a real job. I'll work at the A & P," she says, although even she can't imagine that.

"Absolutely not!" cries Nina.

"Andras," says Aunt Eva, "why should the children work when, thank God, they don't have to? I never understood."

"That's not the point," explodes Nina. "This is not work. This is a camp."

"So, Alex, is this camp really such a terrible place?" Uncle Philip asks in a stage whisper to his little nephew.

" 'S okay," mumbles Alex, who has been eating steadily.

"And are the Lamkins doing a good job?"

"Uh-huh."

"You like the other kids?" presses Philip.

"Yeah." Alex serves himself more kugel.

"I'd rather get a real job," Renée says again.

Andras looks at his daughter skeptically. This is a novel proposition, that Renée could do something constructive. Counseling camp isn't a real job. Not a job independent of Nina's influence. He doubts anyone would actually employ Renée. But that could be a valuable lesson for her. He's never known her to try for anything before. "All right, then," he says. "I'll make a deal with you. You find some other job, and you do it—no complaining—and you don't have to go back to camp."

"Okay." Renée nods, meek with surprise.

But Nina shakes her head. "No," she mouths to Andras. To see her daughter bagging groceries at the A & P! Impossible. She's furious at Andras. To have her judgment so . . . preempted. How could he? How could he pretend to be a believer in the day camp for Renée and Alex, and then sabotage the whole thing later? Doesn't he see she has some pride, some feelings? Or is it all a game between him and his sisters? In which Eva and Maja and Andras all know better than she how to raise the children.

IN KAATERSKILL, Eva and Maja and their husbands share a house. There are no children, and the two couples form a permanent unit, a family of four. They live near each other in the city, where Saul and Philip work together in the diamond business. In Kaaterskill, Eva and Maja keep house together in a large brick edifice with green shutters and a porch in front. While they were not brought up in a traditional home, the sisters are now religious. They have turned to their synagogue in Brooklyn and to the shul in Kaaterskill as to a second family. It is they who draw Andras up to Kaaterskill each summer; they who encouraged, indeed expected, him to buy his summer house. Eva and Maja have a serenity their younger brother lacks. They have a gracious calm and even joy in life, as if somehow in themselves, in their own generosity, they find some comfort for all they lost in the war, some recompense.

The two are legendary for their hospitality. Each of them has a gift for creating an occasion. They nourish their friends and their friends' children with pastries, or honey cake. The sisters have made sociability their life's work. Eva, especially, brightens every gathering with her hot tea and lemon and her fresh berry pies, and above all with her intense interest in her friends' lives. Always she is inviting people in; always baking, whether for bereaved families or new parents. She shares her friends' sadness, and their joy.

Their house is on the way back from shul, and the sisters have a tradition every Shabbes. They invite all their neighbors on Maple to stop in on their way home from services for an oneg. For the children there is a table on the porch with homemade rugelach. Inside, Eva and Maja serve schnapps to Andras and Nina, Elizabeth, Isaac, Cecil and Beatrix, the Ergmans, and the Landauers. A curtain of green leaves frames the children's party. Curtains of lace spun into roses and leaves frame the grown-ups'.

At the Oneg Shabbat this week, Elizabeth sits on the gold sofa, talking about her idea. She tells everyone about the store, her imagined store. It will be a grocery store, the first kosher grocery in Kaaterskill. Everyone complains about the lines in Washington Heights, the men trying to shop on Friday afternoons and the bakery running out every week, and Auerbach's—impossible to get in after eleven-thirty. And of course, there is no other choice. No one from Washington Heights can buy from shops unsanctioned by Rav Kirshner. But Elizabeth will bring meat up from Auerbach's, and challahs from Edelman's, and stock a little store herself, small scale, of course. With a store in Kaaterskill there needn't be any last-minute rush on Friday afternoons. She'll have food in the mountains all during the week.

She's already been making phone calls for wholesale prices on the goods from the city, and she's made a list of all the Kirshner families who would come. Large families. She knows how much money they spend. Then, of course, the other Orthodox people would probably come in to buy, although they haven't got the same restrictions on their shopping, the same need as the Kirshners. And there are also the Kirshner yeshiva bochurs sent up from the city to counsel camp. Elizabeth has filled a steno pad with notes. She'll have a freezer and stock chicken. She'll have shelves of canned goods with cookies and potato chips, bouillon cubes, supervised jam.

"It's a wonderful idea," Eva says.

"But a lot of work," says Maja.

"A lot of work," Eva echoes. "Yes, but it's a splendid idea."

"A kosher store would save so much time," says Nina. "You have to do it. Don't you think she has to do it?" she asks Andras.

Andras sips his drink in the wing chair and he says nothing. What can he say? Elizabeth has never had any experience with a business. She doesn't know anything about inventory; hasn't considered how to transport food from the city or what kind of markup she'll need.

With the transportation expenses, rented space, or at least rented equipment, she won't break even, let alone make money. But there she is, radiant, planning on the sofa. Andras has never seen her so enthusiastic. It's like hearing she gambles secretly. Elizabeth Shulman, mother of five! He's always seen Elizabeth as a certain type. Practical, capable, and warm. Calm and fair with children, a sociable neighbor, and, of course, a pious Jew. That comes last somehow. In religion, Andras assumes, she just follows Isaac's lead. He has always assumed she would behave true to form. And now, suddenly, she seems very eager, very young. He realizes, sitting there, that Elizabeth is probably only thirty-three or thirty-four, and yet he's always thought of her as older, because of all the children. There are people like Nina who always seem young, impulsive, passionate. And then people like Elizabeth, who always seem mature.

Eva and Maja serve strudel to their guests, apple and cherry. They have two sets of good china just for Kaaterskill, and two sets of sterling. They serve on dessert plates painted with acorns and curling brown oak leaves. Eva's hands tremble as she cuts the flaky pastry. "Let me," Nina says. "You sit. I'll do it."

"Who's the guest? *You* sit," Eva tells her young sister-in-law.

"But I'm not a guest," Nina protests.

"In this house. In this house," Eva murmurs, and Nina sits down.

"And where would you put this store?" Maja asks Elizabeth.

Elizabeth hesitates. Isaac looks uncomfortable. She sees he doesn't want her to go on about it. "I was thinking of renting out the back room in Hamilton's."

"Really?"

"I was just thinking about it."

Actually, Elizabeth has gone and talked to Hamilton already. She's gone to see him in his little shingled store, free standing on Main Street between the Taylor building and King Real Estate. Hamilton's was the town grocery on Main Street before the A & P arrived and took all the business. Now Mr. Hamilton sells tourist souvenirs that he brings up from Catskill—postcards, necklaces with Indian bead dolls on the end; trail guides, fishing gear, maple-sugar Liberty Bells.

Hamilton has white hair, and a short white beard, and ruddy skin

weathered from the sun. His eyes are bright clear blue. He is a prickly
fellow, and he's grown worse since the death of his wife, but Elizabeth is not afraid of him. Just yesterday she walked right into his old
storeroom, unused now. It was small and windowless with its Dutch
door opening into the main part of the store. She looked inside. And
then she came up to Hamilton at the register and she said, "I've been
thinking about selling some kosher food, and I was wondering about
renting your back storeroom."

Hamilton said nothing.

"It seems to me that you only use the big storeroom, and you've
got nothing much in the little one. So if I paid you rent and arranged
for deliveries on my own, you'd have a clear profit, and the risk
would be all mine." She told him all about her idea and how much
she'd pay in rent.

"I don't need it," Hamilton said.

"Of course, I'm talking about next summer," Elizabeth told him.

He just shrugged, but Elizabeth wasn't put off. She knows she
can convince him; all she needs is time.

"That little room in the back?" Cecil asks Elizabeth now. "You
know, that used to be the liquor department. Years ago. It's true.
Mrs. Hamilton used to sit there, presiding. At night she locked up the
place with three bolts. Not one, not two."

"He doesn't use it now," Elizabeth says.

"He lost his liquor license ten years ago. Some kids got killed
driving drunk up Mohican."

Elizabeth nods.

"It was before your time," says Cecil.

"Ernestine Schermerhorn told me about it at the library. The
rainstorm," she says. "But now Hamilton's room is empty. . . ."
She does not finish the sentence. She feels suddenly that she has said
too much about the store.

"Did you know they're doing *Iolanthe* at Saratoga?" Beatrix says.
"It's the D'Oyly Carte, so we all have to go. You have to go, especially," she says to Elizabeth, "since you're English."

"Oh, I can't," she says.

"Why?"

"The Three Weeks," Elizabeth says. There are no plays, movies,

or concerts permitted during the Three Weeks. There are no weddings. Every summer on the days the Three Weeks fall out, there
must be mourning for the siege of Jerusalem that led to the destruction of the Second Temple.

"Oh, the Three Weeks," Beatrix mutters. "I don't suppose it
matters that we've got Jerusalem back, and the state of Israel and all
that?"

"The Temple hasn't been restored," Isaac points out.

"Well, you can't have everything," Beatrix says.

AFTER the oneg Elizabeth and Isaac walk into the bungalow, the
children buzzing around them, in and out, up and down the porch
steps. She and Isaac go to their bedroom and shut the door. Quiet and
perfect shade. The children know that on Shabbes afternoon they
can't come in. Elizabeth sits on the side of the bed and takes off her
stockings, but Isaac takes his book and starts out the door. "Where
are you going?" she asks him.

"To read," he says from the doorway.

"Are you angry at me?" Elizabeth asks.

He doesn't answer.

"I just wanted to try out my idea. You didn't think I should?"

He says, "I just didn't think you should talk about it to everyone."

"But it's just an idea."

"Because it's only an idea."

"What's wrong with mentioning it?" she asks him.

"But we haven't even discussed it. We've barely discussed it ourselves."

"Well, why didn't you say anything, then? Why were you just
sitting there?"

"Because I can't sit next to you with everyone there and contra-
dict you," Isaac bursts out. "You don't think about the position you
put me in."

She thinks a moment. Then she says, "It's just that you don't
want me to do it."

"Elizabeth," he says, "there are questions. You aren't thinking about all the questions. The money—"

"I have the money," she interrupts. She has a little money from her grandparents.

"The permission from the Rav."

Of course, she's thought of that. This is the most important question of all. Any business involving food requires permission from the Rav. "You could help me get it," she says. "You could help me if you wanted to."

"It's not an easy thing. It's not such an easy thing for you to suddenly decide."

She sits there on the bed and holds her pillow on her lap, punching her fists deep into it. "Of course it isn't easy. Why should it be easy?"

"A store is risky," Isaac says, swaying slightly back on his heels, holding his book in his arms.

"I know."

"I don't think you do."

"Does that mean I should never try anything or spend my own money?"

"I just don't understand why you're suddenly convinced you want to do this. Why all of a sudden now."

"Because I want to do something."

"But of all the things you could do."

What things? she thinks. What are all the things? All the opportunities to create something of her own. What are all the opportunities for someone who has only been a mother? Not merely a mother, as if it were unimportant, but only a mother. All consumingly. Only a cherisher and a teacher, a feeder of souls, hungry and mysterious, and always becoming more like themselves. What she wants is the chance to shape something that cannot become anything else, only hers. To truly create something, material, definable, self-limited.

Isaac sits down next to her. He puts his book on the bed and Elizabeth stares at the oversized volume of Talmud with the title printed gold on the leatherette cover. The edges of the pages are marbleized a blurry pink and purple. They don't have much money. Of course she knows that. They certainly don't have money to throw away. "Just let me look into it," she says. "At least let me try to find out about it."

"Elizabeth," Isaac says slowly, "this is something—I really think this is something that would be a mistake."

"You wouldn't help me?"

He looks at her in frustration.

"Why don't you just say that you won't let me try."

"I don't think you're being fair," he says.

"No, you aren't being fair," she says.

He picks up his book.

"Isaac," she says, "I can do this myself." She says the words in anger, knowing they are untrue. She couldn't go on if he refused. She couldn't oppose him in that way. And, of course, the Rav would never give permission for her alone to open a store. He wouldn't even see her if she came to him alone. The Rav doesn't really speak to women. Not women outside his family. Not women with business propositions.

2

From the window the Rav can see his people walking up the hill to shul. Before morning services he often stands at the window on the second floor of his house and looks at them; little children running ahead, young parents, older men with canes. He wonders what they are thinking; how they view the world. There are fewer now from Germany in the Kehilla. Fewer every year who once lived in Frankfurt with its great flowing river and the towering, even-spaced trees, the grand stone-fronted houses. The Rav's people are more and more American born. They know only Washington Heights. A jumble of apartments. A hodgepodge. They are not rich as they were in Germany. Their Sabbaths have none of that grandeur, none of that ease. They do not cover their tables with silver and curling candelabra. Their tables gleam with small candlesticks. In America everything is smaller and more private. Missing, and impossible to reclaim, is the old confidence about the world. A holocaust of blood has washed away his congregants' pretensions to a natural place, a decorative culture, a luxuriant liberal education. The inner confidence remains.

Rav Kirshner is unlike the Hasidic rebbes of Borough Park, Crown Heights, and Williamsburg. He is a different sort of rabbi altogether. He is not one to speak often to his followers, stirring them up in crowded halls, demanding and inspiring, imploring. He does not wear a long black frock coat or a shtreimel on Shabbes like those rabbis who dress in the garb of eighteenth-century Polish nobles. His is the modern dress of the nineteenth-century man of business, a suit with a vest and watch pocket, a large gold watch on a chain. He has no flowing beard. In the style of all the Frankfurt rabbis he is clean shaven. He speaks in a clear, direct fashion, without parables or fairy tales, with no reference to Gematria, that cipher of mystic numbers coded in the sacred texts. There are Hasidic rebbes who tie their handkerchiefs to their fingers as they speak of certain things—thus to keep their ascending spirits tied to the ground. Rav Kirshner's handkerchief remains folded in his pocket, starched and ironed. He is no mystic. He is a rationalist, interested in law, not myth. People do not flock to him with supplications, or for blessings on their enterprises. He is not the sort of Rav to whom men pour out their hearts, pleading for words of wisdom and glimpses of hope. As far as he is concerned, their way is laid out before them; they must seek guidance by learning halachah, by living the life prescribed to them. He makes rulings on legal questions, dictates the standards of the community, but he is no counselor or magician to his people. It is not for him to greet them all, accepting petitions like a king on a throne. It is not for him to pull happiness out of a hat, exorcise evil, or divine misfortune in the misshapen letter of a mezuzah. He hates that kind of superstition, and has even written that he prefers doubt and skepticism to that kind of belief. For the skeptic's questions may provide a ground for learning, but the ignorant believer cannot reason. He has written this, and yet he hates both skepticism and ignorant superstition.

The families are quiet as they walk up the hill to the synagogue. Even the children are subdued, because it is Tisha b'Av, the day set aside for prayer and fasting to mourn the fall of Jerusalem, the destruction of the Temple, the dispersion of the Jews. The sun is shining through the trees, illuminating the leaves, but the day is tragic.

Isaiah is knocking on the door, and the Rav checks his watch to make sure it is time. He will not enter the synagogue early or late. His son takes his arm on the stairs and looks at him anxiously. The Rav is under doctor's orders not to fast, but, of course, he is fasting anyway, and no one has dared to offer him breakfast. Together, he and Isaiah leave the house and enter the white synagogue next door.

The Rav cannot see for several minutes when he comes out of the sun into the shadowy sanctuary. He feels, rather than sees, the men parting in front of him, the soft mass of their suit jackets, the hundred curves of their hats. Opening the siddur in front of him, turning the smooth white pages, the Rav waits for the letters to stop dancing. They are floating and jumping over the page, but this does not frighten him. Gradually his eyes adjust to the dark. The letters settle into their proper places, moving into their correct and eternal order. Only after they have settled down does he begin to pray. He davens standing, reading silently, moving his lips. He does not shuckl, swaying from side to side or up and back on his heels, because he does not go in for theatrics. He simply davens. He feels no hunger or thirst. He has always fasted well.

FROM the women's section Elizabeth glimpses the Rav standing. For just a moment she sees his small dark figure between the white curtain and the glass of the mechitzah. The shul is packed. All the men are up because it's Sunday. Tisha b'Av fell on a Saturday this year, and so the fast was put off until the next day. Mourning is forbidden on the Sabbath; it would be wrong to read lamentations on such a joyous day.

Elizabeth leans back. She sits with the girls and her familiar headache, the emptiness of getting up early and skipping breakfast. She got up at six to feed the three little ones. They are too young to go without food the whole day, and so Elizabeth gave them breakfast. She lay down for a few minutes while Isaac helped the girls lace up their tennis shoes. They are all wearing white canvas tennis shoes instead of leather, as a sign of mourning.

Beyla Lamkin is tapping Elizabeth on the shoulder. "Is that seat empty?"

Elizabeth shakes her head. "Chani's coming back."

"I don't know where to sit," Beyla whispers. "It's so warm. Do you feel warm?"

"Sh," Esther Ergman hisses.

"Sit, sit, I don't know where Chani is," says Elizabeth, although she doesn't want to sit next to Beyla with her squirming baby.

"Sh." Esther Ergman is glaring at her. Elizabeth does know where Chani is. She is outside running around, up and down the hill;

she'll come in scratched up from the blackberry bushes behind the shul. Chani hates sitting all this time.

Beatrix isn't in shul, having announced that Tisha b'Av is unnecessary; but everyone else is here. Nina Melish at the window looking pale, her sisters-in-law Eva and Maja next to her, as serene as ever, matching, their straw hats trimmed with clusters of dried flowers. And all the other summer people. The pregnant women in their voluminous dresses and big sheitels, their hair looking too big for their heads. Young Rabbi Shavitz's wife with Chaya and Tova, four and two, in matching dresses, big white collars appliquéd with flowers, Chaya, taller and with longer hair, wearing a hearing aid. The young girls are there, with long legs; the little ones with headbands; the very old ladies with their old-fashioned rings, white gold and diamond clusters. A bride, married a month or two ago, a little zaftig, wearing a tailored suit. The babies with dark curly hair, white dresses, pink sashes. The toddlers squirming on laps in their lace-trimmed socks. The Conservative Rabbi Sobel's wife with her eyes on her book. Leah Landauer sitting alone, because she has no daughters. All her sons sit in the men's section with Joe.

The Rav does not see any of this, of course. It is impossible to see the women even from where he stands on the raised bima. Isaiah supports him at his side, but the Rav holds the carved railing of the bima and nods to his son to let him go. What he sees from the raised dais is the hundreds of men, a shifting ocean of black. Lifted by the day and by the fast, he stands holding the railing like a man at the prow of a ship, all the faces below him floating on a sea of black suit jackets. He sees them floating, and yet he feels the wood railing beneath his fingers. He watches their faces blur and drift, surreal, and yet he stands still, firm on his feet. He can observe to himself that his eyes are playing tricks on him. It is strange to be making that observation, to see himself standing there on his feet and to know that there is no ocean beneath him, that the ground is still, that in truth all the men's faces sit squarely on the correct bodies. For, of course, if he had eaten and taken his medication it would all be clear. Without it he realizes that his perception is faulty. The experience is interesting to him. When he sits down he sees well, but when he stands up, he watches his eyes play tricks. Standing up, he stands outside of himself —a rational ecstasy.

It is time for the reading. For Jerusalem, the city, alone and bereft. Her garments spoiled, her cheeks wet with tears. The Rav fixes his eyes above the sea, and slowly raises his hand to silence the murmur of men praying.

"I will say some words about *Eichah,* the lament which we read last night," he says in his unwavering accented voice. "For in the words of the prophet: *Avar katzir, calah kaitz, v'anachnu lo noshanu.* Harvest is past, summer finished, and we are not saved." He pauses. "And we must ask ourselves, *whose* is this lament? It is ours. And which generation? It is ours. We have lived in confusion; we have suffered, our people lost in flame."

Strange, but again, as he speaks, the Rav can see himself talking, and he can see the men listening, and yet he knows that they are not listening to him. He sees now, quite clearly, their upturned faces, intent on his every word, and yet he feels that this clarity is itself illusory. For they are not listening to him. They are whispering and davening to themselves. Their voices murmur underneath his voice, like the murmur of lazy bees and distant lawn mowers, a murmur of sleep.

"For us the lament is redoubled," he says. His voice is neither angry nor sad, but cold. Chilling. "Once, in Germany, we remembered our nation, Israel, scattered. Now, in America, we remember our families in Germany who were slaughtered, burned to ash. We mourn our ancient land laid waste in injustice, as the prophet has said, and the people dispersed, as the prophet has written. But we have also seen the land of our dispersion laid waste; the just men slaughtered. We must remember both; we must remember each."

He clutches the railing, and he sees his hands clutching it, his fingers white. He senses it all. His sense is almost too keen. On one side his nephew Joseph, on the other, his son, Isaiah, poised next to him, weighing on him. The people below, anxious, waiting. He sees how young the young are; he can see it in the innocent beauty, the slight stupidity, of their faces. He sees them with their mouths open like birds about to swallow. They know, even less than he, why they were born to live instead of die. Their prayers fill their minds; they wash through the room in a tide of repetition, and the sounds double and double back again upon themselves. But, of course, the young know nothing. They remember nothing. There is no experience written onto their soft blank hearts. He is speaking to them, and yet he sees they are not listening. He is reciting, chanting the first kinah, the first words of grief and desolation. They are still murmuring. They are murmuring to themselves, following along blindly in their books, brushing the edge of each word with their lips. He senses it all as he sings: the red velvet on the lectern, his son and his nephew on either side, the gabbai, the president of the shul, the young Rabbi Lamkin. And it seems to him as he reads, his perspective is growing ever broader, the whole room turning about him, the bima gently floating, the memorial lights like white evening stars, the trees brushing against the vaulted windows, trailing their branches as if the glass were water.

His words float into the hushed congregation, and in the women's section Elizabeth follows, swaying in silent concentration. The pause is almost imperceptible, but then she hears a gasp from the men's section and a shuffle. The plain, almost droning, music of the voice breaks off. "Get an ambulance," someone shouts, and then there is a roar of voices.

"What happened? What happened?"

"Hold him up. I'm a doctor."

"So am I!"

"I can't believe it; please, please—"

"Mommy, is he hurt?"

Lifting the lace curtain Elizabeth can't see the Rav, only a crowd of men on the bima. The women are pressing forward. They push to the entrance of the women's section, holding back the children.

"He's hurt."

"It's a stroke," someone whispers.

"God forbid!"

"That's what they said."

"Back up. Back up. Move back."

The ambulance siren sounds in the open doorway, and the town medics burst in with a white stretcher. The children are crying. Elizabeth is holding them, sitting with Brocha's head in her lap. She can hardly breathe. The breath has been knocked out of her. No one ever thinks about the Rav falling, stricken down. No one imagines that. They take it for granted that he stands at the center, that he speaks and chastises and controls. They take for granted what he is and has been for almost fifty years: scholar, judge, historian, witness.

In the knot of men near the bima the Rav breathes painfully, eyes shut. "You, Isaiah, continue," he whispers.

"I'm coming with you, Father." Isaiah bends over him.

"No, stay," the Rav commands, and he feels Isaiah touching his hand, and the warmth, confusion, and trembling excitement of the touch, because he has suggested that soon Isaiah will succeed him. He feels it all, more than Isaiah means for him to feel. He feels them lifting him away. They are carrying him away outside. It annoys him to be touched this way, and annoys him more that Isaiah is coming with him, leaning over him. He would flick him off if he could. He feels the ingratiating warmth of Isaiah's hand, and at the same time the cold intravenous fluid tracing a path through the veins up his arm. He feels his body caught in the moment of transformation, both animate and inanimate, warm to the touch, but cold within. They slide him into the back of the ambulance, one medic to watch the Rav, the other to drive down the mountain to Catskill Hospital. Isaiah climbs in and they speed away down Main Street.

The ambulance careens down the mountain, siren shrieking and sobbing on the curving road. It rips through the shadowy forest and screams into the silence of the trees.

Halfway down the mountain, however, Rav Kirshner opens his eyes. He looks up into the face of the Kaaterskill volunteer fireman, Stan Knowlton. "Where are we going?" he demands.

"Lie still, sir," says Knowlton, "we're taking you to the hospital."

"Thank you, it is quite unnecessary. I am revived," says the Rav. "These things"—he gestures to the IV bottle and tubes above him—"these have revived me."

"We have to take you to the hospital, Father," Isaiah says.

"This is very expensive; it is quite unnecessary." The Rav purses his lips in disapproval. "It is time to go home."

Isaiah touches his father's arm.

"It is time to go home," the Rav says again.

"We can't," Isaiah murmurs.

"How old are you?"

"Thirty-nine," Isaiah answers.

"How old am I?"

"Seventy-eight."

The Rav nods. "That is correct. You may please tell the driver to turn the vehicle around, and tell them to slow on the way up the mountain. I don't like this speed, and it is very expensive. Go. Go and talk to the driver."

Isaiah hesitates. He cannot tell the driver to turn the ambulance around. Of course his father must go to the hospital, but to calm him he goes up front and sits next to the driver as if to consult with him. After several minutes of hushed debate the vehicle does indeed slow down, but it continues to the hospital in Catskill.

From the stretcher the Rav stares at Stan Knowlton. "What is your name?" he asks mildly, as if to make conversation.

"Stanley Knowlton," Stan answers.

"And you live in Kaaterskill?"

"Yes."

"What do you do?"

Stan looks uncomfortable, interrogated by the old man. "I work —I used to work for Michael King, fixing the bungalows, mainly."

"I see. You are married?"

"Yes. I have a wife, Janet, and one daughter, Lark."

"Lark?" the Rav asks, puzzled. "Ah, yes," he says, "I have read in the *Times* about these names after the animals and birds. Star, Fawn, Dawn, Sky."

"No, that wasn't it," Stan explains. "We named her from a line in a Shakespeare play."

The Rav is surprised. "Please quote," he demands of Knowlton, just as he does of his disciples in Talmud shiur.

"Quote what?"

"The verses with the name."

" 'I'll say yon gray is not the morning's eye,' " Knowlton recites. " 'Nor that is not the lark whose notes do beat / The vaulty heaven so high above our heads.' It's from *Romeo and Juliet*. We acted in it in high school.''

The Rav smiles. "Ach! But it's better in German," he exclaims. "The Schiller translation. It is the most beautiful language. Schiller is the best of the German poets."

The ambulance sways and dips and Knowlton steadies himself. "I didn't think you would read them—Germans," Knowlton says.

"But I am German," the Rav answers softly.

"Rabbi!" Stan calls out. The old man seems to be drifting off.

"I was speaking on this subject, Germany, before you came for me," the Rav says. "They were nodding their heads in the congregation, but do you think they understand me? I think not. You have seen my people when you fix the bungalows, have you, Mr. Knowlton?"

"Oh, yeah, of course."

"They are good people," the Rav muses. He speaks slowly and softly. "But they are very *simple*. I notice all the time. They are always working and they are learning. Today I asked myself: What are they *thinking*? Such a simple people. They are afraid of the Mind, and to read. They don't read Schiller and the Shakespeare. How can I say it to you? They keep one thing, the religious, alive. It is the most important, but they have lost the other. They have forgotten the poetry. There is not one of them who is what we used to call an Educated Man. With Greek and Latin, student of the arts. That was what I had in Germany. They do not attend university. They have the one thing and not the other. How did this happen? In this country I think perhaps it is necessary. They make their way—accountants, lawyers; in the banks. Getting and spending, I am afraid. Working all the time. When do they think of the spiritual?" Stern and exhausted, but somehow wondering, he opens his eyes and looks up into Stan Knowlton's face.

"Well, at least they've got jobs," Knowlton says. "In New York City there's decent jobs to choose from."

The Rav doesn't seem to hear this. He is still talking, his voice barely audible as he keeps talking to himself.

THE Rav insisted he wouldn't go into the hospital. He was furious when Stan took him out on the stretcher, but he was too weak to fight it. Knowlton thinks about this on the way back to Kaaterskill. He thinks about his strange conversation with the rabbi. All the old man's questions. Stan had never met Rabbi Kirshner before. He hadn't known he was such a talker.

Knowlton and the driver take the ambulance back to the firehouse, and Stan walks over to Boyd's garage. James Boyd, one of old Boyd's nephews, works there as mechanic. James is the same age as Knowlton, twenty-eight, but much heavier around the middle. He was always stocky, and now he keeps his T-shirt tucked in over his belly. He has a ruddy face and big hands, sandy brown hair and green eyes. The Rubin kid is working there with him, and they've got the radio on and the fan blowing just as they always do in the summer. Ira Rubin's father owns Rubin's Hotel on Main Street, but the kid loves cars. At sixteen he is six feet, as tall as James, but half as wide. His hair is curly brown and his face seems as yet too small for his body. He wears glasses that sometimes slip down his short nose. Even when he was fourteen, Ira hung around the garage. He's like a little brother to James.

"Guess who I just took down to Catskill Hospital?" Stan says.

"I don't know, who?" James asks.

"Guess. Three guesses."

"Michael King," says James.

"Yeah, that'd be a good one," Stan says. "You guess." He pokes his head into the Volkswagen bug where Ira is working.

"I don't know," says Ira. He is cementing the square base of the rearview mirror onto the front window. As the rubber cement drips down the glass he scrapes it up with a razor blade.

"Rabbi Kirshner," Stan says.

"Who's he?" asks Ira.

"You know who he is. The old guy on the hill."

"Which old guy?" James asks.

"What do you mean, which?"

"I mean there's a hundred old rabbis in this town."

"I mean *the* Rabbi Kirshner."

"Does he wear fur? A fur hat?"

"No, I'm telling you this is Kirshner, the one in charge."

"So why'd he have to go to Catskill?" James asks. "Is he dead, or what?"

"He didn't die," Knowlton tells them. "He was just lying there on his back the whole time talking my ear off. Shakespeare, Germany, economics."

"Wouldn't shut up, huh?" says James.

"And you know, he said he's only seventy-eight," Stan muses. "He looks like he's about a hundred."

"You look like an old man yourself," James teases. "What d'you think, Ira? Stan here is twenty-eight."

"Old, I guess," Ira says, grinning. He can see James and Stan are going to kick back and start talking. They love talking about the old days. Ira sits down on the pile of tires with the fan blowing and the greasy radio playing. James and Stan can talk on and on. They talk about when they were in high school and they played basketball, and fought, and got suspended. The times James used to liberate cars from his uncle Boyd's shop, and they went driving around the mountain. The time they went skinny-dipping at Kaaterskill Falls. Ira sits there on the big tires and he takes it all in with his intent freckled face, his ears sticking out as if to listen harder to the stories, all the good times up to the very end—the day they never mention—when Stan, and James, John Curtis, and Billy Walker flew off the road and crashed in Devil's Kitchen.

*

IT WASN'T accurate, what he said in the ambulance. The Rav considers this in his hospital bed. It isn't completely true that his people have forgotten the liberal arts. After all, his own son, Jeremy, did attend university. Columbia. And he did learn those rich and florid ancient languages. His son excelled, in fact indulged, in the arts, history, and poetry. Jeremy was a brilliant scholar, learned in both sacred and secular literature. From the beginning his learning and intellectual ability far surpassed Isaiah's. The Rav thinks of this as he lies there in his foolish hospital gown with Isaiah at his side. He is tired. Tired of his younger son always present, always solicitous. Dutiful. Isaiah does exactly as he is told. The Rav expects no less. This is what he requires. He thinks he can see Isaiah, both his sons, objectively, for what they are. Each has what the other lacks. Isaiah is good. He has a pure and dedicated heart. He is ambitious, but his ambition is turned entirely toward the welfare of the Kehilla. He is pious; he is truly pious. But he is not interesting.

"I would like to see Jeremy," he says to Isaiah. "I would like to see your brother."

"Of course we already called him, Father," Isaiah says.

"And he is coming here?" the Rav asks. "Or to the house?"

"We don't know yet how long you will be here. The doctors have to decide." Isaiah is sitting nervously at his bedside. He is surprised at his father's insistence, and a little frightened. The Rav has never been so anxious to see Jeremy. His words seem portentous to Isaiah. Like a rebuke to him and his wife, as if they have done wrong; as if they have not done enough, so that now, in the hospital, he turns to the other son. "I'm sure he'll come as soon as he can," Isaiah says.

"Then tell him I am waiting," says the Rav. "And where is my *Times*?"

That evening Jeremy arrives. Wearing his light sport coat and cream Panama hat, he walks into the Rav's private hospital room. The Rav seems half his true size, a tiny old man swallowed up in the white bed. On one side Isaiah sits with the water pitcher and the reading glasses. On the other side of the bed sits Jeremy's cousin, Joseph. The two of them with their suits coal-black against the white sheets; they seem like a pair of dark Puritan angels.

"Jeremy." The Rav stretches out his frail arms and smiles.

The warmth of the welcome shocks Jeremy. He is confused by that smiling face. It is unlike his father; it is as if his father were vanishing into a sort of frail pixilated benevolence. "Go, please," the Rav says sharply to Isaiah and Joseph, and his sharp tone is somehow reassuring.

"How are you, Father?" Jeremy asks when they are alone.

"I am a patient," the Rav says, "but I am not patient." His deep-set eyes sparkle. He is enjoying his little joke. "They are holding me for observations, changing my medications, experimenting, and this causes me hallucinations."

"Really? Hallucinations?"

"I see one, for example, right now," the Rav says calmly. "Just" —he points to Jeremy's left shoulder—"there. A figure, I can see, quite clearly."

Involuntarily, Jeremy turns and looks.

"But I know it is a trick of the eye. She has no shadow. It is interesting, isn't it? The eye plays tricks. There is a great difference between what we see and what we know. You have not sent me your essays," he tells Jeremy.

Jeremy studies his father's face. The Rav has rarely shown any interest in Jeremy's scholarly work. In his library in the city he has a bound copy of Jeremy's dissertation, but Jeremy has no idea whether he has ever read it.

"Here I have time to read," the Rav says. "Because they do not like me to do my work. When I get home I will be behind with my correspondence."

"Are you going back to Kaaterskill or to the city?" Jeremy asks.

"Of course, Kaaterskill," says his father. Then he adds, "Your brother wants me to go back to the city." As he speaks his tone is the same, his wording the same as always, only slower. "You remember when we first came up to Kaaterskill."

"Sure," Jeremy says. He must have been ten or eleven at the time.

"Your mother was the one who wanted to come up to the mountains."

"I know," says Jeremy.

"I had not wanted to buy the house in Kaaterskill. It did not interest me then to leave the city. We argued, and she said, it is not good to stay all year in Washington Heights. Not good to have only one thing and not another. The children need air to breathe and other sights to see, and you need it too. I said it was trouble to come to the mountains, to have two houses, and she said, it is not enough to live in one place if it is not beautiful. It is not sufficient."

Tears start in Jeremy's eyes. It is hard for him to hear his father speak of her. They almost never speak of her.

The Rav pauses, and then he says, "She believed in beauty, its power and strength. She believed in beauty and nature and in art."

"And she was right about the house," Jeremy says lightly, just to say something, to deflect the moment because it is so strong.

"I had loved those things," the Rav says. "But I did not believe in them as she did. Except perhaps when I was very young. Before the war when I was young."

"Father." It is Isaiah knocking on the open door of the hospital room.

The Rav looks up irritably.

"Father," Isaiah says again, "Dr. Stein is here."

"I am in the middle of a conversation," the Rav says. Then he turns to Jeremy and confides, "I have no time for this." He gestures to the hospital bed. "They would like to keep me here, but I have no time for it. My manuscript on *Kohelet* is still uncorrected. My correspondents will be waiting for answers to their letters. I have never delayed my replies before."

The Rav looks at Jeremy with his dark impatient eyes, and Jeremy feels a rush of gratitude to be singled out this way. He meets his father's gaze with wonder and with joy.

3

—

"OKAY," Stephanie tells Renée, "so the deal is, we have to get you a job, or you go back to Rabbitville." That's what Stephanie calls Rabbi Lamkin's camp. Stephanie has a way with words. She particularly likes vintage slang, which she's picked up from the succession of baby-sitters she had as a child. She's had baby-sitters from several eras, and she mixes together phrases from all of them. There was Mrs. Boyles, the old housekeeper with support hose who lived in until Stephanie was twelve and played Nanny to Stephanie's Eloise, and there was, of course, Malaya with her women's group and ashram. There was also a tight-lipped divorcée who had a cache of pills in her night table. She left one day, taking nothing but Mom's jewelry. Stephanie remembers all of these women fondly and still drapes herself with their mismatched catchwords. "Say, Steve," she'll tell her cousin—the one with the license—as he drives, "you'd better slow down, there's fuzz on this road."

"Now, for a new job . . . Well, what can you do?" Stephanie asks, examining her friend.

"Nothing," says Renée.

"Sh, I'm concentrating."

Renée watches with anxious eyes as her friend strides out into the living room of the Fawesses' lake house. Balancing like a surfer, Stephanie takes a slide across the polished hardwood floor on a huge white New Zealand sheepskin. She paces around the circular fireplace, which King advertises to the winter renters, and kicks the polished driftwood coffee table contemplatively. Her parents don't care what she does to the furniture; it's not theirs, and they're rarely home anyway. They haven't bothered to buy and furnish a house in Kaaterskill because security is so difficult in the winter.

"What can you do?" Stephanie asks again. She wanders into the kitchen and sticks her head in the refrigerator. "Hmm. What are you good at? Parents. You're good at parents." Stephanie's mother adores Renée, because she's so polite and quiet. Nina's training has left its mark. When Renée comes over she always says, 'Hello, Mrs. Fawess, how are you?' And she thanks Mrs. Fawess for having her over. "Parents. Adults," Stephanie brainstorms. "Goody Two-shoes. Pain-in-the-ass . . . Libraries!" She shouts, triumphant. She slams shut the refrigerator door. "Kendall Falls Library," she tells Renée. "They'll love you. Come on, we have to get over there."

"But what do I say?" Renée asks.

"Come on, come on. I'll pick up the dogs and walk you." Stephanie has started a dog-walking business. Three dollars an hour per client. She calls the dogs "clients."

Renée and Stephanie set off for Kendall Falls. Renée walks her bike, and Stephanie walks her five clients: two terriers, her aunt's hyperactive spaniel, Roberta—named after Redford—and King's gray poodle. Deftly, the aspiring veterinarian untangles the leashes as she talks. "You go in," she instructs Renée on the way. "You tell whatserface you heard she needed help cataloging or something."

"But I didn't hear that," Renée says.

Stephanie glares at her. "Just tell the goddamn librarian you want a job," she orders.

Renée groans. "She knows my mother. She's known me since I was eight years old."

"So obviously she'll hire you," Stephanie reasons. "Look, chick, nothing ventured, nothing gained. There comes a time when you decide: Am I going to be a shrinking violet, or am I going to achieve? Come on, woman, this is your life."

"But I don't know what to say," says Renée as they approach the library.

"Buffalo biscuits," Stephanie says. She leaves her friend in front of Kendall Falls Free Library, turns around with a flick of her hair, and walks off, dogs jumping all around her.

Renée stands alone on the sidewalk, and feels not so much afraid as sad and unimportant. She wants to be original like Stephanie, but she isn't. She looks at the library with distaste. The library's front yard is divided in half by a path from the gate to the front door. The flagstone walk is perfectly straight, like a compass-and-ruler construction. Petunias planted on each side. Two straight lines of purple-and-white pinwheel flowers. Renée trudges up the path. She opens the glass library door.

"Renée Melish," says Ernestine Schermerhorn. Mrs. Schermerhorn's voice carries. She exercises her librarian's privilege not to whisper. "I haven't seen you for quite some time."

Renée smiles nervously. She doesn't want to approach nimble-fingered, keen-eyed Mrs. Schermerhorn. She pretends to browse instead. But the library has grown very small, like Renée's grandmother in Buenos Aires. It is just one room, like a one-room schoolhouse, tall bookcases and short, all facing the desk.

"Are you looking for something, Renée?" Mrs. Schermerhorn says.

Renée hesitates. Then she says, "I was looking for you."

"Well, here I am," says Mrs. Schermerhorn. She sits up, straight and tall behind her desk.

"I heard you need help cataloging or something," says Renée.

"I don't know where you could have heard that," Mrs. Schermerhorn replies, and Renée can feel the library's silence blossoming between them. "We're part of the state cataloging plan now, and I have an assistant, you know, Mrs. Knowlton."

"Oh," Renée says.

"However," Mrs. Schermerhorn says thoughtfully, "I could use help on the bookmobile."

And so Renée is hired and saved from Rabbitville. She starts working on the bookmobile that afternoon. Renée and Mrs. Knowlton load the books into the van. Then Renée gets in, alongside Mrs. Schermerhorn.

Each afternoon they drive to a different town and park while the library customers browse the shelves. Then they make side trips to individual houses to deliver books on order, collect fines, pick up donations of used magazines. It's a bit like the trick-or-treating Renée remembers from when they had the old house in Brooklyn and her mother still allowed the children to celebrate Halloween—that pagan holiday. Renée has to do the running in and out, carrying books and bringing back request slips, money for overdue fines. All of this saves Mrs. Schermerhorn's back. The work is all running up to the door and ringing the bell while the librarian waits at the curb. Mrs. Schermerhorn sits behind the wheel of the big gray bookmobile and toots the horn when she thinks they're getting behind schedule. The van is fitted out like a boat with safety rails on the bookshelves. There are red tulips painted on the windows, but the flowers are small, so that they won't block the view.

"Well, Renée," Mrs. Schermerhorn says as they drive up Mohican, "you came at an opportune time. I haven't had anyone to help for the last eight or nine years. There was a girl at the beginning, but it ended very unfortunately."

Renée looks up, startled.

"And she had been a bright young girl," Mrs. Schermerhorn murmurs as she steers the van. "She had been about your age. Candy Kendall. She's Candy Walker now."

The librarian steers the van into the private road off Mohican. "This is where I live," she says with simplicity and pride as they pass the gatehouse. "We've lived here for twenty-five years. Here in the Mohican Road Community. Of course, my family have lived here much longer than that—before the American Revolution, before there were any Yankees here, before Kendall Falls existed. You know the mountains were Dutch."

The van sails into the gated community, and up the private winding road. They have a covenant, Renée thinks, remembering Stephanie's words. Renée never did get straight exactly what the secret Mohican Road covenant is, but she knows she wouldn't be here inside the gate if she weren't on the bookmobile. The road twists up the mountain, and behind the trees, the great houses reveal themselves, turreted like true castles. Renée has never seen them up close, only from far away, only in glimpses from the road below. She and Chani Shulman used to have names for them all when they were little; Renée had forgotten that. There was the Gray Tower for Rapunzel, and a pillared Sleeping Beauty's palace, the White Castle, and Cinderella's house. She and Chani planned to make a map just like the Fairy Tale map in the glass table at the library, but somehow they could never make their map as beautiful. Depending on the pens they used, some of the palaces stood out very dark and spotted, and some were just dry scratches from old used-up markers Chani wouldn't throw away. Chani believed that Magic Markers last forever, and she said if you just didn't use a marker for a while it regenerated in its cap. Now Renée is inside Fairyland, and when the van stops she can see the whole mountainside below, the forest and the lake and the little houses of Kaaterskill.

Mornings in the library, plucking selections for the bookmobile, Renée hears the verdict on every family passing through the door. Mrs. Schermerhorn makes the pronouncements for the benefit of Renée and Mrs. Knowlton, the assistant librarian. At her desk on Monday before the Bear Mountain run, Mrs. Schermerhorn scoffs at the improvements on Michael King's house. "I've never seen anything so vulgar." She unrolls a fresh-typed library card from her electric typewriter. She says to Mrs. Knowlton, "I can only imagine what it must be like for you and your husband, living across the street from that monstrosity. The Seventh Wonder of Maple Street."

Mrs. Knowlton leans on the new arrival table. "Stan says someday Michael King is going to get too big for his britches. He's trying to rent out a new house each year, and he still hasn't finished repairing the roofs and gutters from when the bungalows got swamped last August."

"Is Stan still working for him?" Mrs. Schermerhorn asks.

"Oh, no—not now," Mrs. Knowlton says. "He's restoring the Lamkin house."

"Where is that?"

"Way back behind Spruce."

Mrs. Schermerhorn knits her brow.

"The gray place," Mrs. Knowlton says. "Two stories."

"I can't quite recall it," Mrs. Schermerhorn tells her.

Mrs. Knowlton glances over to where Renée is pulling out biographies. "Where the Jewish day camp is," she whispers at last.

"Oh, you mean the old Thorne place!" Mrs. Schermerhorn's voice is muffled. "Oh, yes—"

"—little . . . coats . . ." is all Renée can make out of the reply. She strains to hear what Mrs. Schermerhorn has to say about Rabbi Lamkin and his wife, but Mrs. Schermerhorn is back to Mr. King's improvements again.

"Last time I looked," Mrs. Schermerhorn says, "King was having white columns delivered. Four for the front. To make the house colonial, I think was his idea. It looks like the Phoenicia Motel."

"I wonder—" Mrs. Knowlton begins; but the library door jingles.

"Good morning, Candy," says Mrs. Schermerhorn.

Instantly Renée looks up from her pile of biographies on the floor. This is Candy, Renée's predecessor on the bookmobile. The girl with the unfortunate end. Renée stares and stares, and she wonders if the woman eats a lot of it—candy, that is. Candy looks like a great round Russian doll from the back. Long fine blond hair streaming down over round shoulders to where her round bottom begins, with hardly an indentation at the waist; the line of her belt looks instead like the place where the doll comes apart to reveal the next largest one inside. Renée used to have a set with ten nesting dolls, painted and lacquered.

"Just returning these?" Mrs. Knowlton asks Candy.

Candy does not reply. With an indifferent look she casts her eye over Mrs. Knowlton's new-arrival table. Then she passes briefly through the children's section. Like a lady browsing in a store, she picks up a few books, then puts them down. And after only a few minutes she turns and walks out, the door jingling behind her.

The library is silent. There are no other borrowers in the room.

"God has entered her life," Mrs. Schermerhorn says of Candy.

"What do you mean?" asks Mrs. Knowlton.

"I'm simply telling you what she's told me," says Mrs. Schermerhorn. "She says she's going to Kaaterskill Bible Church."

"I don't think she's very happy," Mrs. Knowlton says after a moment.

"I think she's happy enough," Mrs. Schermerhorn says. "For a girl with a history like hers. And she doesn't have to work, you know."

She's pretty well set with her widow's benefits. Wouldn't I have been surprised to look into the future when she was working on the bookmobile."

Renée pauses in her search for *Mary Queen of Scots*. Still as she can be, she kneels on the carpeted floor.

"But the crash . . ." Mrs. Knowlton says.

"Yes. Yes, she lost him. I don't deny that. A tragedy. But as I say, she's well set with her benefits from the service."

"August nineteenth," Mrs. Knowlton says in a hushed voice.

"It was August twentieth!" Mrs. Schermerhorn exclaims. "I'll never forget it was August twentieth."

"I'm sure it was the nineteenth," says Mrs. Knowlton timidly.

"No," Mrs. Schermerhorn declares. "I'll never forget it, because August the twentieth, 1966, my mother came to visit. And you remember the storm. That was the record August rainfall for the last fifty years. I was just terrified to drive. And you remember there were two hikers lost in the mud down in Palenville. But even with the wind that night I could hear the car skidding. And there was a shatter of glass I remember distinctly. I have very keen ears. My dog, poor Caesar, went absolutely wild. I knew the crash was just off Mohican. The driver could have been a Mohican Estate resident for all I knew. I said, 'Ralph, get out of bed; it's an accident! Call the police!' "

"But the phone line was down," Mrs. Knowlton murmurs tremulously.

"Yes, just come apart! And the power too. So Ralph took his big flashlight, and Mother and I crept up to the window with the old kerosene lantern. We couldn't see anything but the trees thrashing against each other."

"I know," Mrs. Knowlton whispers. "I'd been waiting up for Stan to begin with—"

"It was a miracle your husband survived," Mrs. Schermerhorn says severely.

Mrs. Knowlton looks up with her round eyes. "A miracle any of them did. Stan said they fell so fast—"

"Fifty feet skidding on the car roof. Ralph saw the wreck. That old car was absolutely wrapped around the tree. I can only imagine what poor Bill looked like in the driver's seat." Mrs. Schermerhorn shakes her head. "He and Candy only married a day—"

"I thought they hadn't been married at all," Mrs. Knowlton says. "When the storm hit they were driving home from Bill's bachelor party."

"No, no," Mrs. Schermerhorn corrects.

Janet shakes her head, puzzled, but doesn't argue further.

"Well, Judge Taylor took care of it, drew up the papers," says Mrs. Schermerhorn.

"And they'd hardly any time together," Mrs. Knowlton whispers, thinking how she nearly lost her own husband.

"I wouldn't say *hardly*," the librarian corrects. "Candy gave birth just six months later. And as I say, she's well set with her benefits from the service." Then Mrs. Schermerhorn calls to Renée, "Let's get those books into the van, please, or we'll be late."

THE hilly Bear Mountain Road bumps and jolts the van. The forest seems thicker here, because there is less of a town. "I've noticed you don't take out any books yourself, Renée," says Mrs. Schermerhorn. "What do you do with your free time?"

Renée looks down at her cotton skirt. Her arms hurt from carrying stacks of books from the library to the van. She's wearing down the rippled rubber soles of her Famolare sandals.

"I would like to recommend some titles," the librarian tells her. "It's a pity to let a summer go to waste."

When it comes to reading, Mrs. Schermerhorn doesn't approve of anyone's taste in Kaaterskill or Bear Mountain—except for Mrs. Shulman, who always comes in to the library for fat old books and serious nonfiction. As for the bookmobile customers, deadpan Mrs. Schermerhorn announces the name and then the special request of each as she drives.

"Mrs. Juliet Lacy: *Passion Flowers*."

"Mr. Richard Beckstein, MD: *All the Right Moves: Meeting Your Mate*."

"Mr. William Curtis: *Real Estate with Nothing Down*."

"Mrs. Jacqueline King: *French Provincial: Ornaments and Accessories*."

In Bear Mountain Mrs. Schermerhorn pulls up in front of the post office and parks to open for business. Her first customer is already waiting on the curb. Mrs. Schermerhorn tisks as he boards the van and hands a stack of worn paperbacks to Renée. The torn covers are blue and black, covered with galaxies, spaceships, dragons rearing up under women in gold bras. Renée expects to hear one of the titles read out loud, but Mrs. Schermerhorn restrains herself. She lets Renée stamp them and hand them over to grubby, curly-haired Ira Rubin, whose glasses always seem about to slip off his short nose.

"Well. We are what we read," Mrs. Schermerhorn remarks as they pull away from the curb.

"The rock face was brutal, studded with metallic waste," Ira Rubin reads when he gets home, *"but we kept on, clawing, crawling our way up, first Buck, then me, then Xanda. I looked up at the sonar range finder strapped to Buck's pack. Forty feet up, and a higher rock face ahead. No, she was right, there is no moral instinct, I thought. Just the will to survive, keep crawling up to the top. What then? You don't think a lot about the future when you're scaling a decoy crater on the planet Rhea."*

"Ira?" he hears faintly from upstairs.

"What?" he calls back.

"I said come here," his mother calls.

"Why?"

"Now," his mother hollers from the top of the stairs.

He follows her up into his room. "Clean it," she says.

"Oh, yeah," he says, peering into his cavelike room. He was supposed to clean it. It's hard to see the mess. Ira keeps the shades down. There are paperbacks, and his school texts left over from eighth grade—the ones the teachers didn't even want back at the end of the year, they looked so bad. *Catcher in the Rye,* and *Ancient Civilizations,* free weights, newspapers strewn across the floor—he uses the old papers to line the cage of his pet rat, Bester.

"Clean it now," his mother says.

"Okay." Ira thumps back down the wooden stairs with his book and takes it back out to the porch, where the birches rattle with the white summer wind. He finishes a book in an afternoon, racing through it and forgetting it all as soon as he's done. Then sometimes he rips through another one at night, reading in bed until the pages hurt his eyes.

His father, Mark, thinks he should do something better with his time than read sci-fi books and sit in Boyd's Garage. After all, if he wants a summer job, he could work at the family's hotel in Kaaterskill. If he wants to fool around he could play soccer and get some exercise outside. His mother, Felice, is worried about Ira's eyes. He's straining them, reading those trashy novels with his rat at his side. That huge, lumpy rodent, over a foot long, with its thick tail, tiny red eyes, the most repulsive thing Felice has ever seen—she'll admit it, she's afraid of it, lying there indolently on Ira's shoulder, its sensitive nose nudging Ira's ear. They'd let him buy it when their dog died, their German shepherd, Lady, which Felice now associates with Ira's former happy nature. This nocturnal rat—it could be rabid, it could escape!—seems to her a sign of what Ira has become. His parents don't know about Renée.

Ira knows that's her name because he's heard Mrs. Schermerhorn calling to her, "Renée, let's go! Get the door, please." He doesn't know much else about her. He never says anything to her beyond hi and thank-you. He looks at her, mainly. Renée's hair looks brown in the shade and deep red in the sun, and when her brown eyes fill with light they turn gold. She has freckles all over her arms. Once she asked him, "Do you ever do anything but read?" He was suddenly happy. She'd stopped and asked him a question.

Every time the bookmobile comes to Bear Mountain, Ira climbs aboard to browse for books and see Renée. Sometimes she's frowning; she looks annoyed and tired. Occasionally she looks happy; she glances at her watch. She must be thinking about what she's going to do afterward. He's seen her a couple of times on the weekends in Kaaterskill. Once she was walking with another girl and a bunch of dogs. He watched them cross Main Street and disappear down Maple.

No one knows Ira likes Renée. James Boyd would laugh at him, liking one of the summer people. What's the use? She'll only go back to the city. Then Ira won't see her all year, all through the long winter.

4

—

"LISTEN to me," Stephanie tells Renée on the phone. "Do you realize what you've done? You've infiltrated the Mohican Road Community! Why didn't I think of that? You can get in on the bookmobile. You know what we should do? We should put leaflets denouncing racism into all the library books you deliver."

"Stephanie, no!" Renée says.

"Oh, come on," says Stephanie, "don't you care about discrimination? These people are illegally keeping out minorities."

"They are? How do you know?"

Stephanie chomps on something crunchy on the other end of the line. "Because my father tried to buy up there. Seriously, it would be so fun if we could shake them up. We could type up something really small like a bookmark and stick it in all the books."

"I'd just get in trouble again," Renée says.

"God, you are so boring!" says Stephanie. "Haven't you ever heard of Rosa Parks, or Gandhi, or Martin Luther King? Don't you have to take American History?"

"I'm taking it next year," Renée tells her, offended.

Stephanie hangs up.

Renée calls back after dinner. "Why are you angry?" she asks.

"We have to do something to the Mohicans," Stephanie says. "Renée, you have an opportunity here. We can't let it go to waste."

All week Renée worries over her conversation with Stephanie.

She's begun to think her friend is disappointed in her. She feels as if Stephanie is waiting, daring her to defy Mrs. Schermerhorn. But Renée never lives up to Stephanie's expectations. She isn't interesting enough. What has she ever done, after all? She's just a good student in the ninth grade. A plain good student with eighties and nineties in all her subjects and no special interest in any of them. Renée does only what's asked and no more. She finishes her homework in study hall and then forgets about it. She *is* boring, she thinks. Maybe Stephanie is right. Weighted with the problem, she goes at last to her father for advice. "Daddy," she asks on Friday night, "what do you think of agitation?"

Andras puts his copy of *Commentary* on the table next to the sofa. "What are you talking about?"

"Agitation against what you think is wrong," Renée says. "Like racists."

"What racists?"

"On Mohican Road."

Andras throws back his head and laughs. "Sweetheart," he says, "who's going to agitate them? They're just a bunch of rich old WASPs."

"They have a covenant," Renée tells him, "and Stephanie thinks I should do something to them, because I get to go in every week on the bookmobile."

Andras knits his brow. "Well, she can do something herself if she's so offended. If Stephanie wants to go looking for trouble, she doesn't have to use you for that. You can just tell her to mind her own business."

"But she's my friend," says Renée.

"Your friend! Well, there are limits," Andras says. For this is Andras's general feeling these days.

He is drawn to the woods because of the quiet, and the distance from the house. He needs to get away from Nina and her worrying and planning, and the children with their bicycles and friends, Renée and her sulky piano-banging. He needs to get out and walk away under the trees. Most Sundays he walks up Mohican Road. Often he stops at Una Darmstadt-Cooper's cabin.

Una respects silence. She goes about her work, photographing animals and trees and stones. She has a propane tank in back of her shed for fuel in winter, but she also has a woodstove, and Andras brings his mallet and helps her split logs. He splits wood while Una takes care of her animals, her goats and stray cats. Sometimes she just sits with her camera in her lap. She can sit for hours, perfectly still, looking at a piece of lichen. But when she's in the mood she loves to talk.

"What kind of toys do you sell?" she asked him last week.

"Dolls," he told her. "And stuffed animals."

"Do you think that's right?" she asked.

"What do you mean?" Andras looked at her puzzled from where he stood at the woodpile.

"I mean the minds of the little children," she said. "How will they know what real bears look like? Or rabbits?"

"Well, if they've never seen the animals, maybe the toys are better than nothing," Andras said.

Thoughtfully Una walked through her yard and fed the goats. A few minutes later she came back. "I say you teach children to treat animals like pieces of fluff. So they drool on them when they're little and then they shoot them down out here when they get big."

"Well . . ." Andras demurred.

"Aha!" Una said, "I see you feel guilty."

He couldn't help laughing at her joy in finding him so.

Una has removed herself from the company of other people; she chooses animals and trees as her companions. True, she is eccentric, but Andras respects her for her independent old age, and her valiant isolationism. Isolationist politics are something else, of course. Andras opposed the withdrawal from Vietnam, as a waste of the lives lost in the war. He saw there and in Korea echoes of the tragedy in Munich, in Prague, and in his own country in 1956. He believes in aid to democratic nations, monetary support of Israel, an active military presence in Western Europe. And he believes in comprehensive welfare programs, government spending on social services, famine relief, federal funding for environmental preservation. Politically, he advocates engagement, and he takes as moral duties the responsibility to vote, pay taxes, and supply charity. But personally, Andras takes comfort in solitude. He understands Una's impatience with the stuffy houses in town, her disgust with the dirty crawling pace of the city. There is something in him that won't give and won't take part.

"There are limits," Andras tells his daughter when she asks him about Stephanie. But he speaks more of his own experience than in answer to Renée's questions.

Renée looks at him, confused. Andras sees she doesn't understand, and yet he doesn't know how he can explain himself to her. She is too young, and too hungry for friendship, to see how it could possibly be an imposition.

5

   —

ON THE hill behind the shul Elizabeth and Isaac pick blueberries. Small berries, pale dusty blue, and big dark ones, sleek and nearly black, exploding from their tight skins. The girls are strung out down the hill filling all the containers Elizabeth found in the house. Plastic sand buckets from excursions to Mohican Lake, a big colander, the double boiler.

"If the Rav is seeing people, then I think we should see him," Elizabeth tells Isaac.

"I don't think he's really seeing people," Isaac says.

"But how do you know? You could find out."

"Elizabeth, stop," he says. "Stop nudzhing me."

"Ruchel," Elizabeth calls out, "give that back to your sister. You have your own." The August afternoon is hot. The girls' hair is damp on their foreheads.

"But I want to try," Elizabeth tells Isaac.

They continue picking in silence, stripping blueberries from the tangled bushes. Elizabeth can't stop thinking about her idea for the store, and yet she can do nothing about it. It is late, the summer almost over. Without permission from the Rav Elizabeth cannot begin to make plans for next year. Since the episode on Tisha b'Av, the Rav has been in delicate condition. Back from the hospital, but home in bed, he is attended by his nephew, Joseph, and his son, Isaiah. He is surrounded by a cloud of rumors. There is the rumor, for example, that the Rav is going to ask Isaiah to take his place. However, he has not made any positive sign. The morning minyan has moved to his house and meets in the Rav's living room. Each morning the Rav comes downstairs to pray, always exactly on time, fully dressed as usual, but he does not speak to the men, and his son Isaiah does not report on his condition. It is unclear when, or even if, the Rav will again teach his weekly Wednesday shiur, and grant audiences to answer halachic questions, as he did before his illness. Of course Isaac is relieved that it's impossible to broach the subject of a store with the Rav, but for Elizabeth it is agony to wait and wait and not pursue the question. Quickly, she piles berries into her big salad bowl. Her fingers stain purple. The late afternoon sun is beating down. Soon the little ones will be too tired to stay out any longer.

Laden with berries, they stop at the Birnbaums' house on the way home. Cecil and Beatrix are lounging on their porch with two mathematician friends up for the weekend, and the elderly Kaaterskill couple, the Heiligmans. Beatrix is having one of her mathematical arguments.

"My God," Beatrix exclaims, "if I'd wanted to be so absolutely *grungy,* I would have been a physicist. Once you do a thing just because it's *use*ful, you aren't doing math—well, that's just shit work, isn't it? . . . Hello, Shulpeople! Oh, blueberries, Elizabeth. Marvelous."

Beatrix introduces them to her colleagues from Queens College and Courant, and Cecil waves from the wicker sofa, where he sits with old Emil Heiligman and Emil's solicitous second wife, Frieda.

"How Bacchanalian," says Cecil, surveying Elizabeth's little girls, with their blueberry-stained mouths and their overflowing plastic buckets. "Brocha and Sorah would work quite well on each side of the porch. What do you think, Isaac? I've been looking for something suitable to rival King's plaster lions. Would you believe he had the gall to say I was planting bushes on his land? Three currant bushes. He's having surveyors. He's staking out his property. And he's been complaining that Beatrix and I have loud gatherings at night. Loud! A couple of algebrists, and a cryptographer with his dog."

There is a roar of laughter from Beatrix's corner. Something about the dog and King's swimming pool. But Emil Heiligman just looks at Elizabeth's daughters, shaking his head.

"Like a picture," he murmurs in his husky, sad voice, indelibly sad, as it is indelibly accented, German. "Like a picture." He leans over to smile at Brocha.

The little girl backs away, shying from Mr. Heiligman's heavy face, his watery eyes. Elizabeth herself feels a pang of sadness as she tries to draw Brocha toward him.

"Who just had a birthday?" Cecil asks the girls.

"Me," says Chani, who has just turned thirteen.

"Very good, I've got a present for you."

"Oh, Cecil, *no,*" Beatrix calls out. "It's mildewed."

"Nothing of the kind," Cecil replies. "Three silverfish do not a mildew make."

"You can't. *Really* . . ."

Cecil dismisses this protest with a wave of the hand. "Now, listen to me, Chani," Cecil says. "How would you like to have a complete set of the Eleventh Edition *Encyclopaedia Britannica?* Come around here to the basement and I'll bring it out." His voice floats back as he and Chani walk around the side of the house. "I was working in the basement this morning when I discovered them behind my roofing slate. Now, this is the famous edition, you know. Twenty-nine volumes. Nineteen ten. Dedication to George V and President Taft. This is the essential Britannica. The rest is commentary."

He and Chani make more than one trip to the basement. They come back huffing, carrying ancient encyclopedia volumes stacked all the way to their chins. The red leather bindings of the books flake with yellowed tape.

"Here we are," says Cecil. "You hold on to these, Chani, and you can buy a husband with them someday."

"Cecil," Beatrix says. "They're comp*lete*ly worthless."

"Nonsense." Cecil turns to Elizabeth and Isaac. "I ask you— what better gift for a young girl? Here the century is ever young. No world wars, no Russian Revolution. No television." He smiles wickedly. "No Zionist state."

No one replies to this, but Chani looks up from the porch steps, surprised. It had not occurred to her before that Israel did not exist in 1910. In the Kirshner school Chani has learned Biblical rather than modern Jewish history. She was unconscious of Israel altogether until the Fourth of July and the Entebbe raid. Then Israel became a place for her. A country with guns and aircraft. A nation of rescuers swooping down in the night to pluck up hostages from inside enemy walls. When Chani heard about Entebbe, the words of the prophets took human form, and angels from heaven flew fighter planes. She does not know when or how modern Israel first came about. But this summer the state of Israel was founded in Chani's imagination.

The August light softens. There won't be many more evenings like this. Elizabeth and Isaac, and Cecil and Beatrix, and even Beatrix's colleagues, who should start driving back to the city, forget the time. The children play with Cecil's old red wagon under the apple tree. On the street some boys are bicycling, up and back on Maple, circling like birds. Andras and Nina walk over, slight Nina and her tall husband like a shadow. They come and sit with the others.

No one knows when it starts. Only subtly, as the light changes, the conversation drifts to the war and the families lost. Old Emil leans forward on the wicker couch with new animation. "My name, Heiligman, isn't a Jewish name," he says. "It came into the family three hundred years ago when my ancestor was converted by force."

"Converted to what?" Beatrix asks. She hasn't heard the story before.

"To the clergy," Emil answers sternly. "He was a famous clergyman; der Heiliger Heiligmann. Only later it came out he was Jewish. The name stayed in the family, and for that, Hitler didn't take us in the first sweep. In the second time that was a different story. He sent us on the trains. Then in Dachau, when we were starving, he beat us, he kicked us, he sent us in the lines to die. After the liberation when I came to New York I was security on Governor's Island in the POW camps. Then who do you think I saw behind the fence? My guard from Dachau. The same one who kicked me when I was lying on the ground. I recognized his face. So when I saw him, I raised my security gun and I shot him once—and he was dead."

Emil nods tremblingly. The others are silent.

"I told the other guards he'd tried to run away," Emil says.

When the general conversation begins again, everyone is subdued. The mathematicians are quiet. No longer joking, they pace
softly around the porch. They trail propositions like fishing lines in
the evening air. Andras and Nina turn for home, and Elizabeth hunts
for the children in the garden. She tells them it's time to go, and they
drag the red wagon up the hill at the side of the house. Metal wagon
wheels thump over small apples in the grass. Only Chani is still sitting
as she was on the porch steps, with the volumes of the old encyclopedia stacked around her.

"Listen to this, Chani." Cecil reads from the encyclopedia entic-
ingly, as if he were giving her forbidden candy. "Listen to this. 'It is
uncertain whether the settlers in Palestine can survive "the languid
heat; the enervating climate." ' "

NINA takes her husband's hand as they walk home. "It's so sad," she
says.

"What is?" Andras asks.

"Emil Heiligman. His story, I had no idea. And then he killed
the man too. His own guard. Can you believe it?"

"No," says Andras. "I've never believed a word of that story."

She pulls away from him. "How can you say that? Are you saying
Emil is a liar? Why would a man like that not tell the truth? When he
says—"

"Oh, he says what he wanted to happen," Andras tells her as they
climb the front steps. "Emil Heiligman never killed anyone." He
holds open the aluminum-framed screen door for Nina and then lets
it snap shut behind them. He can't tell Nina how he knows that the
story isn't true, but he knows. He has a keen nose for sentimentality
and melodrama. A fine sense of disbelief. He rejects stories and re-
membrances just as he disbelieves ritual and prayer. When he comes
to Kaaterskill and sits among his pious neighbors, when he sits in shul
in the dark-paneled sanctuary filled with prayer, his own inner voice
tells him, no, the words aren't true. None of it is true.

Andras was sitting in shul the day the Rav collapsed. He sat close
to the bima where the Rav stood, and he heard the Rav's words
about the Jews' dispersions, old and new. He enjoyed the Rav's tone,
his formality, although the message was purely conventional. The

Rav's voice and diction were old and polished, and they matched the bima with its dark polished wood. Nina was sitting with the children in the women's section, and Andras sat alone in the sanctuary among the hundreds who were fasting, alone, having eaten breakfast that morning, and drunk his coffee black as usual. He sat, listening to the Rav, and the fast day was foreign to him, the community grieving together in this artificial way. The holiday couldn't move Andras, the day set aside for sadness, the reading of this poetry, all prescribed, as if grief could be expressed that way, as if mourning could be accomplished with these simple and unthinking acts and, at the end of it, put away. This is why he thinks these recitations and acts of prayer are for children—because they are so flat and simple, because magically they are intended to discharge infinite obligations.

When the old man faltered and swayed back, Andras, who was not reading along, was almost the first to realize it. He was there on the bima in an instant. Instinctively, he held up his arms to support the Rav's frail body. He felt the smooth cloth of the Rav's suit. Of course, the panicked Kirshners crowded up and Andras retreated. His heart was pounding. He had seen the Rav's face, and seen the eyes roll back, and he was afraid. Suddenly, in the ornate synagogue, in the midst of prayer, Andras had seen something real.

UPSTAIRS, Nina is sorting clothes in the bedroom closets, packing up the family for the return to the city. She is labeling, making lists, separating new from old and outgrown clothes. Andras carries boxes and old suitcases to the attic for her. "Where is this going?" he asks her, pointing to a large shopping bag.

"Oh, I'm giving those away to Hadassah," Nina says.

Andras touches the heavy plaid blanket on top. He imagines Una could use an extra blanket in the winter. He could try to give it to her, although she probably wouldn't accept it. "I don't like things," she's told him. "I'm not here to pile up a lot of things."

Nevertheless, Andras takes the blanket in a shopping bag and drives up Mohican Road after dinner. With his hazard lights on he parks at the side of the road and walks into the woods toward Una's light, the kerosene lamp that turns her window gold. He hadn't realized how dark the trees would be at night. Insects and tiny animals rustle in the leaves. A thousand creatures he cannot identify. Una must know them all by sound.

Una hears Andras coming. She opens her door and comes out to see him.

"It's late," she says.

"I wanted to bring you this." Andras shows her the blanket. "I couldn't bring it by tomorrow because I'm going back early to the city. Tomorrow's Monday."

Una is amused by this. "I have a calendar."

"I thought you might like this in the winter," Andras says.

"No, no, thank you." She stands in the lantern light of her open doorway with a ratty shawl over her shoulders.

"All right," Andras says. "I thought I'd ask. My wife was going through the closets," he explains. Then he stops. He hopes Una is not offended.

Una's eyes shine. "Fire is best," she says. "Fire takes care of most everything. Old clothes, newspapers, letters, books. When my husband died, I burned all his old clothes and books. He hated waste. This earth is crowded enough, he would say, and it's not for us to clutter it up. When his heart went bad they said he might live five, or maybe even ten, years, but he didn't want that. Being half an invalid. We talked about it. And it was selfish, he decided, to keep consuming without producing his share. So one day," Una concludes matter-of-factly, "he was cleaning out his rifle and it went off."

Andras stares at her speechless.

"I was prepared," Una says. "He did the right thing, you know. The sick shouldn't linger. Whenever one of my friends has a broken wing or gets stuck in a trap, I put an end to it. Those people who try to save every limping squirrel! Pure sentimentality. The little beast can't be saved, nineteen times out of twenty. And there isn't place for those poor half-dead creatures in the world. No, my husband was right. The gunshot was for the best. Of course, you're in the business," she says.

"What business?" Andras asks her.

"Things, things, selling things. Your toys, your stuffed animals. They're idols, don't you think? The worst of it is they make children think the little animals last forever, and then they don't realize what an important thing death is in the world."

"Una!" Andras shakes his head.

"They should learn about death," Una says. "They should be taught. Making room and culling out—that's what death is. Children will never understand that, if they're always buying your plush teddy bears. You're protecting the children with these toys—pretending living things don't eat anything, don't excrete anything, don't struggle against anything, and as a result, last forever. Now, that's a false religion."

Andras walks back to the car with the warm blanket in the shopping bag, and he shudders a little in the cold. He can't make up his mind about Una. Listening to her is peculiar. He finds it funny in a way to hear her cast judgment on him. To hear his warehouse of floppy stuffed animals spoken of as some vast pagan temple. His business, small and profitable, called a false religion. Una is perverse in her views, eccentric, sometimes cruel, and yet at the same time, some of what she says is right; so clearly true. He has never put it to himself that way, what she says about the toys, the plush animals and children. His own Renée and Alex, past owners of numerous toys, really are timid, and terrified of pain. There is some truth in Una's words. That's the bitter good in her. She is a tonic. Not an elixir to live by, more like quinine, an antidote against the big houses and hordes of children, the lacy traditionalism of Kaaterskill in summer, the long pious shadows of the men walking to shul. Una lives in luxury, living alone. She has no one sleeping next to her, no one else to consider. She does not have people to her house, does not invite them to dinner or worry about what they think of the food. She has no garden. All her trees grow wild.

III

September–November '76

It is now September, and the sun begins to fall much from his height. The meadows are left bare by the mouths of hungry cattle, and the hogs are turned into the cornfields. The winds begin to knock the apples' heads together on the trees, and the fallings are gathered to fill the pies for the household.

—NICHOLAS BRETON
   Fantastics: Serving for a Perpetual Prognostication

1

—

THE city is dark, the air thick with noise. From the living-room window Elizabeth sees a stream of cars and delivery trucks. The apartment's bedrooms are quieter, but they face on brick and shadowy cement. Elizabeth and Isaac and the girls share three bedrooms. There is a maid's room as well that Elizabeth has converted into a long, narrow pantry, an annex to the kitchen. One wall of the living room is devoted to Isaac's books—the tall volumes of Talmud, thick commentaries, Seforim in stately colors, black and brown. There is a reclining chair and a sofa Elizabeth would like to reupholster, except that there isn't enough money. A large coffee table. The furniture is big, perhaps too big for the space. Almost half of the living room is taken up by the mahogany dining set Elizabeth inherited from her aunt: a pedestal table and ten chairs, a lovely china cabinet, where Elizabeth keeps the candlesticks and the silver spice boxes—a miniature castle with a filigree turret and flag, a tiny sunflower with curling petals. Isaac's silver kiddush cups stand there as well, the set his grandparents gave him for his wedding, with one large and six miniature goblets gathered on a sterling tray. Isaac's grandfather had joked at the time about the old tradition—for each kiddush cup Isaac would have a son—"a bochur for each becher."

In her galley kitchen Elizabeth is working, preparing food for Rosh Hashanah. She stands on a stool and takes the stockpot from its perch on top of the cabinets. The counters are covered with vegetables and bakery bags. There are eight round challahs, four with raisins, four without. The turkey is in the oven, the honey cakes done. She has just taken them out of their loaf pans to cool. The kitchen is hot, and Elizabeth's legs hurt. The girls are off from school, and she has sent them to the playground with Chani in charge. She needs to use the time. She makes two noodle kugels, one with onions and mushrooms, one sweet with pineapple. She bastes the turkey and turns down the heat on her lentil soup. The refrigerator is stuffed with wine bottles, tomatoes, jars of gefilte fish. She likes to start with a salad for each person: gefilte fish on a bed of lettuce, with two cherry tomatoes and cucumber slices—Malki's with no tomato, Chani's with no cucumber, Ruchel's with no fish. She moves quickly, washing out the pans as she goes, but all the time she feels the pull to stop and sit down. Her imagination is pulling against her, and she has to fight the daydreams slowing down her hands. At last, when Elizabeth is almost, but not quite, done, she gives in. She pours herself some ice coffee and just sits. It's been a month since she's returned from Kaaterskill. The great leafy trees are far away, the quiet of the evening, the cool air. She thinks about her idea for next summer. The store she might have, stocked full of kosher food. Then, of course, she thinks about the Rav.

He has still not spoken publicly since he returned from the hospital in August. He has not conducted his shiur, attended services, or granted audiences. And yet the talk is that he intends to resume his duties, that he is planning to teach again and continue leading the community. His son, Isaiah, has not taken the Rav's place as head of the shiur. The famous Wednesday class has simply been suspended. Nor has Isaiah been allowed to grant audiences to answer halachic questions. There is a committee of rabbis, instead, of which Isaiah is a member. There are no signs that the old Rav is capable of returning to his position, and yet he has not given up and passed on any of his powers or responsibilities. Of course, this is his right and privilege. Like a king he will govern for life. Elizabeth has heard that the Rav will not recover. Some say it's his heart, others that it is the tuberculosis he had as a child. His lungs are scarred from the disease, and now, perhaps, are weak. Whatever the cause, it means that plans for a store must wait.

THAT evening in the crowded synagogue, the sanctuary iced with central air-conditioning against the muggy September night, Elizabeth and the girls sit in the balcony. The Kirshner women are wearing their best fall clothes—burgundy, deep blue, brown, and black, suits with thick jackets, dresses of wool, despite the Indian summer outside. The men below wear black suits and black fedoras. They are milling about, murmuring together, standing in groups, and settling in their seats. Everyone is wondering if this time it will happen. If today will be the long-awaited day when the Rav returns to take his place before them. And then, gloriously, it happens. At exactly the moment the service is to begin, the Rav enters. He is supported not by one, but by both his sons—Isaiah on one side, Jeremy on the other. The congregation springs up, every last one standing, in ardent reverence. They crane their necks to see him, between Isaiah and Jeremy, his frail figure moving to the front of the sanctuary, his face slightly downcast.

From above, Elizabeth watches the three men make their way up the aisle. Such a strange triumvirate. The Rav and his two sons flanking him, an unmatched pair. And she sees, as everyone else must, that something is changing. Jeremy is a presence again at the Rav's side. What could it mean but that the Rav's mood is shifting? Clearly he is honoring Jeremy, bringing him out to be near him. Perhaps whatever divided him from Jeremy, the traveling, or the career at a secular college, is now less important to the Rav. Or perhaps it is Jeremy who has come back to his father's side. Perhaps, as his friend Cecil did, he has suddenly decided to marry. Perhaps he's had a change of heart. Jeremy is a mystery. But the service is joyful with the Rav's presence. The whole community buzzes with delighted speculation, so that every prayer and song is fuzzy with whispering.

Elizabeth's in-laws speak about the Rav at dinner. Isaac's younger sister Pearl and her husband, Moshe, have come with their two girls.

"Wasn't that wonderful? The Rav back in shul," Pearl says.

"I heard he's going to be teaching again," says Moshe.

"Really?" says Isaac.

"He's having his shiur on Wednesday."

"It's wonderful," Pearl says again. *"Baruch hashem."* Blessed be His name.

"And what about Jeremy Kirshner?" Elizabeth asks.

"I heard at the Kollel," says Moshe, glancing at the children, "that the Rav has asked him to lead the shiur next month as his guest, and Jeremy said yes."

"Really!" Isaac says.

"But I don't know if it's true," Moshe hastens to add.

"It's just talk," says Pearl.

LATE that night with the girls in bed, Elizabeth and Isaac clean up. She clears the table and Isaac stands at the sink, washing the dishes with his sleeves rolled up. For a long time they work in silence, except for the spray of water and the clink of silverware in the dish rack.

"Isaac," Elizabeth says finally, "if the Rav is going to hold his shiur, could we find out if he's seeing people?"

Isaac doesn't answer.

"Never mind."

"You know—" Isaac begins.

"I know how you feel," Elizabeth says. "I don't think you know how I feel."

He looks up from the sink where the water runs over his hands.

"What is it?" she asks.

"I'll finish cleaning," he says. "You go to bed."

"There are all the pans, still."

"I'll do them," he says. "Go."

Alone in the kitchen Isaac scrubs the pans. She's wrong about him. He does know how she feels. He knows how she does things, so passionately, so well. But this plan of hers. It isn't that he objects to Elizabeth working outside the home. Many Kirshner women work— in schools, and stores, and even office buildings. But to start her own business. That's something else. To plunge into something like that! And yet he knows why she wants to do it. He sees what it is—her desire to make something from scratch.

He knows he's right. They don't have money to throw away. Elizabeth has a little from her grandparents, but she and Isaac also have five daughters. There will be five weddings to pay for, and they must help each of the children set up house. There will be china and furniture, and presents to buy. There will be the customary set of Seforim for each bridegroom. A whole bookcase full of sacred texts. It will be very difficult financially, but there is no way around it. He knows he's being sensible, but he hates disappointing her. He hates being the one to stand in her way. He tells himself he's right, but as he turns it over in his mind he admits to himself it isn't simply prudence guiding him; it's pride.

Isaac cares little about external things—money, status, advancement in his job. He works hard at the office, but his job is only that to him, simply a way to earn a living. It isn't creative work. It doesn't define him, doesn't express his inner self. The core of his life is his religion, the practice and study of halacha. Isaac is modest in his work, unassuming in the world, because he has so little at stake in it. Inside, spiritually, he is an ambitious, driven man, exacting in his standards. Uncompromising. He is proud of his observance. He cares infinitely about the details of his religious life, the manner in which he prays, the exact timing of each blessing and each fast. The less visible the act, the more he cares about it. His pride is in everything hidden, everything private.

Yet it is not only his inner life that matters to him, but the community as well. And this is where his pride does get the better of him. Isaac can't help considering what the others think, the men in the minyan and in shiur. His neighbors and friends. In his most secret thoughts, self-critical and self-indulgent, he is painfully aware of the hierarchy within the community, the levels defined by scholarship and rabbinic ancestry. He is aware, because in those terms he has so little. His father was a pious man, but not a learned one. He was a CPA and worked long hours. He was a member of the Kehilla's burial society and a loyal member of the synagogue upkeep committee until he died. But he was no scholar. Neither a descendant of a great rabbi, nor—he realizes this about himself—a great scholar in his own right, Isaac has none of that kind of capital. He had wanted a son to teach and learn with, a son to be his scholar, partner, protégé, a son who could dazzle where he could not, but it is not to be, and so Isaac learns alone and davens alone in shul, driven, exacting, careful, wary of standing out, afraid of making mistakes. It is this in him that flinches at Elizabeth's idea, this self-conscious pride in being unexceptionable. His vanity is in self-effacement.

Isaac does not want to consider this, but he forces himself just the same. He admits to himself that his objections to Elizabeth's idea have as much to do with his own fears as money. As so often, he looks inside himself, and he is disappointed in what he sees. Disappointed especially in his old grief and longing for a son.

He dries his hands and sweeps the floor. On the bookshelves Elizabeth has arranged the Rosh Hashanah cards the family has received. Cards decorated with drawings of shofars, pictures of Jerusalem, reproductions of the designs in medieval manuscripts. "May You Be Inscribed in the Book of Life." *"L'Shana Tova."* "Best Wishes for a Sweet New Year." The messages are not clichés to Isaac. Not simply lines of greeting-card verse. These are the fateful days of the year. This is the precious time before Yom Kippur, when God considers the actions and the souls of men. As it is written, on Rosh Hashanah our fates are inscribed, and on Yom Kippur they are sealed. Only repentance, and prayer, and charity, will cancel God's stern decree. Isaac finishes sweeping and throws away the crumbs from the dustpan. He feels a certain urgency. This is the time to take stock. This is the time to change.

THE phone rings a few weeks later, and, when he picks it up, Andras hears Isaac's voice, sounding a bit rushed, a bit blurry. "Hello, this is Isaac Shulman. *L'Shana Tova tikatevu.* How are you?"

"Isaac," Andras says. He is surprised, even a little alarmed. Could there be some emergency? Isaac never phones him after summer ends.

"How is Nina? How are the children?" Isaac asks.

"They're all fine," says Andras. "How are you?"

"Thank God. Enjoying the weather—last year it was so cold for the haggim. Listen, I wanted to ask you a question."

"Go ahead." Andras puts his paper down on the coffee table in his high-ceilinged apartment. It is twice the size of Isaac's, but Nina isn't entirely happy with the place. The kitchen doesn't suit her, and the children's bedrooms are small. She'd like to move out to New Rochelle, but Andras doesn't want to commute.

"We've been thinking more about Elizabeth's idea for a store in Kaaterskill," Isaac says, "and I wanted to ask you what you thought— since it would be a kind of importing. Importing from the city to the mountains."

She must have talked him into it, Andras thinks. He assumes that Elizabeth told Isaac to call. "Well," Andras says, "I have to say I wouldn't get started with something like this—"

"No, of course not. But if she did—"

"Well, she'll lose some money," Andras says. "Or you can think of it as spending money, or even investing. It's just a question of how much."

"How much do you think . . ." Isaac begins to ask.

Andras hesitates. Isaac is embarrassed, and yet he's pushing on. He must think Andras knows what kind of losses or possible gains a store in Kaaterskill will accrue.

"It all depends," Andras says. "You know, it depends on how much you have to play with. For something like this I wouldn't spend money I didn't have. I certainly wouldn't do that. You'll have to sit down and figure out the numbers. Getting the stuff, transporting it, renting a place in town, storing it, of course . . ." He goes on talking, answering Isaac's questions, and in the back of his mind he is thinking about all the things he has to do the next day. "You know, as a matter of fact I have to go up to Kaaterskill tomorrow," he says.

"Tomorrow?"

"Someone broke into our house."

"Oh, I'm sorry."

"Well, it happens," Andras says. "I've got to take off the day and drive up."

"That's terrible."

"Nina is very upset about it, but apparently they didn't take much."

"I wonder who would do such a thing," says Isaac.

"I think it was just a couple of kids," Andras says. "But now I've got to go up and meet with the claims adjuster, get the window repaired. It's a nuisance."

"You have to ask yourself why," Isaac says again wonderingly.

His tone annoys Andras. "Well, why not?" he counters.

AFTER all, Andras thinks, as he drives out of the city, the house was there, the things were there. Why not take them? The burglary isn't so hard to imagine. He can't help but feel the irony that Isaac sits there in Washington Heights in the little Kirshner enclave besieged by drug dealers, muggers, rapists, and yet he can't imagine why someone would steal. Of course Andras is bothered that someone got into the house, but it was bound to happen sooner or later. Obviously in the off season, the townies decided to take a little for themselves.

The October leaves flame over the mountains, more and more colorful as Andras makes his way up. He can't help slowing to look at them, trees turned to gold, green dyed garnet. Somehow he had forgotten about the leaves this time of year. The leaves are changing in the city, too, but you can't see the full effect, the thousands all together. Here the color is so deep, so bright; the forests seem for a moment much greater than the city he's left behind, the worries, the little grievances, and problems. The day off from work, the wasted day, is so beautiful. As he drives, the claims adjuster and all the little errands seem to fade away.

But the insurance claims and the repairs really are a nuisance when Andras gets to town. After the police came and found the broken window, they were supposed to board it up against the weather, but nothing was done on that score. The dining room is wet from the last rainstorm. The rug will have to be replaced. The new window is still on order, and the adjuster has not yet completed his paperwork. The whole business is a mess, one tale of incompetence after another. Andras paces through the cold, damp house impatiently. He'd come up determined to take care of everything at once, but in Kaaterskill neither the adjusters, nor the police, nor the workmen, have been in such a rush. They fully expect him to take off another day of work and drive back up later in the season. When it's clear that there isn't anything more he can do, Andras gets into his car and slams the door.

The leaves are even more beautiful in the late afternoon light. Dusty gold. Andras drives along Mohican, staring out at the thick woods. Then he stops by the side of the road just to sit in the car and look. Slowly he opens his car door and gets out to stand at the edge of the road where it cuts into the forest. The air is cool, but surprisingly mild. Piled high on the ground are yellow leaves still fresh and new, like a river of gold through the trees. Andras stands and looks at them, the masses of leaves like a shifting stream, then walks in a little way, just to see how deep they are. He wades in up to his knees. Slowly he begins to feel the quiet of the woods. He reaches down and touches the golden surface carpeting the ground. Something cracks, then cracks again. A shot breaking the air. In numb terror, Andras scans the trees, but all is still.

The tree trunks stand around him black. The leaves are still golden, but the place is not beautiful anymore. "Andras," he hears faintly. He starts at the sound. He spins around and he sees Una in the trees, holding a long rifle.

"You!" Una exclaims. "What are you doing here? I thought you were a hunter."

Andras stands motionless for a moment, riveted by the sight of the old woman holding the gun. Then he strides toward Una. He towers over her, his fear flaming into rage.

"What the hell are *you* doing?" Andras fairly screams at her.

"I thought you were a hunter," she says. "I'm scaring them off the land." She looks up at him and she speaks calmly. She has regained her composure. "The hunters are attacking my friends, and I won't have it anymore."

Andras wants to shake the old woman by the shoulders. He wants somehow to shake some sense into her. "You're going to kill someone," he tells her.

"And what do you think the hunters do?" she demands. She stands straight and taut before him, her features sharp, gray eyes fierce and clear.

He turns away, disgusted with her, afraid in his anger that he will hurt her. "You're spiteful, cruel—" he spits the words out.

"I'm just the way I always have been," Una says mildly, and she walks away and leaves him there with no apology.

He knows she fired high, but he is still trembling, even with the knowledge that she shot in warning. Even if scaring hunters with a rifle is like her, consistent with Una's stubborn, misanthropic opinions. Trembling, he walks out to his car, clumsily; he fumbles for his keys. Those summer afternoons he had not listened carefully enough to what Una said. He had only appreciated her detachment and independence, her voluble solitude, her more picturesque eccentricities. He had made Una crusty but softhearted in his imagination. And when she suggested to him that she did not cherish life he couldn't believe she was completely serious. He had imagined her a kindred spirit; proud, as he was, so that last summer he left the blanket on a tree stump for her even after she refused it. He was sure when he was gone that she would change her mind.

2

—

THE Rav has been seeing a great deal of Jeremy. He has been asking Jeremy to visit, and even to spend Shabbat. He feels a new interest in his older son, a desire to talk to him about books and articles, even about Jeremy's scholarship. But even as he draws Jeremy to his side, the Rav seems consciously to exclude Isaiah, speaking less to him, suspending their private Talmud sessions. He doesn't treat Isaiah the way he used to, doesn't confide in him, and in fact, looks up at him warily from his white pillows, almost, it seems to Isaiah, as if he were just another doctor. This avoidance hurts Isaiah deeply, and yet he says nothing. He can't speak of it.

Only Rachel, Isaiah's wife, speaks of it. "It isn't right," she tells Isaiah. "He's determined to humiliate you. He's purposely turning against you after all the work you've done for him, after devoting yourself to him." Isaiah feels even more miserable when Rachel talks like this, because she articulates his own feelings so well. She is a fiercely devoted wife, and she makes his cause her own. She wants Isaiah to confront his father and admonish the Rav for treating him this way. She bursts with indignation on Isaiah's behalf. Whenever they speak, she not only reflects but magnifies Isaiah's own sense of injustice. She turns his worries and his fears back at him with such intensity that they cut like accusations. He isn't getting credit; he isn't being treated as he deserves. And what is he doing about it? Why is he allowing this to happen? When she berates him like this, it's easy to forget that she is on his side. They argue in low voices in their apartment directly above the Rav's.

"You have to speak to him," Rachel says.

"What could I say?" Isaiah retorts. "Is he going to listen to me?"

"That's not the point," she says.

"Then what is the point?"

"The point is that you make yourself heard. You have to be——"

"Rachel, stop it."

"More assertive."

"Stop."

Rachel purses her lips. She knows that pressing Isaiah will not change the situation, but she can't help herself.

Their marriage was arranged by their parents when Rachel was twenty-two, and Isaiah a year younger. They had been introduced in the living room of her parents' house and left alone to talk. Rachel was then about to graduate from Barnard with her degree in music. She did not go out. She knew few people at the college because she lived at home. Of course, this was what her parents intended. The Rav and Rachel's father, Rabbi Guttman, knew and respected one another, and they had planned the meeting of their children for some time.

Isaiah and Rachel met in the Guttmans' brick Brooklyn house, the living room decorated in green. Rachel sat on the stiff green silk sofa, and Isaiah sat in the armchair facing her, so that he stared at the framed embroidered birds on the wall above her head. Chinese birds with fanciful tails embroidered on white silk in satin stitch. Rachel's mother had left coffee for them on the table, and a plate of her small dry mandelbrot. Rachel and Isaiah sat with their hands at their sides. They did not touch the mandelbrot. Rachel thought that Isaiah was a good-looking young man. His eyes were a warm brown. She asked the questions. What are you learning? What do you want to do later on? She was trying to gauge his character. Isaiah told her what he was learning, that he learned every day with his father. He said he wanted to be a rabbi. He looked at her as he answered, but his voice was extremely quiet. Rachel said, "What did they tell you about me?"

"You play the piano," he answered.

"Do you like music?" she asked.

"I don't know much—anything about music," Isaiah said. There was a pause and then he added, "But I like to listen."

She liked that answer. He was honest. There wasn't anything put on. She felt somehow that Isaiah would listen to her.

A full five years after their wedding, Rachel became pregnant with their only child. It had been difficult for her to conceive, and the pregnancy was fraught with complications. During labor she bled excessively, and almost died. She was hospitalized for several weeks after Nachum's birth.

Nothing in life comes easily to Rachel. Nor is she an easy person. She is too quick, understands too well the selfishness, competitiveness, the cruelty, in people. She does not let bad behavior pass. She struggles against it. She struggles with herself. Even when she sits down at the piano, the music isn't relaxation for her. She practices relentlessly, and with a kind of existential pessimism, believing that despite her skill she will never really capture the soul of the music, and that for her, music will always be a discipline and not a gift. She believes this although she plays beautifully. Rachel seems to other people to play with great feeling, although she is convinced that the inspiration is missing. She has never considered the possibility that in a performance it might not matter whether the feeling is authentic or merely projected. She believes that there is such a thing as a divine musical gift, a spiritual essence that she lacks.

But Rachel's doubts are centered on herself; she has none about her husband. Her ambition for Isaiah is uncompromised. He is her profession, and his future is her life's work. "It doesn't matter," she fumes to Isaiah. "You should ask him why he treats you like this. Is he angry at you all of a sudden? Is he suddenly upset at something that you've done?"

"Asking won't help," Isaiah says. "You know that." He knows she isn't really suggesting he confront his father. She is just wringing the situation over and over in her mind.

JEREMY has wondered about his father as well. He is baffled by his father's sudden interest in him. After the holidays he and the Rav sit together in the Rav's library on a couch moved in from the living room, and they talk about Jewish and classical philosophy. Aristotle and Rambam, Plotinus, Halevi, Philo. They speak about Jeremy's travels in Italy and the clear simplicity of the Fra Angelico murals in Florence. They speak of the poetry of Petrarch, of Machiavelli's anatomy of the art of war, and Jeremy's work on the frame narrative in Castiglione. They discuss Jeremy's paper on the courtier prince as an emblem of Plato's unity of virtues. The Rav trembles more now; he speaks haltingly, and his face seems creased with shadows. Only his dark eyes are unaffected. They burn with intelligence, black and quick.

Sometimes Jeremy thinks of those people near death who suddenly turn to religion as if afraid of the hereafter and penitent for their former lives. He thinks wryly that his father is doing this in reverse, turning to his prodigal son with a sudden nostalgia for secular learning, for the memory of his wife and his own youth. Jeremy tries to objectify the attention in this way, and yet he can't really think about it objectively. He enjoys it too much.

One October afternoon Jeremy sits in the library on his father's couch and his father says, "I like this very much, the problem of the virtues. They are different and yet they are one. We used to study it in school. Where is my *Protagoras*?"

"I don't know, Father," says Jeremy, glancing around the book-lined room. In 1946 the Rav bought the apartment behind his own, and workers came and broke through the dividing walls. The Rav's library is a double room, made from two parlors back to back, with an arch carved from the wall between them. The front parlor is dark and wintry, with deep leather chairs and brown velvet curtains. The bookcases rise up to the ceiling, and books fill every inch of space on the walls. In the back parlor even more volumes line the walls. Thousands of them rising up and crammed together on the shelves. Low tables are stacked with books. Even the leather ottoman in front of the Rav's reading chair is weighted down with volumes. The Rav probably hasn't looked at Plato in thirty years, and his copy must be buried deep behind the tall volumes in Hebrew and Aramaic.

"I remember Socrates' question," the Rav says. "If the virtues are all aspects of the whole, how can we distinguish them from each other? Are they merely different names for the same thing? Or are they truly separate? If they are separate, then is it possible to have one without the other? Can we have temperance without wisdom? Or justice without holiness? No, of course not. And so we are left with the paradox." He looks at Jeremy with his sharp eyes and says, "And what did Socrates prove?"

"Well, of course—" Jeremy begins.

"He argued that they are united as parts of knowledge, did he not?" The Rav pauses. Then he says slowly, "I think about it differently now from when I first studied it. I think perhaps the virtues are all distinct, that some may be taught and some not. They are all good, all valuable, but separate."

Jeremy is surprised. "But what about their interdependence? How can you have justice without wisdom? and wisdom without holiness?"

"I think," the Rav says heavily, almost sadly, "that in each person they may be developed to a different degree. Goodness is not all in the teaching. Some virtues are born in the soul, and some not. I think this must be. The collection of virtues depends on the individual, on his traits within him."

"But how can you separate wisdom, temperance—"

The Rav smiles and murmurs, "*Baruch atah adoshem, hamavdil bein kodish l'kodish.*" Blessed art thou, our God, who separates holiness from holiness. "I am going to teach my shiur next week," he says.

"That's what I heard," says Jeremy.

"And I am going to hold my office hours again. Did you hear that?"

"No," Jeremy says.

"They don't want me to do it," he says, and casts his eyes ever so slightly upward to the ceiling, to Isaiah and Rachel's apartment. "But I will do it anyway."

"HE SEEMS stronger," Jeremy says to Isaiah and Rachel, on his way out.

"Forgive me, you don't know," Rachel tells him. "You have no idea. It's impossible for him to teach. He's pretending nothing has happened, and he can go back to all the things he did before."

"Why shouldn't he?" Jeremy asks.

"It will exhaust him," Isaiah says.

"I think it will keep him going," says Jeremy.

Rachel shakes her head. "He won't admit that he's ill, but in his condition—the Parkinson's and now the heart—he can't drive himself on and on. He'll have some kind of episode. . . ."

Jeremy looks at his sister-in-law, intense, severe, and, as always, worried. "What are you so afraid of?" he asks her.

"I'm not afraid, I'm speaking from experience," she says, bristling. "Because I care for him. Both of us do. We don't come in and out. We organize our lives around his minyan, his shiur, his meals, his medication. And if he's ill or if he suddenly . . . *we* are responsible."

"I feel just as responsible as you do," Jeremy says.

"Feel," Rachel says, and the word seems to carry the weight of her accusation. Jeremy might feel, but she and Isaiah are there day and night.

"You chose, you chose to take care of him," Jeremy says coolly, "and for him to care for you. I'm not going to feel guilty about your life. I'm sorry you resent mine."

"I resent it that you suddenly come in and start passing judgment." Rachel ignores Isaiah's pressure on her arm.

"He asks me to come. Is this difficult for you?" Jeremy knows he is wounding them and he's glad. "Is it difficult for you that we have things to talk about?"

IN THE library the Rav feels suddenly exhausted. When Jeremy is with him he feels stronger. His speech is clearer when he speaks to his son. Even his body seems to draw itself together, alert and straight and trembling less. But after Jeremy leaves, the Rav is tired, and his illness descends on him again.

The Rav should lie down, but he won't let himself. When he lies down, his head becomes heavy. He has strange dreams; his muscles stiffen and it is difficult for him to get up again. Instead, he heaves himself up from his desk and inches along carefully, guiding himself along the bookcases. Then he eases himself into his reading chair with his large gemara. He wills himself through the dense thicket of text on the page, and hacks with irritation at the little paradoxes and conundrums in his path. His new medication makes him impatient, and agitated. He would rather not take the pills, but without them he cannot move. Stiffly, he sits in his brown leather library chair, and tries to bring the words before him into focus. His head hurts with frustration and with disappointment because Jeremy has gone.

"Do you need a drink?" Rachel asks him. "Do you need a drink of water?" She appears with a glass of water and a straw. The Rav drinks more easily from a straw.

"No, no," the Rav says. "Tell Isaiah we must sort through the correspondence."

"He already has," Rachel says.

"I did not ask him to," the Rav says sharply. "Bring him here."

Then Rachel brings Isaiah and stands silent as the Rav berates her husband for looking at the letters that have come in that day and for organizing the papers on his desk, for touching his manuscripts and looking into his affairs. Rachel burns with indignation to hear Isaiah mistreated in this way and ordered like a schoolboy never to pry into his father's things again. Suddenly this winter, the Rav will not let Isaiah do the secretarial jobs he has done faithfully for fifteen years. He will not let Isaiah assist him with his correspondence or substitute for him in his shiur, or answer halachic questions or lead services. He berates Isaiah instead, and spends his waking hours with Jeremy.

Quickly, angrily, Rachel prepares dinner in her father-in-law's shadowy kitchen at the back of the apartment. The winter light from the one small window is gray. The sky looks strained and over-wrought, about to snow. When Isaiah passes the kitchen door, she gestures him inside.

"I don't understand him," she tells Isaiah. "Why is he punishing you?"

"He isn't punishing me."

"He's taken everything away from you. Now of all times, when he can do the least for himself!"

She opens the oven and checks on her lemon tarragon chicken. She pricks a chicken breast with a fork. "Does he ask your opinion? Does he talk to you about your place in the community? He treats you like a stranger." She slides the oven rack back fiercely and shuts the oven door.

"He's very sick," Isaiah says slowly, as if to convince himself. "I don't think we can expect him to—I don't think he is acting as he usually would. He can't control his actions."

"That's not true," Rachel says. "He knows exactly what he's doing. And he's trying to humiliate you."

It seems to Rachel that the Rav has decided to show the whole community that he doesn't favor his son and his son's wife; that he is not going to abdicate his authority to them or to anyone. And it seems to her that the Rav, having trained Isaiah so carefully, is now betraying him. With a kind of jealous pride he is competing against the learned man his own son has become. She does not make excuses in her mind for her father-in-law. She knows him, and she never underestimates him.

In the library the Rav is getting sleepy. He closes his book and puts it on the table next to his chair. It is a strange childish sensation: he does not want to sleep, and yet he cannot stay awake. He imagines they are talking about him somewhere in the apartment. In the living room or in the kitchen. He knows they talk about him. He knows that Rachel is angry. She has a temper. He has always respected his daughter-in-law, but despite her many virtues, her intelligence and talents, there is something in her character—a selfishness. From the day she married Isaiah, she has wanted him to herself. She wants him to do only as she says.

The Rav had originally planned for Rachel to marry Jeremy, but Jeremy would have none of it. Although he'd only spoken to her once at a dinner his mother had planned, Jeremy announced that he'd taken an instant dislike to Rachel. He refused to call on her, and told his mother he would never marry her. Hearing this, his mother was, of course, dismayed. The Rav was furious. Now, however, the Rav looks back with some amusement at this youthful distaste. Perhaps Jeremy knew more than any of them realized.

3

—

THE synagogue is crowded with men, and warm despite the November chill outside. When Isaac arrives for services on Friday evening, he sees neighbors and friends all clustered together in the entryway. The Kollel students are coming in from the little chapel where they study. Dressed alike in their rumpled black suits, carrying their great black-bound books, they pass through the crowd into the main sanctuary where the older men are arriving, businessmen coming from downtown, the storekeepers from the neighborhood, the retired grandfathers. Young and old mix together, and their languages mix: English and German, a little Hebrew, a little Yiddish. Isaac does not notice the mixture; he grew up with it, and he understands all the languages equally.

"Did you hear that the Rav is holding his office hours again?"

"No, I didn't know."

"He's holding them on Tuesdays again."

"The same hours?"

"Yes. Of course, he's limiting his visitors, but *baruch hashem,* he's well enough."

The men speak cheerfully. For of course this is good news. Isaac is annoyed at himself for being troubled by it. He walks into the sanctuary; and, as the service begins, he tries to put the talk out of his mind. He stares intently at the pages in front of him, although he knows the prayers by heart. He closes his eyes as he sings and tries to concentrate on the words. *Lechah dodi likras kallah, pinei Shabbas nikabelah.* Come, my friend, to meet the bride; let us welcome the Sabbath. And he turns with the other men toward the door of the synagogue. All of them bow to the door expectantly, as if, like a bride in white, the Sabbath were coming to walk down the aisle between them. They sing as if to make it so.

When the short *Kabbalat Shabbat* service ends, Isaac closes his tiny siddur and puts it into its blue velvet tallis bag. Quickly he walks out into the chilly evening, the air filled with voices, "Good Shabbes, good Shabbes," the streetlights shining brighter than stars, filling the night with their dusty light. The men are walking home to their waiting families. They are hurrying along the tar-black city streets, past fire hydrants and blue mailboxes, telephone booths, shop windows covered with roll-down steel grids. All the Kirshner stores are closed, dimly lit only for security. The butcher, the florist, the bakery, and the specialty groceries, Grimaldi's with its pyramids of fruit, Eisen's Bookshop with its hand-lettered placard, GIANT SEFORIM SALE. They are all closed for Shabbes; the shul closed and locked until morning. But the night is filled with the sounds of the city, the sirens, the thumping beat of music pouring out of cars. The screech of taxis, the rumble of the trains.

Hands in the pockets of his good coat, Isaac walks on. He feels distracted and a little nervous. He knows Elizabeth will want to go to the Rav's office hours, now that they have begun again. She is still thinking about the store. Isaac has not spoken about it to Elizabeth or even told her he called Andras. Still, Elizabeth's idea weighs on his mind, his doubts chafing with his desire to make Elizabeth's store possible. Impractical as it seems, beginning her own project would be such a joy to her. Of course he must tell her that the Rav is holding audiences again. Perhaps he should say that he will go with her to see the Rav. The question tugs at him as he hurries, almost runs, home. Above him the apartment buildings crowd against the sky, not tall and slender like the buildings in midtown, but stocky, shouldering against each other like people in a crowded room.

Isaac lets himself into his building. Loosening his scarf as he goes, he runs up the three flights of stairs to the apartment. Then, at last, he opens the door and steps into the warmth of the living room. It's so warm and bright, the table dazzling white, the toys put away, the candles lit. Every Friday he is amazed at the transformation. The apartment is more than clean; it glows with warmth and safety. In Kaaterskill, Shabbes is somehow not such a surprise. It's beautiful there on all the ordinary days. But in the city, and especially in winter, Isaac is amazed at the way Elizabeth makes their home shine against the black streets. Against the sirens and traffic, the dirty ice outside, the apartment seems to rise like a great yellow moon.

The children are scrubbed pink and clean, dressed in their Shabbes clothes. They are playing Chinese checkers on the coffee table. In the kitchen Brocha stands on a chair and tries to wash the pots.

"That's enough soap," Elizabeth tells her.

"But the bubbles are all gone," Brocha protests.

"The soap is still there in the water. It's hiding."

"Hiding?" Brocha echoes dubiously. "Daddy! Daddy! Daddy! I'm washing the dishes."

"Yes, I see," says Isaac.

"Brocha, you aren't supposed to use soap," Malki calls out from the living room. "You aren't supposed to use soap on Shabbes."

"She's just playing," Elizabeth assures Malki. "And it's liquid soap." Isaac puts his arm around Elizabeth. He can hear through the wall their neighbors the Steins, already singing. In Kaaterskill the Steins have a place on Maple. The Buchsbaums upstairs will be singing too. They are old, and bought a big house in Kaaterskill early on, a huge place with a circular drive, and neat symmetrical flower beds and fir trees. The building is full of Kirshner families, and their Shabbes guests, hearing kiddush and drinking the wine. Somehow, their faint voices reassure Isaac. Of course, if Elizabeth opened her store in Kaaterskill it wouldn't be a store outside the community, it would be a business among neighbors, a service rendered among friends.

At the table Isaac and the girls stand next to their chairs and sing to Elizabeth, as all the Kirshner families serenade the mother of the house on Friday night. *"Ashes chayil miyimtza? V'rachok mipninim michrah. . . ."* Who can find a virtuous wife? She is more precious than rubies. . . . She seeks out wool and flax, and works with eager hands. Isaac smiles as he sings the verses from Proverbs. He is thinking about the words. Is it really such a question whether a woman can start a business? This is the work of the virtuous wife, the *"Ashes Chayil"* in the ancient song: "She considers a field and buys it; / With her earnings she plants a vineyard." And *"Ta'ama ki tov sachrah; / Lo yichbeh balaila nerah.* She finds that her trade is profitable; / Her lamp is not snuffed at night." That could be Elizabeth, his wife, his businesswoman.

The children are standing at their places, the gold-rimmed plates in front of them. Chani and Malki tall and thin on one side of the table, Ruchel and Sorah on the other side, much shorter, their hair in their eyes, their faces still chubby, and Brocha is standing next to Elizabeth, only her head showing above the table, her Peter Rabbit plate in front of her. "She makes a garment and sells it, and delivers a belt to the merchant. . . . Let her have the fruits of her hands. . . ." The children are singing, although, of course, they aren't listening to the words; no one really listens. But tonight Isaac sees Elizabeth in that poem, the song everyone sings. He sees that the poem is not simply about the ideal wife, but about Elizabeth in particular. For Elizabeth is the woman who would plant a business, buy and sell, create something with her industry. She is the woman who deserves the fruit of her hands.

The song warms him. Magically, the words open up to him. He grasps them with recognition and relief. At the yeshiva, mastery of halachic arguments never came easily to Isaac, nor did quick recall of the narrative texts. But in his daily studies he still strives to understand, identify, take a text to heart, to reach through the centuries of commentary, those layers of responsa, and grasp a meaning that is strong, believable. And when it happens, and the words unfold for him and touch his life, this is a moment of great joy. The burden of decision falls away, and he is free, for he knows what he should do.

Isaac looks at Elizabeth at the foot of the table. She is clear eyed, smiling and half laughing at them as they sing to her. He is going to tell her that they should ask to see the Rav. After dinner he'll tell her. He will promise to go with her and help her. She will jump up to hear him say it. Even now, standing at the table, Isaac can see her, spinning on her heels. He can already feel it. He is dancing with her in his mind, spinning with her in delight.

———

THEIR appointment is November twenty-second, just before Thanksgiving. Isaac wears his best black suit and his Shabbes hat; and Elizabeth, a good but plain dress, navy blue. The Rav doesn't approve of women who attract attention with their clothes.

They don't speak as they stand at the Rav's door. They wait there, not afraid, exactly, but apprehensive, excited, as if they were about to go up on a stage and perform. Quiet and pale, the Rav's son Isaiah opens the door. In the cool entrance hall he takes their coats. Isaac has been once before to see the Rav, but Elizabeth never. She notices every detail, the black-and-white-tiled floor, the old-fashioned brass knobs and keyholes on the doors, the scent of furniture polish.

Isaiah leads Elizabeth and Isaac through the front parlor into the library's back room. Now they see the Rav's great desk, a table royal in scale, its top covered in red leather, and stacked with folio volumes of the law, covered with cardboard manuscript boxes, and a row of three fountain pens, neatly arranged, lined up behind three glass bottles of blue-black ink. Elizabeth and Isaac stand at some distance from the great desk where the Rav sits wearing his black suit. He is small and bent, but he holds his head up, keeping abreast of the books around him.

Isaiah walks around to the Rav's side of the desk and bends down to his father's ear like a translator. "This is Isaac Shulman and his wife," he announces.

The Rav looks straight at Isaac with keen dark eyes. "Very good," he says clearly, his voice remarkably steady. His voice is bearing up.

Isaac comes forward. "Rav Kirshner," he says, "my wife and I would like to ask your permission to open a small store in Kaaterskill."

Here again, Isaiah bends down as if to translate, but the Rav waves him away with a blue-veined hand. "I hear this," he says. "Now, again, Mr. Shulman, the facts. Who?"

"My wife and I," Isaac replies, gesturing to Elizabeth, who stands at a little distance.

"Your wife," the Rav says. "In addition your wife. And what will be her role?"

Elizabeth shivers at the question.

"What will she do?" the Rav asks.

"Mimerchak tavi lachma," Isaac quotes.

Elizabeth nearly forgets herself and laughs. It's such a lucky refer-ence for him to happen on, a cardinal virtue of the virtuous wife in *"Ayshes Chayil,"* the song sung on Friday nights. She bringeth food from afar.

"She wants to bring up food from the city to Kaaterskill," Isaac says, "so the women can shop during the week, instead of waiting for us to come up on weekends with all the groceries in the car."

The Rav nods with a pursed-lip smile. "We have who and what," he says. "Now, how?"

Isaac explains about the back room in Hamilton's store, and gives the names of the stores in Washington Heights from whom they will buy wholesale. The Rav gives his patent to no others.

By the end of this the Rav is leaning back in his leather desk chair. The explanations tire him, Elizabeth thinks. He was more in-terested in Isaac's textual defense. He pauses now, and seems to forget them for a minute as they stand there, Isaac in front of the desk, Elizabeth nearer the door. Then in an instant he makes his decision.

"Isaiah, the typewriter."

Wordlessly Isaiah rolls two sheets of the Rav's letterhead and carbon paper into the gleaming black manual typewriter. Hammer-hard, Isaiah hits the silver keys as his father dictates a letter of permis-sion:

I, the Reverend Doctor Elijah Kirshner, have examined the business proposals of Isaac Shulman and his family, to purvey kosher food from the city up to Kaaterskill, and to bring this food up to the mountain, packaged and unaltered in any way, and to be sold unchanged.

The proposal seems to me without any harm to the Kehilla.

Isaiah unrolls the letter and puts it on the desk in front of the Rav. "My pen," the Rav says.

Isaiah opens a desk drawer and takes a pen out of its case. It is a black pen, glossy black trimmed with gold, but not, Elizabeth notices, a fountain pen like those on top of the desk. This is a fancy Waterman ballpoint.

The Rav puts on reading glasses and reads the letter. The paper quivers in his hands. With trembling fingers the Rav puts down the letter and signs his name. He writes firmly, almost too firmly, so that his signature is crabbed with his efforts to control it. Then he pushes the paper toward them. "That is all," he says.

They stand there a moment looking at him. "Thank you," Isaac says. "Thank you for seeing us."

The Rav doesn't answer; he just nods to Isaiah to see them out.

Isaiah opens the door for them. Only as they are walking out the door does the Rav's voice drift after them. "Isaac Shulman." Startled, Isaac and Elizabeth turn to where the Rav sits at the leather covered desk with his books all around him. The Rav is smiling faintly, almost imperceptibly. "Isaac Shulman."

"Yes," says Isaac from the doorway.

"I remember your father."

4
—

THANKSGIVING day is cold and rainy. Andras and Nina have to step over mud puddles to get into the car. As they do every year, they are going with the children to Eva and Saul's house for Thanksgiving dinner. Eva lives in a large brick house in Brooklyn. Each house in her neighborhood has a glassed-in porch and a high-peaked roof and a garden. All the houses were built in the 1930s, and they are almost alike. Inside, Eva has carpeted her house everywhere in pale green. The stairs, the living room, the dining room, and even the downstairs bathroom are all soft and padded with carpet. Eva's Persian rugs lie on top of the wall-to-wall carpeting, in yet another layer, so that the house has a hushed feeling, even with company. The windows are covered with filmy white curtains. The furniture is dark wood, elaborately carved, and throughout the house, on side tables, and end tables, and even atop the dark piano, Eva has placed cut-crystal candy dishes filled sometimes with sour balls, sometimes with chocolate drops.

As soon as they arrive, Nina insists on helping in the kitchen. Maja is already at the stove with Eva, and the three women work together. Andras and Saul and Philip sit with the children in the living room and read the paper. The table is already set, and there is nothing for them to do.

Hours later they sit down at the great mahogany dining-room table with its clawed feet. Eva carves her turkey and serves it onto each china plate along with stuffing, cranberry sauce, sweet potato and carrot tzimmes, kasha varnishkas, and pickled red cabbage. With just a little help from Maja, Eva has done almost all the cooking, and she is tired. Her face is flushed, but her eyes are happy. "You're going to play for us this afternoon?" she asks Renée.

Renée says nothing. She just sits in the Shabbes dress her mother made her wear, and she picks at her food. She knows how much her aunts like to hear her play their piano, but she hates to do it.

"Did she bring her music?" Eva asks Nina.

"Of course," Nina says.

"We had the piano tuned," says Eva.

Again, Renée doesn't answer, but she feels her father looking at her. "Thank you," she says. She had talked to Stephanie on the phone before coming. Renée's mother doesn't allow her to see Stephanie in the city, but surreptitiously Renée calls her on the phone.

"They're going to make me play for them," Renée said miserably. "And I just make mistakes all the time, and then my mother tells me I wouldn't be making those mistakes if I practiced, and if I don't practice all the money for my lessons will be wasted. . . ."

"So don't play this year," said Stephanie. "Don't play ball."

"She'll *make* me play," said Renée.

"Not if you don't let her," said Stephanie.

Stephanie said that Renée should go on strike this Thanksgiving. She should use passive resistance, or, at the very least, forget her music at home. Renée tried to forget her music, but her mother remembered it for her.

"I have to drive back up to Kaaterskill tomorrow morning and check on the repairs," Andras tells his sisters.

"You'll have to leave early to get home for Shabbes," Maja says.

"Of course," says Andras. He would never tell his sisters the truth. That it doesn't matter to him if he arrives home before sundown or not. He would say it to Nina, but not to Eva and Maja. His wife would flare up at him, but if he spoke to his sisters coldly like that, if he showed them that he didn't care about Shabbes or their treasured holidays, then it would wound them. He would rather lie to them than make them sad. He would rather protect them, always speaking to them gently, hiding and withholding everything sharp and bitter. In this way Andras is more honest to Nina than he is to Eva and Maja. Nina doesn't understand this, but it is true.

Eva has made three pies for dessert. Pumpkin, pecan, and cherry with a lattice crust. Nina brings them in and cuts them, placing thin slices on the dessert plates—Eva's city china, cream and gold.

"I see for once you aren't complaining about being served," Saul teases Eva.

"I'm happy to be sitting down," Eva says frankly, and she leans back in her chair.

"What about the piano, Renée?" Maja asks.

"Go ahead," Nina tells her daughter.

"Mommy," Renée mutters under her breath.

"What is it?" Nina asks.

"Mommy, I don't want to," she whispers.

"She used to love to play for us on Thanksgiving," Maja says to Andras, half chiding, half surprised.

Renée sits where she is, on strike, tensing for a torrent of nagging and begging from her mother. She sits and ducks her head down, but no one speaks. Then she feels an iron grip on her shoulder.

"Come here for a minute," her father says, and he ushers her into the kitchen and shuts the swinging kitchen door.

"Daddy. Ouch!"

Her father looks her in the eye and he speaks to her so quietly and so seriously that she can scarcely breathe. "You are going to sit down and do exactly what your aunts ask you to do."

"But—"

"Sh."

Renée is terrified by her father's voice. In all her fifteen years her father has never spoken to her this way before.

"Daddy," she whispers, "why do I have to play piano? I'm not even—"

"It has nothing to do with whether you're good or not. Your aunts want to hear it. The reason is that they love you. And so you are going to play. This is not something your mother is asking you to do. This is something I am telling you to do. And if you disobey me, I will punish you."

Then Renée's father holds open the swinging kitchen door, and wordlessly, Renée steps out and goes to the piano. She sits down and looks intently at her music, and with tears of confusion in her eyes, she begins to play.

ANDRAS makes good time on his trip the next day to Kaaterskill. He leaves the city at dawn, and takes care of all his business at the house in the morning. A month after his October visit there is some satisfaction in seeing the repairs finished at last. He examines the new dining-room window, and the new carpeting now in place.

Snowflakes dance on the windshield as Andras starts home. Just a light snow. It won't last, the radio informs him. Andras turns on the windshield wipers and drives down Main Street, past the movie theater and the A & P. A delivery truck backs out of the supermarket's parking lot, streaking mud in long tracks across the gravel. The first ice storm has already hit the mountain, leaving threadbare rattling trees. The older trees are withered and dry, and some of the young trees look damaged. Only the oak in front of the post office is holding on, tattered scarlet, filibustering against winter. The road is icy. It looks like it's going to be a hard winter.

He drives down Mohican, cautious on the slippery road. Una will be digging in, he thinks. He wonders how she can face the cold every year. But she's tough enough, and mean. She prides herself on her endurance. As he drives, Andras looks into the trees. He doesn't want to meet her, not after the last encounter with the gun.

He can see her cabin easily without the thick summer foliage blocking the view: the clearing where she keeps the goats, the path lined with pieces of broken glass, the burial ground for her animal friends. He sees with some surprise that Una has left her ax out by the woodpile, and her toolbox as well. That isn't like her, to leave her tools out in the snow. He looks at the cabin and realizes that although there is a small load of wood by the door, there is no smoke coming from her chimney. Then he sees that the goats are gone.

He parks on the shoulder of the road. Puzzled, he sits there with the engine running. At last he gets out of the car and starts walking. Brambles snap against his legs, and the cold bites through his thin shoes. He walks to Una's door and knocks. Even when they were on good terms, Una never invited him inside. The door is partly open, and gives easily to his fingers.

For a long moment he stands there in the cold, in his double-breasted coat and his cashmere scarf, his leather driving gloves and absurd soft shoes. He has never walked into Una's cabin. He doesn't want to go in. He is afraid to see her. Afraid to look.

The place is freezing inside and dark. There is only the dim light coming through the window. There is the inky smell of the developing table, the books, the photographic paper, the big cameras hanging on hooks next to the door. Just one room, with a table and chair, and a bunk bed. Polaroids pinned up on the wood, several dimes and a few pennies stuck with Scotch tape there as well. The bunk beds, both top and bottom, are piled with blankets jumbled together. She left in a rush, he thinks, looking at the pile on the bottom bunk. Then he sees her lying underneath. Small, stiff, cold, her face buried in her pillow. Suddenly he doesn't have enough air. He wants to run, but he can't move.

"Una," he calls to her, as if she were sleeping.

He should pull the pillow off. He should turn her over. Instead he rushes out and away, tripping over himself to the car. He drives with numb fingers to Kendall Falls. Rushes up the icy path to the library, snow covering its tall peaked roof. He runs in, the glass door swinging behind him. The librarian, Ernestine Schermerhorn, starts up from her desk. She doesn't recognize him in the winter.

"It's Una," he says, "I found her."

"Found her where?" asks the librarian.

"In her cabin."

"But she came in two days ago. I asked her two days ago about the heat," Ernestine says. "I'll have to—I'll have to—" She calls an ambulance, and Judge Taylor, and the police.

Andras stands in the library with its rusty orange carpet and tells the Kendall Falls police exactly what he saw. He watches them as they scribble in their small notebooks. He thinks how Una would have laughed at him, shivering there. Of course, she was right about him from the beginning. She sensed it immediately about him—that he is afraid, simply afraid, of death.

I am numb; I am numb, Andras thinks. The police are gone. He starts the engine in his car, and rubs his hands at the vent of the dry car heater. He feels like ice, alone there, warming up the car in the gravel parking lot of the library. In the summer there are bushes behind the lot, thick bushes and rabbits. There are the petunias marching up each side of the library path. He sits there with the engine running in the snow and thinks about Una, clear eyed, intent, photographing lichen on a rotting log. He thinks of how she spent her years watching, and how he's spent his averting his eyes. How absurd she would have thought him, stock still in her house, bundled up and paralyzed with fear. He couldn't touch her, couldn't take a step closer to her. He, who has never seen the flies cover an animal in the forest and neatly suck away the flesh. He is the one, after all, who doesn't go to memorial services. Not even those wordless ceremonies with the candles illuminating a collective darkness. Which candles would be assigned to them—the people of his childhood? His parents, grandparents, uncles, aunts, cousins. He has never visited the places of their death. He's never seen a body. They'd vanished, left nothing tangible. Did he really believe that? he wonders now. That they weren't flesh and blood? Did he really think of it that way? As if their bodies didn't break and burn. As if their souls left when he did, and had wings to fly from pain.

"Please," he says aloud. His voice surprises him. He didn't mean to speak, but the word escapes him anyway, almost a prayer.

Down the mountain Andras drives and drives, and the car's heater blows hot dry air onto his knees, but he is tight with cold. Shivering. Outside the ashen trees fly by. He scarcely slows for turns as he takes the road down the mountain. He speeds, so he won't have to think. He spins away onto the straight Thruway, with the car radio turned up loud. Only the heavy weekend traffic slows him down.

Andras takes a breath and turns off the radio. He tries to calm his shaking hands. In an hour he will be back in the city. He will drive up to his office and get some work done. Catch up on his order forms. The thought reassures him. Soon he will be back at work. He will be almost himself again. In a day, in a few days, he will walk around without thinking about her, without thinking about any of this. He tells himself this, but his throat is tight. He tries to blink away the sight of Una, but his eyes ache.

On the Thruway he passes cars with fir trees strapped onto their roofs. Christmas trees for apartments in the city. There are station wagons with long skis on top, locked into ski racks. A few cars on the road are loaded with deer trussed onto their roof racks. Each deer stiff on its side, back legs tied together, front legs tied together, brown eyes like glass.

IV

—

July–August '77

The sides of the mountains were covered with trees, the banks of the brooks were diversified with flowers; every blast shook spices from the rocks, and every month dropped fruits upon the ground. . . .

—Samuel Johnson
Rasselas

1

—

BEES cover the goldenrod, the air floats with pollen and barbecue smoke, and Hamilton's store bell rings with Elizabeth's customers. There are Kirshners buying food in bulk, the women wheeling strollers loaded down with bags. Customers come up the road from Phoenicia and Bear Mountain, the weekenders bursting out of their cars like circus families. A Yiddish translator and his wife saw the ad Elizabeth stapled up on the community bulletin board in Palenville. They pull away with three grocery bags of meat and requests from their daughters for chicken pot pies. The Spiegelman family reunion drives up in Volkswagen vans and buys out Elizabeth's entire stock of Hebrew National frankfurters and ground beef. Elizabeth rings up the huge purchase in Hamilton's back room, and she feels strange, a bit jumpy. Even now in midsummer, whenever customers arrive, Elizabeth's heart pounds with excitement; the rhythm of her ambition within her.

In a leaf-green dress elderly Mrs. Sobel picks out her groceries from Elizabeth's stock. The graceful wife of the Conservative rabbi and historian Cecil Birnbaum admires, Mrs. Sobel comes into town from her forested estate, and buys blocks of cheese and frozen rib eye roasts. Cutting in front of her, two boys plunge their hands into the cooler where Elizabeth keeps kosher Popsicles and ice cream sandwiches on ice. Sleek and hungry from swimming in the lake, they throw down their money on the counter, one of the quarters still spinning as they dive back through the door to the street.

Elizabeth knows Hamilton is watching her customers as they walk purposefully through his store. They find their way to the back, and make their purchases only from her, while Hamilton watches with a strange expression, partly annoyed, partly impressed.

"I'd like to put up a sign," Elizabeth tells Hamilton one Friday afternoon, when she's closing up. "A sign of my own."

"I don't want another sign," says Hamilton.

"But it's impossible for people walking by—"

"They seem to find you," he says.

"Just a small sign," she says. "Or something I can set up on the sidewalk. I'd take it down when the store is closed."

Hamilton doesn't answer. Thoughtfully, he walks out to the front of his little building. He opens the screen door and stands out on the steps, looking up at his own red-and-black sign: HAMILTON's, in curlicues, 1890s style. He bought it from a mail order catalog two years ago.

"I don't need another sign," he says, stepping back inside.

"But I need one," Elizabeth says.

Hamilton looks at her. "I may raise my rent next summer," he says.

"Should I look for another place?" Elizabeth asks.

"Well, there aren't so many places to put a store," Hamilton tells her. He lights a cigarette and pulls his wood slat chair close to Elizabeth's Dutch door. "I guess you could rent from King. He'd rent you something."

"We do rent from him," Elizabeth says. "We rent our bungalow."

"Well, there you are. Course, I've known him for years. You know the father?"

"No," says Elizabeth. She's packing up the Popsicles and frozen chicken pieces. Over the weekend she keeps them sealed in boxes in Hamilton's freezer.

"Michael King's father. He was before your time. A dentist; rich. A—" Hamilton was about to say "a Jew," but tactfully he substitutes, "Summer people like you. Name, Herb Klein. A short little man, and dark. Not like the son. Dr. Klein took his summer fees in cash. He didn't declare. Hid the money instead in his summer place. That old house had a black iron stove, potbelly for wood burning, and Dr. Klein kept his money there in bills, stuffed in the back. Maybe fifteen thousand in greenbacks."

Elizabeth leans over the Dutch door.

"One fall, after old man Klein went back to the city." Hamilton taps the ash off his cigarette. "The son, Michael, came back here hunting, with a girl from the city. Thought no one would notice them because the summer people were gone. So there they were, alone together fooling in Klein's old house. There was no water, and the electricity turned off. All of a sudden we had a cold snap. October, and it went down to twenty-three degrees. The two of them were freezing in that house, and there wasn't any heat. So Michael decided to light a fire in the old woodstove. Dragged up apple wood from the basement—"

"How do you know that about the wood?" Elizabeth asks.

"I made up that part," Hamilton says evenly. "But the truth is he got a fire going and burned all that money his father kept in the stove. As long as he lives, no one in this town will ever forget it. He may be rich, but the moral is: Klein is Klein."

Elizabeth laughs. She feels almost like a year-rounder, working at Hamilton's store, and listening to his tales about Michael King. She feels that in some curious way Hamilton is extending his friendship to her, grousing with her about the one man in Kaaterskill they have in common, his interloping neighbor and her landlord.

"You've seen his house on Maple," Hamilton says.

She nods.

"Take a look at the lions. Look at those lions in the front. He bought a pair of plaster lions, you know, with the paw upraised, one for each side of the entrance. But if you take a look, you'll see that they both face right. He's got a dispute now between him and the company. They claim he ordered two identical lions, not two lions facing each other. And I'm sure he did."

As ALWAYS on Fridays, Elizabeth closes early, at two o'clock. She walks home, carrying the cash box along with her purse and a shopping bag full of extra challahs. She has hired one of the mechanics from Boyd's garage, James Boyd, to go down to the city for her every week with his pickup truck, and Ira Rubin, a boy from town, to help him with the heavy lifting. Of course, these are expenses. She has to charge more for everything, but what has surprised her is that people are paying the higher prices. Elizabeth marks up the fresh baked goods in particular, but every week she sells out of challah and babka, cookies and coffee cake. Her customers love the fresh bread and cake she brings up from Edelman's. They will pay for that.

The little girls are playing in the yard in front of the house, but as soon as they see Elizabeth they jump up and follow her inside.

"Can I have a cookie?" Sorah asks her.

"Me too," shouts Brocha.

Malki comes running from the girls' bedroom with Chani after her. "Mommy. Look what Chani is reading. Look."

"Give it back," says Chani.

"Mommy, look," Malki says, flashing a small book.

Chani charges, grabs the book, and pushes her sister so hard that Malki loses her balance and falls to the floor.

Elizabeth rushes over. She helps Malki up and scolds, "You know better than that, Chani. Are you listening to me?"

Chani says nothing. She is fourteen now, tall for her age, her hair thick and dark.

"She's reading books about Israel," Malki says doggedly.

"Are you being a tattletale?" Elizabeth asks her.

Malki's eyes well up with tears.

"I can read whatever I want, stupid." Chani glares at Malki.

"Don't you ever call your sister stupid," Elizabeth snaps. "Apologize. Now."

"Sorry," Chani says grudgingly to Malki.

When the house is calm again Elizabeth and Chani make dinner. "What did you do in camp today?" Elizabeth asks as they work together in the kitchen.

Chani makes a face. "Rav Lamkin talked about the fast days and how we should mourn for the calamities of our people and that we have no home. He likes fast days."

"Does he?"

"That's all he talks about. Calamities." Chani cuts up celery for stuffing. "Why does he pretend Jews don't have a home?"

"The rabbi meant we don't have a homeland," Elizabeth explains.

"But Israel is in the paper every day," Chani says, puzzled. She sees it all the time. That Prime Minister Begin is coming to Washington to talk with President Carter. That Begin is allowing settlements in Judea and Samaria. Just last Shabbes after shul, Chani heard Mr. Melish and Mr. Birnbaum talking about the settlements and the territories and Jordan. Mr. Melish was grumbling about President Carter —that as far as Carter is concerned, he'd give all Israel's land away for ten points in the polls, and that this Middle East peace conference of his is just a publicity stunt.

And Mr. Birnbaum answered with one of his strange sayings: "Blessed are the peacemakers. For they shall inherit the earth."

"Everyone talks about Israel all the time," Chani says now. "You can't just pretend it isn't there."

"Chani," Elizabeth begins. But she doesn't know quite how to put it. She never imagined hearing words like these from her daughter. "I think reading and finding out about the world is good. It's necessary to learn about the world. But the world is one thing and God is another. The two don't fit together yet. And one day they will, and the Temple will be restored, and Israel will be ours again. But the place isn't ready yet, and neither are we."

"I know that," says Chani. "But why do you and Daddy never talk about it? Why are you pretending it isn't real? Look," she says, and she runs and gets the *Times* from the living-room couch, and she holds it up so that her mother can see, right on the front page, the picture of a soldier standing guard while workers are building houses. "See," she says. "It's in the newspaper and in the maps—"

"But we don't want just a place," says Elizabeth. "You can't substitute bare land for—for the mitzvos that must be done, and the transformation of all the lives in every place in the world. . . . We're waiting, you see."

"But if you just sit around and wait, nothing will get done—

that's what you always say," Chani points out, triumphantly practical. "So what good is it going to do if we're all waiting over here in New York? Shouldn't we be in Israel now?" she suggests recklessly.

"Well," Elizabeth says, "if you wanted a house and I gave you a model of a house, would you take it?"

"I don't want a house," Chani says, and she puts the newspaper down on the counter. Houses in Chani's mind are made up of chores. A house means making beds and preparing dinner. Picking up toys and washing dishes every night. But a country, a whole country, would be big and full of mountains. Places to climb and places to swim. Bare land. Those words sound good to Chani, like bare feet.

Elizabeth begins stuffing the capon they are having for dinner. Chani, Chana, Anna, Annette, she thinks. All the permutations of that name. All the different ways she imagined her child would grow up. Weren't they all just variations on the thoughts she had about herself? Of course Chani has her own opinions. They all do, all her daughters. But Chani is so outspoken. That concerns her. Chani's questions in themselves are natural. Bright children don't accept ideas without asking for reasons. The explanations should hold them to belief, not blind obedience. But among the Kirshners questions like Chani's are a private thing. They aren't accepted publicly. There are bounds on discussions and arguments, and talk in public places. There are books that people simply do not read, and subjects that they avoid altogether. Chani is getting older. She needs to be more careful about what she says.

ALL the summer people are preparing for Shabbes. Peaches and nectarines cover the table in Eva and Maja's big old-fashioned kitchen. Quilted appliance covers lie in a heap and all the appliances are whirring—the thirty-cup coffee urn, the white KitchenAid mixer on the counter. Andras sits and tells his sisters about Nina's home improvements. This summer she is having an alarm system installed. She is redoing the bathroom downstairs. For reasons Andras cannot understand, she is getting estimates on finishing the basement.

"She keeps busy with that house," says Eva from the sink.

"Well, she's busy with a lot of projects," Andras says. He wants to be fair. "She's been working very hard with HIAS."

"That's a wonderful thing," Maja says. "The Soviet Jews."

"She's very good at it, coordinating them," says Eva, and she laughs so heartily that tears come to her eyes. You wouldn't know from her laugh that she has been ill. At Andras and Maja's urging she is finally going down to the city for some tests.

"Well, it's true," Maja says, "she finds them schools, apartments. It's hard work."

"And she is always scandalized by one thing or another," says Eva, wiping her eyes.

This is what Andras's sisters laugh at. The edge to Nina's character, the catch to her generosity, the sharp words motivated by motherly concern, the problem that the children might be spoiled or assimilated. The worry that the children should be practicing their music, and that the refugees—some of them take advantage! One family from the Soviet Union was practically *given* an apartment, a luxury apartment. And then it turned out they weren't Jewish at all! Russian Orthodox on both sides!

Nina spent most of the winter organizing the family's annual trip to Argentina. Andras didn't come with them this time—he had work at the warehouse. And so over the Christmas holidays Nina took the children to visit their grandparents. She and the children left for three weeks, and they returned with the sun in their faces and their hair. Then, of course, Nina had to get Renée and Alex back on schedule, back to school.

They are watching him, his sisters. They serve Andras ice coffee at the cluttered table, their husbands' newspapers neatly folded to the side. It's warm in the kitchen. The oven is on, and Eva and Maja are baking rugelach, rolling out the dough, cutting it into crescents with a knife, then spooning in the filling and rolling up the cookies.

"This is very difficult dough," says Maja, "very difficult to work with."

"I think only the two of you can really make rugelach," says Andras.

"And Cecil's mother," Eva amends. "Esther Birnbaum, of blessed memory. Don't sit like that, Andras, with your hand over your mouth. It makes you look old."

"I am old," Andras says. "I'm fifty-eight years old."

His sisters look at each other in mock horror. "No," says Maja, "we can't allow that. What would that make us?"

"You've been spending too much time on the business," Eva says. "You don't take time to enjoy. You should be interested in other things."

Maja nods vigorously as she cuts the crescents from the thin rugelach dough. "Wait, wait, don't rush," she warns Eva, who is ready to spoon the filling in. The dough is sticky, and it makes Maja nervous.

Eva sits back with her bowl and loaded spoon. "You know that Philip's cousin died at only fifty-three!" she tells Andras. "He overworked. He was thinking about the shop even on vacations. He only turned on the radio to hear the news. No music. He never went to see the movies. You should go see what's playing at the Orpheum." Eva brandishes her spoon at Andras—the rugelach filling of raspberry jam mixed with crushed walnuts. "This you have to taste. Taste," she orders. Her eyes are full of light.

AT THE Kendall Falls Library Renée is getting ready to go home. Her mother hadn't wanted her to work a second summer at the library. She'd wanted her to try the Lamkin camp again, but Renée refused to consider that, and her father said she could keep working for Mrs. Schermerhorn.

"Renée," Mrs. Schermerhorn says now, "did you finish reshelving on the adult side?"

"Yes," says Renée.

"All right, you may go."

Renée runs out to where Stephanie is waiting.

"Let's go to Coon Lake," says Stephanie.

"I can't. I have to get home," says Renée.

"Be late," says Stephanie.

Renée looks at her watch. "My father is probably home already."

"Let's go fast," says Stephanie, and she hops on her bike and takes off down the street.

Renée pedals after Stephanie up Mohican Road, past Mohican Lake, and all the way to the smaller Coon Lake. Huffing, she and Stephanie walk their bikes along the overgrown trail to the water's edge.

They take off their shoes and wiggle their toes in the soft, wet sand. They watch the tiny flicks of fish.

"Maybe I'll be an ichthyologist," Stephanie tells Renée.

Renée says nothing.

Stephanie asks her, "How come you never say what you want to be?"

"Because I don't know yet," says Renée.

"You don't have ambition," says Stephanie.

"I don't know what I want to be ambitious *about*," Renée protests.

"Well," says Stephanie, "you'd better be careful or you'll end up like all those other women in Rabbitville."

"What do you mean?"

"Housewives, of course. You've got to open your eyes, Renée. We've got to do some consciousness raising here."

Renée opens her eyes and looks at her friend. She can never tell whether or not Stephanie is joking.

"You can't just spend your life taking the path of least resistance," says Stephanie. "You've got to get out there and do something. And if you don't know what you want to do, you've got to figure something out."

"Okay," says Renée.

"You're hopeless!" Stephanie throws herself down on the sand.

Renée is hurt. "I have to go home."

"You're going to spend your whole life doing what people tell you to," Stephanie says. "It's like you're cursed. You're like a goose or something. Whoever you're with is going to imprint you. Whoever you see first, you'll follow wherever he goes. Your father, your boyfriend, your husband—"

"Boyfriend! Husband!"

"I'm talking about the future. Because this is what's going to happen. It's your trajectory," Stephanie says darkly.

"You're the one who's always telling me what to do!" says Renée.

"I'm deprogramming you."

"No," says Renée. "You're just bossy."

Stephanie gets up and shakes the sand off of her. She grins. "Oh, yeah, well, that's true," she says. "I am."

Renée pedals home, and the wind tangles up her thick hair. She is half offended by and half in love with Stephanie's talk about the future. Offended that Stephanie thinks she's such a follower, bound to do what other people say. Fascinated, and somehow flattered, to hear Stephanie say that she has a trajectory.

2

THEY are forcing the Rav to stay inside. They will not leave him unattended, even for a moment. He is angry, furious at Isaiah and Rachel, but too weak to get up by himself. He has only his voice left to make his displeasure known. He calls to them loudly like a wounded bird, and chastises them from his bed or chair. The Rav is almost immobile. For two months he has been sleeping in a rented hospital bed. Two male nurses carry him up and down the stairs. Rachel tried to convince him to stay in the city during the summer, but he rejected the idea so violently that she did not dare to press the issue further. The Rav insisted on coming to Kaaterskill as he always has. Now, in July, the house is congested with the minyan every morning, doctors coming in and out, the nurses coming and going on their shifts, lifting and carrying him as if he were a bale of hay. And, of course, Isaiah and Rachel, always present, always strained. It exhausts him, all of it—not merely the medication and its side effects, the nausea, the hallucinations—but the tedium and banality of his days, the flow of people, the effort to eat, to sit and stay awake, the grinding, slow mechanics of his life.

Late now, on Friday afternoon, they have moved the Rav downstairs for the evening service. The table is set, the food prepared. Today, at last, Jeremy is to come up for the weekend. He has just returned from his two weeks abroad. When Jeremy left for Italy, the Rav was stronger. He was in better spirits. But in the brief time

Jeremy has been gone, the Rav's medication has become less effective. Even high doses do not loosen his legs and arms or help him to swallow.

The Rav has been waiting for Jeremy. For days he has spoken about the coming visit to Isaiah and Rachel, told them how impatient he is to see his older son and talk to him. But why is Jeremy late? The long afternoon is ending, and Rachel must light the candles. She is putting away books and shuffling papers in her fussy way, moving piles from one place to another. Did Jeremy's car break down on the road? The men have already begun arriving for the Kabbalat Shabbat service. They fill the living room and crowd the Rav in his chair. He must sit, but they stand for him, while Isaiah paces nervously around the perimeter of the room, glancing at his watch.

Why is he late? Was there an accident? The sun is still setting in pinks and golds and flaming orange, but the colors make no difference. The time of sunset determined for this latitude is seven fifty-nine. To be late would be unconscionable. Isaiah is davening with his mouth set. The Rav knows what Isaiah fears—that Jeremy will come in after Shabbes with all these people in the room watching. The Rav himself cares nothing about that. He cares about the time. The start of Shabbes is not a thing to be put off. Not a thing to be delayed. The moment comes, and either one is ready or one is not, either one observes the time or one does not. The moment comes once, and it is gone. Candle lighting is not delayed because someone is late. Shabbes is not an event like the theater or the train, for which it is simply rude or impractical to be late. There will be another show, or another train. There will be other times to meet one's friends, but for candle lighting there is no other occasion. The time of candle lighting is a matter of readiness for God. And to be unready, to put candle lighting off, to delay, or simply to let other concerns govern the clock—that is an offense, that is truly a desecration. And as he sits downstairs in his straight-backed chair, the Rav must imagine there was something on the road, some emergency, a matter of life and death, because there is no other excuse.

The short service over, the men pay their respects to the Rav and to Isaiah, and begin walking down the hill, joining the other men emerging from the synagogue. Jeremy has still not come. The family sits down at the table, the Rav, Rachel and Isaiah, and the Rav's grandson, Nachum. They make kiddush and drink the wine. They wash their hands and say the blessing. Silently, Nachum brings in a pitcher and bowl from the kitchen and pours the water over the Rav's hands. They make motzi and eat the challah. Rachel brings out the soup from the kitchen and they begin eating, but no one speaks. What is there to say? They can only sit expecting Jeremy, dreading his arrival after candle lighting. He will walk in the door late, and it will be like having some filthy thing in the house. They sit in anticipation. Rachel clears away the soup bowls quickly but carefully, as if afraid of breaking them.

AT nine-twenty the sky is inky blue. The stars have begun to gather, tiny, pure, and white. Jeremy takes his overnight bag out and closes the door of his car. He breathes deeply in the fresh air, and tries to steel himself. He had not allowed enough time and got caught in traffic. There had been a terrible truck accident, the truck upended on the road and two cars smashed. The Thruway was backed up for miles. Jeremy had inched along in the traffic, looked at his watch, and even thought about turning back to the city. Now, just outside his father's door, he wishes that he had. He was not ready to come up so quickly after his conference and vacation in Milan. He was jet lagged, his internal clock was off, and he had miscalculated the shift between his professional world and his father's timetable. None of this will matter to the Rav. Jeremy puts his hand on the doorknob. His heart is pounding.

He stands in the doorway, his suit bag on his shoulder. He stands on the threshold of the house, warm and fragrant with Shabbes dinner. And from the dining room the family sees him at the door. For a long moment they look at him, standing in the entryway. They do not speak; they sit frozen at the table, their hands paralyzed, forks in midair. And in the lamplight Jeremy burns with shame. He feels his brother and his sister-in-law, and especially his father, looking deep into him. They see what is obvious, but what nobody has ever stated. That Jeremy, with all his learning, has become someone else, a stranger to them. That he, their own flesh and blood, is alien. The anger is not only because of what he is, but because he has made them look.

Slowly, the strap of Jeremy's bag slides down to the floor. Cautiously, he approaches them and takes his seat at the table where his bowl and plate stand empty. Rachel gets up and serves him, and they eat in silence, without appetite.

The family does not sing the grace after meals. Each of them at the table says the blessings silently. Then the nurses come and carry the Rav up to bed.

"Maybe I should go," Jeremy says after his father has gone.

Rachel darts a look at him as she clears the table. But Isaiah shakes his head. "No," Isaiah says, "don't go."

Of course they don't want him to go because that would mean more traveling on Shabbat.

JEREMY lies awake in the bed that had been his as a boy. As a child he had loved the feel of the cotton sheets against his skin. They were cool and smooth, worn smooth with washings. Now he lies awake, and the sheets are cool against him and soft. But the softness against his skin is a reproach to him. He blames himself for being cavalier about the time and coming late. He blames himself for angering his father. He should have turned back on the road and returned to the city. His father would have been far less disappointed to hear that the traffic was too heavy and that Jeremy would have to come up the next weekend. Why did he keep driving up? Why did he do it? In the past year the Rav approached him and tried to talk to him on his own terms. They had begun to speak again, and now Jeremy has ruined those conversations.

He considers that perhaps somewhere within himself he had wanted to come late. He'd forgotten about the hour on purpose in order to show them . . . to show them what? That like an adolescent he would continue to provoke them, breaking the rules, waltzing in late to take his place at the table. He is a grown man, a middle-aged man. Why did he do it, when an hour would have made the difference? All his father wanted was to see him. And all he, Jeremy, has done in return is take the opportunity to strike back.

Small and narrow, Jeremy's old room is at the top of the house. There is one window and a closet that extends far under the eaves. There are boxes of papers back there, school assignments, college notes. There are old clothes, toys. Even the teddy bear he slept with as a child. The window is covered with aluminum blinds full of dust. Rachel does not clean here. No one comes here. There is a hurricane lamp on the dresser and, on the wall, one of his mother's small water-color paintings. It is too dark to see it, but he sees it in his mind's eye, a painting of wildflowers, bachelor's buttons. When Jeremy was quite small he had told his mother to hang that painting in his room. "I want the bachelor's buttons," he said, "because I'm going to be a bachelor."

He lies there and thinks about his mother. He is glad she is not alive. He could not have borne her disapproval. If she had been sitting there with them at the table he could not have entered the house. Bitterly he tells himself that the rest of the family is of no conse-quence to him. Their rules and ceaseless blessings, their anxieties and damning looks, can't follow him back to the city. They sting here. Here they matter. The old patterns play and replay themselves. Jeremy provokes them and they buzz angrily. He provoked his mother, too, but only because she let him. He teased her as a boy and, as a young man, mocked her desire that he marry. Fifteen years ago, when his mother died, Jeremy began in earnest to withdraw from the family and its expectations; he began to withhold himself.

By the time his mother became ill, Jeremy and his father scarcely spoke to each other. After her death Jeremy left Washington Heights and moved to Queens. He stopped going to his father's synagogue. In fact, he stopped going to synagogue altogether. He began to travel for months at a time, to Israel and Europe. And, above all, he refused to allow the family to make a match for him. The door was already closing, but he shut it with finality—with pleasure. He enjoyed the irony, because he had every accomplishment necessary to succeed his father: a deep knowledge of halacha, a vast talmudic repertoire, flu-ency in legal conventions and midrashic language. He had everything except a respect for the spirit of the law, and a belief in it as more than ancient text and arcane ritual. He would not live the life. He held himself apart. He would not marry.

But tonight Jeremy is not in the city or traveling. He is not doing something else, and he feels it all. Anger and shame. The aftertaste of his own cruelty, like blood in his mouth.

———

SHABBES passes long and silent. The Rav does not speak to Jeremy or even look at him. The men arrive for morning services, and Jeremy stands with them in the living room and listens to his brother read the Torah. He wears his cream-colored suit and a look of indifference. But he does not feel indifferent; he feels broken. He has not simply lost his father's good opinion. He has lost the Rav's interest. Become again a stranger to his father. Breaking the Sabbath by arriving late, Jeremy has become insignificant, his opinions without weight. In his father's community he is not a member in good standing, in his father's eyes he is not a man.

After the service ends and the men have gone, Jeremy sits with the family at the table while Rachel serves her elaborate Shabbes lunch. He will wait it out, the long, bitter day, and he will leave as soon as it is dark. At the table he asks Nachum some questions about what he is learning, and Nachum answers, looking down. The Rav is carried up to his room to rest, and he calls out irritably to the attendants on the stairs to watch where they are going.

Jeremy sits in the living room. He gets up and glances at the volumes on the bookcases. For the most part the books are in German. The Rav has always kept his German books in Kaaterskill. Books of theology and poetry, philosophical treatises by Jeremiah Solomon Hecht and the Frankfurt Kirshner rabbis. Jeremy looks at them on the shelves, but does not take them out to read them. Rachel's piano sits mute, the top down, the lid locked, as always on Shabbes. No music is allowed. Jeremy had brought his father a book from Italy, a large coffee-table book with pictures from the Uffizi. He had thought the Rav would enjoy looking at it, but of course, he cannot take it out now.

Through the screen door Jeremy sees Isaiah and Rachel sitting together on the enclosed porch. He sees that they are arguing, but he cannot hear what they are saying, they oppose each other so softly.

"HE HAS no right," Rachel says. "I don't want him in my house."

"He has a right," Isaiah says. "Father asked him."

"He didn't ask for this. He's been . . . berating us about getting Jeremy to come and now—"

"Rachel, enough," says Isaiah.

"I think now your father might possibly stop using him as a weapon against you," Rachel says in her fierce whisper.

"I don't want to hear you speak like that," Isaiah replies.

His anger startles Rachel. "I'm sorry," she says, after a moment, "but—"

"Don't say *but*," Isaiah tells her.

Isaiah has said nothing to the Rav or to Jeremy about the night before; but in the dark he, too, lay sleepless, thinking. His father has spoken often to him about his brother in the past year. He has said that he regrets the years he spent without talking to Jeremy, the time apart. He has said that it was foolish. They live in the same city and have seen so little of each other. He told Isaiah that he had forgotten how much he'd enjoyed discussions with Jeremy. "Your brother is a brilliant man," the Rav said. "Knowledgeable, but what is more, he is creative. In that respect he is exceptional." When Rachel hears the Rav talk like this, she is angry on Isaiah's behalf, but Isaiah remembers more than she does.

Of course he knows his older brother is brilliant. Jeremy's brillance was the central fact of Isaiah's childhood. From the time Isaiah can remember, Jeremy was striding ahead, quicker, better. Held up to him as an example. It was not simply that Jeremy was older. When they were young men, from the time they were thirteen, they learned with their father, and they were dealt an equal share of knowledge. But even in those early years it was clear that Jeremy was superior. Isaiah would read and read; he would sift through a text repeatedly. Jeremy would shake it once and discover gold. He would pluck out a word or phrase and suddenly illuminate the discussion. Rachel has never seen Jeremy in shiur. Where Isaiah hesitated, unsure what to do, Jeremy could look at a passage and all the commentaries, and say something completely new. Learning was easy for Jeremy; his stunning exegesis an inborn talent. The Rav, and Isaiah, too, would sit back and marvel at Jeremy, for he read like a magician. The Rav's eyes would shine when he heard him; his whole face would brighten, even while he only said one word: "Good."

Jeremy's example and Jeremy's absence have been the central axes of Isaiah's life. Rachel cannot understand it, but Isaiah has always admired his brother's genius, even loved him with an unrequited love. Rachel is frustrated by her husband's hesitation, his self-effacing humility. The humility is real. Isaiah is committed to his father and to the Kehilla, he has dedicated his life to learning and practicing halacha, but he does not have Jeremy's intellectual ability. Isaiah is too fair minded to deny it, too self-doubting to be jealous. He labors to deserve the position Jeremy has thrown away.

"I HEARD they're worried about whether he's strong enough to be moved back down at the end of the summer," Mrs. Schloss says to Mrs. Fraenkel as they wait at Elizabeth's counter. "Braised beef is there, right there." She points to the place on the shelf and Elizabeth whirls around with two cans in her hands.

"Two tins braised beef, three packages soup bouillon, two pounds ground beef, four chicken quarters, two large challahs, one corn rye," Elizabeth totals. A small crowd of women cluster around the Dutch door.

"But he wouldn't stay here in Kaaterskill for the holidays—I can't believe that," says someone else.

"If they can't move him—"

"They'll move him. If he came up, he'll go down."

"I saw your husband," Mrs. Schloss says to one of the younger women, Batya Erlich. "How long is he up for?"

"He has two weeks' vacation."

"Does he accumulate?"

"That's accumulated! Two pumpernickel, one chicken parts. Is that corned beef the lean? I can't see the marking."

"Yes, that's lean," says Elizabeth, "sixty cents more per pound."

"How lean is the lean? Really leaner than regular?"

"All the beef is lean," Elizabeth says. "Lean is extra lean."

"Well, I'll take it, then, and two challahs."

"Let me slice the meat for you first." Elizabeth is doing a landoffice business. She thinks of the expression as she sells the meat wrapped in white paper, pounds and pounds of it. And she imagines those land offices selling claims in the West; uncharted prairie overrun with game. She had dreamed of a store like this. A flood of customers. The bookkeeping alone keeps her up late at night. The plans for new orders; the lists for her driver, James Boyd; phone calls about prices to New York. The Rav is drawing people to Kaaterskill. People from New York who have never come up before. His condition is worse. He does not go out of the house, and now everyone wants to come to Kaaterskill, to be near him. As the Rav's orbit contracts, the Kirshners are drawing closer. They are driving up and spending their vacation time, even extending their vacations. They need to be near him, even if they can't see him. Even if they only catch a glimpse. The Rav's letter of permission hangs outside Elizabeth's door on the wall. She has it framed there for everyone to see, the signature in blue-black ink. Strange the way his permission and then his illness have given her this opportunity. She was busy in June, but now the demand is escalating. The orders are enormous.

Hamilton fusses in the cellar storeroom, then comes up and stares at the long line of Kirshner customers snaking through his store. He must think this is an invasion. He must be wishing he'd charged Elizabeth more for her little kosher concession stand. Elizabeth just keeps pounding on the ancient cash register, emptying out the shelves. Only when she turns her back on them, her crowds of customers, does the worry creep in, the question, What will be next summer? They won't all be here then, these reinforcements from New York. Their husbands won't be up through the whole week. Of course, the Rav could recover. He could come up again next summer. It's possible. And perhaps the habit will be formed. People will be used to buying from her instead of carting up all their food on their own from the city.

"A bottle of dills, a bottle of bread-and-butter pickles."

"I'm out of those," Elizabeth says. "I've got sweet gherkins."

"Can you order?"

"Write it down. Over here. And anything else we haven't got—put it down too."

She feels light-headed. At five o'clock, after she closes for the day, she sits down for a minute on Hamilton's steps facing Main Street. She looks at the sign she has set up on the sidewalk. A plywood sign painted blue and white: KOSHER PROVISIONS. The store fills her days and her nights. It has grown from an idea she could open and close like a book into a living, breathing being, a giant of her creation, a golem with the Rav's magic letter on its forehead. Suddenly she has no time to read or think, she is so busy with the business. Far from possessing what she has made, Elizabeth feels that the store possesses her, and the things she used to do, the little projects with the children, the afternoons on the porch, Shakespeare in the barn in Lexington, have all fallen away. She is thinking about how to keep this pace next summer—even expand. She has an offer from Eva and Maja to cater Renée's birthday party this year, and she is seriously considering taking the job. She has seized on the Rav's permission, taken her opportunity, the sudden surge in Kirshner vacationers on the mountain. Managing the business now is like flying on an untamed horse's back.

She should get up and start walking, but her legs are tired. When she gets home, the children will be waiting for her. They will be home from camp, tired and hungry, and still restless, wanting to go out on their bikes. She'll find them outside, jumping rope, Ruchel and Sorah chanting together, counting out beats for the girl who hopes to jump in: "One a-dibble, two a-dibble, three a-dibble, four." And always in back, Chani and Malki playing tetherball. She'll find them there when she gets home, pounding the yellow ball between them. She wishes they had more space, now that the girls are older. Chani fourteen, and Malki thirteen. The bungalow seems smaller every year, with two in one room and three in the other. Perhaps someday she and Isaac will have a big summer place like Cecil's or Andras and Nina's. Elizabeth imagines idly that maybe if the store does well they could afford it. That's what it's like when you get a wish. It breeds others. She's heard the girls playing outside: "If you have one wish, what would you wish for?" The ready answer: "Three more wishes." Always wanting things. Even the children. Even in summer with their long jump-ropes in front of the bungalow, twanging in the dirt—the bald spot where the grass never gets started.

"Good afternoon, Mrs. Shulman." Elizabeth looks up from the steps. It's Judge Taylor, in his suit as usual, neat and trim. "I see you've opened up for business."

"Yes, I have," Elizabeth replies, a little flustered at the way the judge knows absolutely everyone by sight.

Boyishly, Miles Taylor brushes back the shock of white hair from his forehead. He looks at her with his clever blue eyes. "I hope you aren't planning to leave your sign on the sidewalk like that."

"Well, I—Hamilton said—"

"We have an ordinance about sidewalk signs," the judge tells her. "Two summers ago Edith Wycherly fell and broke her hip just a little farther up the road. She just tripped over a sandwich board propped up on the ground."

"Oh, I didn't know," says Elizabeth. "I hope she's all right now."

"She is not the same," Taylor informs her. "She has never been the same. That's why we established the ordinance."

"But Hamilton doesn't want my sign up in his window."

"Perhaps you could work something out with him," Taylor says. "Or perhaps you don't need a sign at all."

"No sign? But I need advertising," Elizabeth says.

"Do you really? It seems to me word of mouth is always the best way in small communities, don't you think? Your customers all know about you. And those who aren't your customers . . ."

Those who aren't your customers don't want a sign on Main Street, Elizabeth completes the thought silently. She looks at Judge Taylor standing there next to the big blue-and-white sign, a symbol of the ubiquitous Jewish clan of summer people. "I see," she says.

"Good," says Judge Taylor, and he walks on.

Elizabeth folds up her sign. Slowly, she drags it off the sidewalk and up onto Hamilton's porch. Like the Rav, Judge Taylor is a man to be reckoned with, the guardian and advocate of his community. The Rav has his sacred law and his Kehilla of families. The judge, his ordinances and his Kaaterskill. They are men who rule. With their word they command. But Elizabeth isn't used to obeying Judge Taylor. She resents it.

CHANI isn't supposed to bike to the library by herself. She knows that, but she pedals hard anyway along the curving road all the way to Kendall Falls. She is going to take out a book. It's true that Chani has been reading books about Israel. She has a book at home, the one Malki saw her reading. She bought it from the sale box near the glass door, *A Pilgrim's Guide to Palestine,* published in 1924 by the Ladies Guild of Holy Cross Church in Cleveland, Ohio. It was a bargain, for a quarter, and it's full of maps and photographic plates of the tombs and monuments. Where Rachel is buried. The excavations in Jerusalem. The gates of the city. The Temple Mount. Maps fold out and show the places where the Romans breached the city walls of Jerusalem. There are black-and-white pictures of the desert, all shadow and sun, profiles of hills with herds of goats.

While the Entebbe rescue first brought Israel into Chani's mind, the *Pilgrim's Guide to Palestine* fills her with a desire to see the land. Kirshners rarely visit Israel, she knows, and they will not move there until the Meshiach comes. Just the same, Chani dreams of seeing the hills of Jerusalem with their gnarled olive trees. She imagines climbing on the walls of the Old City and hiking in the desert, all black and white, as pictured in her book's photographic plates. Black rippling shadows on hot white sand.

Chani has two real talents: memorizing Tanach and hiking. She has a prodigious memory for scripture, although the memorization does not come easily to her. She picks through the text doggedly, inching her way through hard passages. Like her father she learns slowly and meticulously. And once she has learned a passage, though it might take weeks, she knows it unshakably. She's won the elementary girls' Bible contest three times. At home in the city she has three pairs of candlesticks on the bookcase in her room, her trophies. Chani is even better at hiking. Fast and surefooted. Cecil says she's an intuitive hiker and a first-rate rock hound. She's found samples of nearly every kind of quartz: rose quartz, smoky quartz, white, brown, pale lavender. When she was nine, she made it to the top of Cole Mountain. Only she and Cecil and her father made it up that far.

Those are her favorite things—memorizing scripture and hiking on Cole Mountain. Each has its season: the Bible contest in January with the radiators hissing in the classroom, the hiking in the summer on leafy trails, ribbon trail markers tagging the trees. But it seems to Chani, when she thinks about Israel, that it is all scripture and hiking, with no separation between the two. She pedals her bike up to Kendall Falls and she pictures Israel, where all the trees are markers, and the genealogies themselves are trails. Covenants are places; mountains stand as quotations from the prophets.

When she gets to the library Chani has to stand outside a moment to catch her breath. Tentatively she comes in, uncertain without her little sisters pulling on her arms. She walks around the room, just herself, and it is as though she has forgotten something. The usual posters are hanging there on the walls. Smokey the Bear. Birds of the Northeast. On the children's side are the low bookcases and the reading corner with cushions. There is the long, low table with the map of Fairyland under glass. Chani goes instead to the gray metal bookcases on the grown-up side. She looks at the titles slowly, glad to stand behind the tall shelves. In the front, at her great desk, sits Mrs. Schermerhorn stamping books, and at the smaller desk next to her, Mrs. Knowlton.

"What can I do for you, Hannah?" Mrs. Schermerhorn asks, and she looks straight at Chani through the shelves.

Chani comes out with the heavy book she's found. She comes to Mrs. Schermerhorn's desk and surrenders it. The book is *Exodus,* by Leon Uris.

The librarian takes a long look at Chani. "Hannah Shulman," she says. "How old are you?"

"Fourteen," Chani answers, confused.

"Are you aware," Mrs. Schermerhorn says, "that this book contains adult material?"

Chani's heart jumps. Mrs. Schermerhorn has read it. She knows it has material about Zionism.

"What does your mother say?" the librarian asks.

"She always says . . . read and find out," Chani stammers.

Mrs. Schermerhorn looks at Chani thoughtfully. "If your mother doesn't object," she concludes at last, "then I shall feel no qualms."

She rocks her date stamp on the purple ink pad and stamps the card in the pocket at the back of the book. "Two weeks from today," Mrs. Schermerhorn says. "There you are."

3

EVERY Thursday, James Boyd and Ira Rubin make the trip to the city for Elizabeth Shulman's kosher provisions. They drive back with warm challahs, and coffee cakes, dozens of rugelach, bags of cookies, meat wrapped in plastic and packed in ice, briskets, rib eye roasts, ground beef, corned beef, and roast beef from the deli in Washington Heights. And then the kosher cheese. Blocks of Swiss and creamy Muenster, round Gouda in red wax, crumbly cubes of feta, balls of mozzarella packed with water in white plastic. There are the cartons of ice cream sandwiches, and Popsicles striped cherry, lemon, blueberry—red, white, and blue. And there are special deliveries this week. Smoked fish wrapped in white paper, dozens of miniature Danish, an enormous cake in a pink bakery box tied with string.

They take Washington Irving Highway up the mountain in James's truck. Cheerful, glad they're almost home, James is talkative. But Ira looks out the window at the dark trees, and he thinks about Renée. He has waited and waited for summer and for Renée to come back. Now she has finally come. He sees her sometimes in Kaaterskill on Saturdays walking to services with her parents. And he sees her once a week on the bookmobile. He climbs aboard and he takes out books, and Renée is close enough to touch, but he is afraid to speak to her.

Windows open to the breeze, the truck skims past Phoenicia and

Palenville. They pass Floyd's Georgian-style brick motel, and James grins.

"Let me tell you, right in this spot," James is saying.

"What?" Ira is startled from his reverie.

"Ten years ago, some of us thought we'd take a little drive."

"Oh, was that the time you crashed?" Ira asks, and he is embarrassed that his voice sounds so eager. He has always wanted to hear about the crash, but it's the one story James won't tell.

"The crash was just three weeks later. I'm talking about when me, Stan Knowlton, and Bill Walker were just taking a leisurely little drive. Stan and I'd been out of school awhile, but Bill was just graduated and he was getting married to Candy Kendall. Then he was going into the Marines, to Vietnam.

"We were all sitting around on a summer's night and there wasn't much to do. My girlfriend and Stan's wife were out with Ladies' Bowling League. Candy was working late in Catskill. We had Knowlton's truck, his dad's truck, and we went driving along right along here, and we see this little Corvette in front of us." Boyd leans forward now, as if he sees the car again on the road. "Stan says, 'That's King's Corvette!'—Michael King, you know—'and there's someone in there with him!'

"So we start yelling, 'Chase him down. Chase him down! Run him off the road.' He was one of these summer people then, you know. Just one of these kids with a rich dad. So we start following him.

" 'He's going to Floyd's, I'll bet you fifty,' " Stan says. We all knew King took girls there. So Stan decides to follow him. First he slows down. He's a very subtle guy, you know what I'm saying? We slow down really casual, like we'd lost interest, and we turn off the road like we were really on our way down to Catskill. Maybe the double feature at the Odeon. So we let him loose just outside Palenville. Then we circle back toward Floyd's and park off at the Little Red Hen, so the truck isn't visible. We all get out, and we come at Floyd's through the trees; you know, the swimming-pool side?"

"Yeah," says Ira, although he's never been.

"Well, the doors are all in front facing the road, and pretty much

you park in front of your door, so we came around the sides of the
motel, me and Bill Walker on the left, Stan on the right. Like a pincer
movement. And right there in front of number seven is King's black
Corvette. Bill was doubled over laughing."

"So then what?" Ira asks.

James shifts into low gear and starts up Mohican Road. "Well, we
rush in on number seven. Door was dead-bolted. We were thinking
about chipping in to pay for the window, but Bill had his wedding
coming up and he couldn't afford it. Then Stan thought of trying to
open the window. We talk it over in the parking lot and then we rush
in on it to try. The window slides right open. But they heard us
inside and the lights went on. By that time we'd got Bill in, though,
and I was right behind him.

"There was a scream you wouldn't believe. I jump down into the
room, and Stan scrambles down, and there before our eyes is Michael
King with *Candy*! Bill is in shock. There's his fiancée, running for the
bathroom with nothing on her but the motel bedspread.

" 'Candy!' Bill shouts, and she stops in her tracks.

"When Candy saw him, her mouth just drops open. 'Oh, Bill!'
Just like that. 'Thank God you're here!' She starts crying how King
had offered her a ride and they ended up in this place.

"So she and Bill start screaming at each other, but the rest of us
didn't waste time. We pinned King to the bed and tore into him. But,
naturally, with all the noise, we'd barely started when the manager
came running with the skeleton key and tried prying us off his clien-
tele on the bed. So I guess we all got a little carried away and someone knocked this guy unconscious.

"Candy starts shrieking, 'You killed him, you killed him.'

" 'Shut up, slut,' says Bill. 'Here I am planning the wedding.
Here I am making payments for furniture.' See, he and Candy were
going to have a baby, due in January."

"You mean Billy Walker, Jr.?" Ira asks.

"That's the one. That was the baby," says James. "Named in
memory of his dad. So now, where was I? Oh, yeah. So Bill was
saying how he was trying to do the right thing.

" 'Do the right thing?' Candy screams back—she's still standing
there in the bedspread. 'I thought you loved me.'

"So now King's just about breaking loose, screaming something about prosecuting us. 'Yeah, from Canada?' I ask him. We all figured with his money he'd go up there so he wouldn't be drafted.

"The motel security rolls over and crawls out to call the cops, and Candy is just earsplitting. 'Then you can take back your ring, Bill, I don't want it anymore.'

"King was kicking, and Stan calls out, 'Bill could you move your butt and give us a *hand* here?'

"Bill comes over and grabs King's legs while Candy makes a big show pulling off the engagement ring. 'If you don't trust me, Bill . . .' But I guess she couldn't get it off her finger. It was on too tight. When she saw no one was listening to her she picked up her clothes and locked herself in the bathroom, so she was in the shower by the time the police came."

"What was she doing in there?" Ira asks, fascinated.

"Washing her hair," says James. "That's what she told the judge the next morning after they hauled us all in. But you should have seen when the cops came, the sirens and the ambulance, King on the stretcher—all he had was a broken nose and a few bruises. And then Candy makes her grand entrance out the bathroom door in a cloud of steam in her little halter dress with her hair down her back all golden and squeaky clean, and this look on her face, so reproachful, all hurt and innocent like we'd put her through all this trouble, instead of her being the cause of it! So they dragged us down to the station, and King to Catskill Hospital for his nose, but Candy they drove home. That's how it's always been for her."

"Why is that?" asks Ira.

"Because she had the looks. And she knew how to use them," James declares.

"She just looks . . . kind of fat now," says Ira.

"That's neither here nor there," James says philosophically as they drive through Kendall Falls.

"But then what happened?" Ira asks.

"Well," James says, with relish, "they got us to the county holding block and filed all the paperwork—it was practically Sunday morning. We slept a few hours, and then Judge Taylor came and spoke to us. Crack of dawn he came down to give me and Bill and

Stan our lecture. And you better believe he milked it for all it was worth. It was like being in church. He said we had certain rights and certain responsibilities. We had liberty and we had licenses and either we were going to choose between them, or he was taking one of them away. Knowlton's sweating now, since it was his truck and he was driving, so he figured his license was on the line, but Taylor carries on. It's not just one, but all, who bear the brunt, being an unruly mob, attacking people, disturbing the peace, despite what we thought was the cause. And anger was a sin, and so was violence, and we'd indulged in both, and not taken proper channels for any resentment we might have, and whether there was just cause for Bill Walker —since it was his fiancée there with King—was not up to a lynch mob to decide, but through reasoned action and educated choices, not tomfoolery like this. And he said, we might live up to our family's hopes, and the town's aspirations, becoming young men of probity instead of laughingstocks. Gentlemen, not clowns. And if we would think and watch, using our natural faculties for good, we wouldn't get into this kind of mess. And if we didn't, well then there wouldn't be any hope whatsoever.

"And he looked at us one by one. I'll never forget it now, how he looked at all of us. Like he could see the future. Who would live and who would die." James pauses for a moment. "But at the time I was so tired and so hungry, I didn't care. All I could think about was breakfast, my stomach was growling so much. Taylor just went on and on, and I thought I was going to be sick just from hunger. It was like the judge decided to starve us into submission. But the gist of it was we all got fines and we had to pay damages to Floyd's for drycleaning that bedspread.

" 'But, Your Honor,' I says, 'we never touched that thing.'

" 'Quiet,' Taylor says. 'Bring in the rest.'

"So in comes King to the station house with his nose in a bandage and behind him old man Kendall with his hunting rifle and Candy with that innocent look like her face froze that way. So Taylor looks around at all of us like the detective who solved the crime, but before he could open his mouth Bill turns to Candy's dad and says, 'Mr. Kendall, we've broken it off, Candy and I.'

"But Kendall says, 'Like hell you have. We've got a wedding half

paid for here already, and we're going through with it. As for you'—
he points to King with his long gun—'if you lay hands on my daughter again I'll blow off the rest of your horny nose or any other part of
your anatomy. That's all I have to say, Your Honor.' And he stomps
off."

"Old man Kendall?" says Ira wonderingly.

"That's history for you," says James as they drive into Kaaterskill.
"Gotta see it to believe it."

And they back into the dirt lot behind Hamilton's store, and
James hops out to start unloading. But Ira sits a minute in the truck,
and he tries to picture in his mind those long-ago days of which
James speaks. Stan Knowlton and James a couple of wild kids, and
Candy Walker beautiful like Renée.

ELIZABETH is waiting for James and Ira. When she hears the truck
pulling in, crunching gravel behind Hamilton's, she hurries out back.

"Let me check the fish," Elizabeth says.

"It's behind these boxes," James tells her. "Let's get this stuff off
first." James and Ira start carrying down the boxes of challahs, and the
heavier crates of frozen meat.

"And the cake?" Elizabeth asks anxiously. "It's not crushed back
there?"

"Not to worry." James lifts out the coolers where the whitefish is
packed on ice. "Come on, Ira, carry these in."

Inside Hamilton's store Elizabeth opens one of the red-and-white
coolers and examines the white paper parcels within. They are for
Eva and Maja's party, as are the boxes of cookies and miniature Danish, the miniature loaves of rye bread, and the cake in its tall pink box.
"Put the cake over here," she tells Ira Rubin. "Gently. Thank you."

Elizabeth cuts the string and opens the cake box. Ira's eyes widen.
There in pink icing the cake says *Happy 16th Birthday Renée*. The
cake for Renée. He hadn't realized it when they made the pickup in
the city. Everything was packed in boxes marked *Shulman*. But it is
for Renée, and she is sixteen, a year younger than Ira.

The cake is in perfect condition. With its basket-weave icing and exquisite bouquet of flowers and butterflies, it is more elaborate than Elizabeth's own wedding cake had been. Excited and nervous, a little feverish, a little jittery, Elizabeth is standing there with this bounty around her, writing a check to Boyd, collecting receipts, doing something completely new. In two weeks she's organized the party for Renée Melish's sixteenth birthday; in a morning she's brought up the food from the city. She sneezes and blows her nose. Then, despite herself, she glances up at the Rav's letter hanging on the wall. The cake and pastries, and the fish, come from Eva and Maja's bakery in Brooklyn, and their special deli in Flatbush, all outside the Rav's supervision. Of course, the Rav did not forbid her to bring up food from outside Washington Heights, but he did not give her permission either.

When Maja comes to pick up the food, she stands with Elizabeth and gazes at the cake. "It's beautiful," she says. "You did a wonderful job."

"Well, I didn't make it," Elizabeth says.

"But you deserve some credit for bringing it. For the long-distance catering. We can just put it in the backseat of the car," Maja says. Eva doesn't drive, but Maja keeps a car in Kaaterskill.

"Let me help you with those," Elizabeth says. She helps Maja carry boxes out.

"You sound like you're coming down with something," Maja tells her.

"I've had it for weeks. It's my sinuses," Elizabeth says. "I think it must be hay fever, but I've never had it before this summer."

"Allergies are like that, you know," says Maja. "You grow into them and you grow out of them. Eva had a terrible allergy to certain flowers when she was a child. Gardenias was one. Now they don't have any effect on her at all. And Andras used to have an allergy to grass, the cuttings, and now . . ."

"Now it's gone?" Elizabeth asks.

"No, now it's even worse."

It must be some kind of flu, Elizabeth thinks after Eva and Maja are gone. Standing at the cash register, she is not only congested, but light-headed and exhausted. Her muscles ache, and as the day passes, she feels as though she is watching herself hurrying along. She would enjoy this work, she would savor this day, if she had the chance to catch her breath.

By the time she gets home, she has a throbbing headache. "Chani," Elizabeth calls out.

"What?" Chani calls back from the yard.

"Would you come here?"

"What, Mommy?" Chani runs over.

"I'm going to need your help. I don't feel good. I'm coming down with something. Could you put up the chicken? And there's fresh corn, just boil the water."

Chani is a good cook, and a good baby-sitter too. She gets Sorah and Brocha to husk the corn. Elizabeth takes a shower and stands in the steaming water until her head clears. Soon Isaac will be up from the city, and he'll help her. She would go to the doctor, but she doesn't want to leave Chani with everything just before Shabbes. When Isaac comes home with the car, there won't be time to get to the doctor and back before sundown. She rifles through the medicine cabinet and takes a decongestant.

"You need to get some rest," Isaac tells her when he gets home. Right after candle lighting he and the girls bundle Elizabeth into bed.

"Here, Mommy," Brocha says and she gives Elizabeth her stuffed animals. "You can sleep with Three Bears, because I know they're your favorite."

WHEN Elizabeth wakes up the next morning, she is still tired, but her head has cleared. The house is silent. Isaac has taken the girls to shul. The shades are down and the room is shadowy. It is so quiet, so good to be alone. The time she spent alone in past summers is now spent at the store. She is caught up in the business, the customers and the money, the constant talking. This morning none of that exists. The store has stopped for Shabbes.

"You're making yourself sick," Isaac tells her that afternoon. They lie together on the bed while the children play outside.

"It isn't the store," she says. "Isaac, I've been tired for a few weeks, and I'm starting to worry that—"

"I wish you hadn't gotten started with Renée's birthday party," he says.

"I didn't realize how much extra work it would be," she tells him.

"I don't mean that."

She doesn't answer. Then she says, "I know what you mean."

"Well, I don't think it's right," he tells her. "You're playing with the Rav's permission."

"This is just the food for their party," she tells him as she has before. "It isn't food in the store."

"But you wouldn't eat it," Isaac says. "How can you sell food you would never eat?" The Rav does not sanction Eva and Maja's Brooklyn bakery. He does not certify their stores.

"Is it so terrible to recognize that there are other rabbinical authorities?" she asks him.

"Elizabeth!"

"Just because you follow the Rav—you don't expect all the others to join you. Other communities have strict standards too. They exist; why pretend otherwise?"

He looks at her unhappily. "You could open yourself up, Elizabeth, to—to problems. The standards aren't the same, and you know it. They hold differently in so many cases—"

"Isaac," she interrupts, "then do my parents in Manchester eat treife meat just because they don't eat food sanctioned by your Rav?"

Isaac can't answer that.

Admittedly, hers is an ad hominem argument, but it encapsulates what she has come to believe. Elizabeth looks at the question differently now that she has a business. She has taken one opportunity and she can't help taking others. There are other families up for the summer, not just Kirshners. All those other families come up for the summer with an equal need, equal potential to be customers. She can serve them as well. And many of them will come back next summer, when this sudden gathering for the Rav's sake disperses. Of course, Isaac questions this kind of thinking. And there are questions underneath his questions. Isn't she doing this just for profit? Why should she corrupt her original idea to serve the Kirshners with food from

Washington Heights? What about her original principles? Isaac doesn't ask that directly, but she can see it in his face; she sees it in his eyes.

She doesn't know a way to resolve this argument of theirs. They disagree; neither will retreat. Isaac is a purist, but she pushes against the rules. They have always had this difference. "You think I'm doing something wrong," she says.

"Look," he tells her, "it's something I disagree with; it's something I wouldn't do." He can't call it wrong. The word is too difficult, too divisive. But he is troubled that he hasn't somehow prevented her from taking this action, from expanding her business in this way. This kind of entrepreneurship, increasingly assertive, offends his pure sense of how to act in the community, his sense of the order of things. He has lived in this particular hierarchy all his life, moved within it as through water, slowly, but without a feeling of constraint. Neighbors, teachers, rabbinic authorities, rippling around him in smooth concentric circles. "I just worry about it, this business of yours," he tells her.

"But do you want me to succeed?" she asks him.

He hesitates. "Yes," he says.

They lie on the bed with their differences between them, the seam exposed where they are joined together.

THERE are long tables set out in Eva and Maja's garden. Platters of lox and whitefish garnished with sliced lemon, capers, olives, sweet purple onions. There are small slices of rye bread fanned out on plates, bagels, onion rolls, miniature Danish. Trays arranged with cookies from the city. Nothing ordinary. Only small and delicate cookies. Madeleines, ladyfingers stuck together with raspberry jam and dipped in chocolate, cookies like flowers and cookies like leaves, cookies dusted with crushed walnuts. There is punch and lemonade in Eva's heavy cut-crystal bowls. Elizabeth watches the cookies disappear, the punch ladled out floating with sherbet, the children swarming the dessert table. In past summers Eva and Maja prepared everything themselves for Renée's birthday. They had their husbands bring up some of the food from the city, but they did most of the baking. This year, however, Eva has been tired. She's had dizzy spells and has been seeing doctors in the city. She and Maja have not told Elizabeth what the problem is.

"Elizabeth!" Beatrix calls out from across the lawn. "We never see you. You're always minding the store."

"You can come and see me there," Elizabeth says, and she smiles, because Cecil is standing with his arm around Beatrix's shoulders, just as he had a year ago when they were newlyweds. He is uxorious, Elizabeth thinks. Terribly proud, exceedingly in love with his mathematician wife.

"But what about our badminton?" Beatrix asks her.

"I thought you'd given up playing badminton with me," says Elizabeth.

"Listen to her," Beatrix says to Cecil. "Listen to this arrogance."

"When I'm over this flu, I'll come play again," Elizabeth promises.

"You said that last week," Beatrix says.

"It's been a rather long flu," Elizabeth admits. "But come see me at the store."

"And who is minding the children while you're there?" Beatrix asks.

"I'm open while they're in camp, and on Thursday afternoons Chani watches them for me."

"Oh, Chani. How very clever of you to have a teenager," says Beatrix.

"Chani's my big girl," Elizabeth murmurs, looking over to where Chani sits on the grass with a bowl of ice cream.

"Well, I don't know how you do it all," Beatrix says, throwing her long rough black hair over her shoulder. And Elizabeth realizes with a rush of pleasure that Beatrix is not teasing her. She is really speaking in admiration.

"I hear that you're going to start a franchise, you've been so successful," Andras says to Elizabeth as he comes over with Nina.

"Oh, no." Elizabeth laughs. "No franchises yet."

"I have to admit," Andras says, "when Isaac called me last winter I said it wouldn't work out."

"Oh—I didn't know Isaac called you," Elizabeth says, startled.

"Well, it doesn't matter. You have every right to be proud."

"But I don't feel that way," Elizabeth confesses to him. "I'm too busy."

"And what is it like having a business?" Nina asks.

"It's all come about so strangely," Elizabeth says. "So many people coming up because of the Rav's illness. Unfortunately this isn't an ordinary summer. And the work is different from what I expected. It isn't more difficult, but it's more uncertain. I thought I would feel somehow more"—she pauses to think of the word—"triumphant. But I'm too busy. Too tired! I thought success would be sweeter, somehow."

"Well, success is an acquired taste," says Andras. "But here we are already in July. You should be planning for next year."

"I have records of all my sales, and I was going to study them to plan for next summer, but this year is so unusual. Everyone is here."

"This summer doesn't have to be unusual," says Andras. "You should be compiling a customer list with phone numbers in the city. Then over the winter you can work out orders for next year. You can give discounts for ordering ahead."

"How much of a discount would you give?" Elizabeth asks him.

"Talking shop at the party," Nina admonishes them as she goes to greet the Sobels. But Andras is already considering the question.

They talk for a long time, Elizabeth and Andras. They discuss Elizabeth's profits and expenses; they talk of the possibilities for next summer. And Elizabeth forgets her cold. Her voice is full of energy. Somehow it returns to her—the sense that this is her project, that she has created something of her own, even within the tight weave of associations in Kaaterskill—the family, the Kehilla, the neighborhood. She has knit from this mesh something entirely new.

The long cool evening settles over the party. The guests drift home. The children quiet down. Renée is opening her presents on the grass, Nina trying to keep the cards with the gifts. Elizabeth walks home with Isaac and the girls. She steps lightly, looks everywhere. She watches the maple leaves shifting in the sky. After speaking to Andras, her mind is filled with plans and new ideas. She is bright with anticipation.

Then, as they are walking back to their bungalow, they meet the

Steins, their Kirshner neighbors in the city. "Good evening," Isaac calls out to them.

"Hello, hello," they answer. "Where were you? Estie was looking for someone to play with. You were all away."

"We were at Eva and Maja's party," Elizabeth says. Lightly, recklessly, she adds, "I catered it."

They stare at her, shocked to hear her say this.

Then Elizabeth stands there with Isaac and the children and she wishes she could take back her words. Her cheeks burn. She should have kept quiet. But her confidence spilled over, her joy in her accomplishment. The words escaped her at the wrong time to the wrong people. They belonged to a different conversation.

"I didn't know you were a caterer too," says Leah Stein.

And Elizabeth can't speak. She feels the reproach in her neighbor's words. The sarcasm and the disapproval. She feels it just as if a bee had stung her careless hand. First the soft body of the bee, and then the surprising flicker, and then the pain.

EARLY the next day as the new week begins, Elizabeth's head aches, and she buries her face in the pillow when Isaac gets up to leave. With difficulty Elizabeth struggles out of bed and packs five lunches for the children to eat at camp. She stands at the counter and spreads strawberry jam and peanut butter on five slices of bread. As always she spreads the jam first, and then the peanut butter directly on top. She got into the habit years ago in order to prevent the children from just licking off the jam. Into five brown bags goes each finished sandwich, along with an apple, a can of juice, a bag of pretzels, and two oatmeal cookies. She starts closing up the peanut butter and sways back dizzily. She will have to put up a note at the store. She has to go to the doctor.

After the older girls set out on their bikes, and after Nina drives up and takes the little girls to camp along with Alex, Elizabeth hurries across the street, where Beatrix is working, pacing on the porch, back and forth, back and forth, thinking about her mathematics.

"Beatrix," Elizabeth says, "I've got to get some antibiotics. Do you think I could borrow the car?"

"What, the Minx?" Beatrix asks, looking over at the tiny cream-colored Hillman Minx that she and Cecil drive. "Do you know how?"

"Oh, yes," Elizabeth says. "I learned on a manual. I just have to get to our doctor in Kendall Falls."

"Right," Beatrix says, and she sticks her head inside the screen door. "Cecil? Throw me the keys."

DR. PETERSON, short, heavy, and sandy haired, has an office in one half of a long ranch house set back from the road. Elizabeth always goes to her when the girls are ill, and once she came when she sprained her ankle. She'd returned home with a brochure about sprains, and the children had enjoyed learning what color her ankle was going to turn next.

"Well," Dr. Peterson says, after she has examined Elizabeth, "you certainly have a sinus infection, and we can give you something for that, but all this seems to have gone on for quite a while along with your other symptoms—exhaustion, indigestion, queasiness. Are you thinking what I'm thinking?"

"I hope not," Elizabeth says. She and Dr. Peterson have always been frank with each other.

"Well . . ." says Dr. Peterson.

"It just doesn't make sense," Elizabeth says.

"All right," Dr. Peterson says. "Well, we'll see. Let's give you a quick mono test as well."

Elizabeth drives back to Kaaterskill and hurries to the store. She takes her antibiotics and feels out of kilter. A bit numb. People come and go, and she talks to them from deep within her head cold. Everyone seems very far away.

That night Elizabeth and the girls call Isaac in the city. As always he talks to each of them. "We made tambourines," Brocha tells him. "Brown. I used all the colors, and so it was brown, and there was glitter on top, and then we put on bells."

"I didn't finish." Sorah tries to grab the phone. "Mommy, I didn't finish my turn."

"You can have a turn after Brocha," Elizabeth says.

"How come she gets two turns?" Chani asks.

"She's just going to finish her turn because she got interrupted," says Elizabeth wearily.

"I got interrupted too," says Ruchel. "And I forgot to say something. Mommy, I really need the phone. Mommy, I *really*—"

"Stop it!" Elizabeth tells all of them, and finally she takes the phone away. "I got the antibiotics," she says to Isaac. "Ten days . . . Yes, a sinus infection."

She has a hard time getting the children to bed. At nine it's still light outside, and they want to go outside and play, but finally, at ten-thirty, they are all asleep. Chani's book has slipped down from her bed to the floor. Brocha has stopped calling for a cup of water, and a cup of water with ice, and a toy for her bed—a soft toy—and a blanket for Three Bears, and she lies limp on top of the covers in her nightgown, with her arms around Three Bears' blanket.

At last the house is perfectly quiet. Elizabeth takes a deep breath. Then she steals into the living room and calls Isaac back.

"What? What is it?" he asks, startled from sleep.

"It's all right." She has to whisper in the tiny house. "The doctor gave me a pregnancy test—to rule it out."

He doesn't say anything at first. Then he says, "But that can't be."

"I know, but—it's true. In March."

They sit there on the phone, he in the city, and she in Kaaterskill, and they don't speak. Elizabeth tries to steady her voice. "I don't understand why, now suddenly—"

"But this is . . . a . . . wonderful thing," Isaac says slowly.

"It's just a shock," she says.

"It's a surprise."

"I'm not used to it yet."

"I know—but, Elizabeth, it's no tragedy, it's a wonderful thing."

"But I don't know how—I don't know how I can start again—because I thought we were—it's in the middle of everything. And what about next summer? The store."

"But we could get you some help with the—to watch—"

"Isaac," she whispers. "It's awful."

"It's not awful," he says sharply.

"I meant that suddenly it's happened now. I can't believe it. And where are we going to find the space? And the money is—"

"But wait, think," he tells her. His voice is fuzzy and exhausted, but somehow close, as if his lips were brushing her ear. "It's a miraculous thing, because, because what could be more important than having a child? What work could be more important? A child is everything. The future. The beginning of everything."

Yes, she thinks, but I have five already. I have invested in the future already.

"Elizabeth? We'll find a way."

"I haven't told them."

"Of course not. Who knows?" he tries to joke. He is thinking that it could be a boy.

"It won't be," she says miserably, "I know it won't."

"You need to sleep," he says.

"I don't think I'll be able to sleep."

"But you have to try," he says. Then he admits, "I don't think I'll be able to sleep either."

Elizabeth puts down the phone gently, and she walks out onto the porch. She shivers in the cold night air, but she stands for a long time looking at the towering trees, and the black sky. And she tells herself that even though there isn't enough money; even though she and Isaac are stretched to the point that they haven't any more energy, or attention, or patience, left to give, they will stretch a little more, and there will be joy in the giving. She will not be disappointed; she will not allow herself to be afraid.

4

—

IRA RUBIN has shot up this summer. When he steps inside the book-mobile, his head grazes the roof. Instantly—as soon as he comes in—he sees Renée sitting at the drop-leaf checkout table, but he tries not to stare at her. He browses among the books instead.

During the winter, when he was thinking about Renée, it oc-curred to Ira that she would probably look down on the paperbacks he reads—even the good science fiction. He decided then that when he saw her again in the summer he would take out better books, impressive books—the old ones Mrs. Schermerhorn displays as clas-sics. This summer he has already borrowed *War and Peace* and *David Copperfield*. Valiantly at home he is struggling through *The Red and the Black*. He's even hammering away at *Favorite Works of the Greek Philos-ophers*. Somehow it's never occurred to Ira to return the books with-out reading them. Doggedly he keeps at it—his secret travail, his chivalric service.

Now, in July, bent over in the bookmobile, Ira picks up *The Works of Aristotle*. He takes a copy of *The Odyssey* as well. "Ira," Mrs. Schermerhorn tells him, "you are making great strides. You are giv-ing yourself an education."

He stays as long as he possibly can, putting off the moment when he must check out the books.

At last he comes up to Renée and hands her the classics in their faded red library bindings. She barely looks up as she opens the books and inserts new cards in the back.

But Ira looks at her. He looks at the backs of her arms flecked with freckles, and he looks down at the top of her head, her copper hair. He has never seen that color on anyone else. He has never known—or, in any case, never noticed—anyone so beautiful before.

"Here," she says, and hands him the books.

He decides that he will say something. He resolves to speak.

"Here," Renée says again. She is still holding the books out for him.

"Thanks," he says.

Then Renée looks up at him and Ira knows that she knows. She has sensed the truth. He feels both relieved and wary. She knows he has a crush on her.

That afternoon when Renée comes out from the library, she finds Ira standing near her bicycle at the fence. Just standing there poking at a Smiley's milk shake with his straw.

Ira bends down and picks up an identical large shake from the ground. Fine red dirt clings to the bottom of the paper cup. "I brought you one," he says.

"Why?" Renée asks.

"Do you want it?"

"No," she says, although she is very thirsty.

He puts it down again. "Can I have it, then?" he asks.

She almost laughs at him.

"Mine is almost gone," he explains.

She looks at the tall cup sweating on the ground. "What kind is it?" she asks.

"Chocolate."

"Oh," she says.

"Why? Do you want it now?"

"No, I was just wondering what kind it was." She gets up on her bicycle.

"I see you all the time in Kaaterskill going to temple," Ira says.

"It's not a temple. It's just a shul." Renée leans over the handlebars of her bike.

"My great-great-grandfather built it," Ira says.

"Your great-great-grandfather?" Renée asks dubiously.

"Yeah."

"I don't believe you."

"Well, it's true," Ira says indignantly. And it is true. His great-great-grandfather was old man Rubin, the man Cecil Birnbaum likes so much to tell about, the founder of the synagogue in Bear Mountain who fought with the townspeople and hauled the synagogue building to Kaaterskill with his team.

But Renée doesn't know any of this. She just looks at Ira skeptically.

"So I guess I'm Jewish like you," Ira says.

"Either you are or you aren't," says Renée.

"I am, but I'm not religious," Ira informs her.

She looks at him, a bit surprised.

"But you are, right?" he asks her.

"I am what?"

"Religious."

She nods.

"Why?" he asks her.

She hesitates. "Because my parents are," she says.

"But when you're older you won't have to be," Ira says.

"I might or I might not," Renée tells him. "I have to go."

"Where?" Ira asks.

"None of your business." She pushes off.

"You're mean," he says, but he says it humbly.

She circles back. "I am not."

"Yes, you are."

"You don't even know me," she says diffidently, but she wheels her bike closer. She is almost close enough to touch. He can almost touch her hand.

Without noticing, Ira takes a step. Almost before he realizes it, his fingertips brush Renée's freckled arm.

Then Renée takes off. She shoots away down the road and disappears, pedaling hard. Dust rises around her as she pedals, and she gets dirt in the toes of her sandals. It was so strange, standing there and talking like that. His great-great-grandfather! Stephanie will think it's so funny. Ira Rubin likes her. Ira Rubin with his philosophy books and his glasses nearly slipping off his short nose. And his long arms. He never knows what to do with his long arms. His fingers made her shiver; they were so cold from holding that milk shake. She feels embarrassed somehow, remembering it, but also a little glad. She's got to tell Stephanie about this. Stephanie will laugh and laugh.

Mohican Lake glistens green beyond the currant bushes as she takes the turn into Stephanie's yard. Two dusty white cars are parked in the driveway near Mrs. Fawess's Mercedes. Renée leaves her bike on the grass.

She runs to the front door and rings the bell, but no one answers. The door is ajar, and she lets herself in.

She feels lost when she enters the shadowy living room. The lights are all off. "Stephanie?" she calls.

The house looks strange. The living-room furniture pushed over to one side, as if the place were being closed up for the summer. Beyond, in the dining room, the tablecloth tilts, one end brushing the floor—about to slip off the long glass table.

In a murmur of voices Mrs. Fawess appears with two men dressed in dark suits. Mrs. Fawess's face looks swollen, her eyes puffy; Stephanie stands behind her with a startled face.

"Stephanie?" Renée says.

Her friend stares at her with such hard eyes, Renée is afraid to come closer.

"Leave, Renée," Stephanie orders.

Renée stands still, and then Stephanie walks over. "I said go."

"Wait," Renée says. "What's wrong?"

Mrs. Fawess shakes her head and says, "I'm sorry, Renée, this is not a good time."

"Why?" Renée asks Stephanie. "What happened?"

But Stephanie puts her arm around Renée and she whispers in Renée's ear, "Promise you won't say anything."

"About what?"

"Promise."

Renée looks at Stephanie for a hint of a joke; she looks into Stephanie's face, hoping and half expecting a smile. "I promise," Renée says.

"We're going," Stephanie says.

"You're moving? Why?" Renée whispers back.

But Stephanie doesn't answer. Fear pricks Renée. Where is Stephanie's father? Where are her cousins? Renée doesn't get a chance to ask. Gently Stephanie propels her out the door.

Renée picks up her bike from the front lawn. She doesn't want to go. She wants to run back inside and find out what's happened. She is Stephanie's best friend—at least in Kaaterskill. She has a right to know. But Renée doesn't run back to the house, and Stephanie doesn't come out after her.

WHEN Renée gets home she shuts herself in her bedroom. She clamps her pillow to her and stares at all the things in her room until they look unfamiliar to her. The rosebud wallpaper and white bookcase of books she read when she was little, the blue-lettered spine of her *Pinocchio,* the wicker clothes hamper, the blond doll sitting on the dresser in her blue-smocked dress, legs thrust out in front of her, and the Eskimo doll standing guard with his spear, face peeking out of his rabbit-trimmed hood. Everything in the room is bigger, quieter. When her mother knocks, the sound is muffled and magnified as if underwater.

"Renée, what's wrong?" Nina rushes over. "Did you hurt yourself?"

Renée just shakes her head and clutches the pillow more tightly.

"What's wrong?" Nina begs.

"It's Stephanie," Renée says. She can't help speaking of it, although she promised not to. "Something happened—there were men there with her mother."

"What kind of men? Police?"

"I don't know; I don't know. They didn't have police cars. Everything was all mixed up in the house—"

"It must have been a burglary," Nina reasons. "It was just a burglary, and the security came to see the damage, that's all." Nina takes both Renée and the pillow in her arms. "That's all," she murmurs, "that's what happens when the alarm goes off. The men come down from the company, they make the inventory—that's all. . . ."

But Renée knows there was no burglary. By the next morning Stephanie and her family are gone.

Everyone in town is speculating about where Fawess has gone and why. They are talking about it at Boyd's garage and in the hotel, in the ticket booths at the Orpheum, in the Kaaterskill post office. Fawess and his wife and daughter, his brother and sister-in-law, and their children are nowhere to be found. They left before dawn, and scarcely packed their things. Michael King's twin houses on the lake are full of clothes, dishes, even groceries, but his wealthy renters have vanished. Some people say that the family left simply to avoid paying bills. That Fawess did not have as much money as he pretended. Others argue that Fawess had Mafia dealings and left town because he was told to leave, or because he felt he had to go undercover. Mrs. Schermerhorn is of this school.

"He was working with the wrong kind," Mrs. Schermerhorn tells Mrs. Knowlton in the library.

Renée looks up from the pile of magazines she is slipping into clear plastic sleeves.

"I, for one, suspected it a long time," says the librarian. "Those truck runs to Canada? You remember, Janet, those gatherings they had up at the lake. All those limousines coming up."

In the sunny library Renée feels cold.

"I, for one," says Mrs. Schermerhorn, "particularly noticed the smoked-glass windows in those cars."

Renée swallows, thinking of the Fourth of July picnics at the Fawesses'. She remembers the drums and the thousand almond cookies; handsome Mr. Fawess dancing on the porch, arms above his head. The limousines parked on the grass.

"I think one day the law caught up with him," Mrs. Schermerhorn declares. "Or maybe just the folks he worked for. In any case, he got the signal it was time to go. He got some sign. Of that you can be sure."

Renée ducks her head down and keeps at the stack of magazines. Her mother has ordered her not to speak about Stephanie to anyone. "Renée," her mother said, "if I had any idea those people were, that my daughter was—you have no idea how I blame myself for letting you gallivant around town with that girl—I didn't know—" And her mother's voice trembled. "I telephoned your father in the city. We want you to promise us you will never, ever—and you won't discuss how you know that girl with anyone, do you understand? I don't want you touched by this."

Stephanie always said Renée's mother was overprotective. Renée doesn't think of her that way. She imagines overprotective mothers are sweet and gentle and timid. Renée's mother is fierce and peppery. She has such a temper. She doesn't seem to have any sympathy for Stephanie, or even for Renée.

Renée can't help feeling sorrowful, abandoned there in the library. How could Stephanie leave her here with Mrs. Schermerhorn? At home Renée's brother is sitting with his little friends, playing Monopoly on the porch, sneaking in real dollar bills for the "free parking" bonus. Renée's mother is working in the backyard, repainting the bungalow where the lawn mower and the tools are kept.

On Friday Renée's father comes up, and they all sit down to dinner together. And now that Stephanie is gone, even Friday-night dinner is different. Without any plans to make, without anything else to think about, Renée sits at the table and she pays attention. She hears her mother's insistent questions to her father, and her father's cold replies.

"But why shouldn't we go on a family trip?" Nina asks. "The children have only been to Argentina. It would be good for them to travel. It's educational. They should see Europe. Ruth Fishman was just telling me how every summer the whole family gets away to a new place. They're going to Scandinavia before the Holidays. Last summer they went to Eastern Europe. Renée and Alex are getting older. Kaaterskill isn't as good for them the whole summer."

"They look fine to me," Andras says.

"It would be good for all of us. You haven't gone back once, not even to Paris."

"No."

"What is that supposed to mean?" Nina presses.

Andras pushes away his plate. "It means no." And in silence Nina brings out her apple pie, a magnificent sight with the crust ballooning upward and then sinking down at the point of her knife to touch the cinnamon spiced apples.

Undistracted, Renée sees her parents in a new light—as though they are not her parents, but independent people, strangers. There is something sharp and severe about them, and even sad. Why do they never touch each other? Are they too old?

For so long Stephanie had been Renée's internal audience. Renée feels an echo inside of her now that Stephanie is gone. She'd come to anticipate Stephanie's reaction to everything she saw and did. Already now, Stephanie's voice is fading and she can't consult Stephanie's decided opinions anymore. The whole charmed world Stephanie conjured up has also vanished. The dragon Schermerhorn is only a librarian again; Rabbitville has become again the shul day camp and bungalows of Kaaterskill. And Renée notices the unhappiness in her house. She feels it now, without distraction, without the chance to rush outside with Stephanie into the buzzing summer air. It's as if she'd been spinning, as she used to when she was little on the grass, and then suddenly she stopped, and the world stopped spinning with her; the trees settled back into their places, the scattered house came back together, and the tilted windows slowed and squared themselves.

5

—

THE Rav does not come downstairs anymore. He is confined to his
room and lies in the rented hospital bed, asleep much of the day.
When he wakes, he feels as though he has forgotten something. For a
moment he cannot recollect it, and then he remembers his illness and
his immobility. With great effort he opens his eyes, draws breath,
moves his head.

The men, his many Kirshner followers, pass through the room
downstairs. In the morning the Rav feels them passing and praying.
They are putting on their white tallesim, shaking out the voluminous
draperies. They shake them over their shoulders like wings. The Rav
feels the words in the house and he moves his lips with them. His
mouth is dry, and yet he feels he still has something to say. The men
finish. They fold up their wings and hurry away, only to return again
in the afternoon. For hours Isaiah sits with him, reading aloud from
the gemara in his quiet voice, his voice of restraint. The Rav has
something to say, but not to Isaiah. Rachel comes and goes with
food. She adjusts the black radio on the nightstand, so that he can
hear the news. She brings the Rav's grandson with her, and Nachum
stands next to her, pale, serious, a little frightened. The Rav does not
speak to them. He is tired of all of them, their caution and concern
for him because he is dying, their restrained good health and subdued
youth, their false modesty about living. They seem to live in shadow.

He sees it, but they cannot. They don't have a sense of what was taken. American born, they cannot possibly appreciate the loss. For they did not know the great Kirshner synagogue in Frankfurt which stood like a palace, with windows like jewels. The Frankfurt synagogue was a seat of learning and a soaring theater for prayer. Now that place is ruined, and its burning was like the destruction of a new Temple.

He lies in bed and thinks about Germany, and what was broken there. The good, and the true, and the beautiful split apart. The Kirshners there had lived rich, complicated lives, devoting themselves above all to halacha, but also to art and business, to the German language and its literature, to German music, *"Torah im derech eretz,"* Torah with the ways of the land, as his grandfather would say. But they had been betrayed in that conjunction.

The Rav chose to leave, and he chose a new way, a life of greater separation. He has built a community of vigilance, a careful, cautious American generation. How strange that none of them see their piety is a way of mourning. How strange the way they embrace it in its severity. They don't know the difference. They are born now with the severity within them, although they do not know it. It cannot be otherwise, and yet it saddens him. The Rav remembers the expansiveness of his own youth, and the feeling of possibility. He had read great and beautiful books in German. He had pursued wonderful imaginative voyages. Life was golden to him, and the world his treasure house and laboratory. He could not see it then as he sees it now, a place with neither goodness nor mercy. Where he received his beautiful education, he lost parents and sisters, a family, a people. He cannot believe in the world anymore. Only in God. There is only God.

JEREMY does not want to come up to Kaaterskill, and yet he does. He does not want to walk up the stairs, but his legs carry him anyway. Six weeks have passed since he drove to his father's house after candle lighting. It is now the beginning of August. Jeremy is afraid to see his father now, and yet it is too late to avoid it. He must come with all his fear and confusion, and a slight hope, very slight, that the Rav will speak gently to him. That, as happened once before, the anger won't show itself, and give way instead to better feelings. There is so little time. He does not want it to be bitter.

Isaiah is sitting at their father's bedside, and the Rav is awake, sitting up against the rented hospital bed. "Isaiah," the Rav says, and Isaiah gets up and leaves the room.

Jeremy stands alone before the Rav. "How are you, Father?"

"I am as you see," the Rav says calmly. He is small and distant with all the hospital paraphernalia around him, his eyes heavy lidded. He looks at Jeremy for several long minutes, an eternity, waiting for him to speak.

"I'm sorry," Jeremy says at last hoarsely.

"It doesn't matter," the Rav says.

"I was late and I shouldn't have been," Jeremy says. He sees instantly that this is a mistake.

"Whether you are sorry or not makes no difference," says the Rav. "What does it matter?" He pauses and then adds, "It is characteristic of you to apologize to me for an offense to God."

Jeremy says nothing.

"You have always been quick," the Rav says deliberately. "You are accomplished. You are a scholar. A true scholar. Twice what your brother is. He will always lose himself in the details. You know what you are about." The Rav looks Jeremy in the eye. "However, none of this matters to me. I look at you, and I see what I have always seen. You have been everywhere but where you should have been, read everything but what you should have read, done everything else—"

"Father," Jeremy says.

"I knew it from the beginning," the Rav tells him. "You were a brilliant and a selfish child. You knew what you knew, and you were hard. Hard."

"I was what you made me."

"No," the Rav tells him. "It was there when you were three years old. Indifference."

"You can't know that about a three-year-old child. You can't simply discard a life like that."

"But I did know," the Rav says. "The indifference was there. It was wrong from the beginning."

"There is no such thing as wrong from the beginning."

"Yes, there is," the Rav says.

"God," Jeremy whispers in his anger and his grief to hear this. Even now his heart is confused. The bitter, confident voice within him is laughing at the hope, the very idea, that he would come to his father and they would forgive each other.

The Rav sees the pain in his son's face, but he does not alter his words. He believes, from the depths of his loss, in an immutable evil in the world, and a hard grain of evil in the worldly. To what has Jeremy devoted himself? Never to God, never to the holy and the eternal.

"You know nothing about my life," Jeremy says.

"You did not direct your soul to what is good," the Rav says. "The rest does not mean anything."

"I didn't come here for you to berate me like this," Jeremy cries out.

"Go," the Rav tells him.

Then Jeremy runs down the stairs and out of the house, and he turns his face so the others won't see the tears in his eyes.

CHANI is breathing hard, pedaling up the street. She feels the importance of her message, and the heaviness of the day weighing on her. She gets to Hamilton's store and practically throws her bike down in front. She runs up the front steps two at a time. Her face is streaky and her hair disheveled. "Mommy," she calls out as she runs to the back of the store, and then, with a winded gasp, "he's dead."

Elizabeth starts, and Mrs. Lerner, who had been buying meat asks sharply, "What did you hear?"

"I saw people walking down from his house," Chani says, "the doctors, a lot of them, and I asked what happened, and they said, he's dead."

Mrs. Lerner lets out a cry and she bursts into tears. Elizabeth does not cry, but steadies herself against the high table she uses as a counter. She seems to Chani determined not to cry. Tired and pale, but determined. Chani stands there, relieved of her burden, glad to have said it. Relieved as well that her mother is not sobbing like Mrs. Lerner. She feels somehow that if her mother had cried she would have too. Chani hadn't known what to do. She had raced all the way, not only to tell her mother the news, but to see how to respond to it.

Chani has only seen the Rav from a distance. Pushed aside by his black-suited aides, she has glimpsed his old old face, white as a moon caught in the black branches of trees. He was a great figure to her, a commanding presence, a tower of learning, but never a person.

THE funeral is in New York, and the Rav is buried in the family plot next to his wife, Sarah. The family sits shiva in the city as well. They sit on low benches in the Rav's apartment and receive the streams of downcast silent mourners. Rachel and Isaiah, along with Isaiah's cousin, Joseph, and the Rav's other nephews, each of them rabbis. Jeremy comes each day as well, but he remains somewhat apart. He does not speak to anyone, but sits with his mouth set, as if willing himself to stay. When the week is over, the family returns to Kaater-skill, but Jeremy does not come with them.

The Rav's memorial service is on a Sunday afternoon in Kaater-skill, and not only the Kirshners, but the whole community of sum-mer people, walk up the hill to the white synagogue. It is a cloudless day, and as the mourners walk, the sun warms their backs. But the Kirshners bow their heads as if bracing against a cold wind. They are bereft. They are a people without a leader. They do not yet see Isaiah as their Rav. Isaiah has worked in his father's shadow for so long that they cannot suddenly view him that way. The Rav alone kept them together. He was both their navigator and their memory. Until the end he was their guide, and even in the last stages of his illness, he never abdicated his authority. He did not leave instructions for the future, or even indicate that he meant his son to take his place. While Rav Isaiah is now the de facto leader of the Kehillah, he never re-ceived a public sign from his father. Until his father's death he re-mained the heir apparent, but never the anointed.

When it came to the end, when Isaiah stood beside his father, there was no final blessing, no sign, or even hint, that Isaiah was to become the future Rav. Everyone knows this, and, of course, Isaiah is aware that they know. He had been afraid, even at his father's bed-side, that the Rav would not give him his blessing. Isaiah stood with his wife and cousins by the Rav's side during the last moments, and he asked his father for some words. Just to speak to him once. Isaiah asked, in agony that the Rav would not speak at all, that he would not even utter his name. But when at last the Rav opened his mouth, it was not to endorse his son, or even to encourage him. He simply said, "I am tired." And then later, "I have been very angry. I have been angry at your brother." And those were his last words. Even at the end the Rav's passion was spent on Jeremy. Isaiah, who had always been at his father's side, was never an object of concern. Isaiah thought of this on the day his father died. Somehow Jeremy's sins were more important than Isaiah's loyalty. The disappointment in Jeremy's academic vocation, more compelling than any of Isaiah's rabbinic scholarship. Always the Rav thought about what hadn't been. He did not once consider what Isaiah himself had become.

The shul is crowded for the short afternoon service, and the building hot. The men pack the seats, and spill into the aisles where they daven, sweating in their dark suits and hats. The youngest of them, long limbed and angular, perch like blackbirds on the window-sills. In the back, behind the glass-topped mechitzah, the women press against each other and lift the edges of the lace curtain that blocks their view. Isaiah stands with the dignitaries on the bima, all rabbis; his own cousins and his brother-in-law, and other rabbis as well, the leaders of other small and strict communities. They have all come to speak about his father, but the Kirshners are crowding the synagogue, waiting to hear what he has to say. Each of the other rabbis will give a drash, but the Kirshners are waiting for Isaiah.

Pesach Lamkin speaks first. He is the youngest of the rabbis, only a young man, and only the director of the summer camp, but he is also the rabbi of the Kaaterskill shul, and so he is allowed to begin. In deference to the more senior rabbis who will speak after him, Pesach limits himself to just a few minutes. He talks of sorrow and of conso-lation, and although his words are not freighted with experience or erudition, they are coherent. His beard wispy and his eyes eager, he speaks of the wicked thriving like grass, but the righteous enduring

forever. He talks about eternity with a rapture in the moment. He is
entranced to speak in this convocation with these hundreds of men
and their families, and to be heard by these rabbayim, the heros of his
generation. "The Rav, *olav hashalom,* was a great light on earth, and
his qualities will endure. Truth and goodness and the word of the
Torah will last throughout time. The tongue that never utters a word
of evil, the mind that never swerves from learning, all will outlast the
wicked or the flawed heart; they will pave the way for the Temple,
may it be rebuilt in our day."

Isaiah's cousin, Rav Joseph Butler, speaks next. He is a slight man
of fifty with a strong voice, dark hair, and heavy brows. Isaiah has
always known his cousin to be his rival. The Rav never liked his
nephew Joseph, but Joseph has a vital role in the Kehillah as the
director of the yeshiva. The directorship is a post of tremendous
influence, and Joseph uses it. He is popular with the young men. A
charismatic teacher, close, perhaps too close, to his students. When
he eulogizes the Rav, he speaks with an extraordinary energy, as if he
were arguing a case before his audience. He declares that the Rav was
a Tzaddik, a saintly man, a chosen one, almost an angel on earth. He
speaks as a flamboyant advocate for the Rav's righteousness, and his
rhetoric and passion are extreme. But Isaiah understands the real argument, because it is an argument against him. The Rav is a Tzaddik,
and he cannot be replaced. The Kehilla should not shift its loyalty to
anyone else, but should continue to serve the Rav's memory. Isaiah
watches the men drink in this performance; they are eager for it,
stirred by it. They are susceptible, because the Rav, when he was
alive, never allowed them to indulge themselves in this way. He
scoffed at this kind of talk and reined in speculations about his holiness. Now, in their grief, the Kirshners' adoration wells up within
them, the more intense because it was repressed.

What will Isaiah say to them? How will he answer this? For it is a
challenge to him, a direct challenge, pitting his father's memory
against his own new authority. Reb Moshe Feurstein is speaking
now, a tiny man, no more than five feet three inches, the head of a
small Hasidic community that vacations every summer in Kaaterskill.
With his frock coat and great beard, his hands clasped behind his
back, his face lifted up, Reb Moshe's self-important voice belies his

little body. He is speaking of the great tree in the midrash from which, if you shake it, abundant fruit will fall. Was not the Kirshner Rav like such a tree, from which his fruit, his mitzvos, would fall for all to partake? Isaiah hears Reb Moshe talking, but his own questions course through him rhythmically. What will he say to them? How will he answer this? He will have to rise up and plead his own case. He will stand before them as his own counsel.

Rav Yaakov Guttman, Rachel's brother from Brooklyn, is speaking about the Rav's scholarship, about the deep friendship between the Rav and Rabbi Guttman, Yaakov's father. The depth and breadth of the Rav's learning and his precise rendering of the text, his devotion to truth and his ability to impart that truth to his students. Isaiah only hears half of what his brother-in-law is saying. Already the blood is rushing to his head; his cheeks are hot. He must speak next, and he must speak well. He has never spoken before such an audience, never stood before his people as their Rav. In the next moment his fate will be decided. When his brother-in-law finishes, Isaiah will stand to prove himself before his father's community. And yet he is not afraid. Isaiah is not an experienced speaker or a charismatic man, but he knows what he knows. For years he has thought about the Kehilla and the role he would play in it if he had the chance. For years he has imagined this time—not, God forbid, his father's death, but his father's retirement. He has waited to come to his people, and say the words he has so long held in his heart.

When Rav Guttman takes his seat, Isaiah rises to speak as in a dream. He sees the men looking at him on this day of mourning with expectant eyes, with a kind of hunger in their grief, as if the death has set them loose, and all their reverence is now turned wild. But Isaiah is strong, as he stands before them. He opens his mouth and the words come.

He speaks about constancy despite change, and unity despite the pressures of the outside world. He talks of dedication to Torah, not merely as something learned, but as an instinct, so that there is no hesitation and no question about its teachings. He quotes the most famous of verses: *"V'ahavta et adoshem elokeha, b'kol levovcha, uv'kol nafshechah, u'v'kol me'odechah"*—And you shall love the Lord your God with all your heart and all your soul and all your might—and he talks about this kind of love as deep within them, in their blood. That their observance should be a second nature to them, habitual. He talks about what must be inconceivable to them—that they should ever compromise their beliefs, that they should ever give way to any pressure or temptation.

"The world is full of false gods and enticements," Isaiah says. "But it should be impossible even to imagine serving them. Our work is to build the Kehilla like a fortress, so strong that inside it each member can devote himself to God; not to struggling against the outside, but to striving within. Our energies should not be wasted on defense against what is false. What is false should be understood without saying; our energies should focus on what is true. Halacha permits no compromise and no negotiation, but if it is the center of our lives, then we are free. We are free to dedicate ourselves to God. This is what it means to love the Lord with all your heart and all your soul and all your might. Nothing is wasted on the extraneous, or the evil, or the false."

He talks about his father and the example of his life. His father as the architect of a community which is precious but also unfinished—a Kehilla left of necessity to the future, for all its members to uphold and perfect in each of their lives. And, as he talks, Isaiah feels his words charge the air; his voice penetrating the stifling room. He knows, as he talks, that he is not just speaking well, but with a sudden brilliance. It is not that his words are so powerful intellectually, but rather the way they come from him, with such force and clarity. They seem to catch fire in the room and flare before the Kirshners, dazzling their eyes.

It is exhilarating to hear Rav Isaiah talk this way. In the sweating, dark-suited audience of men, Isaac listens intently, and he is proud of the new Rav's drash. The message is strict, perhaps even harsh. Isaac himself would never express himself this way, and yet the drash is everything he could hope for. A rallying cry, a call for unity and strength. There is a sense in which Isaac expects his Rav to be a soldier and to maintain a defense against the outside world. For the Rav stands guard over the bulwarks his followers take for granted. It is he who provides the security that allows for dedication from within, and that is why so much depends on his presence, his powerful stance, a voice strong and confident, ideas unwavering. Rav Isaiah is going to maintain the community; he will ensure its safety and consistency. That is what he has come before them to declare. Isaac listens, and he is relieved.

But Elizabeth hears the Rav differently from where she sits. She has come late with the girls, and there are not enough seats for all of them in the women's section. There are beads of sweat on her face as she sits with Brocha on her lap. She feels the heat in the shul; and, within her, the familiar waves of nausea. The Rav's drash goes on and on. His voice is bright and strident, shrill, and he repeats himself often. Again and yet again he underlines his point. There is no room for compromise, there is no sustenance outside the community.

"Our strength comes from within, from our own convictions, our own families, and our own institutions. There are those who argue for leniency, for making exceptions. There are those who maintain dealings and friendships with Jews who do not observe Shabbes, or who intermarry or eat treife. What, then, is the message that they send to their children? That these people are still good; that they are still worthy of attention and uncritical friendship. This is what our children learn: that we will tolerate this kind of behavior. Is this the lesson we want to teach them? How then should we explain it? That it is wrong for us, but right for other people? Or that it is wrong for anyone, but that people who do wrong are still worthy of our respect, and of our friendship? Is this what we want to teach? Only consistency will sustain us. Only consistent thoughts and actions will keep Judaism alive."

Of course, Elizabeth has heard all this before. This is Rav Isaiah's first major drash, but the message is familiar. She is used to these formulations, and although she listens to them, she does not believe them. She has never seen the Kehilla as a fortress. Now, more than ever, the outside fascinates her: the people there, the way everyone moves about, the complexity of a world with such loose days and weeks, the time never delineated between work and Shabbes, the food never separated, the men and women mixed together as well; so many decisions made rather than received. Where to live, what kind of work to do. She sees it now; it was never the poetry she was after, never the secular books, the paintings, or the plays; it was the diversity of choices. The quick and subtle negotiations of the outside world. Elizabeth listens to the Rav, but she hears him from a distance. Deep within her she knows that she has scaled those bulwarks of which he speaks. She has scaled the Kehilla's wall and softly lowered herself down to the other side.

When Rav Isaiah finishes, a surge of voices rises from the men surrounding him. They push forward to shake his hand and follow him out of the synagogue, a mob of black, hundreds and hundreds of men. The people are relieved. They leave the synagogue with a fierce joy, the women streaming out in their dark dresses, the children dancing into the sunshine. Isaiah has drawn them to him. He has proven himself his father's son.

Elizabeth hurries out with Brocha and scans the crowd for Isaac and the other girls. Nausea rides up the back of her throat, but she pushes forward anyway.

"Elizabeth," Isaac calls out as she reaches him, "are you all right?"

"Tired," she says. "A bit queasy."

"Let's go home. There's Chani. Chani, get your sisters."

"Mommy, what does *queasy* mean?" Brocha asks.

"A little sick. Not very. Really nothing," Elizabeth answers.

"He spoke well," Isaac says as they walk home. "Didn't you think so?"

"I suppose so," Elizabeth says. "I was so uncomfortable for most of it."

"Could you hear?"

"I heard him," she says.

❦

NINA bursts in from the memorial service, the metal screen door snapping shut behind her. She is dressed in a dark green suit, tailored and crisp, and she wears a hat with a matching green band. "He gave a brilliant drash," she says to Andras, who is sitting in the living room. "He spoke for an hour and it felt like a few minutes. It was a—a brilliant thing. Such an experience. Rav Yaakov Guttman was there, the rebbetzin's brother—"

Andras looks up from his paper at Nina, and she sees suddenly that something is wrong.

"What is it?" she asks him. "What is it? Eva? What did the doctor say?"

"She has cancer," Andras tells her.

"Andras!" Nina rushes to his side. She wants to know if Eva and Saul are going back to the city early, and whether Maja and Philip are going with them. She wants to know if they should all go back early, if Eva needs help. Andras tells her what he knows, but Nina keeps darting around and around with her questions. Will she have surgery? When will it be?

In the evening Alex comes in from outside with his hands dirty, and Nina makes him wash with soap. And then Renée comes in, clean and wistful, as if there is nothing to do in the summer without Stephanie. They sit down to dinner, and Nina serves them. All the time she is talking, asking Andras what will be and whether there is a second opinion yet. She is worrying, she is concerned, but her chattering grates on Andras. He leaves the table as soon as he can.

When the children are asleep Nina comes to Andras in the living room and says, "I think we should talk about it."

"I'm sorry," he tells her. "I don't want to talk about it. Not now."

"Not ever," she says. "Not with me. Not ever."

"I'm just not . . . talkative," he says with a weak smile.

"You are with her," she tells him, "and with Maja. You talk to them every day. You talk to them for hours."

There is nothing to say to this. It's true. With his sisters Andras feels free. They are like him, part of him. They have been parents, friends, and teachers to him. To lose them . . . he cannot imagine living without either of them.

That night Andras drifts in and out of sleep, and restless in the bed, he begins to dream. He walks in the forest in the evening, wading through piles of leaves. He hears a woman calling him. Faintly he hears someone calling his name. He recognizes Eva's voice and hurries on, past lichen-covered boulders and the dry, empty beds of streams. He hurries toward the voice, and finally he sees Eva crouching down, hurt. He sees her familiar plump figure, her reddish-brown hair, her reading glasses fallen at her side, and he struggles to lift her in his arms. Only then does her face reveal itself. It is not Eva at all, but Una, her face a mask of white with slits for eyes.

Andras wakes with a start. His breath comes quickly, but the dream does not leave him. He is afraid, but he can't stop looking at it. Una's face, the white face, the object that is death.

He lies for a long time, stricken. Next to him Nina is sleeping, oblivious, her face buried in her pillow. How trivial their life is. How insignificant. It is all put on. Tomorrow the week will begin. He will go down to the city and mind his business. He will work the days away, and the days will be light and inconsequential. They will slip through his fingers. They will mean as little to him as a handful of loose change. Now it is the nightmare that is real. The fantasy that is fact.

Two o'clock. Two-thirteen. Two twenty-seven. Andras gets up and puts on some clothes. He walks down the hall and down the stairs, treading carefully on the edges, where they won't creak. He steps outside and begins walking along the silent street. He walks up and down Maple. All the way up, and all the way down. Rhythmically, he walks and walks. He looks at the houses under the trees. The Birnbaums', the Curtises', the Landauers', the Erlichs', the Shulmans', the Knowltons', the Kings'. How small the houses are in the darkness. Up and down the street all the lights are off. He can only just make out the shape of a bike lying on the grass at Joe Landauer's place. There is the tire swing, hanging in front of Isaac's house. Andras cannot see but he knows there is a clothesline tied farther up on Isaac's tree, the Shulmans' metaphoric wall marking off the property so that the children can play ball in the yard on Shabbes.

What would it be like to live like that? To mark off the yard for the Sabbath? To speak to God morning, noon, and night. To believe in God—and not only to believe in him, but to believe that he listens to prayers. What would it be like to have that reassurance? That God would take an interest, and approve or disapprove one's life. How comforting to believe that one's life is significant in that way. That it is guided by God's will, and not left to chance. Andras has none of this reassurance. He has only the conviction that there is nothing in heaven but cold space and stars, and that if there is a God, he scatters his creation and lets lives fall where they may, seeding good and barren places alike.

He walks and thinks about his children. He does very little with them. He does not join them in their games, or take them to summer camp, or scold them when they come inside. When they were younger he never put them to bed at night or sat there with them in the dark. He buys the children presents because he doesn't know what else to do. Nina nags, and his sisters worry. They sense the truth; that there is something lacking in him. If he could be like Eva, that would be something. If he could be one of those radiant people in the world who seem to warm the ones around them like little suns. If he could be like that. But he cannot generate the heat.

Andras looks at himself with a mixture of self-pity and disdain as he walks there alone in Kaaterskill. He is alone, even here in this small place, even under these trees, not entering into his neighbors' religious belief, not holding God in common with them. His neighbors sing together like birds in morning, afternoon, and evening. They are a thousand voices enlivening the air and calling to each other. There is nothing Andras can contribute to that, nothing he can add, although he lives there with them and watches them. His own soul is silent, his experience and ideas hard and dry, having to do with business and money, with economic rather than spiritual transactions.

Just before dawn he hears the birds. He hears doors closing, the trees rustling in the cool air. An old car starting. Then the men begin walking up the street. They are carrying their blue velvet tallis bags and walking up the hill to shul for morning minyan.

"You're up early, Andras," Joe Landauer calls over to him.

"Coming with us?" someone else asks.

"No." He has to clear his throat. "Just out for a walk." He is hoarse from the night air. He watches them as they hurry on toward Main Street and the shul. Joe Landauer is taking three of his sons with him, and they jostle along behind him, thin versions of their father.

Andras watches as they disappear up the hill. The sun is rising. He is going to be late.

As always on Monday mornings, Andras rides with Isaac down the mountain. As usual they listen to the news. But when they reach Cooksburg, Isaac turns off the radio. In silence Isaac drives the sleeping Andras to the city.

6

—

ALL afternoon Isaiah and Rachel sit in the library of the Rav's white Kaaterskill house. They are sorting papers together at the desk, and they are exhausted, overwhelmed by the Rav's unfinished business, months of correspondence with halachic questions from members of the community, stacks of notes, drafts of essays, bills. They are tired from the events of the past weeks; they are overwrought. The Rav never sorted out his papers, or allowed anyone to look at them when he was alive. He was never interested in writing explanatory notes or putting his manuscripts in order for future executors. His work simply lies where he left it on his desk.

"What are these, the new letters?" Rachel asks.

"Yes," says Isaiah.

"These have to be answered."

"I know," Isaiah tells her. "But I have to look through these too."

"What's this?" she says. "Isaac and Elizabeth Shulman. A request to reopen their store next summer. And these"—she sifts through another pile of paper—"his manuscript on"—she looks closely at the handwritten pages—*"Kohelet."* All the Rav's manuscripts are written out by hand in blue-blue ink. But the Rav's handwriting deteriorated in his last year. Even Rachel can barely make out the words he has penned on *Ecclesiastes.* "Under the sun there can be nothing lasting, and there can be nothing new. The fixed, the eternal, and the original lies in the Holy One. . . ." Rachel unfolds a cardboard manuscript box, places the papers in it gently, and writes out a label in her own dark, compact script. She and Isaiah work together in the library like a pair of archaeologists among the towers of books. Dust motes float before them in the late afternoon sun and settle on the overloaded shelves. The work is slow and still, and yet they are pressed for time. In just three weeks they must return to the city, where the other library, in the Rav's apartment, awaits them.

"You need to have your cousin start sorting the papers in the city," Rachel tells Isaiah now. "The letters there can't wait until we come back."

"I don't want Joseph in the apartment," Isaiah replies.

"But you can't do all of it alone."

"I think I may have to," he says.

Rachel turns on him. "You are a scholar," she tells him. "You are the Rav. You are not a secretary anymore. You are not an assistant. This is not your job." She gestures to the cluttered desk. "You have a job, and that is to lead and to teach. Not to spend your time filing. Not to be editing, or—transcribing his manuscripts, his notes."

"We are not going to leave all of this lying here," Isaiah says.

"I'm telling you"—Rachel's voice is urgent and soft, although there is no one else to hear—"We cannot do this alone."

Isaiah doesn't answer. Silently they continue working on the correspondence, arranging the letters by date.

"What are you going to do about this business of the store?" she asks him, again holding up the Shulmans' letter.

He takes the letter and reads it. "The store was useful this summer," he says. "Next summer it might be a good thing."

Rachel looks over his shoulder and reads the letter with her small intent face. Her eyes are dark and fierce.

"They act as if they are asking to renew a library book," she says. "No. No," she tells Isaiah. "This is not your job. This is not your responsibility. The Kehillah doesn't need to have stores here and stores there, and you managing it all. Let them buy in the city like everyone else. Your father, *olav hashalom,* spread himself thin. Of course he did. He had you to work for him. You are going to have to set your own standards. If he did something or made you do something, that does not mean that necessarily it continues. No. They heard you when you spoke at the service. That is how you should be. You are not a bureaucrat. You are not a slave."

"Rachel," Isaiah chides her.

"What?"

"I'll consider the case on its merits."

"Exactly," she says. "You'll need to speak to them. Do they want permission to bring up food from the Heights, or are they also planning to bring up from other places? I heard that they catered a party."

Isaiah knits his brow. "The Rav didn't give them permission to cater parties."

"Where is the copy of his letter of permission?" Rachel asks him.

"It should be there," he says, pointing to one of his father's old filing cabinets.

"There was no mention of catering as I recall," Rachel says as she looks for it. "He didn't give permission for anything but the store." She pulls out the carbon copy and puts it on the desk. "And he had very little interest in that. I really think he gave them the letter to make work for you."

Isaiah holds up his hands to stop this talk. "I don't think that's true."

"What does it matter now?" Rachel says, "Now it has to be taken care of. Now you are the one who has to straighten it out."

ELIZABETH stays late on Monday afternoon to balance the books. Hamilton is puttering in front, seeing to his stock, straightening the shelves, and Elizabeth works in the back room with her pencil and her ledger. She is tired, but she finishes up anyway. She forces herself. When she is done, she checks her delivery days on the wall calendar, *Compliments of Auerbach Butcher*. She has the calendar from Auerbach's and a set of refrigerator magnets from Miller's cheese. Hamilton has a whole clock from Budweiser with a holographic-style picture of a team of Clydesdales drawing the Budweiser Wagon through a stream, and a moving waterfall in the background, splashing white behind the clock dial.

"Till tomorrow, then," Elizabeth tells Hamilton.

"Mm," he answers.

The afternoon is warm and quiet as she walks home, the breeze drifting with the hum of lawn mowers. In the cooler shade of Maple, little children are scampering over the sidewalk, carefully skipping over the cracks left by long-forgotten ice. Stan Knowlton is working on his car in front of his red bungalow; Cecil is raking up under his apple tree at the side of the house.

Inside Elizabeth's bungalow the scanty mail still lies on the doormat. The girls never bother to pick it up. A two-for-one ice-cream offer from Smiley's, a phone bill. There is a third envelope from the Rav's office.

"Mommy!" Brocha hurtles across the room. "What's for dinner, Mommy?"

"Just a minute," Elizabeth says, and she opens the envelope as she walks into the bedroom.

The Rav's letter is only one line long: *Dear Mr. and Mrs. Shulman: We would like to discuss your request for next summer with you.* The words are typed in clear round pica, the sharp carbon letters of an electric typewriter. Nothing like the Rav's 1938 manual machine. *Please call and make an appointment. Rav Isaiah Kirshner.* The letter could have been generated by the bank, or by the credit bureau. The message seems so bland and mechanical. But what does it mean?

"I'm hungry, Mommy," she hears Brocha from the living room.

"Chani, could you get her an apple?" Elizabeth calls back from the bedroom. She sits there on the bed with the letter. The Rav and rebbetzin must have heard about her deliveries for Eva and Maja's party. They must be calling her in to ask about it. She didn't have permission. Isaac had warned her about that, but she had gone ahead anyway. Now she frets about it. Not about whether it was wrong, but about whether the Rav might think it was. She has never felt this way before, uncomfortable about the Rav's opinion. Elizabeth has never had occasion, simply living in the Kehillah and running her household. Well, there are going to be questions with something like this. Her business is a new enterprise. And yet she does not want to go in to see the Rav and answer to him. The store is hers alone. Her creation, or so she'd fancied it.

Before she'd received permission, the Rav's decision had loomed large in her mind, but afterward, once she had the letter, she took it for granted. It was like securing a loan. Taking the money and forgetting the debt.

How gratified she'd been at Eva and Maja's party when everyone complimented her, told her it was wonderful the way she'd brought up all the food herself. She was flattered by that. She'd not fully considered that they were thinking that she'd done well, despite the limitations she was working with. They were impressed she'd managed to pull off the party and the store. But it wasn't her, it was her position that they marveled at. Elizabeth holds the Rav's letter in her hands, the pure white typing paper with its two neat creases. The envelope, ripped open, has fallen to the floor. What a contortionist she must seem to her Kaaterskill neighbors, making a business in Hamilton's back room. What a marvelous object she is to them. A ship in a bottle. How did she get in there? How could she get out?

With nervous hands she picks up the phone and calls the Rav's office. The rebbetzin answers the phone.

"This is Elizabeth Shulman," Elizabeth says. "I—my husband and I received a letter from the Rav. We need to set up an appointment."

"Let me look at the calendar." The rebbetzin's voice is thin and distant. "Thursday?"

"Would it be possible to do it Sunday?" Elizabeth asks. "My husband is in the city during the week."

"The Rav doesn't have hours on Sunday," Rachel Kirshner says.

Her tone pricks at Elizabeth. She is so cold, as if Elizabeth were asking some presumptuous question. And then Elizabeth realizes something. She must not get Isaac involved in this. She mustn't get him tangled in her mistake. It would be unfair and cowardly for her to bring him all the way up to Kaaterskill for this meeting, as if he should somehow defend her for decisions she made independently— indeed, against his advice. "I suppose I can come Thursday," she says, "but I'll have to come alone. My husband will be in the city then, because he works there, and I don't want to ask him to lose a day because—because it's mine really," she says. "It's not his store at all. It's mine, so it isn't necessary for him to be there."

SHE wakes up many times on Wednesday night, and once she wakes shivering, the blanket having slipped onto the floor. Drowsily, reaching for the blanket and pulling it over her, Elizabeth searches for and remembers the events of the day, and what is worrying her. Her dread of the next day's audience with the Rav brings back a long-forgotten memory of the night before a contest at school when she woke up shivering in the dark, thinking of the teachers waiting for her to recite a pasuk from *B'reishit.* That's what it's like, isn't it? Like school. Like her daughters in the corridors. She has been called out of school to explain herself.

All the next day on her stool behind the Dutch door, Elizabeth rings up groceries for her customers. The young mothers pushing strollers with ungainly babies, some of them sprawled in sleep, some awake and screaming. The older women, who come in pairs, clutching their square-cornered, short-handled pocketbooks, and ordering her about peremptorily. She is nervous even as she marshals her defense. She hasn't done anything wrong, she tells herself. But her conscience is troubled. She knows that there is something wrong, if not in what she has done, then in the way she has done it. She feels guilty, as if now at last she is being held accountable for thoughts and feelings that have become strong and disrespectful, perhaps even opportunistic. Stop, she tells herself. Stop imagining the meeting this way—as if it were a court-martial, for heaven's sake. She tries to shake off these thoughts as she closes up early and puts out her handwritten note, *Closed at two today.* She smooths the back of her skirt where it always creases from the stool. It is ten to two.

Heart pounding, she climbs the hill past scraggly blueberry bushes and ragweed and approaches the Rav's house with its glassed-in porch. Silently, Rachel Kirshner shows her into the Rav's library and leaves her there in the dark, book-lined room, almost exactly like the library in the city. The furniture is the same, the desk placed in the center of the room with the large table behind it. But instead of the old Rav, the middle-aged Rav Isaiah looks up from his desk, a much younger face. "Good afternoon," Isaiah says. "Where is Mr. Shulman?"

"He is in the city," Elizabeth answers, steadying her voice.

"I see," the Rav says mildly enough. Clearly, he won't refuse to talk directly to women as his father had. "Please come sit down."

She takes a red leather chair near the desk.

"Mrs. Shulman," the Rav says, "I have some questions about the store." He pauses there.

Elizabeth says nothing. Instinctually she holds back. She needs to see where he's going.

The Rav keeps waiting. He waits until he makes her silence uncomfortable. Until it seems there in the library that she is keeping something from him.

"What has disturbed us," he says at last, "is that there are reports you have been selling food that is not sanctioned by our community." He leans toward her across his desk.

She has never seen him this close. Behind his glasses his eyes are warm brown, not black. His hair is threaded with white.

"What are you asking me?" she inquires respectfully, but with precision, as if she were in court.

"I am concerned," Isaiah says, "that you have been pushing your letter of permission from the Rav, *zichrono tzaddik livracha,* farther than it was meant to go. Bringing up food from outside, catering events—if in fact you have been doing these things. These were not provided for in the original license. And what I am asking, first of all, is, were you doing this? Bringing up food with other hechshers."

She stiffens slightly. "Yes," she says.

"And did you bring up food for a party?"

"Yes," she says.

He knits his fingers and rests his two hands together on the desk. "Well," he says, "of course, you understand that this is well beyond the scope of the permission given to you."

"But it wasn't forbidden," Elizabeth says. "It wasn't clear—"

"If it wasn't clear, then you should have asked," the Rav reminds her. "Unfortunately you did not ask. You took it upon yourself to interpret his permission as you wished. Then you sent me a request to renew your license. Now"—he picks up her letter. There is a hard quietness about him as he sits there in front of her and silently reads her request to reopen the store next summer. "I am in a position," he says, "—have a responsibility—to uphold the halachic standards of this community, and I don't think I can renew a license that has not been honored. It may be true that you did not violate the arrangement, such as it was. But it is clear that you did not honor it either." He puts the letter down, simply places it, her store, her idea, on the desk.

"No," Elizabeth says, "I don't think that's entirely true, because the work I did was good work, and I did it in the way I had presented it to him—"

"A license from the Rav is not a blank check." Rav Isaiah speaks more quickly than before. "And the Rav's signature is not to be misapplied. His name on a document is a matter of trust—"

"And trust in me?" Elizabeth asks. "Is it an agreement if only one party determines what kind of trust it is, if only one side writes it and signs it, gives it and takes it away?" As soon as she speaks she regrets her words, but she could not help herself. She sees that the Rav is angry, but she is angry too.

Rav Isaiah looks at the frank-faced woman across his desk. One thought galls him; one thing enrages him. She would never have spoken to his father this way. She would never have dared. He takes a breath; he collects himself before he speaks. "I can't allow this to continue," he says. "You are not honoring your commitment. You will have to close the store."

"Let me explain the situation," Elizabeth says, her face reddening.

"I think I understand the situation quite well," the Rav tells her. "It will have to stop. Immediately."

Then Elizabeth can say nothing. He has made his decision, and there is nothing else to say.

SHE walks back to Hamilton's store. She strides down his narrow aisle to her Dutch door in back. James Boyd has already arrived with the week's delivery. He and Ira are unloading the truck together, stacking boxes and carrying two at a time up Hamilton's back steps.

"Hello," Elizabeth hears James calling. "Hello, anybody home?" They walk into the little storeroom where Elizabeth stands among the boxes and the freezer cases.

"I'm sorry," Elizabeth says, "I'm going to need your help pack-

ing up these things. I'm going to have to return them to the city—
and the ones you've just brought too."

"Now, wait a second," James says.

"Of course, I'll pay you anyway," she tells him.

"Hold on—we drive to the city and pick up this load and now
you say you don't want the stuff?"

Pale, Elizabeth stands before them. "I'm going to have to close
the store," she says.

"I don't understand," James says.

"Well . . ." She hesitates. She doesn't know how to put it. "I
had permission. I had a sort of a license, and I don't have it anymore."

"You lost your license? I didn't know you needed a license to sell
frozen chicken breasts," says Boyd. "And why didn't you tell us this
before?"

"It just happened. This afternoon," Elizabeth says. "You were
already on the road."

"Can I put this stuff down?" Ira asks from behind.

"Look, if you think I'm driving all the way back to the city—"

"Oh, no, not today, of course not today," Elizabeth says. "We'll
set another day. Next week. I'm going to have to call the suppliers in
the city."

James starts to speak and then stops.

Elizabeth sees that he is almost afraid to make her talk. Another
word and she'll be crying.

She tells him she will call later. In a few days. She writes him a
check and records it in her checkbook. She writes a check to Hamilton for the whole month's rent. It is a lot of money. A lot of wasted
money. She closes up her gray cash box and puts her ledgers in her
old canvas tote bag, silk-screened *Kendall Falls Library*.

She cannot explain it to James Boyd or to Hamilton. The Rav
has taken her store away from her. He has decided to take it away.
And there is no recourse for her. No way to appeal or argue her case
before the Kehillah. The decision is made. She can't negotiate.

Elizabeth has never questioned the Rav's judgment before, the
old Rav's decisions on halachic matters. That self-cleaning ovens are
acceptable for cooking on Pesach, but continuous-cleaning ovens

should never be used on that holiday. That families should eat in their sukkahs on the eighth day of Sukkot. His determinations about education for the children, the tunes sung on Shabbes, the kind of clothes the men should wear, or the hair coverings for women. They were all such small things, transparent, and easy, like air. She never experienced disapproval; she never did anything to merit a rebuke. But when she made something new, the Rav took it from her. When she found something for herself and for the community, then he took it away. He looked at her across his desk as if she existed only on sufferance.

Tremblingly, Elizabeth packs up her makeshift store. She takes down her fluttering calendar. Of course everyone will talk about it. Of course everyone will know. She is shaking, angry to the tips of her fingers. She pulls the Rav's framed letter off the wall and it drops from her hands. The cheap glass cracks, and one piece shatters on the floor.

"What's that? What's that?" Hamilton calls out from the front of the store over the grinding of the ice machine. "You break it, you buy it."

But Elizabeth closes the Dutch door. She shuts herself into the windowless storeroom. Sitting with her feet up on the rungs of her stool, she ignores the ice machine and the bell ringing as customers come in Hamilton's front door. She holds herself and rocks softly back and forth, hot and flushed from the close air.

BY EVENING all the summer people know about the store's closing. The women talk about Elizabeth on their porches, and in their lawn chairs. When they call their husbands in the city, they tell them that Elizabeth Shulman has lost Rav Isaiah's permission and shut down her business. Even the children know something of the story. They talk about the store as they pedal up Maple. They call to each other in their flock of bicycles. "Ruchel's mother closed her store. Did you know that?"

"The Rav made her close it down."

"Ooh."

"What did she do?"

"Nothing!" Ruchel shouts.

Even Beatrix has heard about Elizabeth. She and Cecil have heard from Nina that something has gone wrong with the store, and that Elizabeth has closed up shop. Beatrix thinks it over, pacing on the porch. Back and forth she walks, considering Elizabeth's situation. Then at last Beatrix says to Cecil, "I'm going over to talk to her."

"All right," says Cecil.

"Aren't you coming?"

"I'm far too comfortable where I am," Cecil admits. Deep in the wicker couch, he is reading his *TLS*.

Beatrix sighs. "It was such a lovely image I had in my mind, Elizabeth twiddling her toes in the twentieth century with Hamilton as her sort of duenna. I don't see why she had to close. I wouldn't have done it—"

"You are not Elizabeth," says Cecil, "to state the obvious."

"I meant in her position."

"You would never be in that position," he says.

"Don't be so literal. Could I tell her?" Beatrix calls back from the porch steps. "Are we telling people?"

"If you want," says Cecil.

In the twilight Elizabeth's children are playing with an old soccer ball. Elizabeth is watching on a lawn chair in the grass.

"Elizabeth?" Beatrix lopes around the side of the bungalow in white jeans and a hooded sweatshirt. "How are you? Nina told us there's been a rabbinical eyebrow raised at you. I was just coming to say My God, and how awful, and—you know—how absurd. Are you all right?"

"I'm fine," Elizabeth says.

Beatrix looks at her carefully. "No, you aren't," she says.

Elizabeth smiles. She cannot describe to Beatrix how she feels, so small and sick and cold.

"Well," Beatrix says, "I wanted to tell you something. I hope it cheers you up. You're the first one I'm telling. We're reproducing ourselves. We're having a baby in March."

"B'sha'ah tova!" Elizabeth uses the traditional formula, May the

baby be born at a propitious hour. She does not mention her own pregnancy.

"I'm a bit . . . terrified about it," Beatrix says, sitting down on the grass before Elizabeth. "Not just the pregnancy and the labor, but the child. I've been working so long on my papers and my lectures. I'm only used to thinking about my mathematics, and my career— I've never *liked* distractions. And the thought of having something so distracting as a child . . . You'll have to advise me. You'll have to tell me how I'm going to manage."

"You'll manage beautifully," Elizabeth exclaims. "You'll see that when it happens and when you have the child you'll forget all about not having distractions. . . ." She speaks reassuringly and, she hopes, cheerfully to Beatrix. And as Elizabeth talks, she finds to her relief that her voice does not betray her. She does not sound like a person whose heart is broken.

V

September-October '77

"It is winter," said the swallow, "and the chill snow will soon be here. In Egypt the sun is warm on the green palm-trees, and the crocodiles lie in the mud and look lazily about them. My companions are building a nest in the temple of Baalbec, and the pink and white doves are watching them, and cooing to each other."

—OSCAR WILDE
The Happy Prince

1
—

WHEN the High Holidays come again, Elizabeth goes with Isaac and the children to the Kirshner synagogue in the city, and they walk inside with the other families, dressed up in their best fall clothes. She sits with the girls in the balcony, and the other women nod to her, or touch the children as they walk by. The women who speak to Elizabeth ask when the new baby is due. The others just look at her. They know something about the store. Elizabeth senses their curiosity and turns away.

She sits among them, but she feels perfectly alone. She hears the voices of the congregation; she sees the letters in the book in front of her, and her lips move, but she is muffled by her own thoughts. She knows she has lost something. She does not belong to them in the same way anymore.

Elizabeth read one summer in Henry Adams about the monastery on Mont-Saint-Michel, which is surrounded by water on three sides at low tide. The tide came in each day and transformed the place into an island, sometimes trapping tourists overnight. Elizabeth has been that kind of tourist, taking day trips, and staying longer each time, until, at last, entranced, she forgot about the time. But she was a tourist in the other direction, traveling off the island to tour the mainland, leaving her small and perfect world. The water rushed in behind her.

She shouldn't be thinking these things in shul. Feeling sorry for herself on this day. What is she, if she can't sit among her neighbors without knowing she has their approval? What was she thinking all those years? Was all her time in shul really only about other people, so that now, isolated, she cannot pray? Disappointing, unflattering, but perhaps it's true. Perhaps a certain sociability and desire to please are all she ever had for God.

Despair and confusion wash over her. She has to steady herself, steel herself to sit there during the long morning Rosh Hashanah service. She finds the pages for Sorah and Brocha. She listens to Rav Isaiah when he talks about tshuvah, return, repentance, and redemption.

"Have we been the people we should have been?" Isaiah asks, far below in the sanctuary. "Are we now the people we should be? Every act we do should be *al kiddush hashem*—for the glory of God. Every deed to make his name holy. In our homes, in our streets, in our work. Our lives should be lived with one purpose. There should be no division. We must never think: Here, I am a good pious Jew, but there, in the office, something else. We should be the same in every place, at every time. We should be conscious of His presence. All the days of our lives."

Rav Isaiah's voice floats up through the hushed building to the balcony, and Elizabeth can just make out his small dark figure. She knows that what he says is true, and yet the message is distasteful to her; she cannot separate the words from the speaker. She cannot forget her audience with him in Kaaterskill. The Rav spoke to her then; and, when she tried to reply, he dismissed her and her ideas, he ordered her to give up her project. He crushed her utterly.

They troop back to the apartment, Elizabeth and Isaac and the children along with their guests, the Krackowers, an English couple with their son. The girls set the table for ten: the heavy white cloth, with a pale, almost imperceptible, wine stain, the palest pink, where Sorah once knocked over a glass, the white dishes and crystal, the silver challah plate and the silver knife; two round challahs, covered with the embroidered challah cover, garlands of embroidered flowers, and looping silver fringe. Elizabeth looks over at the table from the kitchen, and it is ready. Every spoon and decorative leaf. She is pouring honey from her big jar into the silver honey bowl with its long silver spoon. At the last minute, after they make motzi and eat the challah, she will cut the apples, because the girls won't eat them when they're brown. She will dribble the apples with honey for a sweet new year. Brocha will complain she didn't get enough, but the honey will be sweet and smooth on her tongue. And Elizabeth will be sad. She feels her sadness growing within her. Weeks have passed, and her sadness is starting to show, as the baby shows now. As always, she carries round and low.

She is angry with herself for always thinking about her loss. She calls everyone to the table and Isaac says kiddush. She serves the food —salad with gefilte fish, chicken soup with kreplach, roast turkey and stuffing, tsimmes, orange and gold with sweet potatoes and carrots, two kugels. She serves from one end of the table, and Isaac carves the turkey at the other. The apartment is warm, because they have left the oven on low to reheat the food for the two-day holiday. Isaac talks to the Krackowers' teenaged son about what he is learning at the yeshiva.

After dessert and the grace after meals, after the Krackowers are gone, the girls go to their rooms to play. They play for a long time quietly by themselves. Elizabeth only hears a murmur from the two bedrooms.

"You should lie down," Isaac tells her as he puts away the ben-schers.

"All right," she says.

"Elizabeth. You seem so tired."

"I am tired," she says.

"You've been working too hard," he tells her. "Cooking all this, and cleaning."

She brushes crumbs off the tablecloth. "That's what it is," she says.

"What did you say?"

"That's the strange thing. The holidays feel like work, suddenly. I suppose they were work before, but they never felt that way. It never used to be so hard."

"You know why it's hard," Isaac says. He assumes she means the pregnancy, but he misunderstands her.

This year cooking and cleaning and even the praying are hard, because Elizabeth is divided from what she used to be, and the tide is in, and she didn't get back in time. She is standing on the shore; she is clearing the table, shaking out the tablecloth over the water. Preparing the house for Rosh Hashanah was sweet before. It was sweet to begin the new year by listening to the Rav. Elizabeth had listened to him with the others and rededicated her life each year. Today, when she heard the new Rav's words, she believed that they were true, and when she watched him speak, she knew that she would follow him, but following is work. She admits to herself the conflict between her own desires and his decisions; she admits the disjunction between her ideas and his plan for the Kehillah. The disjunction was always there, but it was inside of her. Private, familiar. The Rav broke it open, wounding her, making her confess it.

She walks down the hall and passes the little girls' cramped bedroom. Sorah, Ruchel, and Brocha are playing there, still dressed up in their pretty dresses, still wearing their lockets. They are playing hospital, with their dolls as patients on the beds. The hospital is full of sick dolls and teddy bears tucked under white guest-towel sheets. Medicine is distributed, shots given, the sash of Sorah's purple dress serves as a Band-Aid, wrapped several times around the head of Brocha's bear.

"I'm going to take his blood pressure," Ruchel says.

"No, me!" says Sorah.

Of course, all the girls are playing they are nurses.

2

THAT autumn the leaves turn late in the little parks. Red edges brighten the slight elms that line the streets. The tree in front of the Rav's building is small and protected by a black wrought-iron enclosure, but when the sapling turns, its scant leaves are transformed into a shower of gold. Inside their apartment Isaiah and Rachel hardly have time to notice. They are still grappling with the mountain of paperwork in the library, the bills and taxes, the Rav's will.

Many years ago the Kehillah bought the Washington Heights apartment for the late Rav. The deed was written out for him, in his name, Rav Elijah Kirshner, and there was no mortgage. The Rav owned the apartment free and clear. The house in Kaaterskill, however, was not paid for by the congregation. The rebbetzin Sarah bought the place in 1948 with reparation money sent her as the sole survivor of her family. She went up to Kaaterskill that summer and found the white house near to the synagogue. She chose it for its placement on the hill and for the large front porch, the beech tree at the side, and the large sloping garden. After picking out the house, Sarah wrote a check for the entire cost, ten thousand dollars. For five thousand more she could have purchased the two lots behind it on the hillside. The rebbetzin had the money, but the extra expense seemed extravagant to her then. The two lots were later subdivided, and Sarah regretted her decision. After her death Michael King

bought the lots and subdivided them again. That was something Sarah
Kirshner had never envisioned. She could not have imagined that—
the land chopped up that way. But, of course, there were many things
she had not dreamed of—that her porch would be glassed in, and her
beech tree cut down. She had not realized then that her Schumacher
curtains would fill with dust, or that her garden would be overgrown
with blackberry bushes, or that her son Jeremy, her treasure, would
turn his back on the family. How could she have imagined any of it?
Even when she was dying, Sarah could not picture the future without
her guiding hand.

Regretting her mistake passing up the lots behind her house,
Sarah Kirshner bought another property in Kaaterskill. Few people in
the Kehilla know of this. She bought land fronting Coon Lake, a
beautiful arched piece of land, covered with trees and wildflowers,
stretching in a curve into the soft muddy sand, sucked by the water.
The Rav never went there after Sarah died. For twenty years the lake
property stood untouched and unvisited, but the Rav did not forget it
in his will. He wrote, "The apartment in Washington Heights and
the house in Kaaterskill, as well as the property at Coon Lake purchased by my wife Sarah, of blessed memory, I leave to my son
Isaiah."

Short and tersely written, the will's major section is devoted to
Isaiah's inheritance. A few paragraphs spell out the Rav's provision
for the Kirshner yeshiva; the gift of a certain set of books, the Rav's
volumes of Talmud, his tomes of Mishnah and the works of the
Jewish sages. These books were given to the school long ago and
form the core of the yeshiva library. All this is in order. Years ago the
Rav told Isaiah and Rachel of his wishes, and they have already made
their own plans. They will sell the Coon Lake property to raise
money in the Rav's memory for the Kollel of advanced and needy
Talmud students.

When the Rav's attorney opens the will in the Rav's library,
Isaiah and Rachel just glance at it together. They know what the will
contains. They scarcely have to read the document. Then one sentence stops them short. Just a few words at the bottom of the page,
but Isaiah catches his breath when he reads them. Angry tears start in
Rachel's eyes. In disbelief they read the words twice, and then three

times. "All the books that are not part of the gift to the yeshiva, my entire personal library in the city and in Kaaterskill, I leave to my son Jeremy." The words are typed neatly, dated March 1977, the last year of the Rav's life. Initialed by the Rav, *E.K.*

Isaiah and Rachel, and the Rav's nephews, can scarcely believe it; they don't want to believe it, and yet there it is, the gift to Jeremy of the Rav's entire library, his thousands of precious volumes. His rare commentaries and philosophic treatises, theological works in rare German editions, interleaved with notes in the Rav's own hand, the hundreds of volumes of German literature and poetry. The collection is magnificent in scope, an irreplaceable record of the Rav's intellectual development. And the Rav has left the treasure to Jeremy. A sudden and spectacular inheritance.

For months no one in the family speaks of the will. There is the funeral, and then the tremendous work of the transition, shouldered by Isaiah and Rachel. Knowing of the bequest, Jeremy, too, is silent. He goes away to Italy for the High Holidays, as he had often done in the past. On the library shelves and on tables throughout the Rav's locked apartment, the books wait, their spines hooped with gold, their gilt-edged pages shining in the dusty light. They are uncataloged, many unread for years, many touched only by the Rav's own hands.

However, in November, the holidays are over, and Jeremy has returned. It is time to speak of these things. Jeremy comes to his brother's door, and walks into the apartment above the Rav's locked and silent home. Isaiah and Rachel usher him in and take his coat. Their apartment is the same. They are still living as they were above the Rav's rooms, working like bees next to the sealed honeycomb.

"How are you?" Jeremy asks his brother.

"Thank God. And how was your trip?" Isaiah asks.

"It went well. I gave a paper in Milan."

"Come, sit down," says Rachel, and they sit, the three of them, in the living room. Isaiah and Rachel take the long old-fashioned sofa, and Jeremy the high-backed chair opposite. On the coffee table between them Rachel pours tea. She offers mandelbrot, her mother's recipe.

"These are very good," Jeremy says. "Delicious. No, thank you, this is enough. Look, as I said earlier, on the phone, I want to talk about the books."

"We had an idea about them," Isaiah says. "We wanted—we thought the best would be to give them to the yeshiva library and to keep them together with the others for the students."

"No, I don't want to do that," Jeremy says.

His blunt dismissal startles them. Isaiah looks up, surprised and pained. "I don't understand," he says.

"What don't you understand?" Jeremy asks.

"We thought," says Isaiah, "there are so many. They are so specialized—"

"I think I'm capable of reading them," Jeremy says.

"Yes, of course, but you don't, you don't learn from them—and they are part of the whole collection, the family collection."

"But father didn't leave them to the family," Jeremy says. "He left them to me."

"But, you know . . . well, what use would you have for them?" Isaiah asks.

"It's not a question of the use," says Jeremy. "They belong to me."

Rachel looks at Jeremy sharply. "But what would you do with them?"

"What do you care?" he asks. His voice is light, but his words are cold.

They just look at him, their eyes confused and full of grief.

"But I don't understand," Isaiah says again.

"This is my inheritance, and I'm planning to take it," says Jeremy. "You got the houses, the property at Coon Lake, free and clear. I don't suppose you need the books as well."

"It's not for us. None of it is for us," Isaiah says.

"Well, I'm going to take them," Jeremy says. "I'm hiring movers to pack them. I need to bring them in downstairs to make an estimate. And in Kaaterskill."

"I think you should reconsider," Isaiah says.

"I'm not going to reconsider." Jeremy is impatient. "I was left one thing by our father, and I don't need to reconsider. You've taken everything else."

"We didn't take," Rachel says. "We gave constantly. And the houses aren't free and clear. We've had to mortgage both of them. Do you think we got the money to care for the Rav out of thin air? We had twenty-four-hour nursing. Do you think that was free? How dare you say we took. We gave constantly, and the money was the least of it."

"I need to get in with the movers to make an estimate," Jeremy says again.

"But what are you going to do with them?" Isaiah asks. "Where are you going to put them all?"

"I don't know. I might sell them." Jeremy sees them flinch at this, their eyes widen.

"You will," Rachel says slowly. "You will sell them, won't you?"

Jeremy's brown eyes are lively. He watches his brother and his brother's wife. After a moment he says, "I'll sell them to you."

"Sell them to us!" Rachel exclaims.

"How much would you want?" Isaiah asks slowly.

"I don't know. It's hard to put a price—I'd give them to you for fifty."

"Fifty . . . ." Isaiah's voice drifts off.

"Fifty—thousand dollars?" Rachel echoes.

Jeremy has shocked them. They sit there on the sofa helpless and miserable like a pair of children whose parents have gone away. They are good at that, acting childlike. Obedient. They have served and they have given. Of course, it is more complicated than mere filial love. Isaiah and Rachel depended on the Rav. They depend on him now. They would like to make Jeremy obedient to the Rav's memory, but he did not cling to his father, and he will not obey.

WHEN Jeremy has gone, Isaiah and Rachel don't speak. Rachel clears away the teacups and puts away the uneaten mandelbrot. Isaiah goes into his study, a smaller room than the Rav's library downstairs. He works at his desk, preparing for the shiur he will teach that afternoon, and he shakes his head as he reads. He doesn't understand. Even if Jeremy doesn't want to keep the books in the family, he doesn't see why he would deny them to the students, to all the young men at the yeshiva and the Kollel, the young minds desiring only to learn.

Isaiah goes to the kollel to teach his shiur. No one calls him the Rav. He is too new. He has been Rav Isaiah for too long, and now, in his forties, he is still to some extent thought of as the Rav's son, an aging but wholly conscientious Prince of Wales. He walks up the street to the yeshiva, where his class is waiting for him. They are young men dressed in dark trousers and white shirts, black hats and flyaway black jackets. They are nineteen and twenty years old, newly married; the first of them beginning their families in small apartments near the school. They have bright and eager eyes; they are anxious to please him.

Rav Isaiah opens his books and they open theirs. They are learning Talmud, and they are working their way through the teachings about contracts. For two hours Rav Isaiah guides them through the texts on the table. He explains the intricacies and nuances of language that binds and language that divides. Isaiah tests his young students, pressing them to look more carefully at the meaning of each word. But the conversation with Jeremy still rings in Isaiah's ears. It is the motivation Isaiah cannot fathom, the emotion underlying his father's bequest and Jeremy's flippant response. These trusts, these contracts, these things are freighted with feeling. This is the mystery; that these things can cause such pain.

At home Rachel is thinking about Jeremy too. She sits at the piano and as she plays, she thinks that she understands him very well. Her eyes are on the music, Bach. Her fingers pluck the notes from the keyboard, a thousand dark ripe berries; and as she plays she shakes her head because she knows Jeremy, and this is what she should have expected from him. It is a shanda. He is a disgrace. Rachel opens the piano bench and puts her music inside. Then she takes the extra set of keys she keeps there and she walks downstairs.

Gently, Rachel lets herself in to the Rav's large first-floor apartment. Softly, she walks through the living room and dining room with its long polished table and twelve chairs. The Rav's rooms are cool and perfectly quiet. Although the Rav has only just passed away, the apartment feels eerily still, as though no one has lived here for years. Rachel stands at the doorway to the Rav's library and looks at the books lying there on the shelves. They are dark, and their bindings smooth. They fill the shelves and cover the walls up to the ceiling. There is something eerie about the books, something sad, but she does not know what it is. Rachel looks at them and thinks simply that it would be tragic if they were sold. Isaiah must not give them up.

&

IN KAATERSKILL, the first week of November, snow falls thick on the houses and banks up high on the piles of dead leaves. The trees drift in sudden white. The gardens where the summer people played at badminton and growing vegetables are now white and still. Laden with snow, the branches of the Birnbaums' fir tree swoop down to the ground. And the town belongs again to the year-rounders. Old Hamilton stands on the porch of his store and looks out at the street.

It's coming down fast. Hamilton measures his cane against the rising snowbank. He can compare the accumulation to that of other winters, this storm to other early storms. He remembers as far back as the blizzard of '39. He remembers more about this place than any of the summer people ever could. The way in fall the mountain turns all at once as if it were catching fire. The way the winter comes down— an avalanche of ice.

Michael King is walking home from his office. This winter is like a fresh white page after his disastrous summer. After his renters' disappearance King spent days on phone calls and interviews with the police. But despite the best efforts of the police, neither Michael Fawess and his brother and their families, nor any of their money, could be traced. Fawess's deposit check did not clear at the bank, and King was left with the two huge empty houses built on speculation.

But now, in winter, as the snow comes down, King's eyes are bright, for he's found a buyer for the two lake properties. He can already feel that huge mortgage lifting from him, and his cash-flow problems easing up. He'll have the money now to bid on some new land. He'll have the money to start again.

As soon as he gets in the door, he sits down in the den and calls his father, Herb Klein. "Great news, Dad," he tells his father in Miami. "I've got a buyer."

"You're kidding," Herb says. Michael can hear how surprised his father is, and how glad.

Herb and Michael are close. There were times when Michael sorely tried Herb's patience. Not least of these, when Michael changed his last name from Klein to King. Herb tried to talk his only son out of the name change, to no avail, and when Michael went ahead anyway, Herb burst out in aggravation, "I just want to ask you one thing: Tell me, please, just what are you going to be King *of*? Windsor Castle? What are you going to name my grand-children? Louis Quatorze? Catherine the Great? Was Klein so bad?" Nevertheless, despite the name change, and Michael's non-Jewish wife, Jackie—despite everything—even the money burned in the old potbelly stove—Herb is proud of his son. He invests in King's Real Estate enterprises; about half his savings. He is his son's confidant and tax advisor and—as he himself admits—his son's greatest fan.

"A buyer. Wonderful," Herb says.

"And they paid cash," says Michael.

His father doesn't speak for a moment. Then he says, "What kind of money is this cash?"

"What do you mean what kind of money?"

"I mean, where has this money been?"

"No trucking. No drugs," Michael says. "A Hasidic family. Five kids and the grandparents."

"A Hasidic family. *Veyismere*," says Herb. "With the white beards? The black hats?"

"Yeah. Cash on the table."

"And they approached you like this? In the black coats?"

"The father came, the lawyer came. They're in diamonds."

"Michael, you're going to sell to these people?"

"What are you so worried about, Dad?"

"I don't trust them."

"You don't think their money's good?"

"I didn't say that. I've never trusted them, the Hasidim. They're a crazy group of people. They have a crazy way of looking at the world. Michael, this is why I stopped coming to Kaaterskill in the first place. These people started coming up. They were walking up and down the streets. It's like a funeral, all dressed in black, the black suits. I've always been proud of being what I am, a Jew first and last, but—"

"Dad, I thought you swore by cash. Remember?" Playfully, Michael recites his father's mantra: " 'Cash was my philosophy since *dental* school. Cash payment before I even looked at them. Before they even opened their *mouths*.' "

"All right, all right. I'm not going to tell you what to do," his father says. "I'm just saying that—"

"Listen, listen, I've got my eye on a new property," Michael interrupts.

"What, you're spending already? You get out of the hole and you want to spend?"

"This is the best property in the three towns."

"You said that last time."

"Listen, it's huge. Half a mile on Coon Lake. There's room for five, six cabins there. Belonged to the old Kirshner rabbi, but he just sat on it. Now the son is selling."

"Kirshner owned all that? Who would have thought," Herb muses. "Who's listing it?"

"Schermerhorn," says King.

"Victoria Schermerhorn? An anti-Semite."

"What are you talking about?"

"Do I have to spell it out?"

"She's like any other listing agent—"

"Michael, be careful—"

"She just wants the best price like anyone else. And I've heard the rabbi and his wife are motivated. They want to close out the deal fast."

"Ha," says Herb. "Buyer beware."

"Dad," says Michael.

"Listen to me," Herb says. "I'm going to tell you about Schermerhorn. You see those Hasidim coming up, the ones from Borough Park, the ones from Washington Heights? The way they look to you. That's how you look to her."

"Oh, come on—"

"Just you listen. Don't do any business with that woman Schermerhorn."

"Dad, she's the listing agent," Michael protests. He can't help laughing at his father's voice.

After dinner Michael and his wife and their little girl, Heather, sit by the fire. The poodle, Duchess, curls up at Michael's feet. "You see, Jackie," Michael tells his wife, "I told you it would work out." For it seems to him that the past few days have erased all of the summer's difficulties. He is full of hope again; his wife, proud and happy. The future expands before them as generously now as when they married, and Jackie, just graduated Sarah Lawrence, said she couldn't wait to leave the city, with all the crime and vandalism. They pour champagne and give Heather a sip. They play Monopoly and let Heather win.

As for the conversation with his dad, Michael doesn't give it a second thought. He isn't afraid of Victoria Schermerhorn, or even Judge Taylor. And all the dark predictions would be more convincing if his father had enjoyed them less.

VI

March–May '78

Pale, where the winter like a stone has been lifted away, we
emerge like yellow grass.
Be for a moment quiet, buffet us not, have pity upon us,
Till the green come back into the vein, till the giddiness pass.

—Edna St. Vincent Millay
Northern April

1
—

Eva is home from the hospital. In early March, the trees stripped bare, she comes home with Saul and all her flowers, an orchid plant, a small blooming gardenia, and roses from Andras and Nina. Her favorite color, yellow. She is still sick, but she is home, frail but grateful. She and Saul sit together in the living room of their brownstone with Maja and Andras. They talk about the children, Renée and Alex, who are home with Nina.

"Listen, the truth is she plays badly," Andras says of Renée.

"Not so badly," says Eva.

"Oh, she does. Very badly."

"She is a young girl, a child," says Saul. "Admittedly, she is no Mozart."

Andras says, "But Nina is determined she should play the piano. She sits with her, and she works with her—"

"Did Nina play once?" asks Maja.

Andras shakes his head. "Now Renée has to play in a recital."

"Oy veyismere," says Eva.

"It's the old expression," says Maja. "It will end in tears."

"What do you mean? It's already beginning in tears," says Andras. "She has to practice. She has to practice *right,* or she'll only be practicing her mistakes. She should memorize. She should do it with the metronome. Nina spends hours on this. She worries about it constantly—that Renée isn't exerting herself. She isn't living up to her potential. I think the only solution is for Nina to play the recital herself."

Maja laughs at this, and Saul says he's sure Nina would do a good job, even if she doesn't play, and then Maja and Andras laugh some more. But Eva says sharply, "No." She looks at Andras and says, "No, Andras. Stop. She is your wife. You must never say this kind of thing. You mustn't laugh. You must defend her."

They look at her, confused. The laughter is gone.

"It's all right," Andras tells Eva. "Please. Don't upset yourself."

"It isn't all right," Eva says.

"No, of course not," Maja reassures her. "It was only in fun."

"But don't." Eva looks at Andras. "Don't do it anymore."

"No. We won't," he tells her, not even sure what he is promising.

"Do you want something to drink?" Saul asks Eva. "Are you hungry?"

"I want to talk to Andras," she says to Saul and Maja.

"Of course," Maja says. "Let's take the flowers in the kitchen. Let's get the roses into some water."

"You know," Eva tells Andras when the others have gone, "I feel the way everyone does coming out of the hospital."

"And how is that?" Andras asks her.

"I feel how . . . the time is short," she says. But this isn't really what she wants to say. She doesn't know how to put it. She has realized something about Andras. Suddenly she saw it when they were talking about Nina. Her mind keeps whispering it. He doesn't love his wife.

"Oh, don't worry about me," Andras is telling her.

"But I do worry," she says.

"Just get better," he tells her. "The rest doesn't matter."

"The rest is all that matters," she says.

Then it seems to Andras that the whole day, the relief to see her home, the giddy silliness, is gone. He can't keep the front up any longer, and he sinks down next to Eva and takes her hand.

"If you are happy . . ." Eva begins. She is trying to find the words. "You just have to decide. If you . . . mind about her, about everything. If you allow yourself to be happy, then I wouldn't worry anymore. You mustn't still hold on to me. Not me."

"We don't need to talk about this now," Andras says. "It's not important now."

"It's the most important thing. There is nothing else."

Andras lets go of Eva's hand, but she grips his tightly.

"You were like my child," Eva says. "Maja and I loved you like our own child. We were selfish of you, and we didn't want to part with you. And after the war when you were just a boy—a young man coming to us, we thought we would be to you two mothers because you had none. But, Andras, you don't need two mothers; you need your wife. Are you listening?" she asks him.

"Yes," Andras whispers. His sister's voice is so many things to him, experienced, and sweet; both playful and commanding.

"It was wrong of us to laugh at her and talk about her. And it was wrong of you to let us, Andras," Eva adds sharply. "You should never let anyone speak against Nina."

"Not even you?" Andras says.

"Especially not me. You should—you should live as you deserve. You should be in love with your wife. And think of her and hold her in your mind so that you have no room for thinking your sad thoughts."

Andras looks away for a moment. He sees Maja and Saul coming in from the kitchen.

"This is what you must promise me," Eva tells him. "That you will be happy."

"Eva, that's not something to promise."

"And why not?" she asks.

He looks at her. Being happy is not something anyone can decide. It's not as simple as that.

Why isn't it simple? she is asking with her eyes. She expects it of him.

ALL that week in the evenings Nina cooks for Eva and she sends Andras over to Eva's house with food. Of course, Maja is there every day to help, but Nina insists on doing all the shopping and the cooking for her sister-in-law.

Andras sees that Eva is trying to be gracious as she accepts the help. Eva feels overwhelmed by Nina's groceries and kugels; her kitchen is invaded; her pantry rearranged. But Eva does not say anything. Eva does not argue with the facts. She can no longer take care of the house and the meals herself. She cannot dress herself. Her husband must do that for her. Nor can she laugh out loud as she used to. The illness and her constant knowledge of it have not crushed Eva's spirit completely, but they have snuffed her laughter out.

In the weeks to come Andras sees these changes in Eva, but he does not speak of them. He goes to work, and he takes the children to visit their aunt. He delivers Nina's meals. And when he sees Eva he tries to encourage her and speak to her. He always tries, although Eva is less interested than she used to be in Andras's life. This is the hardest change of all. Eva no longer has the strength to be Andras's advisor and confidante; his wry and indulgent listener. Andras had not realized before how much he had depended on her. But he feels the loss when he visits Eva alone. The day Eva came home from the hospital was the last time Eva spoke to Andras in the old direct way. Now she neither questions nor encourages him. Just as she no longer bakes for Andras, she has no chiding advice to buoy him up.

One raw March day as Andras leaves Eva's house, his throat catches. As the door closes behind him, he stands on the brick steps and almost cries. And a kind of prayer rises up in him, although he knows no prayer he makes will do Eva any good. The ideas are confused in his mind but they rush out of him. The words are on his lips, although incoherent; partly a prayer to God and partly a resolve to himself. If he could be like Eva. If he could see what Eva sees in the world. If he could become more like her, then maybe she would live.

THE spring is late, and the days cold. The ice has not melted when Andras drives gingerly through Brooklyn to Cecil's house. He and Nina and the children glide past buildings in worse and worse repair, the front steps chipped and cracked, the brick town houses desolate in the gray weather. There are kids drinking and vaulting over fences, houses with sheets strung up in the windows instead of curtains. He parks as close to Cecil's house as he can, and Nina hurries Renée and Alex out of the car. She is holding a gift for the Birnbaums' new baby. Cecil and Beatrix have a baby girl.

"We're having a shalom bat," Beatrix told Nina on the phone.

"What is that?" Nina asked uncertainly.

"A welcoming party. Instead of a shalom zachar," Beatrix said. "I thought it was absolutely barbaric that there are welcoming parties for boys but not for girls. We're having a naming too. I suppose you didn't have them in Argentina."

"Is it an English custom?" Nina asked. Girls are always named in shul. Never at home.

"No, I think it's American. Apparently they're quite common now," Beatrix said in her breezy way.

Despite what Beatrix has heard, it is clear that most of the guests at Cecil's place on Brooklyn Avenue have never been to a shalom bat. The brick house is crowded with Kaaterskill families. The Landauer and the Shulman children are there, dressed up and looking around curiously, wondering what will be done to the baby. The Sobels are there, and Beatrix's mathematician friends from Queens College and Courant. There are colleagues of Cecil's in rumpled jackets and the occasional tie, as if unsure exactly what the occasion requires. In chairs Cecil's elderly aunts sit with paper plates at a slant on their short laps. They are buttoned up in dark dresses, their pocketbooks standing like small ottomans at their feet. Cecil's parents have long since passed away, and they peer down at their house from black-and-white photographs on the bookcases. The furniture is all the same as it was thirty years ago, if shabbier. The piano is there as it was.

In his freshly pressed suit and tie, Jeremy Kirshner stands a little apart, watching with his sharp brown eyes. Cecil's sister, Regina, is organizing the food and drinks. The glass doors between the living room and dining room are open, and the dining-room table is laden with Cecil's favorite food, a Scandinavian smorgasbord of the most exotic kinds of herring, smoked and cured fish. It is all tangy and salt encrusted, and there is a great need for crackers, cheese, and seltzer.

Cecil stands up. He is holding his sleeping week-old baby, small and curled up into herself. Beatrix stands next to him wearing a lime-green mohair sweater and a necklace of amber crystals that hang like rock candy from a string.

"Thank you for coming," Cecil says to the assembled.

Then Beatrix announces, "We are naming our child Attalia Ada Kahan Birnbaum. Attalia is for Cecil's grandmother Ottalie, Ada for the great English mathematician, Kahan is my surname, Birnbaum, Cecil's. No hyphen," she adds.

There is some confusion among Cecil's Kaaterskill friends. What a strange compound name; what an odd assortment. And the first name, Attalia—its connotations are not good. Everyone looks at the sleeping baby. The name is just short of Jezebel.

"And there is something else we wanted to tell you," says Cecil. "As some of you know, Beatrix has been offered a post at her old college in Oxford, Somerville. We have thought about it and discussed the question exhaustively—"

"Exhaustingly," says Beatrix.

"It is a fine position for Beatrix," Cecil says, "and an excellent research opportunity for me. As you know, my work focuses on manuscripts in Oxford itself. But I have lived in this house all my life —and, of course, in Kaaterskill. And I am a New Yorker. I promised myself long ago that I would never be driven out of this neighborhood or participate in any sort of white flight. But the state of academia in this country is another story. The condition of the arts, the stagnation at the Met, the complete decay of legitimate theater. These are conditions that are becoming intolerable. The decline of the great scholarly institutions in particular. Deteriorating academic standards, grade inflation, and corruption at all levels. I have decided to go back with Beatrix to England. I am going to leave the city."

Having made this pronouncement, Cecil gives Beatrix the baby and begins pouring schnapps for his startled friends and colleagues.

"Slivovitz?" he offers Jeremy Kirshner.

"A little," says Jeremy.

He is still holding his baby gift, a copy of *Mots d'Heures: Gousses, Rames,* with its bilingual puns: "*Un petit d'un petit / S'étonne aux Halles / Un petit d'un petit / Ah! degrés te fallent. . . .*" He sees how pleased Cecil is to have caused such a stir.

"What about the house?" Nina Melish is asking Cecil. "What about the house in Kaaterskill?"

"Well, of course I'll have to sell it," Cecil says.

"Are you going to give it to Regina?" Nina asks.

"This I can promise," says Cecil. "I will never sell the place to Michael King. Never. If I stood to lose all the money I've put into it over the years, I would never sell to him."

"I think we'll have to rent it at first," says Beatrix.

"Preferably to a large family." Cecil is still thinking of avenging himself on King. "With noisy children so they can run around in back. Boys with peyyes, screaming and playing baseball with their tallit katan hanging out."

As Cecil is speaking, Jeremy catches a glimpse of Cecil's sister, Regina, bringing out some cake, and he sees her face, half averted but soft with disappointment. Ah, he thinks, but the parents didn't give the house to Regina, and Cecil won't give it to her either. The house will never be hers. Jeremy is an expert on such matters, and he knows. Regina will never live in that house again. That is the truth about inheritances. That they have nothing to do with continuity, the maintenance of property. The power of legacies is all in separation, in the conflict between the older and the younger, the alienation of the living from the dead. What a marvelous fiction, he thinks, that places and things, or even ideas, can be transmitted over time, that property can be kept in families, or that the families themselves will remain intact. That Cecil would continue to come up to Kaaterskill every summer, and Regina with him, brother and sister in their old rooms with their storybooks and toys. Why not? their parents wonder from their black-and-white photographs on the bookcases. Why shouldn't everything continue as it was, in perpetuity? Why should Regina be married and living in Los Angeles? Why should the house be sold, when it is Cecil's? The white porch is there waiting for him, the tulip and iris bulbs in the cellar. Cecil's bicycle and Regina's, waiting in the garden shed.

Avoiding the crowd at the buffet table, Elizabeth sits in an arm-chair next to the sofa. Above her head, heavy drapes are pulled back to reveal windows gray with the dirt of the city. She is tired. Her own baby is due in two weeks. Everyone asks her how she is feeling, and she says, Thank God, I'm fine. They ask her if she thinks it will be a boy or a girl, and she says it will be a girl—that she can't imagine having anything else. Someone backs onto the couch carefully with a plate of food. Andras.

"Oh. How are you?" he says to her. He hadn't seen her there in the corner.

"I'm fine," Elizabeth says automatically. She looks at Andras. There is something about him. He looks subdued and suddenly much older. His face is gaunt. There is something tired in his eyes. How different people look in the city.

"How is Eva?" Elizabeth asks him.

"Somewhat better," he tells her.

"Thank God," Elizabeth says.

"And how about you?" Andras asks. "Are you looking at new business opportunities?"

"Oh, no," she says. "There will be the baby, for one thing. I suppose I've lost enough money playing store. I won't do it again."

"Why not?" he asks. "You did well last summer."

She doesn't answer. Then she says, "I was rather disappointed."

He considers this. "I thought you were doing remarkably well," he says gently.

She just shrugs, a little defensive.

"The way it ended was unfortunate, but you should try again."

"No—I don't think so," Elizabeth tells him.

"But you enjoyed it."

"It was very hard work," she says lightly.

"Of course. But you seemed to like it."

"Well, I did enjoy it. Briefly," she says.

The party buzzes around them. Brocha comes and asks if she can have some candy.

"Just one? One? Not even *one*?" Brocha asks tragically.

"You could do something new," Andras says.

Elizabeth shakes her head.

"Why not?"

"Well, I suppose I don't really have the time, or the energy. In another life," Elizabeth says, wryly, "perhaps I'd be a great retailer—

or a playwright or an aviator. A farmer. Who knows what? As it
is—"

"Elizabeth—"

She looks at Andras. She is surprised, somehow, to hear him call
her by her name. Andras leans over, speaking conspiratorially. "Elizabeth," he says, "this is the United States of America. You can do
whatever you damn well please."

She stares at him. She has not heard words like these spoken to
her before. No one has ever put it to her this way. As if she could act
without questions and considerations. Without permission. As if she
could really do what she wanted and weren't connected to anybody,
the Kehilla or the children.

She bursts out laughing. All around her the party is humming and
the children are dashing in and out. The coatrack is melting away
under its load of coats. Beatrix is having a heated argument with one
of her colleagues. Elizabeth just laughs. It is delightful; it is funny.
Not so much the truth of what Andras has said, but the novelty of
hearing it.

2

—

MILES Taylor is a great walker in all weather. At seventy-three he is a
little bent, but wiry. He was a sprinter in high school, and he used to
run outside in summer, racing the deer, in his younger days. He walks
now. Walking gives him time to think. This is one of the secrets of his
composure. On newly shoveled sidewalks and on hard-packed snow,
he walks up to Coon Lake. Small and serene, it is not as big as
Mohican Lake, but to his eye it is more beautiful even in winter, the
surface frozen and pure white, marred only by the orange traffic
cones warning of thin ice. At one time the better part of the lakefront
belonged to the Taylors. Taylor's whole childhood, the place was in
the family. Years ago the judge's uncle sold it to old Mr. Rubin.
Rubin took half for himself and then subdivided again. The land
changed hands several times, but the biggest parcel went intact to old
Rabbi Kirshner and his wife.

Taylor looks across the ice to where the lake curves. Great trees,
bare and black, have grown up to the frozen water's edge. When he
was just a small boy he found arrowheads here, and fox. When he was
older he camped there, and one summer when he and his father
fought, he hid out at Coon Lake for three days, until at last he
decided to come home. His mother came to him in tears and forgave
him everything, and his father beat him for making his mother cry.

He walks on with his gloved hands in his pockets, his breath
pluming out in front of him, his step sure on the ice. He walks to

Kendall Falls, to a small house. Just a converted summer bungalow, really. Nothing much. There is a little snow pit of a yard, a picket fence that's down in places, revealing chicken wire. Taylor opens the low gate. "Hello, Billy," he calls to the little boy in the yard. Billy is working on some snowmen, a snow family, rather short and stocky, with ski hats and prunes for eyes. "How are you?" Taylor asks.

"Good," says Billy.

"Is your mother home?"

"Yeah, she's here," says Billy, looking up, round faced, round eyed. He's been chubby all his ten years.

Taylor raps on the door, and it opens to reveal Candy Walker, her long hair spread out over her purple sweater like spun gold.

"Hello, Judge," she says. "Come in!" He follows her into the living room and she turns off the television.

"I hope I'm not intruding," he says. "Stopping by like this."

"No. It's good to see you," says Candy. "Come in. What can I bring you? Cocoa? Would you like a drink?"

"Why, thank you," he says. "Cocoa would be fine."

Candy heats up the kettle and Taylor sits still on the rust plaid sofa.

"What brings you out here. To Kendall Falls?" she asks.

"Well, I thought I'd come by," Taylor says. "To talk to you, to see how you are. And Bill junior. He's a fine boy."

Candy nods. "Thank you."

"And what grade is he in now at school?"

"Fifth," she says.

Taylor shakes his head. "How fast," he says, "how fast they grow. I don't suppose you've heard about Coon Lake," he says.

She shakes her head.

"I'm afraid he's going after it."

"Who?" she asks, and then answers her own question in a hushed voice. "King."

"He seems bound and determined to ruin what's left of Kaaterskill," says Taylor, "and ruin it quick. He rented half Mohican Lake to the Arabs, and now that they're gone, he turns around like that"— Taylor snaps his fingers—"and sells it to the Jews. Now he wants to build up Coon Lake. You know, I grew up on that lake."

Candy nods.

"I had a little boat when I was, hmm, about the age of Billy junior there. You know what I christened her? Yes, we christened her with a cider bottle, and she was called the *Mayfly*. Peter Wycherly used to take her out. She was a most unseaworthy wreck. We capsized regularly. But we used to take her out fishing. We thought we were real fishermen. And astronomers . . ." He trails off, remembering. He and Peter had a telescope in those days, and they built radios and tried to invent things, some more and some less useful gadgets.

The kettle is boiling. Candy fills two mugs.

"Well," Taylor says, "I've got an idea to keep Coon Lake from King."

Candy hands the judge his cocoa. She is looking at him intently.

"I've come," he says, "to ask you for your help to do it."

She looks a little nervous. "I said before. I said at the beginning I would speak against him."

"I'm hoping you won't have to," says Taylor.

"You don't have to worry about me."

"Oh, I hope it won't come to that," Taylor says again. Then he asks after Candy's family. Her father and her cousins. He does not want to pursue the subject of the lake and Michael King.

But Candy thinks about it all after the judge walks off, declining to impose for dinner. She runs over Taylor's words in her mind. Of course, she'll help him. She doesn't question that. She owes everything to Judge Taylor. After the crash, when she lost Bill just one night before their wedding, the judge fixed things for her. Bill had joined the Marines already, and he was due to ship out just after the wedding. Judge Taylor drew up a wedding certificate for Candy and dated it one day early, so that she would be eligible for the service's widow's benefits. He drew up the wedding and the death certificates together.

Candy couldn't have raised Billy without that help from Taylor. She never could have had her own place. She'd be living at home even now. Still, it worries her, getting up in front of people and talking. She imagines that's what she would have to do—get up and tell everything.

She calls Billy in for dinner, and they bow their heads and say grace. They eat meat loaf, peas, and Tater Tots. Then Candy's home-made cheesecake for dessert, tall and creamy, topped with crushed pineapple. After she puts Billy to bed, Candy sits on the sofa in her narrow living room and curls up under her afghan of neon-bright acrylic yarn, no two squares alike. She is afraid of what it might do to Billy, hearing some of the things his mother did in her younger days, one thing in particular. Of course, she was a sinner then. She has told him that. But she's avoided telling him the details.

She takes out her Bible and opens it at random, and her eye falls on the opening of the book of Joel. And it is amazing to her. Now and always the words are like fire, bright and changeable. They are a mystery and prophecy to her: "That which the palmer worme hath left hath the locust eaten; and that which the locust hath left, hath the canker-worme eaten; and that which the canker-worme hath left, hath the caterpillar eaten. Awake ye drunkards, and weepe, and howle all yee drinkers of wine. . . . Lament like a virgine girded with sackecloth for the husband of her youth." She comes to this line and she gasps. For she, Candy, is the one mentioned in these lines, a widow in her youth, and really, like the virgin on the page, a widow before she was even married—although technically she was no virgin. She highlights the lines with her fluorescent pink marker. She repeats them underneath the afghan, the locust and the canker-worm and the caterpillar, the virgin lamenting for the husband of her youth. It is a sign to her. She is meant to speak out. It is a mission upon her. She will stand up and tell the truth about Michael King, and she will stand up and speak about Christ. How she came to Him and was reborn, washed, in his mercy, clean of her young fast life.

She will have to stand before the town and tell the truth. She will have to get up and speak about Michael King.

Her mother used to say, "Candy just grew up dramatic." That's the way people still think of her. For years now she's lived by herself with Bill junior, but they haven't forgotten what she was as a girl. She's a celebrity in Kendall Falls. Candy sees them watching her—what she does, the way she walks. She just had her tenth reunion at the high school, and she came with Bill junior. Everyone was there. They looked at her with curiosity, but also, Candy thought, a kind of respect. Even her cousin Janet Knowlton, who had always hated her.

It is because she is independent; because she is her own woman. Because now she is a Christian.

FRIDAY afternoon in Washington Heights, Elizabeth picks her way through the slush still covering the sidewalk. It doesn't feel like April. She is walking home from the bakery with challahs for Shabbes.

She was due last week, and she is tired all the time. She tries to rest while the children are in school. As always at the end, her lower back is hurting. Only walking helps. She tries to get out every day, even though it's so cold. Every day she goes out in her boots and her long down coat. The sights are not inspiring; the brick buildings, the steep flights of cement stairs.

Rivka, Elizabeth's neighbor from upstairs, comes along with her double stroller, and they walk back to their building together.

"A week late!" Rivka says when they get inside. She laughs. "You'll be having a bris on Pesach!"

"It will be a girl," Elizabeth says.

"How do you know?"

"I'm sure."

"Does it feel the way it did with the others?"

"Exactly the same," says Elizabeth.

"You never know," says Rivka, who has two of each.

Slowly, Elizabeth climbs the stairs. She unlocks her door and puts her purse and the bags of challah on the dining-room table. Any minute the children will be home from school, Isaac home from work. They don't talk much about the baby. What is there to say? It will be. As for names, they haven't picked a girl's name. If it is a boy there is the same boy's name they've had from the beginning. Chaim, for Isaac's father.

She and Isaac will have to bring up the crib from the basement and squeeze it into their bedroom. Once the baby is sleeping through the night, they'll rearrange the girls' rooms. Ruchel will move in with Chani and Malki, and the baby will sleep in the little girls' room. The desk Chani and Malki share will have to go in the living room. In the corner by the window.

Elizabeth straightens up the bookshelves, sorting the piles of papers, and the folded bills that collect there. Her glossy Olana catalog shines white among Isaac's dark books. She pulls it out and leafs through it, flipping through the Hudson River School pictures. There is the picture "Falls of the Kaaterskill," with the flaming trees and the rushing waterfall. There are notes next to the picture about its history and composition, but she looks at the color plate. Of course, it's only a picture of a picture. The plate can't do justice to the real painting, let alone the original experience.

She should vacuum, but her back is still hurting. The carpet needs to be replaced. It's all stained. She paces around. The apartment seems cluttered. There are no real paintings on the walls. There is only a mizrach, and a large family portrait, a photograph of all of them sitting in their best clothes, the children big eyed and serious.

Elizabeth sets the table for Friday-night dinner. Seven place settings. Six with the gold-rimmed china, and the seventh for Brocha with the good Wedgwood Peter Rabbit bowl and plate. She straightens the bookcase and sets the table, but this is not what she wants to do. She wants to stop feeling defeated. She wants her confidence back.

ON SUNDAY, after Isaac comes home from morning minyan, he takes Sorah and Brocha grocery shopping in the car. Chani, Malki, and Ruchel carry the laundry down to the basement as they do every week, load after load, whites, colors, delicates separated. In the kitchen Elizabeth puts up a lentil soup on the stove. An enormous soup, with flanken, lentils, black-eyed beans, carrots, celery, potatoes. She makes halishkas for the week as well, rolling ground beef mixed with rice into the steamed wet cabbage leaves. None of it seems particularly appetizing to her, but she keeps cooking. They'll eat some and freeze some. She is starting to feel now that she should make the most of the time. Her backache is getting worse.

"Elizabeth, sit down," Isaac says, when he and the younger girls return.

"I would rather move around," she says.

"You need to save your strength," he tells her.

She shrugs. "You know, it just hurts more when I sit," she says.

Isaac looks at her carefully. Of course they have been through this many times before, but it seems suddenly that they have skipped ahead in the conversation. "How much does it hurt?" he asks.

"Just the way it always does," Elizabeth says.

"But I mean, are you having contractions?" he whispers. He doesn't want the children getting all excited.

"No, just a backache," she says. "I think if I could walk around . . ."

"It's cold outside," he tells her.

"We could go somewhere after these finish cooking." She gestures to the halishkas in the slow cooker. "We could go to a museum, maybe." Isaac picks up the phone on the kitchen wall. "Who are you calling?"

"I'm calling my sister. You always want to go to museums before you go into labor."

"That's not true," she says.

"What about with Sorah?" he reminds her.

"That was one time."

Isaac tells Pearl on the phone that they might need her to come, that it's a possibility.

Elizabeth walks up and down in the hot kitchen. She makes a couple of kugels, goes through the refrigerator, and throws out some moldy fruit. The little girls go upstairs to Rivka's apartment to play and Elizabeth has Isaac rearrange the freezer. She is having mild contractions. She sips some water and lies down in the bedroom. "They're going away," she tells Isaac. "When I lie down they go away." She lies down and she sleeps.

Pearl comes at dinnertime, and Elizabeth calls the doctor. "They said I should come in and get checked," Elizabeth admits to Isaac.

"All right, so let's go," he says.

"Just let me get the dinner warm."

"Pearl can do that," Isaac says. He is starting to get nervous.

"Just let me get the dinner on the table," she says.

"Mommy, I can do that," says Chani.

"Mommy, you should go to the hospital, you really should," Malki tells her.

"We're going now," says Isaac, and he gets his car keys, his siddur, his tefillin, in case he'll need to be there in the morning.

"You can give them the halishkas," Elizabeth tells Pearl, "and the potato kugel. You can heat up these frozen vegetables." Isaac is pushing her out the door.

IT IS just a dull pain, bad only intermittently. There are long intervals when she is fine. And as they drive to the hospital Elizabeth feels better than she has in weeks. Driving away is a bit like getting on a plane and lifting off into the sky with all one's bags checked. There is nothing that can be done for the next few hours. They sit together in the yellow Mercury wagon and feel how strange it is to be driving without the girls in the back. How quiet the night is, the white-and-gray slush spinning up in front of the wheels. They do not speak. They are both feeling the strange pleasure of being alone in the car, driving somewhere alone together—even if it is to the hospital. Elizabeth keeps thinking how peaceful the drive is, the thought constantly breaking off, interrupted by each contraction, and then returning.

If she could have slept longer in the afternoon, the pain might have gone away altogether. If they had kept on driving, Elizabeth almost believes the contractions would have washed over her. But when she is admitted to the hospital everything comes apart. Her water breaks. The familiar pangs rip into real agony. She cannot think or feel anything else. The doctor is asking her, "Why did you wait so long?" but she cannot answer. They are wheeling her into the delivery room. They are asking Isaac, "Aren't you going to stay?"

She is gasping for air. She needs to slow down but she cannot. "You're almost there," the nurse tells her, but the crushing on her back won't stop.

The doctor is putting on her clear plastic jacket and her gloves; she is standing as if in a rainstorm to catch the baby. She is crouching down, prepared, but Elizabeth is not ready; she has not had time to think about it. She should have been excited; she should have been grateful, but she is not. In her unreadiness and her confusion the baby will be—the baby is—born.

It is more than she deserves. The baby is already born. They bring Elizabeth the screaming infant, perfect and wet, and they say, as she knew they would, "It's a little girl."

They change the sheets and her hospital gown, wash and weigh the baby, and give her to Elizabeth to hold. The nurses leave, and Isaac comes in.

"Do you know what we have?" Elizabeth asks.

He nods. He doesn't trust himself to speak. He sits down next to her and they look at their sixth daughter. She is curled up, tightly wrapped in a receiving blanket with a tiny white hat on her head. She opens one eye and looks at them balefully. She looks like Malki. Her face is solemn, one eye open, and the other shut.

"Half awake," Isaac says.

Elizabeth touches the baby's chin. It is as small as her fingertip. As she touches it, the chin retracts, drawing back into a point. Then even the point disappears. "Isaac," she says anxiously, "we forgot the camera."

"That's all right," he says.

"But we need it."

"I'll bring it tomorrow."

"Could you get it now?"

"Do you want me to?"

"Could you?" she asks. She feels suddenly that they must have the camera and take pictures. For they did not think about this baby; they did not pray for it, and still, by itself, the baby grew, developing without any help or any anticipation. They need to take a roll of film. They must do something. They can no longer neglect their child.

"All right, I'll get it," Isaac says. "I'll bring it up to your room."

HE DRIVES home and trudges up the stairs. As soon as his key turns in the lock, he hears them running to the door. There is a scuffle, and finally his sister opens it. She stands in the doorway with the children pushing behind her.

"Nu?" Pearl asks.

"What'd we get?" asks Chani. Their eyes are lit with expectation.

"A sister," Isaac says.

The children are hushed.

"Mazel tov," Pearl tells him.

"Why do we only get sisters?" Ruchel mutters.

"And Elizabeth is all right?" Pearl asks.

"She's fine and the baby is fine. Seven pounds ten ounces. Do you need to get back?"

"No, Moshe's home with the kids. I thought I'd be spending the night."

"If you'd wait just a little while, I need to bring the camera to the hospital. She said she wanted it."

"It'll be too late," Pearl says. "It's almost ten. They won't let you up."

THE next morning Isaac takes the girls to visit Elizabeth and the baby. They bring her food from home, drawings of rainbows, and smiling flowers, balloons. Brocha brings the baby a bag of toys. The newborn lies on her side in her hospital bassinet. Her five sisters fill the hospital room, all talking at once; but the baby sleeps through the whole thing.

"Isaac," Elizabeth says, "you have to get the bassinet back from Pearl."

"We already did, Mommy," Chani informs her importantly.

"And there is the box in the basement."

"We got it out," says Isaac.

"The zero-to-six-months box?"

"Yes," he says. "Don't touch that button," he tells Sorah, prying her away from the nurse's call button on the bed.

"Is someone knocking?" Chani asks.

"Hello, I'm the registrar," a small young woman tells them. "Congratulations. Are you ready to name the baby?"

"We can't name her yet," Isaac tells the registrar. They never record a baby's name until she is named and blessed in shul.

"You have thirty days," the registrar tells them. She reminds Chani of Mrs. Schermerhorn at the library. "You need to come back to the registrar's office on the fifth floor within thirty days to register the name on the birth certificate."

"All right," says Isaac. "Could you take our picture? Girls, come over here around the bed."

"Oh, you brought the camera," Elizabeth says, relieved.

She stays in the hospital one more night. Her tiny private room is high up on the tenth floor. Elizabeth lies in bed and looks out the window at the squat brick buildings below. In the bassinet at her side the exhausted baby sleeps, bundled up in her blanket, her little eyes closed.

Isaac will never admit he is disappointed. They will never speak of it, but Elizabeth knows. Isaac has wanted a son for such a long time. He has so wanted a son to sit next to him and daven with him at shul, to learn with him. A son who might be a scholar or even a rabbi and lead his own shiurim. A brilliant son of his own.

Elizabeth is disappointed too. She feels it more than she used to, the difficulty with girls, the confining of expectations. The difficulty that they are expected to be careful always and responsible, practical, nothing more. You don't magically become something else when you are responsible for six children. You don't magically create something when you have to ask permission just to try. There is always money to think about, and time, and then the rabbinic permission. The Kehilla is a tight little world, and a tighter one for women. A narrow place. Always safe and always binding.

Elizabeth looks at the infant lying there. She is sound asleep, even though her parents do not have a girl's name. Of course, the baby does not care that she has no name. She sleeps there with all her life before her. And yet so much has already been decided. Elizabeth feels that now.

On other nights like this she felt differently. What futures she had imagined for her daughters. What careers. They seem in retrospect like wild fantasies. She gave her girls English names, grand, she thought, sophisticated. Annette, and Margot, Rowena, Sabrina, and Bernice. It seems quixotic now, the way she used to sit with the children in the dark. On the edges of their beds she used to dream about her daughters; she used to spin lives for them out of books. As if the girls could be part one thing and part another; take flight from the rooftops of the brick apartment buildings and soar through the night sky—journalists, travelers, philosophers—and then somehow return home, floating down as in fairy tales, gliding down over the Heights, television aerials barely touching their feet.

3

———

VICTORIA Schermerhorn is nothing like her older sister. Ernestine was the artistic one in the family, studying dance and choreography, traveling to France and Spain. Since childhood Ernestine planned to be a dancer, and only after injury and illness and a failed first marriage did she return to the mountains and become the Kendall Falls librarian. Victoria also had artistic impulses, but she never left home to pursue them. She decided early, and partly from observing Ernestine, that she would become a businesswoman and that she would never marry; that she would earn enough to support her aged parents and to live as she pleased.

She sits at her desk at Victoria Schermerhorn Realty and she fills out paperwork, printing neatly in black ink. The radiator hums, and her assistant types in the outer office, and Victoria just works her way down the legal-sized forms in front of her, the purchase-and-sale agreement for the shore property on Coon Lake. She does not mind paperwork. In fact she likes it. She enjoys writing in the numbers and the names and terms. She looks up a moment. "Catherine," she says to her assistant, "who's there? I heard a car."

She comes out in time to see Catherine open the door for the black-clad couple from the city.

"Why, hello, Rabbi, hello, Mrs. Kirshner," says Victoria Schermerhorn. "I didn't expect you quite so soon. I'm writing up the P and S right now. I'm still drafting it, you see. May I get you something? Won't you come in and sit down? You must have got up early, would you like some coffee?"

"No, thank you," Isaiah says.

"All right, then," says Victoria, and she looks at Isaiah and Rachel with kind but appraising hazel eyes.

"We thought we might take care of the signatures this morning," Rachel says.

"That would be fine," says Victoria. "Although, to tell the truth, I wouldn't mind waiting another day or two. There is still a chance Taylor will raise his bid—he's fond of Coon Lake, you know. Then King, you see, will have to up the ante."

"No," says Rachel urgently, "we need to take care of this before —Isaiah's brother is coming up tomorrow, and we need to finish the business before then, set the closing date."

Victoria knits her brow at this. She wonders what the rabbi's brother has to do with the sale of the land, but she doesn't pry. "We've got everything ready to go with the sale to King. But, if you could hold out a few more days. I can only advise, but I know these characters, both of them, and we would be in a good position if we just"—she says the words slowly—"eased up, and played for time. I'm just the broker, I know that. It's your deal, but if it were my land I'd play it nice and slow. I'd take care, you see, not to sell myself short."

"We are quite anxious about this," says Isaiah. "About setting the closing date with King."

"We have to go back in the morning," Rachel says.

Victoria Schermerhorn looks at the two of them across her desk. She knits her fingers together and rocks back and forth ever so slightly in her chair. She speaks softly, as if thinking aloud. "It's quite a property you have; it's quite a plum there on the lake. I just don't like to see it go for less than fifty. Now, Taylor has the money, but he's tight with it. He'll take a position and he'll stick to it. He said forty, and he meant forty. But he could raise it to King's forty-five. He could go higher. I've known Miles Taylor for thirty-five years, and I know that when he wants something nothing keeps him from it. I'm wondering what he's planning with his poker face."

"But we're only here until tomorrow morning," Isaiah says. "We have commitments at home."

"But it's all a question of how we play it," Victoria continues. "You know, my old dad used to say to me when I was a young girl, don't fix on the first young man who comes your way, not the first one in your sights. You have to look at the competition. He used to say, Victoria, you've got to play the field."

Isaiah and Rachel sit there across her desk with their tired, anxious faces. The pair of them, worrying in their sober clothes. They want to take care of the purchase-and-sale agreement. They want to set the closing date. Rachel's broad gold wedding ring shines on her slender hand. Her parents never gave her this kind of advice. She has not, nor has Isaiah, ever felt the slightest inclination to play the field.

Meanwhile, in his Kaaterskill office, Judge Taylor is fielding calls. Sometimes he tells his secretary to put them through and sometimes he does not. Victoria Schermerhorn has already called several times threatening that this is his last chance. If he would raise his bid five thousand, to forty-five, then he wouldn't lose the lake. If he would do that, she can promise he will still be in the running. Taylor listens to her go on and says as little as possible. He is not interested in a bidding war. He shrugs off Victoria's attempts to keep the fire of competition alive. At last she calls him and says, "Look, the sellers are in my office now. They want to sign with King and I'm going to let them. We're going to sign the purchase-and-sale agreement right now."

"You go right ahead," Judge Taylor tells Victoria in his quiet voice. His voice is thin and colorless, dry and mean as a martini. He puts down the phone carefully and then at last he gets up from his desk. He asks the young woman in the waiting room to come with him down the street and they walk together to Michael King's office. The young woman is Candy Walker.

"Now, don't worry about a thing," Taylor tells Candy.

"I'm not worried," she says.

Taylor holds the door open for her as they enter King's offices.

"I'm sorry, Mr. King is in conference right now," the receptionist tells them, but they walk on in.

Michael King looks up from his desk. He is speechless for a moment. Then he gets up and closes the door. "What are you trying to pull?" he asks Taylor. "What is she doing here?"

"Well, it's like this," Taylor says. "I would like to buy the lakefront property Victoria Schermerhorn's got listed, and I thought, as you would like to buy it, too, I would speak to you about it directly."

"I'm not interested in speaking to you about anything," King says.

"I was hoping you would be," Taylor says, "because the sale of the thing is dragging on. I have great respect for Victoria, but I thought perhaps she was doing a little more than necessary trying to auction off the place. I've never been one for bidding or bargaining, I guess you know that, and I've always been open in my dealings. So I've come to put my cards on the table, as it were, and say, I would like very much to buy the lakefront, as it belonged to my family for many years. You know I used to go fishing there when I was a boy."

"But my bid was accepted," King says, trying to keep cool.

"Yes, I suppose it was," says Taylor. "But I thought I'd stop in to see if I could persuade you to change your mind."

King looks at Candy Walker. She stands next to Judge Taylor in a corduroy skirt and blouse, and above all shines her long fine hair, gold, brushed over her shoulders. She opens her round mouth and her voice is round too, and sweet, with the slightest quaver in it, like caramel.

"Michael King, so help me, if you take away the judge's land I am going to stand up personally at the town meeting in April and I'm going to say that you, nobody else but you, are the father of my son Billy Walker, Junior. I'm going to get up to that microphone and say it, loud and clear."

"No, you won't," King says.

Candy flushes. She comes closer to him, and leans in, and she says it emphatically, in short breaths, "I—most—certainly—*will*."

"You won't," King says, "because it's not true. Your child could have had ten different fathers."

She raises her hand as if to slap him, but she doesn't. She says instead, "Billy Walker, Junior, had one father, and it was you." She pauses a moment and then says quickly, "And when I get up there I'm going up with my Bible and I'm going to swear on it, and they will believe me. What'll you swear on? Who in this whole town is going to believe you? I'm going to go up there, and I—"

"But I hope it never comes to that," says Judge Taylor. "I don't want it, I know you don't want it, Michael."

"You're threatening me with this if I don't withdraw my offer," King says.

"*I'm* not threatening you with anything," says Taylor.

"Go to hell," King says to the judge.

"I hope you'll think about this," says Taylor.

King does think about it. He can't help it. His visitors gone, he sits alone in the office. He has two black Rolodexes on his desk, and he begins spinning them, first one and then the other, so that the cards whiz by alphabetically. The cards whiz around and around, too fast to read. Of course, he can defy Taylor. He can go ahead with the purchase and sale. But he knows Taylor well enough to see there will be damage. King feels anger welling up inside of him. For a moment he is so angry that he doesn't care. He will get a lawyer. He will sue Taylor and Candy both for trying to blackmail him, planning to libel him. But he knows that the problem remains. The damage will be done.

He thinks about Jackie, and about Heather. They wouldn't believe the things Candy says about him. Jackie would never believe him to be the father of Candy Walker's child. She would stand by him. But, of course, she did not know him then, and she never knew Candy. The people in town, the ones who hate him anyway, ready to believe the worst, would jump on her story and talk and talk about it. And his friends? What would they think? The Rubins, the Butlers. Being old-timers, part of the place, their reaction would be more complicated. They would stand by him in the end, though it might cool things between them for a while. The respect they have might dampen a little. In the end, of course, they would stand by him. They might be loyal more for Jackie's sake than his. The place is too small. The people too close together, all alike at bottom, armed with the same prejudices, sharing and exchanging the same gossip, a public library of hearsay. Jackie would believe him, but she would be pelted on all sides. His enemies would mock her, but the worst might be, their friends would pity her. And as for Heather—on the bus, and at school—he can't help thinking about it. Children being what they are, so cruel to one another.

He doesn't think about himself, only about them, his family. He himself would deny it ever happened. He would get a lawyer to show that Candy is a liar. But he worries he can't stop the talk. The stories would circulate, despite what any lawyer could say or any judge could find. And poor Jackie, to have to live with that.

"Michael, what's wrong?" Jackie asks him that night at dinner. "You're so quiet."

"Nothing's wrong," he tells her, and he looks at her across the table where she sits with her shining brown hair and big brown eyes, and he asks her about her day, and Heather about her homework.

But at night he dreams. He dreams of the floodlit gym at the high school filled to capacity and strung with red, white, and blue bunting, the decorations bought by the selectmen for the Bicentennial. The three mayors are sitting there in chairs on the gym floor, official in their suits: the mayor of Bear Mountain, the mayor of Kendall Falls, and the mayor of Kaaterskill. The gym is packed up to the rafters far above the basketball hoops. Pink-cheeked kids in their quilted parkas, the parents chatting above their heads, the old gentlemen and ladies escorted to the front benches. Hamilton, Kendall, the old-timers of the town. Up top, the burly lift operators from Bear Mountain, and the slim young ski instructors.

"One, two, three," the mayor of Kaaterskill tests the microphone. "Ladies and gentlemen, please welcome the Kaaterskill High marching band."

The band plays, the anthem is sung. The mayor announces, "Ladies and Gentlemen, please welcome a man prominent in the development of Kaaterskill, a man running for his second term as selectman. Michael King!"

And he rises from his seat and stands before them all on the golden varnished floor. There are a thousand people under the basketball lights, the scoreboard shining. But when he opens his mouth he cannot be heard. The microphone is not working, and though he tries to raise his voice he cannot make a sound.

It is Candy Walker whose words rise up and float over the public address system. Her melt-away voice fills the gymnasium. Standing in the center of the polished wood floor, she keeps one arm around Billy Walker, Jr., and she clutches her Bible in her other hand.

And Candy says, "This man is not developing Kaaterskill. This man is ruining it, and he came here from the city to ruin us all. I know about it personally. He almost caused the breakup of my wedding to Bill Walker, my late husband, and no one knows, hardly, but Michael King—he is the father of my child, Billy!"

"You don't have a shred of evidence," King shouts, but no one can hear him. No matter how he screams, no one hears a word he says. They are all against him, rising in the bleachers, hissing. They are starting up against him, pouring onto the gym floor, and in vain the three mayors try to keep them back. Everyone is rising. Stan Knowlton and Curtis. Hamilton, and old man Kendall, Candy's father, with his long shotgun.

"Michael," Jackie says to him.

"What? What is it?"

"You're mumbling in your sleep," she says. "You're very funny."

Jackie pulls up the blanket and closes her eyes, but Michael lies there, aggravated, too tense to fall asleep again.

THE next morning in Victoria Schermerhorn's office, Isaiah and Rachel review the terms of the purchase and sale. "The closing date," Victoria says.

"As soon as possible," says Rachel.

"Well, now let me see, we have to allow for the bank's appraisers and the mortgage approval and the . . . let's see, six weeks from today would put us at May thirtieth, but it would be better to do it on a Monday. . . . Good morning," she says, over their heads. "Judge Taylor, what an unexpected pleasure. I didn't expect to see you, of all people, coming through these doors."

Isaiah and Rachel turn around and look at the judge. They take in his dark suit and neatly combed white hair.

"Have you come to raise your bid?" Victoria Schermerhorn asks him.

"Well, no, I'm afraid I haven't," says Taylor.

Victoria knits her brow and waits a moment.

"I've spoken to Michael King," the judge says. "He has had some second thoughts."

"What do you mean, second thoughts?" Victoria asks sharply.

"Just what I said," says Taylor.

"And what, I wonder, did you say to him?" Victoria asks. She is furious that he spoke to King behind her back.

Taylor doesn't answer.

"Excuse me," Victoria says to her clients. She ushers Taylor into her back office. Isaiah and Rachel are left with the purchase-and-sale agreement, its legal-sized pages flopping in their hands.

"We'll see," Victoria mutters to Taylor at her desk as she dials King's number. "We'll see whether you can get away with this or not."

In the outer office, Isaiah and Rachel wait uncomfortably. They look at their watches. Long minutes pass, until at last Victoria reappears, looking rather flustered and angry. Taylor follows her, looking exactly as he did when he came in.

"Cold feet," Victoria Schermerhorn tells them. "He'll do it. I know he'll execute it, but he says that he needs time."

"We don't have time," Rachel says. "We really don't." Jeremy will be coming up in the afternoon with his movers to make estimates. He is planning to start the packing this week and move all the books to his apartment in the city. Rachel and Isaiah must finish this business. Not tomorrow, not the next day, but this morning. They need to sell the land and give the money from the sale to Jeremy. It doesn't matter to them, five thousand here, five thousand there. They want somehow to preserve the Rav's library, to prevent it from being sold and scattered.

"He asked for a few days," Victoria Schermerhorn says.

"No, we don't have the time," says Isaiah.

"I can see you're in a hurry," Judge Taylor tells them. "And I'm still willing to offer forty if you'll take it."

"Forty." Schermerhorn spits out the price contemptuously.

"The offer stands," says Taylor, "and I'm ready to sign now."

———

IN THEIR small cheap car, a Toyota, Isaiah and Rachel drive back to the Kaaterskill house. Jeremy will be arriving within the hour. Just after lunch, he'd warned them on the phone. Isaiah and Rachel do not speak. In their silence the car whirs along the road, faster and faster. Isaiah is driving recklessly, but Rachel doesn't say anything. In his black suit and black wool fedora, Isaiah is speeding on the curving mountain road.

Rachel is nervous. When they arrive at the house she unlocks the door with shaking fingers. But all is still. Jeremy has not yet arrived. In the living room and on the tables, in the library, the Rav's books stand, all in their places, as yet untouched. Rachel and Isaiah sit in the cold living room and wait. Isaiah walks around through the dining room and the library. They wait for an hour, and then an hour more. They move out to the glassed-in porch and watch the road.

"Should I call him?" Rachel asks.

"No, no, he's coming," says Isaiah.

"It's two o'clock," she says.

"He'll be here," Isaiah tells her.

AT LAST, at almost three Jeremy drives up and he sees them waiting for him on the porch. He takes out his house key, but Isaiah gets to the door first and holds it open for him.

"Hello," Jeremy says to his brother.

"Jeremy," Isaiah says, and he extends his hand with a kind of wistful formality. "Come in."

Awkwardly Isaiah and Rachel stand with Jeremy in the living room.

"The moving company will be here in just a few minutes for the estimate," says Jeremy.

"Well, we were hoping—" Isaiah begins.

"We want you to cancel the movers," Rachel says.

Jeremy smiles wryly and shakes his head.

"I have something for you," says Isaiah, and he gives Jeremy an envelope.

Jeremy opens it and takes out a piece of blank paper folded around a check. It is a check for ten thousand dollars.

"This is for the books," Isaiah says.

"We're getting the other forty from the sale of the lake property," says Rachel.

Jeremy flushes. He looks for a moment as though he doesn't know whether to laugh or to cry.

"But I don't want this," he says at last. He returns the check to his brother. "No, I really don't want it."

"You said you would sell us the library," Isaiah tells him.

"I was—I never meant it," Jeremy says.

"But we have the money and we want to buy it," says Rachel.

"No," Jeremy says. "I can't do that."

"You led us to believe—" she starts.

"If I led you to believe something, then I'm sorry," Jeremy says. "I'm not selling the books."

"I don't understand," says Isaiah.

"Why do you want to keep them?" Rachel bursts out.

"I want to keep them," Jeremy says, "because they are mine."

4

—

EARLY morning, while it's still dark outside, Elizabeth wakes up in her bedroom in the city. Her eyes open easily. Her thoughts are clear. When she looks at the lighted numbers on the clock, she sees why. It is five in the morning, and the baby has slept all night. Isaac is awake too. They look at each other in disbelief. This is a miracle. They have never had a baby sleep through the night this early. They lie still, afraid at first to speak. As quietly as she can, Elizabeth leans over the side of the bed and looks into the battered wicker bassinet. There she is, not even a month, and fast asleep on her stomach, her head pillowed on one arm. The apartment is perfectly quiet. Not a sound from the girls' bedrooms.

"They're all asleep," whispers Isaac.

"It's like the alignment of the planets," Elizabeth whispers back.

Isaac begins laughing.

"Sh."

They want to lie there silent. They don't want to make a sound. Any minute the spell will be broken. The baby will wake up. Brocha will start calling, "Mommy! Mommy!" from her bed. But they can't keep themselves from talking. It is so rare to have time for conversation at the beginning of the day when they are both awake and fresh.

"How did the pantry go?" Isaac asks Elizabeth. She has been cleaning out the pantry for Passover.

"I'll finish today, I think," she tells him. "Then you can bring up the things from the basement."

"I didn't realize you'd done so much," he says. "She must be a real sleeper."

"She watches me," Elizabeth says. "I put her in the carrier and she looks around."

"Like Sorah," he says.

"She's quieter."

"Oh, I was meaning to tell you." Isaac turns to Elizabeth on his pillow. "When I went down to Grimaldi's for the onions he had a sign up."

"What kind of sign?"

"Help wanted."

"Oh, no," she says. "Isaac."

"I thought you might be interested," he says.

"And what about the baby?"

"You know my sister would watch her if you wanted to try it."

"I don't want to run a cash register in a grocery store! And he—"

"He's a little grumpy," Isaac admits. "Still, I thought—"

"That's not what I'm interested in," she says again.

"I know," Isaac says. "It wouldn't be the same as your own business. I was just thinking that you could start there, and then, you know, you would get to know the old man. Eventually—we'd save— we'd be rich. You'd buy him out and have the store for yourself."

"And then a chain, and then an empire of Grimaldis," she says.

"Or Shulmans," he tells her, lightheartedly.

"Oh, please," she says.

Elizabeth watches from the bed as Isaac gets up and puts on his slippers. He has to go to the synagogue for morning minyan. He will put on his tefillin there, wrapping his arms with leather straps. He will wrap the straps so tightly that they will leave their red impression on his arms. He will bind himself with the words of the Sh'ma: Hear O Israel, the Lord our God; the Lord is one. And I will love the Lord with all my heart and all my soul and all my might. Elizabeth will pray in the house as soon as she can, in the time she finds. She will not put on tefillin, but, like Isaac, she will bind herself with the commandments. She will not fold herself in a tallis, but like him, she will fold herself in prayer.

She will never cast the life away. But when, she wonders, will she view the pattern of her days as brightly, or say her prayers as gratefully? When will she observe the holidays with the pleasure of past years? When will she cook again with such joy?

Isaac leans down and kisses her. "You should go in," he says, "and look around."

"Into Grimaldi's?"

"Why not? You can say you have experience—" he begins.

Then the baby starts to cry. The girls wake up all at once and start calling. In a moment Elizabeth is out of bed and looking for hairbrushes and schoolbooks, and trying to tape up Sorah's broken diorama of the crossing of the Red Sea. Sorah is wailing that it's no good, and Elizabeth is telling her, "But you did a wonderful job. It's a very hard thing to show in a diorama." And it's true, it *is* hard to depict Moses leading the children of Israel across the sea, the waves parting, and the pillar of fire before them—this was what had fallen off—with only cardboard, markers, and construction paper.

ALL week Elizabeth is home with the baby. She is cleaning for Pesach, turning the house upside down. In the newly scoured kitchen the Pesach pots and pans and dishes fill the cabinets. All the regular utensils, dishes, glasses—are packed away in boxes. The oven racks lean against the wall ready to go down to the basement. Elizabeth has put away the toaster and the knife rack, emptied and scrubbed the inside of the refrigerator and freezer. Now she is vacuuming the couch. She's taken off all the cushions and she is collecting puzzle pieces, a stray sock, barrettes, and pennies. She vacuums the crumbs, directing the long extension hose with both hands, and the crumbs crackle as the hose sucks them up. On the armchair the baby sleeps, bundled in her blanket. She looks like a small pile of clean laundry, except that she is breathing softly, up and down. They have named her Chaya.

She is a good baby, easy like Brocha was. Elizabeth holds her, rocks her, walks with her. She weighs nothing, and she dozes off quickly. When she is awake, Elizabeth carries her around the room and shows her the house. She props her in the baby carrier and puts her on the dining-room table, so that she can see out the window. It is mild today, and the sunlight shines in pale yellow. She should take Chaya out. She needs to buy wine, meat, matzo, gefilte fish, farfel for stuffing, eggs. Her mind is filled with lists, all the things she has to clean, and all the things she has to buy. It is a buzzing of details, noisy and somehow reassuring, like the roar of the vacuum cleaner. And yet beneath this roar of details, somewhere underneath, she feels her imagination pacing, wounded, restless. She feels the questions muffled under the litany of errands. Where will I go? What will I do?

After lunch Elizabeth pushes the stroller to Auerbach's, where she buys meat and receives compliments on the baby.

"How old?" the saleslady asks.

"Three weeks," says Elizabeth.

"Aren't you brave taking her out at three weeks. I never would have dared."

"So this is number six," one of Elizabeth's neighbors says, as Elizabeth makes her way up the street with her bags hanging from the stroller.

"Yes, this is Chaya," says Elizabeth.

"Oh, very nice. For Isaac's father?"

Elizabeth nods. She makes a little joke. "If we have a seventh we'll have to name her Batsheva." The name means "seventh daughter."

The air is cold, but it feels good on her face. The dirty snow is melting in the bright afternoon sun. Rather than take the groceries all the way up to the apartment and then come down again, Elizabeth puts the bags and the baby in the old yellow Mercury, the poor car spattered with mud and stained with salt. She drives to the car wash at the very edge of the neighborhood, where some of the buildings are derelict and some abandoned, the sidewalks littered, the kids on the street rough. The block is almost, but not quite, too dangerous to visit even during the day. The car wash, however, is the best in the city. It is like a mikveh for cars.

Isaac always laughs when Elizabeth says they should wash the car. Of course, for Pesach, they must get it cleaned. Elizabeth enjoys the luxury, the water sheeting over the windshield, the long flannel strips like jungle vines that slap and slide over the station wagon.

After she pays for the wash, she sits for a moment in the gleaming car. She has finished all these little chores. Now her own thoughts come rushing back at her. Where should she go? What should she do? It comes to her. There is one thing, if she can manage it. She takes a deep breath and begins driving.

She drives with Chaya to the hospital and takes her upstairs in the elevator to the little office tucked away on the fifth floor. With effort she manages to carry the baby, along with her diaper bag and purse. She is sweating in her long winter coat, but she has to wear it because her hands are full. In the office she says to the woman registrar, "I've come to record the name of my baby. We left it blank, and we were supposed to come back and record it."

"All right," the registrar says, and she takes out her book. "Date of birth? All right. Time? . . . Female, Shulman. Here we are. And the name as you would like it to appear on the birth certificate? Last name Shulman. First name . . ."

"Celia," says Elizabeth, shifting Chaya in her arms. They will never use the name. No one will say the name aloud, but in sharp black print the registrar is typing onto the official New York state birth certificate, the English name Celia. C-E-L-I-A.

5
—

THE buds on the bushes in front of the apartment buildings are still clenched shut like tiny fists; the thin trees in May look like upended brooms. Elizabeth walks home from the dry cleaner at the end of the block. Edelman's Bakery has reopened, now that Pesach is over. Its door is propped open, and the smell of fresh bread wafts out to the sidewalk. At the corner Grimaldi's window is stacked high with oranges and apples, improbably bright. She sees it now, the sign Isaac mentioned weeks ago. HELP WANTED. She wonders briefly what kind of help Grimaldi needs. He has never seemed to want help before. The place has been here for years with its odd assortment of produce and tchotchkes and imported food. Perhaps she should go in. But what would she say? Mr. Grimaldi does not much care for his Kirshner neighbors. She might tell him she would like to learn the business and go into it herself. That she has had some experience. A little. Working in a store might be what she needs. She might like to start her own someday. They don't sound very persuasive to her in her mind, these ideas. They are small, idle thoughts. The main thought is that no, she wouldn't want to take a job, really. She has the baby, after all. As Isaac says, Pearl could watch her. But she doesn't want to start again now, start making a fool of herself. And the business wouldn't be hers.

Elizabeth looks at the window and feels awkward standing there on the sidewalk loaded with the dry cleaning. Of course, there is nothing wrong with going in and asking. Introducing herself to the old man. She might have liked to—perhaps she will someday. What is he going to do to her? Putting herself forward might be a little embarrassing. She will seem completely inexperienced and odd, naive.

She begins walking again. Chani is watching the baby at home, and Elizabeth should get back and put up the meat for dinner. And she'll heat up the sweet potatoes. Malki doesn't like them, but she has some frozen vegetables. There are peas. Malki eats peas if they're bright green. Only from frozen, not from a can. The girls love them fresh, of course. In Kaaterskill they break open the pea pods and pop out the tiny peas, smooth and pale. Well, all Elizabeth has is canned. She is no farmer, or great retailer. She stops short. She remembers how she said those words to Andras, sitting in the back of Cecil's crowded living room. In another time, maybe, in another life, she might have been these things, businesswoman, philosopher, traveler, artist. And it comes back to her suddenly, what Andras said to her. His words, half whispered, his voice conspiratorial and dry. "Elizabeth, this is the United States of America. You can do whatever you damn well please." She laughs softly at the memory. She turns around and walks back to Grimaldi's door. She ducks her head down and walks in.

Grimaldi looks over at her from where he sits on his high stool behind the counter. He is bald and heavy, with a pink, weary-looking face, and long yellowish fingernails.

"What can I get you?" he asks.

Nervous, Elizabeth takes six grapefruit and puts them in a bag. She browses the cluttered shelves. She examines Grimaldi's jams and teas and coffees, the china picture frames, and Lladro porcelain figurines.

"Anything else," Grimaldi states rather than asks, when he rings up the grapefruit.

"Yes," Elizabeth says.

He stops and waits.

"I mean, not to buy. Just a question. My husband mentioned—I saw a sign in the window mentioning you might need help."

"That's still up there?" Grimaldi says. "Where?"

"Oh," Elizabeth says. "It's over there." She points to the place in the window.

"Forgot to take it down," Grimaldi says.

"You found someone?"

"No, no, no," Grimaldi says. Carefully, with his nails, he peels off the tape from the window and takes down the paper sign.

"I'm not much of a collaborator," he says. "Know what I mean? I've run the place thirty years, and I don't collaborate well with people coming in, their attitudes." He hands her the grapefruit.

"Thank you," she says.

"I don't like to delegate," he says.

"What," Elizabeth begins, "what sort of help did you, were you interested in?"

"Doing the books," he says, looking at her. "Taking care of the register some hours. Someone in the neighborhood."

"I live in the neighborhood," she says.

"I know."

Elizabeth feels foolish, because of course he knows she lives in the neighborhood. How could Grimaldi help knowing, seeing her every day walking up and down the street, seeing the children coming home from school, Isaac and the old car.

"See you all the time, and your older daughter pushing the baby carriage," Grimaldi says. "How many kids do you have?"

"Six," she says.

He lets out a long, sympathetic whistle. "I have three sons," he says. "All grown now. Youngest one's got a good head on him. He's in college now."

"What I meant before," Elizabeth says, "what I meant was, since I live in the neighborhood I was thinking I might apply to work—to do books."

He makes a face. "What'd you want to do books for? No one wants to do books. It's a lousy job. Boring, and"—he pauses searching for the word—"tedious," he says at last.

"I'm interested in learning the business," Elizabeth tells him.

"Oh, you are, are you," he says.

She says nothing.

"You're one of the Kirshners, aren't you?" he says.

"Yes," she tells him.

"You know, I remember when they came into the neighborhood," he tells her. "A lot of turnover in this neighborhood. I've got cameras now." He points up to the upper corners of the store where the little security cameras hang. "I don't see a lot of the women like you working in stores."

"Well," Elizabeth says again, "I want to learn the business." She does not tell him that she had a store once of her own. She cannot speak of that.

"Why?" Grimaldi asks her. "No offense. I'm wondering why you'd be interested. My own sons wouldn't be caught dead in here. Working all day from the crack of dawn, worrying about your windows, keeping these kids from breaking them. You know how much one of these costs?" He waves at the dirty glass.

She says nothing.

He looks at her. "I'm wondering what your reasoning is."

She hesitates. "The same as yours when you started out," she says at last.

"Ha," says Grimaldi. "I don't think so."

6

—

RENÉE'S chest is tight. She breathes painfully, and her legs are stiff in new sheer stockings. She clutches her music to her. It does not look like her music; her body does not feel like her body. She hears herself walk across the stage, her shoes tapping on the floor, and she looks shyly around at the audience applauding, all the parents of her teacher's many students. This is the annual recital at the end of May, the night Renée dreads all year. The beginning students have already played, and then the intermediate. They are done, and sitting happily in the audience. Now the advanced students have to play. Now Renée has to take her turn at the black concert grand, wheeled in by the music school for the occasion. She sits down and props her music onto the piano. She was supposed to memorize it, but she is afraid to play without the notes in front of her. "Your fingers know the way," her teacher told her in the wings. "Let them feel the music." But Renée's fingers don't know anything. She is afraid to let them feel the music; they'll run away from her.

So she sits down, and she stares at the Chopin, the subject of so many conflicts, the pages covered with pencil markings, and her teacher's exhortations. *"Bright!"* and *"Count!"* and she rubs her fingers and dives in, just as if she were diving into Coon Lake. She does not think of her fingers as feather dusters on the keys. She does not think of anything but icy water. Renée is pushing against the cold, and her fingers are numb, but she keeps them moving. She swims on, and every once in a while a wrong note nips her, like a little fish, but she keeps moving, and her fingers behave mostly as they were taught, hitting the keys brightly, and she concentrates, her eyes on the notes, and her foot ready to pedal, and she keeps counting, no matter what, although sometimes her counting is faster and sometimes slower, and it gets faster at the end, a little blurred as she pushes to the last chords, and stands up, panting for air, because while she was counting there wasn't time to breathe.

They are all clapping for her as she bows, and the noise warms her. She is filled with thanks to be done and then, immediately, irrationally, she wishes she could do it all again, and do it right this time. She looks out at the audience. Her mother and father are there, and little brother. Aunt Maja and Uncle Philip. They are all sitting together in the front. Aunt Eva and Uncle Saul had to stay home, because Aunt Eva is still sick. Renée sees the other families there as well, and the other piano students, and—she can't help imagining it for an instant—there is Stephanie. Just for a second she sees her, and then her friend is gone. She is always imagining Stephanie turning up —although she knows she won't. She is always thinking of her, and even phones her sometimes, although the recorded message says Stephanie's number is not in service at this time. "All right, come on, move it or milk it," she hears Stephanie saying, and so she walks offstage.

Maybe Stephanie is in Canada. Maybe she's driving trucks on her own. Those heaving trucks Renée and Alex always watch as they drive to Kaaterskill, the eighteen-wheelers with names like Lurlene, or Miss Lucy. Renée can picture Stephanie driving cross-country, cracking purple bubblegum, carrying cargo into the Northwest Territories. The wind is blowing Stephanie's hair as she sits there at the wheel in her blue jeans. There are books next to her on the seat. Books about the Cold War and Women's Liberation, and Rosa Parks, and Large Animals, and How to Be a Veterinarian and How to Run a Dairy Farm. Stephanie is studying all these things, with her long straight hair trailing out the window.

At home, riding up the elevator to celebrate in the apartment, the family crowds around Renée.

Nina is ecstatic. "So proud!" she says.

"Well done," says Philip.

Renée can't help smiling in her exhaustion and relief. The day of reckoning is over. Summer is finally here.

"You see," Maja tells Renée, "your mother was right that you should continue. The music will be a joy to you all your life."

Renée's smile fades.

"Am I right?" Maja presses.

"I guess," Renée whispers.

Andras looks over and he sees his daughter's face. She has a look of forbearance that surprises and touches him. Of course, this is exactly what Renée dreads; that she will be playing piano all her life. Poor Renée, as Eva would say.

The elevator doors open and they all walk into the hall. Everyone is talking at once, but Andras puts his arm around Renée and he tells her, "The piano won't last forever. Don't worry; it will end. Every year you'll get older, you'll see. You'll be more independent."

Renée looks up at him, startled. Andras keeps on, speaking softly so that no one else can hear. He tells Renée that she won't be a child, or even a piano student always. She will grow up and decide what she wants to do with her own time. His voice is gentle, but his words are frank, and matter of fact. For although Andras never had fairy tales or lullabies for his daughter, now he sees that he has something to tell her. He speaks in sympathy as Eva would. The gentleness is Eva's; the words his own.

IN HIS apartment in Queens, Jeremy sits at his desk trying to work. He has lived here for fifteen years. It is a two-bedroom apartment on the third floor of a large old high-ceilinged building. A brick building set back from the street with a courtyard in front and a cement fountain that does not work. Jeremy sleeps in the smaller of the two bedrooms; the master bedroom is his study, lined with shelves and filing cabinets. In the living room small glass bookcases hold his antique volumes. There are shards of pottery in cabinets.

He has done what he can with his father's books. He has stacked the boxes neatly in the dining room and the living room, and then again down the length of the hallway to his bedroom, against his bedroom wall, and in towers in his own study. Of course he has no bookcases for the Rav's volumes. Jeremy's own library is large. His shelves are full, and his father's books will fill twice the space of his own books when they are unboxed. Jeremy knows they are more than his apartment can hold.

He sits with his work before him. He must open the boxes and sort through them. He will have to transfer some to his office. He will get some appraised. Perhaps he will even donate some to the Queens College Library. His own manuscript lies before him on his desk, but he cannot stop thinking about his father's books. The boxes sit there on the floor, always in sight, whether Jeremy is working, eating, or sleeping. He cannot avoid looking at them snaking through the rooms. They fill him with fascination and a certain dread. Several times he has taken a knife and begun to open a carton, and then stopped himself. The task is overwhelming. The culling and sorting out of volumes. It is too much to begin. The work is too painful. He simply looks at them. At night he falls asleep with the shadows of the boxes darkening the floor.

The books are a legacy characteristic of the Rav. A confusing gift. Praise and rebuke at the same time. A blessing and a curse. Jeremy must sit now and wonder how to interpret it. He must ask himself what his father meant by this inheritance. Whether it was intended to give him something of his father's mind, to teach him and reconcile him to what his father was and then became. Whether it was meant to remind his younger brother that it was Jeremy who was the superior intellect. That while Isaiah could read and teach the older Jewish texts, he would not appreciate the philosophical works from Germany, the Rav's Kant, Hegel, and Fichte, his books of German poetry, the great leather edition of Schiller's Shakespeare, and then the modern treatises of the Kirshner rabbis, and the diverse volumes of theology, mathematics, and history culled from Jeremiah Solomon Hecht's own collection. By this the Rav would be showing that his younger son, Isaiah, would be his successor in all ways but one. Isaiah would be heir to his father's rabbinic authority, but not his scholarly understanding. Or is this a test for Jeremy? A challenge for him in the value and sheer number of the volumes. Will he be prepared to catalog these books? To study them? To give them to a proper library? Is he capable of preserving them?

The Rav's library could be a test of Jeremy's abilities, but more likely it is intended as a test of his soul. The proof case for the Rav's long-ago decision that Jeremy is selfish; that he has a fine mind, but is a flawed man. The Rav would have guessed that Isaiah would want the books, but that Jeremy would never give them up. He would have assumed it would be so, knowing, prejudging, his sons as he did, coldly assessing their characters. Isaiah above all dutiful, and Jeremy above all . . . how did his father put it? Hard. Grasping. This, perhaps, is the hypothesis motivating his father's experiment, his gift, directed like an arrow toward the future.

Jeremy thinks of all these things. For days he has been agonizing about these questions. He is weary of them, but he cannot stop. At last he stands up. He takes a knife and slits the tape on one box and then another. There they lie, the works of the German Jewish theologians, the translations of the classics, the thousand commentaries. The little ones like orphan children in their tattered bindings, black and blue cloth. The long flat tomes like small monuments, gold and leather, and somehow funerary, their covers shut like praying hands.

The books smell of mildew. Jeremy can barely look at them. He feels for the books a kind of pity and disgust. They are stained and battered, and where they are edged with gold, the gilt is slick and soft with dust. Their companion volumes, his father's dark-covered sacred texts, lie at the yeshiva, open on tables, studied and taught, discussed and still alive. These, here, alone, separated from that library, lie readable but dead in their stacks. The mind that organized them is dead, the spirit and the world in which they were born is gone—their context killed.

In the next few days, open boxes all around him, Jeremy forces himself to grade his students' final exams. He wades through their looping handwritten essays, the pale ballpoint and the sputtering black ink, the smooth round cursive, and the words that knot together on the page. *In what way does Machiavelli appropriate and transform the literary tradition of the courtier prince?*

The apartment is hot. Jeremy hates this time of year, the first muggy days, the end of the semester. As always in May he is tired of his students. He is sick of his class and his apartment, and the city. At this time of year when Jeremy was a boy, the family packed up to go to Kaaterskill.

The students' essays are all the same; transcriptions of his lectures, some more and some less accurate, some more and some less detailed. Jeremy is sweating. He leans over the boxes against the wall and stretches to open the windows. He can barely do it, and strains to pull the windows up. Suddenly, he has had enough. He overturns the boxes at his feet and dumps the old books on the floor. He dumps them all together in piles, the theology and the German poetry, the old history books. The dust flies up at him, as he throws the tomes onto the carpet. Bindings crackle. White pages fall open, exposed. He dumps the books until his arms hurt. A hundred and two hundred more, until they lie there like a pile of junk, and he is not angry anymore.

He picks some up again, just a few from the top of the pile, a volume of Plato and a collection of poetry, some Goethe, and Moses Mendelssohn, and he sets them on his desk. It is a kind of apology for the act. Jeremy touches them. He opens one and then another, and then he sees with a shock of surprise and recognition, not his father's, but his mother's signature on the inside of each cover. The handwriting perfect and small, the signature constant, tightly curled in every volume in black ink.

He opens more books. Quickly he checks each flyleaf. There, in almost half the volumes, the inscription reads *Sarah Kirshner*.

What a fool he is. What a fool he had been, sitting at his desk and pondering what his father meant, puzzling over his father's will. Half these books were hers. It was obvious, if he had only opened them and looked. Jeremy opens the books and then stacks them up, neatly in tall towers. He opens the thick Shakespeare volumes with their pages edged in slippery gold, and there, inside, his mother's name is inscribed. He opens the two volumes of Aristotle in German, the leather Tocqueville, the romantic poets, and the German commentaries of their religious contemporaries, the first Kirshner rabbis. These were all his mother's. They have been given to him, as he is his mother's child. The son she took for herself to educate in the literature of the rest of the world, the vast empire of art outside his father's yeshiva.

Jeremy sits at his desk and looks out at his parents' shared library. He is tired. He puts his head down on his arms, but his eyes are open. He gazes at the ruined pinnacles and minarets of books stacked on the floor. He looks at them with clear eyes.

Jeremy's parents had been only partly happy together. They lived and worked together, and even enjoyed each other in conversation and in their partnership leading the community. His parents were joined in their mission; they shared their strict belief in Jewish law, and the desire to establish the Kehilla in America. But Janus-faced, they looked in opposite directions—his father always turning toward the future in his insistence on transmitting to coming generations the exact letter of the law, and his mother turning always back to the life in Germany, the houses and the music there, the riches of European literature. The Rav was establishing a new order based on the ancient and medieval sacred texts. But Jeremy's mother was nostalgic for the recent past, for the modern languages and for eighteenth-century philosophy. Always, she missed the paintings of Vermeer and Rembrandt, always she was remembering the Enlightenment. Jeremy was her instrument, not simply his father's prisoner. His elaborate education was her singular achievement, his learning her triumph of self-expression.

Jeremy looks intently at his legacy piled on the floor. He stares down at the inheritance toppled at his feet. He does not want to be, nor is he, the vessel of his mother's dreams. Nor can he be anymore his father's tragedy. His parents are gone, and his place between them is gone too. His father's objections have been silenced, as has his mother's praise. All his father's rebukes have not effaced the learning the Rav nurtured in him. And all his mother's books, all her poetry and German theology, cannot now shape him into her idea of a man.

7

—

AT THE end of May a delivery truck's passing darkens the windows of
Grimaldi's store, and Elizabeth looks up from her work, reconciling
the books with pencil, paper, and an ancient adding machine. She
looks around the shadowy room cluttered with packages. The jars of
Swiss jam shine like jewels in the low light, gooseberry, raspberry,
blueberry. "We should get some better light fixtures," she says to
Grimaldi.

"You buying?" he asks.

Elizabeth turns back to the adding machine. She is thinking that
Grimaldi should sell jars of herring. He could sell herring as well as
anchovies and sardines. There is a brand sanctioned by Rav Isaiah that
would sell well in the neighborhood and Grimaldi should carry it. He
should think about his customers. Different kinds of herring, and
some good crackers. And he should sell some Jewish articles along
with his figurines. Some porcelain seder plates. Some mezuzahs, the
Lenox porcelain ones with fourteen-karat gold. Those are pretty.
Some menorahs. Those would sell. He should work on attracting
younger customers. His regulars are quite old. They speak German
still and buy the Swiss jam and chocolate. He could sell some Barton's
candies, packaged. That would work well for the holidays. And the
boxes of marzipan. The little baskets of marzipan fruit, the tiny marzipan challahs. The ideas come to Elizabeth in spite of herself. Despite
the fact that the store is not hers. Perhaps someday she will have her

own store, maybe even buy out this one. Then again, Elizabeth would not want to set up shop on this very street, right here in the neighborhood with its tight line of stores and bitter politics.

Just three doors down Edelman's Bakery briefly lost Rav Isaiah's hechsher because of a perceived laxity about closing for Pesach. The scandal is over now, but it was a great shock to the community and, Elizabeth thinks, a deft show of force by Rav Isaiah. The Rav is establishing his standards in the Kehilla, his public persona, meticulous, efficient. Not just Rav Isaiah, but his wife, Rachel, presents herself this way. Elizabeth remembers Rachel's officious voice on the phone in Kaaterskill. The rebbitzin is zealous in support of her husband's severity. Rachel's ideas are played out in her husband's actions, the giving and the swift taking away, the hard and almost royal granting of favors, patents, and permissions. The Kirshner family and their school and synagogue administrators are like a Tudor court in Washington Heights: the king and his queen, their favorites. Elizabeth sees it that way now, the clever and dangerous politics of the neighborhood, the shows of force and fealty. The aristocrats of the community, like the Rav's cousin, Joseph, at once allies to Isaiah and potential threats.

Isaac would never accept this view of things. After all, it omits the central point of Rav Isaiah's rule. That he is no king, but simply a scholar in the service of God, simply more knowledgeable and discerning in the law. A judge, not a dictator. The Rav's authority is not a matter of politics to Isaac. And following the Rav is, and always will be for Isaac, an issue of aspiring to the best life. Elizabeth had been innocent like this, but curious. She envies her husband his devotion.

She wonders, even now, what her daughters will inherit and discover. Whether they will shake themselves and venture out, even if only to touch the larger world; the city with its thousand neighborhoods and businesses, its traffic, its steel bridges, pointing to far places. Whether they will take exotic paths, researching in libraries or entering law school, learning languages, and she doesn't know what else. Or whether, like their father, they will absorb themselves in the life and turn, heart and mind, toward the Kehilla. And there is beauty in this. Such observance is ordinary to her mind, but there is something beautiful in the constant conscious and unconscious work, the labor of it, ornamenting each day with prayer, dedicating each month, and season, and every act, to God.

*

WHILE her mother works, Chani walks the baby in the stroller. She has already brought her sisters home from school. They trooped home together in their pleated skirts and white blouses, knee socks and scuffed-up shoes. They were wearing backpacks and carrying homework papers. Chani brought home her graded Social Studies essay, laboriously written out in cursive, on every other line: *President Jimmy Carter is going to give the Panama Canal back to Panama on December 31, 1999. Why? Some people said it is really theirs. Some people said, "Save our canal, and give* Carter *to Panama!" It's a big machlochet.* She took her sisters upstairs and gave them milk and oatmeal cookies.

Now Malki is watching the little ones up in the apartment, and Chani walks up and down the block pushing the baby's stroller through the familiar neighborhood, the buildings of brick and shabby cement. She doesn't go far, not beyond the Kirshner buildings, the synagogue and the school and the cluster of stores. Every afternoon she walks up and down, repeating to herself her verses for the Bible contest: *"Va-yomer Moshe el Adoshem: Bi Anoni lo ish dvarim. . . ."* And Moses said unto the Lord: O Lord, I am not a man of words, I am slow of speech, and of a slow tongue. *"Ha lo Aharon achicha halevi? Yadati ki daber yidabber hu vigam hinei-hu yoztei likratecha. . . ."* Is there not Aaron your brother the Levite? I know he can speak well. . . . And he shall be to thee a mouth, and thou shalt be to him in God's stead. She repeats the words over and over into memory. The Bible contest is not until next January, but she is training in the off season. She recites for her father in the evenings, and he follows along in his Tanach, checking for mistakes. Next year Chani will enter the high school competition, and she wants to win.

In the stroller Chaya peeks out at the world, but Chani scarcely notices the familiar shops and streets. Even as she recites her verses, Chani is thinking about Israel. She is imagining the place with its mountains and stone cities, the wells and gnarled old trees, as she has seen in pictures. She is imagining hiking there, up

to the tops of the mountains, or walking in the desert. She will
grow up and become an archaeologist. She will uncover the places
that the ancient words describe, the camps and the passages, the
old walls. Or she will work in the orchards. She will grow grapes,
and, as it is written, she will sit under her own fig tree. She will
make the words come true. The place will be like the map of
Fairyland come to life. The verses will become real. She will dig
up their original vessels and find their source in the dry wells. She
will grow up and be a nature guide in the desert, follow along the
wadis, tracing their meandering paths.

In her long skirt and long sleeves, her feet clomping along in
dirty white running shoes, Chani walks on, down the street. Of
course Chani doesn't say these things aloud. She hasn't said anything
to her parents, but when she graduates from high school, when she
grows up, she will convince them about Israel. First her mother and
then her father. She will find a way. They will worry, and protest.
Still, she cannot imagine that they will refuse her. She will argue with
them and persuade them to let her go there. She will be grown up,
seventeen, old enough to marry. By then, for all she knows, the
Meshiach will be here on earth, the Temple rebuilt, all of them in
Israel together. She walks on with the squeaking stroller, dreaming as
she repeats the words, settling them in memory: *"Vediber hu licha el
ha-am ve-haya hu yihye lecha le-fe ve-attah."* And he shall be your
spokesman unto the people.

She looks up. A moving truck is blocking the street, its engine
heaving. Chani pushes the stroller closer and sees that a crowd has
gathered. There are people from school, and young men from the
yeshiva. Neighbors stick their heads out of upper-story windows.
They are watching the truck standing there with its ramp down right
in front of Rav Isaiah's building. Two men are wheeling handcarts
into the open doorway. They move rapidly, wheeling towers of boxes
into the building, five boxes in each trip.

Inside, hidden from sight at the entrance to the Rav's old first-
floor apartment, Isaiah and Rachel are watching the deliverymen.
They stand side by side, the two of them. They cannot speak. There
was no word from Jeremy, no explanation. Only the call from the

delivery company, the men at the door. The boxes flow down the ramp, hundreds of them. They come continuously without a break. They have all come back. Not some, but all. Every single volume of the Rav's collection returning. A river of books flowing back smoothly into the Rav's shadowy apartment.

VII

June '78

*From the rising of the sun to its setting,
let the Lord's name be praised.*

—Psalm 113:3

In June, the longest Shabbes of the summer, Andras and Nina sit at the dining table with Eva and Saul, Maja and Philip. Nina has cleared away the lunch dishes and the wineglasses, and she brings out cups of tea and more rugelach.

"Have another," she urges her sisters-in-law.

"I can't," Maja says.

"I've had too many already," says Saul.

Eva tastes one more. "My last," she says, smiling. And she turns to Nina. "I never knew what a fine baker you were. Andras, I didn't know we had such a baker in the family."

Nina says modestly, "It's because I didn't often have a chance. You did so much and so well."

Eva accepts the compliment in silence. She just sips her tea.

"Andras, I don't know why you complain, the garden looks green," Maja says, looking out the window.

"The grass is too long," Andras says. "I'm actually quite aggravated about it. I didn't like the job the Curtis boy was doing and I went out to mow it myself yesterday."

"I told him to wait," Nina says.

"Your allergies," Maja says, concerned.

"It doesn't matter now," Andras tells them, "I've managed to break the tractor mower."

"Look, we'll get someone else to take care of it," Nina says in her quick way. "There are services, yard services. You don't need to go out there exhausted and do yet another thing. You shouldn't take that big mower out yourself."

"I can handle a lawn mower."

"A tractor!" she says. "This is a dangerous machine. You could have had an accident. You were lucky no one was hurt."

"Would you like to see the roses in back?" Andras asks Eva.

Eva looks at Saul. "Another day," she says. "I'm a little tired. I need to rest."

"They're lovely," Nina says.

"I really should go home," Eva tells them.

"We'll go too," says Maja. It does not occur to any of them to go out to the garden without Eva.

"Thank you for the delicious lunch." Saul rises from his chair.

"Thank you, thank you," Eva and Maja call back as they walk down the porch steps.

"They really were good, the rugelach," Nina tells Andras as they walk back inside.

"They were perfect," says Andras.

Nina looks at him, surprised and pleased.

"They were. It was a perfect lunch."

"I didn't think it would be," Nina says. "I was worried the kugel would be too crisp in that pan—"

"But it was perfect," he says again. He doesn't just mean the food. Sitting down together at the table, and having Eva with them, is the purest joy he has ever known.

Nina washes the dishes in the kitchen. She rinses out her crystal goblets, while Andras sits on the porch with his *Commentary*. After a bit he puts the magazine down and walks along Maple. There is the Curtis place, the long, narrow prefabricated house, adorned with window boxes now. Next to it the Birnbaums' house stands, white and quiet without Cecil and Beatrix. It is rented for the summer to the Landauers and their five sons. Cecil is going to sell the place, but he is waiting for the right offer, and a strong dollar. Across the street he sees some of the Shulman girls in their small and leafy yard. Still wearing their Shabbes dresses, they are running in and out of the yellow bungalow with old soccer balls, swinging on the tire swing.

There is Knowlton's red bungalow with its chimney still unfinished, where Stan ran out of flagstones. Kaaterskill is all the same. Andras does not take the road all the way up Mohican. He loops back toward home.

He walks back into his garden through the long grass. There are leaves scattered over the back lawn. Even some weeds. He'll pull them up tomorrow. If he did it now, it would scandalize Nina and the neighbors. Working in the garden is forbidden on Shabbes.

He walks out to his arbor of lilacs and looks at the strawberry plants that grow underneath. Firm green strawberries cover the vines. The fruit is beginning to ripen, and a few are red. Andras plucks one and eats it. The strawberry is small and tart. In a bowl with sugar, that's the way his sisters serve them to the children. His tongue loves strawberries with sugar, the sweetness crunching and then melting away. Eva would be delighted by these plants. If she were still baking, she would buy rhubarb and mix together a strawberry rhubarb filling. "This will be a good pie," she would say if she were well, and she would make pies and load up the sideboard with them. She would serve them in the evenings in the garden. Pies and mandelbrot and prune cake.

In her kitchen Eva offered him rugelach filling on her spoon. Andras had laughed at her then, his older sister offering him the raspberry-and-walnut filling as if it had powers to change or cure. Now, to his surprise, he tastes what she means. Only that it is sweet to grow strawberries, and to eat them when they are just ripe. That it is good to rest in gardens and to sit in lawn chairs, the Sabbath lasting late as the long summer day. That it is good to serve and to eat, to sit and to receive the work of the baker's hands.

Andras walks through the garden and looks at the cascading lilacs growing over their trellis. He looks at the Japanese maple and the dogwood trees. At last he walks into the house. Quietly he walks into his bedroom to change his clothes. He is startled by the shape on the bed. Nina lying there asleep. He had assumed she was still in the kitchen or on the front porch. She almost never sleeps during the day. She tired herself out from all the cooking, from entertaining his sisters. Of course, they are not the easiest women to bake for. Polite, but critical. Quick to judge. Nina must have exhausted herself yesterday preparing everything, trying to meet, even to exceed, his sisters' standards.

Andras stands and looks at Nina lying there on the bed. She is curled up with her face against the pillow and her red hair flaming out around her. He looks at her and feels how beautiful she is. He has walked and walked, trying to outwalk the impulse to join himself to his wife, young and necessarily ignorant, unknowing, and, of course, confused by his history. It is his fault, choosing and then blaming her. He has blamed her and accused her in his mind, blamed her for being young. He kneels down next to her sleeping there. He wants to speak to her. He wants to ask her forgiveness, except that it would wake her. She would wake up, and she wouldn't understand.

He only dares to watch her sleep as he kneels next to her. He only speaks to her in his mind. And because he cannot wake her, asking her to forgive him, silently he forgives her: for being well in body and in mind, for remembering without pain, for living and dreaming apart from him, in her own time.

"You would not believe what these people are bringing in," James Boyd tells Ira in the garage late that afternoon. "It's a lawn-mower epidemic." He strides through the garage, swatting a whole line of the driver-mowers with his oily rag. "Come on, let's close up."

"Why'd they all break at once?" Ira asks.

James shrugs. "Summer people mowing over crab apples." He kicks Andras's lawn mower. "What are they trying to do? Make apple sauce? They all want them fixed immediately. They aren't getting done today, though. Monday we'll do Melish. First come, first served. Then King. He'll be Tuesday the soonest."

"He wanted it for tomorrow."

"So sue me. Sunday we're closed. Always have been, always will be. Hi, Stan," he says, as Stan Knowlton walks in.

"Thought you might join me and Curtis for some refreshment," says Stan.

"Love to," says James. "Ira, let's get a move on. Time to lock up." He looks over at Ira, who is leaning against King's tractor mower. The boy takes one of the blue wipes for windshields and cleans his glasses.

"You know, you've got to get out and do something, kid. When I was your age, fine weather like this . . . we waited all year for nights like this."

"You got a girlfriend?" Stan asks him.

"No," says Ira.

"You should work on that," says Stan.

"That's what I tell him," says James.

"You got anybody worth going after?" Stan asks.

Ira says nothing, and they both laugh at him.

"What's her name?" James teases.

"Oh, what's in a name," says Stan.

"Come on, who is she?" James asks Ira. "Who's the lucky gal?" But he won't tell.

CHANI and her sisters watch the lilac sky for the three stars that mean the end of Shabbes. They sit on the grass in back of the Birnbaum house, and Renée sits near them, but a little apart. She spreads her dress around her, feeling the air ruffling the blades of grass. Tomorrow is Sunday, but Stephanie won't be there waiting with her bike. There won't be anyone to swim with or to check up on the cows at Lacy Farm. She is filled with loneliness for Stephanie, for her funny slang and her conspiracies. Renée can't make up any of that by herself. She can only sit on the grass all alone, the summer stretching out before her with no one waiting for her or telling her to hurry up. She does not know that there is someone waiting for her. From the Birnbaums' backyard she cannot see Ira Rubin, pedaling the slight hill on Maple. He rides, faster and faster, until he whooshes past at breakneck speed, only to turn, pedal up the hill and down again, wind in his ears, sky rippling over him. Renée does not know it yet. Over and over, every time he speeds by, he is hurrying to see her.

The Landauer boys are running races in the garden, their white shirts flapping, their black jackets in a pile on the ground. As Cecil had hoped, the garden next to Michael King is filled with small boys in peyyes. There are loud games of flag football and crashing through hedges. More than once King has found stray soccer balls on his property. He has complained to Joe Landauer, and even demanded Cecil's telephone number in England. King says he would move if Jackie were not so attached to the house. Of course, there are a lot of things you can do if you are willing to move and start over. If you don't have roots in a place, as he and Jackie have in Kaaterskill.

They are all outside waiting for havdalah, the Landauers, Andras and Nina, Elizabeth, Isaac, Eva, Maja and their husbands, and Regina, Cecil's sister. She has come back from Los Angeles to get some of her things before Cecil ships the furniture to England. They are all sitting there on the rose-patterned chaise longues, even Mrs. Sobel and her husband—the old Conservative rabbi, frail under a plaid carriage blanket.

"I guess that was the last time," Regina is saying, "the wedding reception we had for Cecil and Beatrix. Two years ago. That was the last time I came up here."

"No. Has it been that long?" Eva asks.

"And now this is my last look at the house," Regina says. "I spent every summer of my life here until I got my Ph.D. Can you believe that?"

Nina shakes her head. "And it's the most beautiful on the street." She looks back at the sweep of the lawn all the way down to Bramble Creek. The rise of the white house before them on the hill, its porches and carved posts, the gambrel roof and bright windows.

"Is Cecil really going to sell it?" Eva asks.

"It's his to sell," Regina says, and her voice is sad.

"You must miss the seasons," Maja says.

Regina shakes her head. "We have seasons in Los Angeles. No, I'm going to miss the house."

"I think you might find a new one," Elizabeth says cautiously, but Regina doesn't answer.

"Elizabeth has taken over a store in the city," Andras tell Regina.

"Oh, no. Not at all. I've been doing the books," Elizabeth says. Working for Grimaldi is nothing like having her own store. She does not feel as she did then, when she carried that idea inside of her— exuberant, unstoppable, on the wind of her imagination. Still, she is pleased to hear Andras speak of it. Taking over a store! She is tickled by the exaggeration. "I just fell into it, working there," she tells Andras. Then she says, "That's not true. I thought of something you said to me."

"Something I said?"

"I'm sure you don't remember. At the naming of Cecil's baby you said, 'Elizabeth, this is the United States of America.' "

He looks at her, puzzled.

" 'And you can do whatever you please.' "

He smiles now, leaning back in his lawn chair.

"That's what I thought of when I decided to . . . go in, and inquire."

"You thought of that?"

"Just the way you put it stuck in my mind—" She stops.

"No, go on," Andras says. "It's just strange you took it so seriously. I was just—"

"I didn't know whether I should bother going in," Elizabeth tells him, "and then I remembered what you said. I thought that you were right."

"But people dream about living in Los Angeles," Nina is telling Regina.

"Well," Regina says, "everyone has different dreams, and I dream about Kaaterskill, right here."

"What do you dream?" Nina asks.

Regina thinks about the question. Then she says slowly, "I dream about being right here in this garden with my parents alive, and Cecil a little boy. My dolls, Cynthia and Nancy, in the doll carriage. And you, Eva and Maja. Your onegs and garden parties. My mother's rugelach. My fir tree." She looks up at the blue-green fir towering above them. "It was planted when I was born. It's the same age as I am. The sunsets here, the blueberry picking, the Escarpment Trail. The rainstorms. We used to sit on the porch in the rainstorms. We always felt safe here. We thought the summers would last forever. I remember looking up at the falls, and everything rushing and white and beautiful. You looked up there and you felt that you could do anything. That absolutely nothing could ever stop you. Do you know what I mean?"

No one answers. The stars are drifting over the sky. They were all watching for them, but no one saw them come. Yes, Elizabeth thinks. I do know.

They get up and go inside the house to make havdalah. The Landauers get out the spice box and kiddush cup. Brocha holds the braided candle, and Isaac says the prayer marking the end of Shabbat. After he says the last words, *Hamavdil ben kodesh lihol,* Nina asks, "What do you think is the best translation for that?"

"Blessed be he who separates the holy from the profane," Isaac says.

"The sacred from the secular," puts in Elizabeth.

"The transcendent moment from the workaday world," suggests old Rabbi Sobel in his quavering voice.

"Mm." They pause around the smoking candle.

"Take some cake home with you."

"What about the Orpheum? We could see what's showing."

"Renée has her lesson tomorrow. I don't know."

"Tomorrow you said we could go to the lake."

"We'll see, Sorah. We'll see."

And so they walk home under the canopy of trees.

Allegra Goodman's first collection of stories, *Total Immersion*, was published in 1989, followed by her critically acclaimed collection *The Family Markowitz*. She was a recipient of the Whiting Writers' Award. Her work has appeared in *The New Yorker*, *Allure*, *Food*, *Vogue*, *Commentary*, and *Slate*. She lives with her family in Cambridge, Massachusetts.

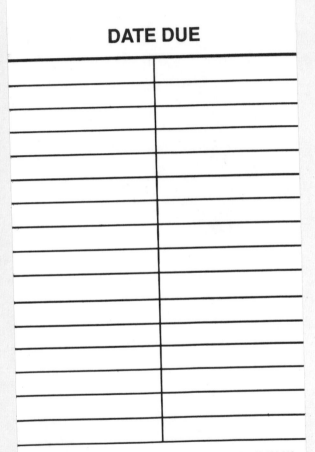

DATE DUE